ROCHELLE ALERS

Butterfly

Recycling programs
for this product may
not exist in your area.

BUTTERFLY

ISBN-13: 978-0-373-83199-9

www.kimanipress.com

Printed in U.S.A.

My lover speaks; he says to me,
"Arise my beloved, my beautiful one, and come!"
—*Song of Solomon* 2:10

Prologue

The sun was high in the heavens, burning off the haze blanketing the countryside, when Hans Lindquist maneuvered into the driveway to the two-story, tile-roofed gray stone house. The ivy covering the antique stones reminded him of a network of spider veins. Shifting into Park, he cut off the engine and stepped out of the SUV, inhaling a lungful of cool, sweet air. He was in California's wine country, but it wasn't the smell of ripening grapevines that permeated the air. It was sweeter, heady.

Turning slightly to his right he saw where the scent came from. Several hundred feet from where the house had been erected on a slight rise was a field of lavender. There were more flowers, climbing roses entwined on a pergola shading a slate path leading to the rear of the house. Visually he was transported back to the small villages in Normandy and the Loire Valley where he'd spent more than a year photographing gardens and window boxes for his award-winning coffee-table book.

He hadn't come to photograph Seneca "Butterfly" Houston, but to interview her for his latest project: *A Pictorial History of Models of Color*. His publisher had granted him a two-month extension, but not one day longer. Just when he'd believed he would have to submit his manuscript and accompanying photographs, he'd gotten a call from Butterfly saying she would make time to see him. At first he'd thought he would interview her in her Beverly Hills mansion, not in a rustic structure nestled in the Napa Valley.

Not only had she agreed to meet with him, but she had also invited him to spend several days at her family's vacation retreat. The extended stay would give him an opportunity to meet her husband and children. Once he'd relayed this information to his editor the word came back that he should take all the time he needed to get whatever he wanted on the elusive former supermodel.

Leaving his luggage and camera equipment, which he always carried with him, in the rental, he walked up to the front door and lifted the iron knocker fashioned into the shape of a lion's head. Hans hadn't realized how fast his heart was beating when the door opened and he came face-to-face with the woman who'd taken the fashion world by storm with her first high-heeled glide down a Paris runway.

The woman blessed with million-dollar genes was even more stunningly beautiful in person. The mane of curly hair framing a light-brown face stripped bare of makeup was liberally streaked with red in various hues. Seneca Houston wasn't quite forty, but she was graying at an alarming rate. Hans predicted that within another ten years she would be completely gray. She wore a pair of fitted jeans, a man-tailored shirt and ballet-type slipper shoes with the same aplomb as she had haute couture. He doubted whether she'd been nipped and tucked, but if she had then it had been by the very best plastic surgeon in the country—if not the world.

Seneca Houston smiled at the tall, blond man who looked as if he'd been impaled with a sharp object. "Good morning, Mr. Lindquist."

Hans blinked and then realized he'd been gaping. He offered her his hand. "Good morning, Ms. Houston." As she shook his hand, he registered the soft warmth of her palm and the subtle fragrance of the perfume that was the perfect complement for her exotic face.

Stepping aside, Seneca opened the door wider. "Call me Seneca." It was a direct order. "Please come in. I'm sorry I couldn't meet with you earlier, but I had to complete a paper."

Hans glanced around the entryway, recognizing exquisite antiques and reproductions that truly made him feel as if he was in a French country home. Vases lining a long wooden table overflowed with roses in every hue.

"You're still in school?" he asked, following Seneca across a limestone floor worn smooth by countless footsteps over the years.

Seneca smiled at the photographer over her shoulder. "I've been in college off and on for the past two decades. With the submission of this paper I'll finally get a degree in fine arts. It was something I'd promised my grandmother on her deathbed. Have you had breakfast, Hans?" she asked, deftly changing the topic. "Do you mind if I call you Hans?"

He blinked once. "Of course I don't mind. And no, I haven't had breakfast." Walking into a sun-filled kitchen with pale plank flooring, matching cabinetry, brick walls, exposed ceiling beams and a large fireplace, Hans stopped short. Somehow he couldn't correlate the rustic retreat with the woman who'd been the epitome of glamour and sophistication.

Seneca smiled. "Neither have I. I usually have something to eat before now, but I wanted to wait for you. What's your preference? Continental or American?"

Hans returned her warm, sensual smile. "American."

She winked at him. "I'd hoped you'd say that."

Reaching into the pocket of his jacket, he removed a small, handheld tape recorder. "Do you mind if I tape you?"

Seneca remembered another time when a man had taped their conversation—a man who'd changed her and her life forever. Wherever he was, she hoped he was safe and content.

"Not at all." She pointed to a stool at the cooking island with a stovetop grill. "You can sit there while I get what I need to put together breakfast."

Waiting until Seneca had gathered the ingredients, Hans positioned the tape recorder where it could pick up both their voices. "We can begin anytime you want."

She gave him a sidelong glance. "What do you want to know?"

"Anything you want to tell me about Butterfly."

Seneca placed several strips of bacon and sausage links on the grill; the circle of diamonds on her left hand gave off blue-white sparks under the warm glow of an overhead light. "I can't talk about Butterfly without first telling you about Seneca Houston." Her dark, slanting eyes met a pair in a shimmering topaz-blue. "How much do you want to know?"

"Everything, Seneca."

"I'm not going to edit myself, but when I say cut that means it's off the record, and I'd want you to honor that. If I see it in print then I'm going to sue you and your publisher."

"You have my word that I'll honor your request." Shrugging out of his jacket, Hans hung it on the back of the stool. He pressed a button, activating the tape. "Today is May twelfth, and I'm meeting with former supermodel Butterfly. She didn't begin as Butterfly but as Seneca Houston. For the record, how old are you?"

"I'm thirty-seven. And before you ask, I'll celebrate my thirty-eighth birthday July fifteenth. The date is auspicious because it was the same day Butterfly emerged from her cocoon."

"How's that?" Hans asked.

"I'd attended a birthday party in Southampton, Long Island, hosted by a prominent film director, and my former agent, who'd invited me to come with him, introduced me to everyone as Butterfly."

"Can you identify your former agent?"

"Booth Gordon."

"There are reports that you and Booth Gordon had somewhat of a stormy and passionate relationship."

Seneca's hands stilled. "Passionate implies a romantic liaison, and what I shared with Booth was anything but romantic."

"Didn't you spend time at his home in the Caribbean?"

"Yes, I did. He offered the house because I was close to burnout."

"Tell me how you met Booth Gordon."

"I was introduced to Booth Gordon by Mitchell Leon."

Part One

Seneca Houston

Chapter One

Seneca Houston adjusted the three-way mirrored panels until she could view her full-length image from several angles. The navy draped silk taffeta dress Luis Navarro had designed for her was a perfect fit. The garment, ending at her knees, was reminiscent of old Hollywood glamour with a modern twist—asymmetric, one-shoulder styling.

"I love it," she crooned, "but are you certain it's not too dressy?"

Luis shook his head and waved his hand as if swatting away an annoying insect. "Don't go there, Seneca. What you don't want to do is look like everyone else."

Her friend was right. She didn't want to look like anyone else, but stand out. After all, she was a model, and it was her job to perfect her personal three Ps: preening, posturing and strutting like a peacock.

She'd recently celebrated her second year as a model, and her career was stuck in a rut. It wasn't as if she didn't get offers. However, they weren't the offers Seneca needed to advance in her profession. The monies she earned as a commercial model paid the rent on the two-bedroom brownstone apartment she shared with an aspiring actress, but left her unable to indulge in her only guilty pleasure: a monthly Broadway play.

What she didn't want to do for the next ten to twenty years was spend hours under hot lights doing catalogs and magazine shoots. Seneca knew she had the face and body for runway, yet that would not become a reality unless she signed with an agency.

Although working as a freelance model afforded her the freedom to accept or decline assignments, she worked longer hours than runway models, earning far less. Doing print ads kept, as her grandmother used to say, "the wolf from the door," but she was tired of having to count pennies to make ends meet.

Unfortunately, frugality had become a part of her day-to-day existence, which was totally the opposite of her generous personality. If she had one cookie she would share it with anyone who wanted a piece. And she was willing to do anything short of prostitution to avoid moving back home with her domineering mother. That, Seneca vowed, was not an option.

Hopefully, everything would change tonight. A photographer who'd befriended her when she did a major department-store catalog shoot had promised to introduce her to the head of BG Management Agency. Mitchell Leon told her Booth Gordon was always looking for a new face and new talent, and he'd told the talent agent that she was fashion's next "It" girl. Seneca knew she had the goods. Now all she had to do was sell them.

Reaching for a necklace made of a double row of carved twelve-millimeter lapis and pale green jade beads with a large clasp encrusted with pearls, she slipped it around her neck and adjusted it until the butterfly-designed clasp rested at the base of her throat. She had debated whether to wear her hair pinned up or down around her shoulders, then opted for a loose chignon. Luis had complained that the hairstyle was too severe for her age, but Seneca had overruled him, leaving wisps to fall around her ears and conceal her pierced lobes.

Dangling the straps of a pair of dark blue, silk-covered stilettos from his forefinger, Luis approached Seneca. If he hadn't been involved with an extremely wealthy and much-married older woman who'd financed his own fashion collection, he knew he would've asked Seneca Houston to become his wife. Seneca knew he liked her. But what she didn't know was how much. Not only had she become his muse but also his obsession.

Going to one knee, he grasped the ankle of her right foot and slipped the slingback onto her narrow foot. Luis felt the warmth of her hand on his shoulder as she leaned down to keep her balance. He eased the strap up and over her heel, then repeated the motion with the left foot. The heels put Seneca's head over the six-foot mark, four inches taller than his own five-ten height.

Reaching for her hands, he brought them to his mouth, kissing her knuckles. *"Buena suerte, mia mariposa."*

Seneca smiled, rose-pink lips parting. Straight, professionally whitened teeth in a face the color of toasted pecans pulled his gaze to linger on her mouth. "Thank you, Luis." She pressed her cheek to his while affecting an air kiss.

Luis stared at the tall young woman whose curvy body belied its slimness. Whereas most high-fashion models were waiflike, Seneca Houston was slender and womanly. Viewed from the front or rear, no one would ever mistake her for a tall, thin boy. Her face was as exquisite as her body; the first time he saw her he'd stared rudely, as if entranced by a creature who had cast her spell over him. It was only when he mustered enough nerve to approach her that he'd discovered she was a freshman at New York University.

He'd convinced her to try modeling part-time, hooking her up with professional photographer Mitchell Leon, who'd taken the photos she needed for a portfolio. Luis had tried to get her to sign with an agency, but Seneca refused, declaring she wanted independence and a semblance of autonomy when it came to selecting her assignments. He knew she was destined for more than just being a commercial and print model, and with Mitchell's intervention he was able to convince her to meet Booth Gordon. If anyone could make Seneca a super-model it was Booth "the Barracuda" Gordon.

Seneca glanced at the clock on the bedside table in Luis's cramped bedroom. She knew the designer could afford to move out of the fifth-floor walk-up apartment building, but she suspected he didn't want to leave the Hell's Kitchen neighborhood where he'd been born and raised. His parents, grandparents and many cousins still lived in public housing within walking distance of Lincoln Center.

"I have to leave now. The driver is probably downstairs waiting for me." She smiled at the designer, who on occasion had been mistaken for Marc Anthony. The only thing Luis and the talented singer shared was culture. Both were Puerto Rican.

"I'll go downstairs with you," he volunteered.

Walking out of the bedroom, Luis following, she left the one-bedroom apartment and managed to navigate the marble stairs to the building lobby in the stilettos without mishap.

It was late spring, and dusk was descending on the island of Manhattan. It was also Seneca's favorite season. The days were warm and the nights cool enough to sleep without the incessant drone of the air-conditioning unit. She spied a black Lincoln town car parked halfway the block.

The driver got out of the limousine at their approach. "I'll call you with the details tomorrow," she whispered to the man who'd not only changed her, but also her life. She slipped onto the rear seat of the limo, waving at Luis standing on the sidewalk until the driver maneuvered away from the curb.

The driver opened the rear door to the town car, surreptitiously shifting his gaze so he wouldn't be caught gawking at the long, smooth legs of the most beautiful woman he'd had the privilege of driving for his family-owned livery company.

He inclined his head as if she were royalty while handing her his business card. "Please call me when you're ready to leave."

Seneca Houston nodded at the man, whose head came to her shoulder. She stood two inches above the six-foot mark in four-inch stilettos. Folding the card in half, she slipped it into the tiny evening purse looped over her body and suspended from a midnight-blue silk strap.

"I will," she promised.

Seneca had borrowed money from her roommate to rent the limo rather than take a yellow cab to a dinner party hosted by Booth Gordon. She'd promised to return the money once she landed another modeling assignment, but Electra Reece-Jacobs had brushed her off with a wave of her bejeweled hand and a "whateva."

Seneca couldn't brush off things with *whatever,* only because she wasn't where she wanted to be. She'd begun modeling within five months of graduating from high school. But renting the limo had become an extravagant extra. Living in Manhattan had its advantages and disadvantages. The advantage was she could take public transportation to go-sees and the disadvantage was that everything, especially rent, was higher than it was in the suburbs or other boroughs. Tonight, she prayed, that would change—if she could convince Booth Gordon to take her on as his client.

Turning on the silk-covered designer heels, she walked toward the entrance to the canopied, doorman Upper East Side high-rise luxury building with views of East River bridges connecting Manhattan to the outer boroughs.

"Mr. Gordon is in apartment 2410. The even-numbered floors elevators are through the lobby on your right."

Seneca gave him her most dazzling smile, a smile that she could turn on and off like a spotlight. "Thank you."

She had to psych herself up before she met the manager/agent extraordinaire. There were circulating rumors that Booth Gordon could sell ice cream on the summit of Mount Everest. Whatever the rumors, Seneca wanted to discover if the man was as good as everyone said he was.

Walking into the elevator, she punched the button for the twenty-fourth floor, and within seconds the doors closed and the car rose silently and swiftly to the designated floor. The doors opened and she found herself face-to-face with the man who was much shorter in person than Seneca had expected him to be. Perhaps it was his leonine head that made him appear taller and larger.

For a man in his early forties, he was in good physical condition. She estimated he stood about five-nine and weighed about one-seventy. His rakishly long black hair was graying at the temples, and brilliant blue-green eyes in a deeply tanned face directed attention away from his too-large nose and thin lips. Although casually dressed in a white linen shirt, black slacks in the same fabric and imported slip-ons he radiated power and confidence.

Professionally arched eyebrows lifted a fraction when she tilted her chin and gave Booth a curious stare. "Mr. Gordon?" Seneca knew exactly who he was, and knew instinctually to play to his inflated ego.

Booth Gordon couldn't bring his rapt gaze away from the woman with a golden-brown complexion, large, slanting dark eyes and perfectly symmetrical features usually seen in the paintings of Renaissance masters. She could've been Sandro Botticelli's model for the wood nymphs in his "Primavera" or his famed "Birth of Venus." Even her hair was perfect. It was raven-black, with wisps framing her extraordinary face.

Taking her hand, Booth examined her long, slender fingers. Her nails were natural and covered with a pale beige polish. "Miss Seneca Houston, I presume."

Seneca gave him a demure smile. "You presume correctly."

His gaze fused with Seneca's, Booth brought her hand to his mouth and kissed it. "When Mitch told me he was inviting someone I should take a look at I never would've imagined someone like you."

There was something about the way Booth Gordon was leering at Seneca that made her feel as if he were undressing her with his eyes. He had to know what she looked like, because Mitchell Leon had sent Booth a number of photos of her. "Are you going to continue to entertain me in the hall, or are you going to introduce me to your other guests?"

Annoyance swept over Booth like an electric shock. *Who does this bitch think she is?* "What makes you think you're one of my guests?" he spat out nastily.

Seneca refused to take umbrage at his tone. She'd grown up with a waspish, controlling, condescending mother who complained about any and everything, so if Booth Gordon thought he frightened her he was mistaken. Although she wanted him to represent her, she had no intention of letting him intimidate her.

"If I'm not a guest, then why was my name on the guest list?"

Booth released her hand and crossed his arms over his chest. "Maybe it's because I was curious. I usually take Mitch's word when he asks for something."

Holding her arms out at her sides, Seneca pivoted slowly, giving the egotistical man a good look at what he was about to lose. "Was Mitchell telling the truth?" she crooned.

Booth bit his lip to keep from smiling. The beautiful Amazon definitely had him at a disadvantage. She was perfect coming and going, and the dress she wore appeared to have been designed expressly for her. He couldn't stop the smile spreading across his deeply tanned face. He stared at her shoes, recognizing the designer's signature red soles, but the design of her dress was unfamiliar. As an agent with several models on his roster, he'd familiarized himself with every major and upcoming clothing designer.

"Who are you wearing?"

It was Seneca's turn to conceal a smile. "Luis Navarro."

"I never heard of him."

"But you will," she promised.

Booth's black eyebrows flickered. "When's that?"

"When you agree to represent me," she said confidently.

"Are you that certain I'll agree to represent you?" Booth countered with a note of annoyance creeping into his normally soft modulated voice.

Suddenly Seneca felt as if she'd been given the challenge to try and push a boulder up a mountain with the aid of only a teaspoon. She'd grown up basking in male attention, and by the time she'd entered adolescence she'd come to realize her power over the opposite sex. A demure smile was usually all she needed to get what she wanted from them. But Booth Gordon was proving her wrong. Mitchell Leon had told her that she would have Booth eating out of her hand within seconds of their meeting.

"If not you, then there will be someone else." Turning, she slapped the button for the elevator, then found her wrist caught between Booth's fingers.

Using a minimum of effort, Booth pulled Seneca Houston to stand between his outstretched legs. "There's not going to be anyone else. And there's another thing," he said cryptically.

"What do you want to know?"

Booth smiled. It was as if she could read his mind. "I need to know if you have any skeletons in your closet like pregnancies, abortions, and husband, ex-husband or crazy-ass boyfriends."

Seneca smiled. "No to any of the aforementioned."

He knew it was time to stop playing mind games with the woman who was even more stunning in person than she was in her photos. "If you give me absolute control of your career I will make you a bigger supermodel than any that has come before you."

The seconds ticked when Seneca met Booth's resolute gaze. "I'll agree if it doesn't interfere with my personal life."

Booth released her wrist, threading his fingers through hers. "I'll call my attorney and have him draw up a contract. We probably can get everything executed within a week. If you don't have a passport, then get one. I'm going to make a few calls and hopefully get you into a show in Paris for the fall."

She shook her head. "I'm not going to sign anything until my lawyer says it's okay."

A hint of a smile softened the agent's thin lips. "You have a lawyer?"

Seneca nodded. "My roommate's father is a lawyer, as are

her brother and grandfather, and I won't sign anything without their approval."

A full smile deepened the lines around Booth's brilliant eyes. "And I don't want you to. I've monopolized you long enough. Come and let me introduce you to my other guests."

Chapter Two

Seneca walked alongside her soon-to-be agent and into an apartment boasting black-and-white vinyl floors and floor-to-ceiling and wall-to-wall panoramic windows. Booth's guests were dressed to the nines in ubiquitous New York City black. Ribald laughter and hushed conversations ended when dozens of eyes were directed at her and their host. She stiffened slightly, then relaxed when Booth's arm went around her waist.

"Ladies and gentlemen, I'd like to introduce my very special guest and the world's next supermodel. Seneca Houston." A spattering of applause followed his announcement.

Seneca flashed the demure smile that was to become her signature expression as her eyes met and held a pair that literally and figuratively ate her up. Her smile grew wider as she caught the wink of the NBA's highest-scoring point guard.

She didn't move as the tall, lanky ballplayer wove his way through the small crowd that had gathered in Booth's enormous condominium, her gaze watching the fluid motion of his approach. He was even more breathtakingly beautiful in person. Olive-skinned, with chiseled cheekbones and defined features he'd inherited from his African-American father and Korean-American mother, Phillip Kingston had become the sports world's latest heartthrob.

"I know who you are," Seneca said when he offered her his hand.

Phillip smiled, exhibiting a wide mouth filled with straight white teeth. "Then we must even the odds, because I know nothing about you. May I get you something to drink?"

She exhaled in an audible breath. It was refreshing to have to tilt her head to look up at a man who towered over her when she wore heels. "No, thank you."

He went completely still. "You don't drink?"

A beat passed. "I don't drink because I'm not old enough to drink," Seneca explained.

There came another pause before Phillip asked, "How old are you?"

"Twenty."

"What about a soft drink?"

Seneca smiled. "I'll have sparkling water."

She wanted to tell the ballplayer that soda drinks were loaded with sugar and that she'd made it a practice not to drink them. Even the low-calorie drinks were not a part of her diet. She didn't starve herself like some models, but monitored any and everything that she ate or drank.

Phillip leaned closer, inhaling the subtle fragrance clinging to the exposed flesh of the woman who stirred emotions he didn't want to feel. Since being signed to the NBA he'd found himself somewhat indifferent to women who literally threw themselves and their underwear at him. It was the ones like Seneca Houston, who were caught up with their own sense of self-importance, that intrigued him. And if Booth had announced her as the next supermodel, then that meant the crafty agent had signed on to represent her.

He hadn't wanted to attend the agent's party because he'd wanted to return to Los Angeles to reconnect with his family after his team had lost their bid for the play-offs by one point. But Booth had insisted he come. To refuse the Barracuda was like jumping out of a plane without a parachute.

Phillip thought of the agent as a legitimate mobster. A single telephone call from Booth would find a former client either blacklisted or the victim of an assault that made one pray for a quick death. Whenever Booth called, he came. Now he was glad he had come to the boring gathering.

"Don't run away, Miss Almost Legal. I'll be back with your water."

Seneca stared up through her lashes at the most delicious man she'd ever seen. His skin was nearly poreless, and she wondered whether he had to shave every day. There was enough of a slant in his large eyes to verify his Asian heritage. However, it was his chiseled jaw and strong square chin that held her enthralled. Her gaze moved up his coarse, close-cropped straight black hair before moving slowly over a pair of broad shoulders under a chocolate-brown silk jacket, matching shirt and linen slacks. Phillip Kingston was more than eye candy. He was comparable to the confections found in Jacques Torres Chocolate Haven. In other words, he was a visual feast.

"I won't be going anywhere for a while," Seneca said.

She hadn't realized she'd been holding her breath until Phillip walked over to the portable bar to get her drink. Luis had wished her luck, and apparently it was with her. Booth Gordon had promised to represent her, and Phillip Kingston appeared to be as attracted to her as she was to him. No doubt it was going to be a remarkable evening.

★ ★ ★

Seneca glanced around the expansive living room. Dimmed recessed lights, dozens of flickering tapers in silver holders, votives in tiny glass vases on every flat surface and baskets of white flowers in every variety added a festive touch to the all-white décor. Partially opened pocket doors revealed a table in the formal dining room. The many bulbs in a massive crystal chandelier sparkled like stars over the table set with silver, china and crystal stemware.

"I see you've caught the eye of my latest prize."

A shiver swept over Seneca when she felt Booth's moist breath in her ear. She peered over her shoulder at the agent. "Who are you talking about?" she asked, feigning ignorance.

She knew he was referring to Phillip Kingston, but there was something in his tone that reminded her of someone who'd just purchased a spectacular thoroughbred. And she wondered if he regarded all of his clients as prizes, or just those who earned six, seven and occasionally eight figures, from which he'd netted incalculable sums in commissions for his ability to ink unheard-of deals.

"Kingston," Booth said in a velvet whisper. "FYI, he's very particular about the women he usually consorts with."

Seneca turned, glaring at the man who'd promised to make her a supermodel. But, she mused, at what cost? "I am not consorting with Phillip Kingston. He just offered to bring me a drink."

"As your host, I should've offered to do that."

A hint of a smile played at the corners of her mouth. "But it looks as if your prize beat you to it."

Booth clamped down on his teeth to keep from spewing expletives. He'd vowed to curtail his colorful language after one of his employees sued him. He'd called a gofer "a dumb-ass, dick-sucking faggot," and a month later he was charged with sexual discrimination. The agency's lawyer agreed to settle out of court, and the little weasel accepted a six-figure check on the spot, then signed documents with a gag order that he would never mention the incident again or he would be subject to a countersuit for defamation. One thing Booth detested was giving away money, and if the snitch hadn't been the son of one of his uncle's friends he would've personally blown his brains out.

An innate instinct told him that Seneca Houston wasn't going to be an easy client. But instinct also told him the exotic beauty was going to make a great deal of money in commissions for him. He would put up with her sharp tongue until she got a taste of fame and fortune. Then the ball would literally be in his court, where he'd have the upper hand in all her bookings.

Fortunately, he had been blessed with acute instincts. Within minutes of meeting someone, he knew whether to give them the time of day or totally ignore them. Booth hadn't become the lawyer his social-climbing mother had wanted him to be. However, he was blessed with something money and higher education couldn't buy—a heightened sense of survival. He was also a visionary. The clients who signed with his agency weren't just actors, models, performers or athletes. BG Management Agency had turned them into megastars.

Phillip returned with a glass filled with a clear sparkling liquid and a sliver of lime, and Booth's gaze darted from the ballplayer to Seneca, his mind awash with ideas. Both were tall and exotic-looking. Tom Brady had married supermodel Gisele Bündchen, and as the agent for Phillip Kingston and Seneca Houston he would market them as a celebrity couple.

Waiting until Seneca took a sip of her beverage, he reached for her free hand. "I had the waitstaff rearrange the place cards at the table. You and Seneca will be seated together," he informed Phillip.

"Where's Mitchell?" Seneca asked, her eyes darting around the living room as she looked for the photographer.

Booth gave her fingers a gentle squeeze. "He called earlier to say he was running late. He should be here before the second course is served." The words were barely off his tongue when Mitchell Leon strolled into the living room. Tall, thin and with salt-and-pepper hair fashioned into shoulder-length twists, he had dark skin reminiscent of sculpted mahogany African masks. He'd hoped the talented photographer would've opted to wear a shirt and jacket instead of the misshapen cotton sweaters he favored regardless of the season. Booth sighed inaudibly. At least he'd exchanged his ubiquitous jeans for a pair of slacks. With his approach he noticed the pants were slightly wrinkled. Was it, he mused, too much for the man to take his clothes to a dry cleaner?

Reluctantly, he released Seneca's hand and extended his to Mitchell. "Mitch, my boy, I'm glad you could make it."

Frowning, Mitchell Leon ignored the proffered hand and leaned over to plant a kiss on Seneca's cheek. "Hey, beautiful." He gave Phillip a nod. "I'm sorry you guys didn't make the play-offs," he said to Phillip. "I need a drink," he said, switching the topic of the conversation without taking a breath.

Three pairs of eyes followed the emaciated-looking man with strangely colored gold eyes as he headed for the bar. "Now, that's one strange dude," Booth muttered under his breath.

Seneca smiled. "His genius outweighs his eccentricity." She owed her modeling career to Luis and Mitchell. One dressed her and the other photographed her and had made it possible for her to meet Booth Gordon. "Excuse me, gentlemen, but I need to speak to Mitchell."

Talking long, fluid strides, she sidled up to her friend as he asked the bartender for vodka on the rocks. "He announced to everyone that I was going to be a supermodel," she said in a hushed whisper.

Smiling, Mitchell gave her a sidelong glance. "And knowing Gordon he will make it happen. The Barracuda could never resist a beautiful woman. Especially one that hasn't been surgically altered."

"Why do you call him that?"

"That's because he is one," Mitchell said. "Booth Gordon is aggressive and at times a tad bit unethical. He will do whatever he has to do to get what he wants for his clients."

Seneca took a sip of her drink, staring over the rim at the model-turned-photographer. Mitchell was only thirty-three but was graying prematurely, the gray totally incongruent with his youthful-looking dark face. His features were more European than African, and with his light-colored eyes he'd garnered a lot of attention from both men and women.

Mitchell had lived with a model, but their relationship had imploded when he returned home to find her in bed with their next-door neighbor. Seneca, fearing that Mitchell, after he'd had an emotional meltdown, would harm either himself or the unfaithful woman, invited him to stay with her until he found another apartment. She'd offered him her bedroom while she'd slept on the convertible sofa in the living room. Six weeks later he moved into a Tribeca loft.

"Does that include you?"

Mitchell took a deep swallow of his cocktail, grimacing when it slid down the back of his throat before a warming spread throughout his chest. "Booth spearheaded my modeling career, but when I told him I wanted to photograph models he made it happen for me. However, when it stops being good, then I'll look for another agent."

Seneca wanted to tell him that she hoped that wouldn't happen for a very long time. She and Mitchell had connected, he with her and she with his camera lens, the instant she'd stepped onto the set for a Macy's Christmas catalog. When she was told that she would do the shoot with M. Leon, she'd believed it would be with the international male model. However, much to her shock, he wasn't a model but the photographer. There was something in the luminous golden orbs that was mesmerizing and electrifying, and for the first time since she'd begun modeling she came alive under the lights.

Seneca met Mitchell's eyes. "Do you miss modeling?"

Mitchell's lips parted in a sensual smile. "No. Rather than posing with beautiful women I get the bonus of peering at them from behind a camera lens." Without warning, he sobered. "You're going to become a sensation, Seneca," he predicted sagely. "Working with Booth isn't going to be easy, because the man has an ego as big as Mount Rushmore. But on the other hand, he will make you a supermodel. Just make certain you don't sign away your soul."

Mitchell's warning stayed with Seneca as she sat with Booth on her left and Phillip on her right with ten other couples. Booth sat at the head of the table opposite his latest barely legal girlfriend, presiding over the assembly like a Roman emperor at a banquet. With a mere wave of his hand or a nod he silently ordered the waitstaff when to bring or clear away each course.

She ate slowly, sparingly, as she sipped her drink. No one seemed to notice that she'd left more food on the plate than she'd consumed. Unlike many women who had a career in modeling, Seneca had never resorted to bingeing, then regurgitating her food. Rice, pasta, potatoes and bread topped her restricted-foods list. She'd made allowances for protein intake: chicken, fish, beans, peas and no more than four ounces of red meat each week. Booth's personal chef had prepared a rack of lamb with an herb crust, but Seneca found it too undercooked.

"Is there something wrong with the lamb?"

Seneca nodded. Booth had read her mind. "It's a little rare for my tastes."

Raising his hand, he beckoned a waiter. "Please bring Ms. Houston a well-done portion of lamb. Take her plate, fool," he rasped, noticeably annoyed with the man's incompetence.

She opened her mouth to chide Booth for his rudeness but just as quickly changed her mind. Her objection was not to what he said but how he'd said it. His tone was a constant reminder of how her mother had ordered her children about as if they were her slaves. It would never be "please," or "would you," but "do this or that, and be quick about it." And if she'd dawdled too long, then Seneca would find an object sailing within inches of her head. She didn't know how she did it, but Dahlia Houston's aim was near-perfect. She never hit any of her children, although she'd come very close too many times to count.

"Why don't you take my plate," Phillip suggested, picking up his plate and setting it down in front of Seneca, "and I'll take yours."

"Are you sure?" she asked him, her voice barely above a whisper.

Phillip beckoned the waiter. "I'll take that." Picking up the knife at his place setting, he cut into the fork-tender meat and popped it into his mouth. "It's good."

Seneca found herself watching him chew until he swallowed. He had the sexiest mouth of any man she'd ever seen. She'd never been one to gawk or go weak-kneed over a good-looking man; however, she was willing to make an exception with Phillip Kingston. He was tall, at least six-six, his body beautifully proportioned. Even his hands were perfect.

She picked up her knife. "I don't eat much red meat, and when I do I like it well-done."

Phillip leaned to his left, his shoulder brushing against Seneca's bare one. "Do you eat?" he teased. "You hardly touched your soup and salad."

"You noticed?"

He smiled, attractive slashes creasing his lean jaw. "You're impossible to ignore."

"Are you flirting with me?"

He pressed closer. "What do you think?"

"You are, Mr. Kingston."

A low chuckle rumbled in his chest. "Damn, baby, don't call me that."

"Aren't you basketball's phenom King Phillip?"

"Don't believe everything you read."

"I only know what I've read," Seneca countered, smiling.

"I think it's time to set the record straight. After this is over, why don't we go somewhere and talk?"

She tried to ignore the feeling of uneasiness shaking her. How many times had she heard the same suggestion from countless men? To them going somewhere to talk meant trying to get her into bed—something she refused to do no matter how much they pleaded or begged. If she was going to sleep with a man, then it would be at her discretion, not his.

"I'll give it some thought, Phillip." His name came out in a sultry drawl.

"Now, that's better. But don't think too long, gorgeous, because I intend to blow this party before coffee and dessert."

Seneca rested a hand atop Phillip's much larger one, recalling Booth's statement that Phillip was very particular about the women with whom he consorted, which led her to believe he wouldn't do anything to tarnish his good-guy image. "Let me leave first, then follow twenty minutes later," she said sotto voce. "I'll be waiting downstairs."

If he was surprised by her suggestion, nothing in his expression indicated it. There was little doubt that Phillip Kingston was used to women coming on to him. But Seneca wasn't coming on to or flirting with him.

Was she attracted to him? Yes.

Did she want to know more about him? Yes.

Would she sleep with him? No.

Seneca had had one serious relationship, and unfortunately it ended badly. It was also unpleasant enough to make her very wary of the opposite sex.

Chapter Three

Seneca wrote her address and telephone numbers on a cocktail napkin before passing it to Booth. "Call me and let me know when you want to meet." She pushed back her chair, Booth and Phillip rising together.

Booth placed a hand at the small of her back. "You're leaving now?"

"I have another engagement. My driver is waiting for me." She'd mentioned the driver because she knew it would make her departure a smooth one.

She curbed the urge to stiffen when his fingers moved to the curve of her waist, then lower to her hip. She didn't want to believe he was attempting to feel her up, not only with his girlfriend looking on, but a room filled with other people. "Call me, Booth."

He dropped his arm. "I'll walk you out."

Seneca wanted to tell the man she could find her way to the door without his assistance, but didn't want to create a scene. Even if she had been interested in the agent she'd seen firsthand how he'd disrespected the woman who appeared as if she was going to burst into tears at any moment.

"No. Please stay and entertain your guests." Not giving him a chance to react, she turned on her heels and walked out the dining room.

A woman in a pale-gray uniform led the way to the door, opening it while inclining her head. "Good evening, miss."

Seneca angled her head, smiling. "Thank you. Good evening to you, too."

The elevator arrived seconds after she'd pushed the button. The doors opened. She hesitated when a couple sprang apart, the man turning his back while adjusting the front of his slacks. It was apparent they'd been engaged in some form of sex play. They weren't old enough for retirement, but Seneca thought them too mature to make out in public.

"Sorry about that," said a deep male voice behind her. Soft laughter followed the apology.

"Whateva," Seneca drawled, using Electra's favorite rejoinder. Opening her purse, she removed her cell phone and business card. When the elevator reached the lobby she'd called the driver to tell him to pick her up in front of the building.

Phillip wasn't able to depart until half an hour after Seneca had taken her leave. Booth had picked the wrong time to want to talk business. He thanked his agent and host for his hospitality and practically ran out of the apartment to the elevator. During the ride to the building's lobby he couldn't stop thinking about the beautiful woman who'd enthralled him. Since joining the NBA Phillip had found himself constantly bombarded with female attention, and not having Seneca batting her lashes or draping her body over his was not only welcome, but refreshing. He always preferred doing the chasing, not the other way around.

Nodding to the doorman on duty, he walked out into the warm night, glancing to his right, then his left. Yellow taxis swerved in and out of bumper-to-bumper traffic while horns from frustrated motorists blared loudly, adding to the cacophony of sounds in the city that never slept. He felt a sinking feeling the pit of his stomach when he realized Seneca hadn't waited as she'd promised.

Turning, he beckoned the doorman. "Please hail me a cab."

"Mr. Kingston, Miss Houston is waiting in the car for you," said someone behind him.

Phillip smiled. "I guess I won't need that taxi," he told the doorman. Following the driver, he walked several feet to a black Lincoln town car. The driver opened the rear door and he ducked his head to slide onto the leather seat beside Seneca.

The light from the small lamp positioned behind the rear seat cast a warm glow over Seneca's face. "What took you so long?" she asked, smiling.

"Booth wanted to talk," Phillip said, stretching out his legs until he found a comfortable position.

"Didn't you tell him you had to meet someone?"

Phillip gave Seneca a lengthy stare. "When Booth Gordon wants to talk you usually acquiesce."

"Are you saying that when Booth Gordon speaks, everyone listens?"

"Only those who count on him for their next paycheck," he confirmed.

Seneca digested this information. First Mitchell and now Phillip had made veiled warnings about the agent. She wondered, for the first time, whether she was getting into something she wouldn't be able to control. *If you give me absolute control of your career I will make you a bigger supermodel than any that has come before you.*

She didn't know why his prediction was branded on her brain like a permanent tattoo. Seneca wanted to up the ante on her career, but would it be at the cost of losing her independence? Independence and control were paramount to her. All her life she'd had to submit to the will of a controlling and domineering mother—a woman who never told her children that she loved them, a woman who barked orders and commands like a drill sergeant and a woman who complained every day of her life.

"Where do you want to go to talk, Phillip?"

"What about your place?"

Seneca shook her head. "It can't be my place." There was no way she was going to invite a man to her home within hours of meeting him for the first time—even if that man was Phillip Kingston.

"Then we'll go to my place."

"Where do you live?" she asked.

"I'm staying at the Ritz-Carlton in Battery Park. We can hang out in the lobby or the club lounge."

Seneca was certain he could hear her sigh of relief. One thing she didn't want to do was spend her time with him fighting off his physical advances. "That sounds good to me."

Leaning forward on his seat, Phillip gave the driver the name and location of his hotel, then settled back to enjoy the passing landscape and the hypnotic fragrance of Seneca's perfume. He made certain to keep a comfortable distance between them when he'd wanted to pull her into his arms and hold her. Reaching over, he grasped her hand, holding it protectively. She turned to look at him, smiling. He returned her smile and then stared out the side window as the driver maneuvered smoothly into southbound traffic.

★ ★ ★

Phillip surreptitiously slipped the driver several large bills when he exited the car, asking that he wait around indefinitely. The man palmed the money, nodding. "Just have Miss Houston call me when she's ready."

Phillip extended his hand, assisting Seneca out of the car, his gaze lingering on her long, bare legs. His breath caught in his lungs when he fantasized about having her legs around his waist—or better yet, around his neck. He didn't know what it was about the model, but just looking at her sent his libido into overdrive. She was approachable, yet a part of her remained aloof. And there was a sophistication about her not usually common in someone as young as she.

He was twenty-six, and there were times Phillip felt years older. He'd been a first-round draft pick even before graduating from college, and with Booth Gordon as his agent he'd been catapulted into the glare of cameras and spotlights as the ink was drying on his six-figure contract. If it hadn't been for his strict upbringing, he knew he would've succumbed to the temptations faced by a young man becoming a multimillionaire at the tender age of twenty-one.

Phillip thanked the doorman as he opened the door when he led Seneca into the hotel with views of New York Harbor and the Statue of Liberty. He'd grown used to the stares and whispers when hotel personnel and guests recognized him. The lack of privacy came with the territory. It was only when he closed the door to his suite that he was afforded complete privacy.

He stopped at the concierge, checking whether he had mail or packages. There were none. "Would you like to freshen up in my suite first?" he asked Seneca.

Seneca noticed people had stopped to stare at her and Phillip. She knew they'd recognized him from television commercials and print ads. Several flashbulbs went off at the same time, and she pressed her face to his shoulder.

"I don't think it's a good idea to talk in the lobby," she said.

Putting his arm around Seneca's waist, Phillip pulled her closer to his length. "If you want we can talk in the club lounge." Reaching in the breast pocket of his jacket with his free hand, he removed the card key.

"I wouldn't mind hanging out in your suite." Seneca had changed her mind. Having people take pictures of her with Phillip had become unnerving. She'd just met the man, and didn't want her photo splashed across the pages of a supermarket tabloid.

"You have to learn to ignore the gawking and picture taking," Phillip said as he escorted her into the elevator. He punched the button for the twelfth floor.

She glanced up at his distinctive profile. "How long did it take you to get used to it?"

"Scouts were taking pictures of me in high school. It escalated in college, and by the time I was drafted into the NBA it was something I'd learned to deal with."

"Do you give autographs?"

He smiled. "Most times I do—especially if they're kids. You can't rely on the public for your fame and fortune, then snub them when they ask you to scrawl your name on a piece of paper."

"Will you give me your autograph?" Seneca asked, giving him a sensual smile.

Phillip winked at her. "How many do you want?"

She returned his wink. "I'll let you know."

He moved closer, their chests rising and falling in unison. "Why can't you give me a straight answer without having to think about it first?"

Seneca was saved from answering his query when the elevators doors opened. She followed Phillip down the carpeted hallway to his suite. Inserting the card key in the slot, he waited for the green light and pushed open the door. "Please come in and make yourself comfortable."

She entered the suite as if pulled by an invisible wire, her mouth gaping in awe. Phillip hadn't drawn the drapes, and the lights of the city, New York Harbor, Statue of Liberty and Ellis Island were clearly visible. She noticed the telescope directed at the windows.

"These views are spectacular!" Seneca gasped.

Phillip slipped out of his jacket, leaving it on a chair in the Art Deco–decorated living room. "That's the reason why I live here."

Turning away from the window, Seneca gave him an incredulous look. "You *live* here?"

"Yes. Why do you look so shocked?"

"I thought you would've bought a house either in the suburbs or across the river in New Jersey."

Emptying his pockets of his cell phone, loose change, credit-card case and money clip, he left them on the coffee table. Picking up a remote, Phillip turned on the Bang & Olufsen audio system, soft jazz filling the room. "I would if I'd had a family. I'm single, so living in a hotel is the next-best thing. I have every convenience that I'd want or need. There's a twenty-four hour fitness center with personal trainers, restaurants on the premises, in-room dining and concierge 24/7, twice-a-day maid service, laundry and dry cleaning, and around-the-clock security."

If he'd bought a house, then there'd be the nuisance of a mortgage or paying taxes. He would always have to hire people to maintain the interior and exterior of the property and concern himself with around-the-clock security. Once the basketball season began he was constantly on the road, and during the home games he usually spent most of his time relaxing in his hotel suite. He slept with women, but not so many that he couldn't remember their names or their faces. Those who took it upon themselves to come unannounced were always escorted off the premises by hotel security. To Phillip Park Kingston, his privacy took precedence over everything else in his life.

Seneca angled her head. "I suppose it makes sense when you think of the upkeep of a house. How large is this suite?"

"It's about twenty-one hundred square feet. There's a connecting one that's a little less than five hundred." Phillip extended his hand. "Come. Let me give you a tour."

Slipping out of her shoes, Seneca placed her small purse on the table, then took the proffered hand. Without her heels, the top of her head reached his shoulder. Her bare feet sank into the deep pile of the carpet as she followed Phillip out of the living room, through the separate area with a dining table, pantry with a microwave, sink and refrigerator, and into the bedroom with a king-size bed. Someone had turned down the sheet and blankets. As in the living area, the drapes were pulled back to take advantage of panoramic views of the city.

She managed to stifle a gasp when she walked into the marble bathroom with a deep soaking Jacuzzi tub and windows overlooking the harbor. She thought of the functional claw-foot bathtub in her apartment where she had yet to take a bath. Since moving in, she'd always taken a shower.

Her shock was magnified when Phillip opened the door to a connecting suite that was a little smaller than the apartment she shared with Electra. It contained a king bed, marble bath with the deep, full-size bathtub and separate shower. The living room had a large, flat-screen television, Bose stereo equipment, a work desk and a fully stocked mini refreshment bar.

"My parents stay here whenever they come to New York," Phillip explained. "A few times some of the guys on the team stay over when they don't want to travel back to Long Island, Westchester or Jersey."

Seneca smiled when she saw the Bulgari bath amenities. The hotel offered the best of the best. "How often do your parents visit you?"

"They try to make it a couple of times during the season. I get to see them whenever we play on the West Coast, and of course during off-season."

"When are you leaving?"

Phillip met her eyes, trying to read the expression in their mysterious depths. Had he detected a hint of regret in her voice? That she hadn't wanted him to leave? "I have a standby reservation for Monday," he lied smoothly.

He'd had a reservation to fly to the West Coast earlier that morning, but with Booth summoning him to attend the dinner party he'd had to change it to Monday morning. Now that he'd met Seneca he didn't want to leave New York. For her, he was willing to delay his return to L.A. up to a week. A week was more than enough time to ascertain whether he'd want to hook up with her for more than just a sexual encounter.

"That all depends upon you," he said in a deceptively quiet tone.

"Me?"

He smiled. "You have to know by now that I like you."

"You like me, hoping I'll agree to go to bed with you. Forget it," Seneca said, not giving him the chance to refute her. "I don't drink, do drugs, nor do I sleep with men."

Crossing muscular arms over his chest, Phillip angled his head. "Who do you do sleep with—women?"

Seneca's right hand swung up an arc, but before her palm could connect she found her wrist caught between fingers that tightened like iron manacles. "You sonofabitch!" she spat out. "Just because I haven't shown you my crotch you think I prefer women?"

Phillip glared at Seneca. Not only did she have a wicked tongue but also a wicked temper. "You've got it all wrong."

"No, Phillip, you've got it wrong. I should've never come here with you." She tried extricating her hand. "If you bruise me I'll sue the hell out of you!"

He loosened his grip. "I'll let you go if you promise not to try and hit me again."

Some of the fight went out of Seneca as the light went out behind her eyes, successfully concealing her innermost feelings from the man staring so intently at her. The incident in the hotel lobby continued to nag at her. People had reached for their cameras and camera phones not because of her but Phillip.

She was willing to do whatever it took to become a successful runway model and if she were to be photographed it was to further her own career, not because she'd been seen with basketball phenom Phillip Kingston.

Exhaling audibly, her eyelids fluttering, she nodded. "I promise." He dropped her hand. "And for your information, I don't sleep with women."

The smile spreading across Phillip's handsome features was mesmerizing. "That's good, because if you did then it would make it impossible for me to react naturally whenever we're photographed together."

"What are you talking about?" Seneca asked.

He reached for her again, this time cradling her elbow.

"Come with me and I'll explain everything." Phillip led her back to the living room of the larger suite, easing her down to the sofa and sitting beside her. "The reason I was late coming down was because Booth wanted to talk about you and me."

Pulling her legs up under her, Seneca shifted to face Phillip. "What about you and me?"

"Booth wants to market us as a couple."

The very thing she hadn't wanted to occur was already on her agent's agenda. "You're kidding, aren't you?" Even as she asked the question she knew he wasn't kidding.

Phillip, who'd divulged more than he should have, shook his head. "No, I'm not kidding. Booth didn't want me to say anything to you until he told you, but I didn't want the Barracuda to blindside you and you go off on him like you did me."

"I doubt if Booth would represent me if I punched him out."

"Don't be so certain about that. I've heard rumors that he likes to be spanked."

Seneca scrunched up her nose. "Kinky."

"You don't know the half," Phillip crooned, smiling. He rested a hand on her bare knee. "Are you a virgin?" He knew he'd shocked Seneca when she emitted an audible gasp. "Are you?" he repeated.

A beat passed. Seneca's eyes narrowed. "Where are you going with this, Phillip?"

"You don't drink, do drugs or sleep with men."

"I don't drink not because I'm not twenty-one, but because they're empty calories. One cocktail and I'm reaching for the chips and nuts. I don't do drugs because I saw firsthand what it did to my cousin. She sold her body, then her infant son for two hundred dollars worth of crack. She died last year from AIDS. I'm currently celibate, because a man I'd believed loved me was sleeping with me and my best friend at the same time."

"I guess that translates into you having trust issues when it comes to men."

"Big-time," Seneca confirmed. "I have guy friends, but they're just that—friends."

Phillip removed his hand from her knee. He had his answer. Any hope he'd had to sleep with Seneca was dashed with her "I don't sleep with men." But he wasn't about to give up. In fact, he liked the fact that she was playing hard to get. That made the chase even more challenging.

"Can I be one of your guy friends?"

Seneca stared at the man who probably could have any woman he wanted even if he hadn't been a high-profile athlete. He was an exquisite physical specimen, and he was a rare find because he wasn't the stereotypical brawn and no brains. Phillip had put off going into the NBA to attend college, majoring in premed.

Peering up at him through a fringe of long lashes, Seneca met his penetrating gaze. "It looks as if *our* agent has already taken care of that. Didn't you tell me that we're going to be a *couple?*"

Phillip's eyebrows lifted a fraction. "So, you're willing to go along with Booth's proposition?"

"Do I have a choice?" she asked.

"You could always say no, but be prepared for the backlash," he warned. "What Booth is proposing is very commonplace in the movie and recording industries—hip-hop stars hooking up with music divas, rockers with supermodels and actresses with athletes. You and I have chosen careers with a very short shelf life. I give myself another ten years before I retire—that is, if I can stay healthy.

"You're twenty trying to make it big when there are fifteen- and sixteen-year-olds out there who think of you as old and a has-been. But you have something special, Seneca, and Booth knows that. Barracuda, Svengali or Machiavelli aside, the man knows his business."

Seneca studied Phillip for a full minute, digesting what he'd said. "Have you done this before? Hooking up with a woman for publicity?"

Phillip's expression was a mask of stone. "Yes." The single word was pregnant with revulsion. "He asked me to escort a singer, who will remain nameless, to an award show. Her breath was horrific and I spent the entire time holding my breath every chance I could. Booth wasn't too happy when I refused to see her again, and I told him that the next time he decided to pair me up with someone I had to meet the lady beforehand."

There was only the whisper of their measured breathing and the bluesy jazz piece floating from speakers placed strategically throughout the suite as Seneca contemplated the turn her life had taken in a matter of hours. She wanted an agent, and she was about to get one. An agent who'd built his reputation as a risk taker. And even before she'd signed a contract with him he'd planned how he'd wanted to market her. What better publicity for his client than to have a supermodel date a superstar athlete?

Smiling and leaning closer to Phillip, she brushed her mouth over his. "How's my breath?"

Phillip placed a hand along the delicate curve of Seneca's jaw and deepened the kiss. He felt resistance, then her mouth relaxed and he caressed her lips with his.

"It's perfect—just like the rest of you," he whispered against her parted lips.

Seneca placed a hand on his chest, pushing him back. "Could you please get me some water? I'm feeling rather parched."

Phillip went to get her water. He took a bottle of Fuji water from the refrigerator, emptied the contents into a glass and then retrieved a bottle of beer for himself. Returning to the living room, he found Seneca peering through the telescope. His hot gaze lingered on the curve of her hips, then moved lower to her long, bare legs and narrow feet. The flesh between his thighs stirred to life and it took Herculean self-control to repress his erection.

"What are you looking at?" he asked, as he approached her. He handed her the glass of water.

"Phillip, I can see the pedestrians on the Brooklyn Bridge."

"I'm more of a stargazer than a people watcher."

She touched her glass to the neck of his beer bottle. "Your secret is safe with me."

Vertical lines appeared between his eyes. "What are you talking about?"

"When Booth proposes I go out with you, I promise to act very surprised."

"Don't act too surprised or you'll arouse his suspicions."

It was Seneca's turn to frown, although she'd made it a practice to keep her face expressionless to lessen the ravages of laugh lines. "Why would you say that?"

"There's no doubt his doorman has already reported back that you were waiting for me. Booth Gordon has legions of spies and paparazzi on his payroll. If there is no scandal, then he'll fabricate one."

She took a swallow of water, watching Phillip over the rim of the glass as he took a long, deep swallow of his beer. "Why have you managed to remain scandal-free?"

"My endorsements come with a morality clause. And that

means no substance abuse, sex with underage girls, drunken orgies or brawls and an endless laundry list of don'ts."

"Do they actually spell it out like that?"

He nodded. "Either I adhere to their rules or give up several hundred million in endorsements."

Seneca whistled softly. Her long-term goal was earning a hundred thousand a year, while Phillip earned nearly a half billion in brand sponsorship for sports drinks, men's fragrances, sneakers, pain medication and a world-renowned clothing designer.

"I suppose I would behave, too, for that kind of money."

"It's not that hard to stay out of trouble. It all comes down to making the right choices—whether it's your friends or a woman."

"Tell me about the private Phillip Kingston—the one the camera doesn't get to see."

"Tomorrow."

"Tomorrow?" she repeated.

Phillip flashed his sensual smile. "Have dinner here with me tomorrow night. I'll send a car for you and arrange to take you back home."

"I'd love to, but I have to go to D.C. for my nephew's baptism. What about one day next week?"

"It can't be next week." He'd changed his mind again about leaving for L.A. now that Seneca had agreed to go out with him. "Remember, I'm going to see my folks."

Seneca lifted her shoulders. "Then we'll get together when you get back." She handed him the half-empty glass. "I only have another hour before my driver is off-duty, so I'm going to leave now." Phillip watched as Seneca put on her shoes, retrieved her cell phone from her purse and called the driver. "I'll be ready as soon as I use your bathroom."

Reaching for his jacket, he slipped his arms into it. By the time she'd returned, he'd filled the pockets with the money clip, cell, and card case with his ID and was waiting at the door. "I'll ride down with you."

Chapter Four

This time Seneca was prepared when she stepped out into the hotel lobby. Hand in hand they strolled across the marble floor, ignoring the bold stares and whispers. What she'd discovered when first moving to New York City was that everyone regarded themselves as a celebrity. There were times when she passed an actor, recording artist or athlete on the sidewalk that she'd noticed people barely gave them a cursory glance. It was tourists who wanted to take pictures or asked for autographs.

Her driver had maneuvered up to the curb and had opened the rear door with her approach. He inclined his head. "Miss Houston. Mr. Kingston."

Seneca got in, and much to her surprise Phillip slipped in beside her. "What are you doing?" she whispered at the same time the door closed with a solid slam.

Reaching for her hand, Phillip laced his fingers through hers. "I want to make certain you make it home safely."

She sucked her teeth loudly. "Of course I'm going to make it home safely. That's why I hired a driver."

He gave her hand a gentle squeeze. "If ever you need a driver, just call the hotel and tell the concierge you need a car."

"You're kidding, aren't you?"

"No, I'm not. I'll add your name to my account."

Seneca wanted to ask Phillip why her, or if he extended the courtesy to all his women. Although appreciative of the offer, she doubted whether she would take him up on it. "Thank you," she said instead.

"You're not going to call." His query was a statement.

"Did I say I wouldn't?" she retorted.

"You won't, only because you want to prove that you're a strong, independent woman who doesn't need a man for anything."

"That's not true. Men are good for a few things."

"Please list them for me, baby."

Seneca went completely still. It was the first time he'd referred to her by the endearment, and whereas she intensely disliked it, just hearing it roll fluidly off Phillip's tongue sent shivers of warming over her body. How, she mused, could one man be the complete package, possess everything most women looked for? He claimed looks, intelligence and physical prowess and exhibited what she'd found lacking in some of the boys with whom she'd grown up: good breeding. However, since meeting Phillip it was as if she were waiting for the other shoe to drop, for him to exhibit a negative side of his personality that would confirm her belief that she couldn't trust a man.

Turning her head, she stared out the side window. "They're useful when I need them to move something heavy."

Phillip smiled. "What else?"

"Checking the oil in the car and/or changing a flat tire."

"What else?"

"That's about it." Seneca turned to see Phillip's startled expression.

"What about making a baby?"

She waved a hand. "I don't need a man for that. I can always go the test tube route."

"That's no fun," he mumbled.

"It is if I don't want to be bothered with a baby daddy. It will be just me and my baby."

Stretching his right arm over the back of the seat, Phillip touched the wisps escaping the intricate twist of thick dark hair. "Is that what you want, Seneca? To have a child and not give your son or daughter the option of having a father in their lives?"

"It would depend on the father."

Phillip caressed the nape of her neck. "So, you punish the entire human male species because of one jackass. Grow up, Seneca. You're not the first and you won't be the last woman who will sleep with a cheater."

"You think I don't know that?" she spat out.

"Then what's your problem?"

"My problem is that the SOB told everyone in our school that we'd gone to a party and after I had a few drinks I went into a room where guys stood in line while I gave them oral sex. He lied, because I never gave him oral sex."

"Damn," Phillip drawled under his breath. "I can see why you have trust issues. But remember, not all men kiss and tell."

"That may be true, but I had the misfortune of sleeping with one. Luckily it was my last year of high school. Instead of attending a local college, I chose one that was downstate."

"Where did you grow up?"

"Ithaca." She told Phillip she'd been accepted into Cornell

University intending to major in theater, film and dance, but Seneca knew she had to leave her hometown or endure the snickering and sly looks from those who'd rather believe a lie than the truth.

"My second choice was NYU. Moving downstate frightened me at first, but now I wouldn't live anywhere else. I had to go from full-time to part-time, because I have to be available for shoots. And now that I'm going to sign with BG Management I'll probably have to drop out."

"Forfeiting or putting your education on hold can't be an easy decision for you," Phillip said in a quiet tone. He also wanted to tell Seneca that she was young and shouldn't judge all men because an insensitive idiot sought to enhance his sexual reputation at her expense. The one who she should've been angry with was her so-called best friend.

Seneca closed her eyes for several seconds. "You're right. It isn't easy." She couldn't imagine what her family's reaction would be once she revealed she wouldn't be going back to classes for the upcoming semester.

The remainder of the ride uptown was conducted in silence, with Seneca contemplating how she would break the news to her parents that she was to become a college dropout. Willing her mind blank, she closed her eyes and sank into the unyielding, muscled body of the man with whom she would be linked romantically as a marketing ploy.

Seneca opened her eyes when the driver got out of the limo and came around to open the rear door. Extending his hand, he helped her out at the same time as Phillip opened the door closest to the curb.

"What are you doing?" she whispered when he reached for her hand.

Phillip gave Seneca a smile parents usually reserved for their well-behaved children. "I'm going to make certain you get inside safely."

She shook her head in exasperation. "Phillip, I live in a very secure building in a safe neighborhood, so there's no need for you to walk me upstairs."

Phillip glanced up at the four-story brownstone on the Upper West Side half a block from Central Park West. There were brownstones and townhouses lining both sides of the tree-lined street, giving it a suburban feel rather than being in the middle of Manhattan with its high-rise apartment and office buildings.

"Which floor do you live on?"

"The fourth," she said, sighing.

"Let's go, baby." Phillip nodded to the driver. "I'll be right back." The man had double-parked in front of Seneca's building.

Seneca had no choice but to follow when he practically pulled her along. "Slow it down," she demanded, "or I'll turn an ankle in these shoes."

"Nice shoes and very nice legs," Phillip said matter-of-factly.

She ignored his compliment while she unlocked the wrought-iron outer door, then another solid oak one with stained-glass insets. When she'd first come to look at the apartment, Seneca couldn't believe her good fortune. The brownstone, erected around the turn of the prior century, had been restored to its original magnificence with marble floors and carved banisters and newel posts. Each apartment boasted parquet floors, tall windows, working fireplaces and claw-foot bathtubs.

Electra, who'd evicted a former roommate who'd refused to pick up after herself, had asked Seneca if she knew of anyone willing to share a two-bedroom apartment only blocks from the Museum of Natural History. Seneca knew she'd surprised the drama student when she told her she would consider moving in with her. Riding the subway uptown and touring around the trendy neighborhood was all she needed to see. Two days later she moved out of the cramped Alphabet City apartment she shared with three other NYU students. Her rent had more than doubled, but at least she didn't have to step over winos and crackheads to get to or into her building. Then there also had been the problem of someone indiscriminately ringing intercom bells in the hope that they would be buzzed in.

"Are you staring at my ass, Phillip?"

Throwing back his head, Phillip laughed loudly. "When I first saw you I never would've imagined you would have a wicked temper with a mouth to match."

She glanced at him over her shoulder. "That's what you get for judging a book by its cover."

"That's true," he crooned. "But you've been a delightful surprise."

"In what way?" she asked.

Phillip stepped off the last stair, following Seneca down the pristine hallway to the rear of the building. "I thought you'd be stuck-up like some of the other models I've met."

Seneca removed her keys from her purse. "All of us are narcissistic," she said in defense of her peers, "but it all depends on what degree. I have a theory that the size of one's ego is usually linked to the number of zeros in their contracts. The more zeros, the more they feel they don't have to adhere to the rules." She unlocked the door, then turned and smiled up at Phillip. "We'll continue this conversation when we see each other again." Leaning closer, she pressed a light kiss to his jaw. "Good night."

Bracing a hand on the door frame, Phillip angled his head,

covering her mouth with his, caressing and tasting the sweetness of her parted lips. He eased back, smiling. "Now, that's a good night."

"Go home, Phillip."

"Not until you go in and lock the door."

Giving him one final sweeping glance, Seneca pushed open the door, stepped inside, closing and locking it behind her. She stood motionless, listening for movement and/or sound from the other side of the door. Then she heard it. Phillip whistling as he retraced his steps, the sound fading with his descent. Bending slightly, she slipped out of the stilettos and walked in the direction of her bedroom. The floor lamp in the living room was turned to its lowest setting, an indication that Electra had decided to visit her parents in Connecticut.

Neither she nor her roommate liked walking into a dark apartment, so they'd agreed to leave a light on. Electra teased, calling their place Motel 6, where they always left the light on.

Seneca touched the dimmer on the wall, and her bedroom was flooded with light from one of two bedside lamps. She undressed, walked into the bathroom to remove her makeup, brush her teeth and shower. Her nightly ritual of applying moisturizer to her face and body and brushing her hair and braiding it into a single plait was something she would be able to execute in a blackout. And, like she'd done as a child, but only if her mother wasn't looking, she raced out of the bathroom and jumped onto her bed. Even at twenty some habits were slow to be relegated to childhood.

Settling herself on the bed, she reached for the remote, flicking on the television and activating the DVD feature. As a serious film, theater and dance student, she filled the empty hours in her life viewing movies. It didn't matter the decade in which they'd been made, whether black-and-white or with

CGI—computer generated imagery—the art of moviemaking had become her passion.

At the recommendation of her professor who taught the history of Hollywood films she'd embarked on a retrospective of Bette Davis and gangster films that included *White Heat, Little Caesar, Bonnie and Clyde,* the *Godfather* trilogy, *GoodFellas* and *The Departed.* Tonight she didn't want to be disturbed by blood and the sound of gunfire, so she selected the Bette Davis classic *Now, Voyager.*

Shifting the mound of pillows supporting her back, Seneca read the opening credits and watched the movie with a critical eye. As a student of film, she had become more than aware of camera angles, dialogue and Paul Henreid suavely performing the archetypal two-cigarette trick.

What she didn't want to acknowledge was how closely her life would've paralleled the Bette Davis character's if it hadn't been for her paternal grandmother. If there was anyone who could put Dahlia Houston in her place, it had been her mother-in-law. Seneca's eyelids felt heavy as the closing credits scrolled down the screen, and she flicked off the television and the table lamp. She would sleep in late, because she'd made a reservation to take an afternoon train to D.C. The last time she'd seen her nephew he was only hours old, and not only was she an aunt, but she was to become a godmother for the first time.

The taxi maneuvered into the driveway behind an SUV with New York plates to a century-old farmhouse in suburban Washington, D.C. Seneca's parents had arrived before she did. Her brother, Jerome, and his wife, Maya, had closed on the property a week before she gave birth to their son. The four-bedroom, three-bath house was advertised as a fixer-upper or a handyman's special, and the couple had poured all of their savings into making the house habitable. Peeling paint and cracked windows with broken sashes had been replaced with white vinyl siding, black shutters and new energy-saving windows.

Seneca paid the driver, retrieved her overnight bag, got out and walked up the porch steps. She smiled. The brick steps and the porch floor were also new. Her brother and sister-in-law, both teachers, had married after a whirlwind courtship. No one, Seneca in particular, had expected Jerome to settle down. He'd dated so many women from every race and ethnic group that she'd thought of him as a modern-day Casanova. She didn't know what it was about Maya, but the high school biology teacher had succeeded where the others had failed.

The door opened before she could ring the bell. She grinned broadly at her sister, who seemed to have grown at least an inch since she last saw her earlier that spring. The similarities between the sisters were startling. Both had curly hair, but Robyn's was a shade lighter, with reddish highlights. The fourteen-year-old had hinted she also wanted to model, but Dahlia had dashed her dream when she said one wannabe model in the family was enough.

Seneca hugged Robyn. "What's up, kid?"

Robyn hugged her back, tightening her grip around Seneca's neck. "Not much. Mom's complaining...as usual," they chorused, laughing.

Seneca had tried analyzing Dahlia and failed completely. Dahlia had become a mother for the first time at sixteen, when she'd found herself pregnant with a married man's child. Her life changed dramatically when she met and married Oscar Houston—a man nearly twenty years her senior. Jerome was six when Seneca was born, and six years later Dahlia gave birth to her second daughter.

Leaving her bag in the entryway, she walked arm in arm

with Robyn to the kitchen, from which wafted the most delicious smells. It was apparent Oscar was cooking. He'd honed his culinary skills during a ten-year stint as a merchant seaman, and when he returned to civilian life he'd continued to cook most of the family's meals.

Jerome held his son, gently patting his back to stop his crying while Maya shook a bottle filled with formula. Dahlia was setting the table in the dining nook as Oscar removed a roasting pan from the oven. A smile softened Seneca's face at the scene of domesticity.

Dahlia noticed her first. "I thought you were coming in earlier."

Seneca's smile disappeared as she bit her lip until it throbbed. "Hello, Mother."

Although Dahlia had recently celebrated her forty-second birthday, she could easily pass for a woman in her early thirties. She was tall and slender, with smooth dark skin, and her chemically relaxed hair was fashionable styled to frame her perfectly rounded face. Intense black eyes, a short nose and a full, lush mouth had most men taking a second look.

It had been her sultry looks that had attracted the attention of an older man who'd seduced her with money and gifts before taking her innocence and leaving her pregnant with his child. When Dahlia's police-officer father came looking for him, the man and his family were gone—never to be seen again. She'd had to endure the shame and humiliation of being an unwed mother until she married Oscar.

Dahlia frowned. "What's with this mother business?"

Seneca caught her brother's warning look, but decided to ignore it. "You are my mother, aren't you?"

"Of course I am," she snapped, "but when did you start calling me *Mother?*"

Waving a hand, Seneca walked over to her father and kissed his cheek. "Hi, Daddy."

Oscar smiled, tiny lines fanning out around his light-brown eyes. His cropped black hair was liberally streaked with gray. "Hey, baby girl. How've you been?"

She kissed him again. "Wonderful. Love you," she whispered sotto voce. "Can I feed him?" Seneca asked her sister-in-law.

Maya set the bottle on the countertop, then tucked wisps of sandy brown hair behind an ear. Her light-green eyes crinkled when she smiled. "Of course you can."

"Let me wash my hands first," she said, walking in the direction of the half bath off the kitchen.

Minutes later, Seneca sat feeding James Scott, who sucked greedily from the bottle. Jerome and Maya had named their son for her father, who'd succumbed to kidney failure four months before the birth of his first grandchild.

James Scott Houston was a gorgeous baby. He'd inherited his mother's fair coloring, hair and eye color, but his features were undeniably his father's. There was no doubt he would be called exotic, which had become the politically accepted designation for mixed-race children.

"The house looks nice," Seneca said to her sister-in-law.

Maya crossed her arms under her breasts. "We decided to complete the exterior first, before concentrating on the interior. We just finished the nursery last week."

Jerome took the platter with a roast turkey from his stepfather. "I told Maya I wanted to remodel the kitchen first only because we spend so much time here."

Seneca stared at her brother, who looked like a very young Miles Davis. Several of his former girlfriends had nicknamed him "Dark Chocolate." With his delicate features and sable-brown coloring, she could see why women had flocked to him in droves, but it was Maya with her flashing green eyes and open, friendly smile who'd enthralled him as the others hadn't been able to.

"Some people take up to five years to fix up their homes," Seneca told her brother.

Jerome frowned, the expression reminiscent of their mother's. "I don't want to take that long. I would've preferred having a post-baptism dinner here at the house instead of in a restaurant."

"I told you I would pick up the tab, son," Oscar said.

"You shouldn't have to, Dad. As a married man I should be able to take care of my family."

Oscar rested a hand on Jerome's shoulder. "Dahlia and I were where you are when we first got married, but we had a lot less in those days. You'll make it, son, but you have to be patient."

Listening to the exchange between her father and brother made Seneca aware that Jerome was more like their mother than she'd realized. When, she mused, had Jerome become a complainer, or had he always been one? She'd come to D.C. to become godmother to her brother's son, not become embroiled in a heated family discussion. As teachers, Jerome and Maya didn't earn six-figure salaries, but they fared better than many young couples in their mid-twenties. They owned their own home.

Seneca knew that living on her own had matured her. Although she shared the apartment with Electra, they rarely got to see each other. They had classes on different days, and when Electra wasn't rehearsing with a theater company, she was waiting tables at restaurants that catered to those in the entertainment field, hoping to get discovered—even if for a minor role in an off-Broadway production.

She kept her bedroom neat and clean and shared cleaning

duties: one week on and one week off cleaning the kitchen and bathroom, dusting and vacuuming the living room. She did her own laundry, shopped for groceries and prepared her own meals. There were no boyfriends, thereby eliminating angst in the romance department, and the times she sat in Starbucks drinking lattes or espressos with a man didn't necessarily translate into a date.

When Phillip had disclosed Booth's plan to link them romantically as a couple, Seneca felt the ruse could work well. After all, she was attracted to the delicious-looking ballplayer, and as long as he didn't pressure her into sleeping with him, then everything would be perfect.

James Scott was asleep before he finished the bottle. Seneca removed the nipple from his mouth with a soft popping sound, then took the cloth diaper Maya handed her and placed it over her shoulder. Lifting the sleeping infant to her shoulder, she waited until he expelled a loud burp. He squirmed, whining softly, before settling back to sleep. She handed him off to his mother.

"I don't mind splitting the bill, Dad," she volunteered.

Jerome shook off his father's hand and glared at Seneca. "Did I ask you for a handout?"

With wide eyes, Seneca stared at her brother. "No, you didn't. All I did was offer to help pay—"

"I heard what you said, Seneca. Just because you sell yourself to the highest bidder like some half-dressed, painted, overpaid mannequin I don't want you to think I need your so-called charity."

"It's not charity, Jerome."

"So, it's a handout," he countered. "You probably earn more in two hours than I do in a week teaching, so don't try to act so fuckin' smug."

"That's enough," Oscar warned.

"What's not enough is my busting my ass teaching kids who could give a shit less about math, while Miss Supermodel here doesn't get out of bed in the morning unless they offer her five figures."

Seneca threw up her hands. "Forget I offered. I'll keep my charity." Turning her heels, she went over to take the silver-ware from Dahlia to finish setting the table.

Chapter Five

Dahlia, who appeared to have forgiven Seneca for calling her Mother, was in rare form. She'd embraced grandmother status with an attitude that shocked most sitting at the table. She talked incessantly about the outings she planned to take with James Scott.

Oscar stunned his children when he announced that he'd decided to retire at the end of the year. "Working thirty years at the same place gets a little boring."

"How boring can it be, Daddy?" Seneca asked. "You're a supervisor."

"That's why it's boring," Oscar said. "When I was a letter carrier there was always some excitement."

Dahlia gave her husband a tender smile. "Excitement or gossip, darling?" she questioned softly.

Oscar winked at Dahlia. "Both. If you ever want to know someone's business, then ask their letter carrier. I could tell you what credit cards someone had, what magazines they sub-scribed to and if collection agencies or the IRS was hounding them. Then don't forget the Family Court summonses for nonpayment of child support."

"How is getting into someone's business exciting?" Robyn questioned.

"You'll understand once you're older," her mother explained.

Robyn affected a scowl. "I've been hearing that all my life. I'll be fifteen in a couple of months. Will I be old enough then?"

Dahlia rolled her eyes at her youngest child, contemplating whether to chastise her for her impudent tone. "What you should concern yourself with is pulling up your grades," she said instead. "You're never going to get into a good college with seventies."

Robyn, mimicking her mother, rolled her eyes, too. "I only got a seventy in science. I got nineties in my other subjects."

"And you only have three weeks before you have to take the Regents."

"I know that, Mama!" Mother and daughter glared at each other in what was certain to end in an impasse. Robyn was just as stubborn as Dahlia.

"Why don't you let me tutor Robyn while I'm on leave," Maya volunteered. She looked at Jerome, who nodded his approval. "The carpenters are scheduled to put in new flooring next week, and I'd planned to stay at my sister's house because they're going to apply polyurethane as a finish. If you don't mind an extra couple of houseguests, James Scott and I can ride back to Ithaca with you."

"Please, Mama," Robyn wailed. "Now that Seneca's classes are over, can she come, too?"

Seneca swallowed a portion of turkey. Although she'd always enjoyed hanging out with her sister and sister-in-law, Robyn had picked the wrong time to arrange a sisterly get-together. Five pairs of eyes were trained on her, and she knew everyone sitting at the table was waiting for her answer.

"I'm willing to help with the driving, but I can't go to Ithaca with you." Uncertain whether her parents had planned on staying in D.C., she'd purchased a round-trip ticket. "I've committed to signing with an agency, and that means I'll probably get more modeling jobs."

Dahlia set down her knife and fork. "What's going to happen in September when classes begin again?"

A beat passed before Seneca said, "I'm planning to take a leave from classes."

"Don't you mean drop out?" Dahlia countered.

She counted slowly to three. "Yes, Mom, I'm going to drop out."

"But…but what about your degree?" the older woman stammered.

"I'll get my degree, because I promised Grandma I would."

"It shouldn't be about what your grandmother wanted but what you want, Seneca."

She didn't want to get into it with her mother, especially with an audience of onlookers. "I want a degree and I will get my degree—just not at this time. I've given modeling full-time a lot of thought, and if I don't do it now then it'll never happen."

Dahlia shook her head. "But—"

"You let her model, and when I asked you if I could you put me down," Robyn interrupted angrily.

Dahlia shook her finger at her younger daughter. "You're not going to drop out of school so you can shake your half-naked ass in front of a bunch of freaks."

"Amen to that," Jerome mumbled, still smarting because he felt Seneca saw him as a charity case.

Oscar narrowed his gaze at the same time he reached over to cover Dahlia's fisted hand. "Robyn, please, let's not talk about this now."

A rush of color suffused the teenager's face with her rising temper. "But—I want to talk about it now!"

"Enough, Robyn," Oscar cautioned softly. "Seneca is a grown woman who can make her own decisions. You forget that your mother and I are responsible for you, not the other way around. And I would like you to watch your tone, young lady."

Oscar Houston rarely got involved in the verbal altercations between his wife and their children, but lately he'd noticed Robyn behaving oddly; she'd begun exhibiting signs of being extremely short-tempered. A single word would set her off, and Robyn seemed bent on seeing how far she could go before Dahlia lost her temper.

"Daddy, the turkey is delicious." Seneca had to say something—anything—to lighten the mood. What she wanted to do was kick Robyn under the table.

Oscar winked at her. "Thank you."

Jerome extended his plate. "I'll have another helping of turkey and dressing. And don't forget to ladle on the gravy. I'm eating for Seneca," he joked. "Ya'll know models are notorious for not eating."

"Since when did you become a stand-up comedian?" Seneca drawled. Her voice was filled with sarcasm. "For your information, I do eat."

Jerome opened his mouth to come back at Seneca, but a warning look from his father quickly ended the interchange. "I'm sorry about that," he said, apologizing. "I have to admit that you're the only model I've ever seen who doesn't look anorexic in person."

She smiled. "I'm probably that rare person who doesn't photograph heavier."

Maya touched her napkin to the corners of her mouth. "Are most photos touched up or airbrushed?"

"I suppose the ones for the glossy magazines do get Photoshopped."

Seneca spent the rest of dinner fielding questions about modeling. She was offered a reprieve when the sound of the baby's cries came through the baby monitor. James Scott was awake.

Seneca maneuvered up the empty space in front of her building, shifting into Park. She'd driven from the restaurant in northern Virginia to New York City, stopping once to refuel outside of Philadelphia. She shook her father gently, rousing him from sleep. Oscar, along with the other occupants of the Toyota Sequoia had fallen asleep before they'd left the Capitol District. The sound of snoring was drowned out by the music flowing from the many speakers in the large sport utility vehicle.

"I'm home, Daddy."

Oscar's eyelids fluttered as he struggled to focus his gaze on the lighted dashboard. "What were you doing? Speeding?" It'd had taken Seneca only a little more than three hours to make the two-hundred-mile drive between New York City and Washington, D.C.

"Traffic was light," she said, rather than tell her father that she had exceeded the speed limit whenever possible. "Are you sure you're going to be alert enough to drive, or should I wake Mom?"

Oscar, stretching out his arms, shook his head. "No. I can drive."

He unlocked and opened the passenger-side door, got out

and came around the vehicle as Seneca slipped from behind the wheel with a large quilted sack that doubled as purse and overnight bag. She hadn't changed out of the suit she'd worn to the baptism and the dinner that followed but had exchanged her heels for a pair of running shoes.

She hugged and kissed him. "Get home safely, Daddy."

Oscar tightened his hold on her waist, lifting her off her feet. "When are you coming up for a visit?"

"I'll try for the Fourth. Maybe I'll bring Robyn back with me and have her stay a week or two."

He kissed her cheek. "I'm certain she would love that. Don't forget I'll be in Pennsylvania the first, second and third for the Battle of Gettysburg reenactment. But I promised to be home by the Fourth."

Seneca smiled. Her father, well versed in military history, was a Civil War buff and had joined a group who reenacted battles from the Revolutionary and Civil wars. "Be careful, Daddy."

"Don't worry. I've heard the speech from your mother at least half a dozen times. 'Sit it out if temperatures go above eighty-five.'"

"Please listen to her." Stepping back, she watched her father get in behind the wheel, adjust the seat and mirror, then drive away, watching until the red taillights disappeared when he turned the corner.

Seneca climbed the steps to the brownstone, unlocked the outer door, then slowly made her way up the stairs to her apartment. She'd volunteered to have Robyn stay with her for several weeks to give her sister a look at another way of a life—a faster, grittier and more dangerous environment. Ithaca, with its magnificent gorges, lush forests, pristine lakes—billed as the gateway to the Fingers Lakes—also had its share of social ills that weren't as apparent as in larger cities. One day Robyn would come to appreciate their mother monitoring her every move.

She unlocked the door and was greeted with a blast of frigid air. Electra had left the living room air-conditioning unit on the highest setting. She closed and locked the door, walked into the living room and picked up the unit's remote device, readjusting the thermostat. Seneca had lost count of the number of times she'd shown her roommate how to program the timer and temperature, but Electra claimed she always forgot. The sound of Electra's low-pitched, distinctive laugh, followed by a deeper chuckle, meant that the aspiring actress was either rehearsing or entertaining in her bedroom.

"Go for it, girl," she whispered. Electra's bedroom was far enough from hers so she wouldn't be disturbed by loud voices or music. Closing the door to her own bedroom, Seneca noticed the flashing red light on her phone. Punching the code to the voice mail, she activated the speaker feature.

She froze, listening intently to the beautifully modulated female voice: *Mr. Gordon has arranged for a car to pick you up at eleven forty-five. Lunch will be at La Grenouille.*

Seneca's eyes narrowed. It wasn't an invitation but a command.

She would shower, then go online to look up the restaurant, only because she didn't want to appear gauche if she showed up wearing the wrong attire. Thanks to Luis, she didn't have to rush out to buy an outfit whenever she had an appointment. Luis had called her his *mariposa,* and that's how she wanted to be promoted.

Peering into the mirror over her dresser, she angled her head. A slow smile found its way over her features. "Please permit me to introduce myself," she drawled in a sultry whisper. "I am Seneca Houston. Better known as Butterfly."

Chapter Six

The driver was standing on the top step holding an umbrella when Seneca walked out of the brownstone. He extended his free arm, and she looped her arm over his suit jacket as he led her down the stairs to the black Mercedes Benz parked at the curb.

The rain that had started earlier that morning was tapering off to a light drizzle. In deference to the weather, she'd changed outfits several times until deciding on a black pencil skirt, black patent leather pumps and a red blouse with a mandarin collar piped in black. Upon closer inspection one could see tiny embroidered butterflies on the silk fabric. The black obi sash accentuating her tiny waist pulled her winning look together. She'd taken the time to flatiron her hair, styling it into a bohemian knot. Her only jewelry was a pair of pearl studs. With the warmer weather she tended to go bare-legged, but today she wore a pair of sheer black nylons.

Smiling, Seneca thanked the black-suited chauffeur as he opened the rear door; she sat on the leather seat, then swung her legs around. Having a driver at her disposal was a far cry from trying to flag down a taxi in the rain. She'd discovered that taxis mysteriously became as scarce as hen's teeth whenever it rained in New York.

Earlier that morning, she'd had a lengthy conversation with Luis, giving him an update on Booth's dinner party, her becoming godmother to her nephew and the scheduled lunch date with Booth at La Grenouille. What she hadn't told Luis was that she'd gone with Phillip Kingston to his hotel suite.

She could hear the excitement in Luis's voice when he told her she was about to make it big. Then his tone changed when Seneca promised him that they were to be a package deal. He'd told her not to worry about him, but that was something she couldn't do. If it hadn't been for Luis she never would've given modeling a passing thought. Now she was on the threshold of signing with one of the premier agents, who'd promised to make her a supermodel.

Relaxing against the supple black leather seat, she detected the lingering scent of Booth's cologne. He'd sent his car and driver to pick her up. Why, she mused, did she feel like a lamb being led to slaughter? Shaking off the uneasy feeling, she stared out the window at the passing landscape as the driver took the Seventy-ninth Street transverse road through Central Park to the east side. The uneasiness fled, and Seneca was in complete control when she was escorted through the doors of the exquisite dining establishment and ushered to Mr. Gordon's favorite table.

Her vermilion-colored lips parted in a warm smile when he rose, hands extended, to greet her. His hands were cool, soft. "The restaurant is lovely," she whispered against his smooth-shaven jaw. La Grenouille was a garden where food just happened to be served.

Booth stared numbly at Seneca before a smile parted his thin lips. He still found it hard to believe that she was even more beautiful in person than in her photographs. She was like a rare D-colored diamond. Seneca Houston was flawless.

"You are lovely, Seneca," he said, pulling out a chair at the table and seating her while he lingered over her head longer than necessary. She lowered her chin, the demure gesture enchanting. He stared at the coil of hair on the nape of her long, slender neck. How he longed to place his mouth against the velvety skin to see if she tasted as good as she looked.

"Thank you, Mr. Gordon."

A scowl replaced his smile as he retook his seat. "Please call me Booth."

Seneca peered at Booth through her lashes. His navy-blue suit with a faint pinstripe must have set the agent back several thousand dollars and there was no doubt his shirt and silk tie hadn't come off a department-store rack or shelf. His fingernails were square-cut and buffed. Booth Gordon was the epitome of sartorial splendor. The exception was his hair. It was too long and much too oily.

"But you're old enough to be my father," she said in a quiet voice.

Booth moved his chair closer, placing his hand over hers. "But I am not your father. Call me Booth." It was a direct order.

Seneca stared at him, her eyes narrowing slightly. "Okay, Booth. What do you want to talk about?"

"Do you have another appointment after lunch?"

She shook her head. "No. I'm free for the rest of the day."

"If that's the case, then I'd like to eat, then talk. Is that all right with you, Seneca?"

She lifted a shoulder. "It's fine with me."

Resting his elbows on the table, Booth tented his fingers. "Is there something about me that bothers you, Seneca?"

To say his query caught her off guard was an understatement. What did he expect her to say? That the way he was leering at her made her feel as if he were a pedophile preying on younger women, although she was past the legal age of consent?

"Your hair is too long." It was the only thing she could say without openly insulting him.

Booth resisted the urge to touch the hair falling over the collar of his shirt. "How short should I cut it?"

Her eyebrows shot up, mirroring her surprise. "You'd cut your hair for me?"

An unnamed emotion darkened the blue-green eyes. "Let's say I'd take your suggestion under advisement."

His response puzzled Seneca. "Does it really matter what I think?"

"To a certain extent it does," Booth countered. "Whenever I consider taking on a prospective client I ask them the same question, and I expect an honest answer."

"Do you always get an honest answer?" she asked.

"Nine out of ten times I don't. Most are so eager to please they lie to me and to themselves."

"So, this was a test."

Booth smiled. "And you passed. The next time I meet with my barber I'll have him cut it shorter."

Seneca gave him a sidelong glance. "Is there something about me that bothers you, Booth?" If her question shocked him, he gave no indication as his gaze lowered to the pristine white tablecloth.

"It bothers me that I can't seduce you."

The seconds ticked before she was able to form a response. "And why not?"

Booth's head came up, he giving her a long, penetrating

look. "Because I've made it a practice not to shit where I have to eat."

There was another pause. "It looks as if we have the same practice," Seneca said. "I will not sleep with you and pay you commission. That would make you my pimp and me your whore."

Booth's face paled with annoyance. It wasn't often that he met a woman like Seneca Houston. She continually challenged him, without regard to the fact that he held her future in his hands. All it took was a single telephone call or the scrawl of his pen to make her a very wealthy young woman. And like all those who'd come before her and would come after her, she wanted fame and fortune.

Some would say she had a great attitude, while he believed she had a chip on her shoulder—a chip directed at authority figures. What Seneca Houston hadn't realized is that she'd just used up her first strike with him.

"Did anyone ever tell you that you have an acid tongue?"

Seneca gave him a sensual smile. "Yes. In fact, Phillip Kingston said the same thing to me the other night." She'd decided to broach the topic of Phillip before Booth did. "When I told you I had another engagement the night of your dinner party, it was with Phillip. We had an arrangement to leave separately, then go somewhere and talk."

"If I'd known you two were getting together I wouldn't have held him up."

"Why did you hold him up?" she asked innocently. Seneca knew Booth's doorman had reported back to him that she'd been waiting for Phillip, but neither of them knew what Phillip had confided to her.

"I'd hoped you and Kingston would hit it off, because I'd like to market the two of you as a couple. I got an offer from General Motors to sign Kingston as a pitchman for the Cadillac

SRX. I was thinking that maybe you could also appear in the ad with him."

Twin emotions warred inside Seneca. Appearing in an ad with Phillip Kingston would thrust her into the media spotlight, but only because of the ballplayer. "You've told them about me?"

Booth shook his head. "Not yet."

"What makes you think they'll accept me?" she asked.

"I'm certain they will once they see photos of you and Kingston together."

"What photos?"

"The ones Mitchell Leon will take this coming weekend. Kingston has agreed to come back to New York for the shoot."

"You want me to do an ad with Phillip Kingston before I sign a contract with BGM?" She'd asked yet another question.

A mysterious smile tilted the corners of Booth's mouth. "Your contract is being drawn up as we speak. All I need is the name and fax number of your attorney and it will be on his desk before five o'clock today. I'll attach a memo asking them to expedite it. And don't worry, Seneca, I'll pay the billable fees out my own pocket."

The uneasy feeling was back. Why, she wondered, was Booth Gordon in such a rush to sign her? Did he see something in her that made her that marketable? What was so different about her that he knew with a single glance that he could make her a supermodel?

Seneca knew she was only one of millions of women with a unique face and body who were able to live uneventful lives away from the cameras and spotlights if they weren't sucked into the world of modeling. When Luis had approached her with the possibility of modeling his designs, initially she'd turned him down. But, Luis was relentless. In the end she agreed to model a collection of evening gowns for a private client. And the rest, as they say, is history.

"It's not an ad," Booth corrected, breaking into Seneca's musings. "It's a television spot."

Seneca was certain Booth could hear the runaway beating of her heart through her blouse. Her first television commercial would pair her with none other than Phillip Kingston. Unable to get out the words locked in her throat, she managed a barely perceptible nod. Within three days she'd gone from part-time student and part-time commercial model to one with infinite possibilities.

"I'm glad you didn't lie to me about meeting with Kingston," Booth continued. He knew Seneca was stunned by his pronouncement that he wanted her to team up with Phillip for a television commercial. What he hadn't disclosed was that the ten-second spot would preview during the Super Bowl.

"There's no need to lie to you, Booth. Phillip and I are consenting adults," she said after she'd recovered her voice. His comeback was preempted when the waiter approached the table to take their lunch selections. Seneca studied the menu, then flashed a demure smile. "What do you recommend?"

Resting a proprietary arm over the back of her chair, Booth leaned closer to Seneca, inhaling the subtle woodsy notes that made up her perfume. The fragrance matched her looks and personality: unabashed sensuality.

"The corn crêpes with sautéed chicken livers and sherry are always good."

"How's the endive salad with pears, walnuts and Roquefort cheese?" she asked.

"It's also quite good."

Seneca stared up at him through her lashes. If she'd been like her mother and sister, she probably would've found herself entranced by Booth Gordon. Dahlia and Robyn liked older men, while she preferred them closer to her own age. That was why she hadn't been receptive to Luis Navarro's subtle advances.

"What are you having?" she asked.

"I'm leaning toward the chicken paillard with sage and squash gnocchi."

"Please order the salad for me."

Booth beckoned the waiter closer, giving him their selections. "I'd also like a bottle of Laurent Perrier Rosé and Perrier for the lady."

The waiter bowed slightly. "Thank you, Mr. Gordon."

Booth settled back to enjoy the youthful beauty of a woman who was completely unaware of her marketability. When the photos Mitchell Leon had taken of Seneca Houston ended up on his desk, he'd found himself mesmerized by the face that made love to the camera.

He'd seen and been with more beautiful women than he could count or remember, but there was something about the up-and-coming model that was different. With or without makeup, with her hair in a sleek, sophisticated style or curling naturally around her face, she was stunning. Whether fully or half clothed, she was spectacular. He hadn't missed the admiring glances directed at Seneca from the other patrons when she was escorted to his table. His only consolation was that he would have her undivided attention for the next two hours.

"What are you smiling about, Seneca?"

"I'm wondering why you would select a romantic restaurant when you want to discuss business." White-bone English china, napkins, exquisite wineglasses—all set on white tablecloths—provided the backdrop for a breathtaking arrangement of white camellias.

"La Grenouille is the unofficial headquarters of top fashion designers and many of their best customers. Speaking of designers—you'd mentioned a Luis Navarro. Who is he?"

Seneca told Booth about meeting Luis at party in the Village and how he'd approached her to model his designs for a private client. "He says I'm his muse—his *mariposa*. That's Spanish for butterfly," she explained, seeing his puzzled expression.

Booth stared at the embroidered butterflies on her blouse. "Didn't you wear a necklace with a butterfly clasp Friday night?"

"Yes, I did."

"Do all of his designs have butterflies?"

"No," she said, laughing softly. "However, whenever he makes something for me he'll include a butterfly somewhere on the garment."

Their drinks arrived, the sommelier uncorking a bottle of wine, filling a wineglass and a goblet with sparkling water. He backed away from the table as they raised their glasses in a toast.

Booth winked at Seneca. "To Seneca."

"To Butterfly," she crooned, bringing Booth's gaze to linger her parted lips.

Seneca declined dessert in favor of a cup of imperial green tea while Booth, who'd finished the bottle of wine, ordered espresso. She'd gleaned a lot about the man who was to become her agent while she'd watched him eat. He was attentive, his table manners impeccable, and he had asked several times if the meal was to her liking.

Booth touched the napkin to his mouth, then placed it to the right of his cup and saucer. Reaching into the breast pocket of his suit jacket, he removed a minute tape recorder, activated the Record button and set in on the table.

"Now we can talk."

Seneca noticed his voice was slightly raspy, attributing the change in timbre to the amount of wine he'd consumed. "Why the tape recorder?"

"I don't want to have to repeat what you've said to your celebrity public relations consultant."

A slight frown appeared between her eyes. "I thought you would be my publicist."

"No, baby," Booth crooned. "You'll have your own publicist, makeup and hairstylist."

"How much is this going to cost me?"

"Twenty-five percent of everything you earn. I get fifteen, the publicist five and the makeup and hairstylist split the remaining five evenly."

"Do all of your models give up twenty-five percent of their earnings?" She couldn't imagine earning a hundred thousand, then just handing over twenty-five thousand to Booth.

"No."

"Why not?" She literally spat out the two words.

"They're not you, Seneca. None of them will ever earn what I project you'll make. Of course BGM will get them assignments, but we don't go all out to promote them. They're only as good as their last job. If a designer likes them, then they ask for them again. If not, then they're shit out of luck."

"Why did you sign them up if you weren't willing to market them?" Seneca asked. Booth closed his eyes, seemingly deep in thought. When he opened them they appeared more green than blue. "You're using them." Her query was a statement. When he didn't confirm or refute her question, she asked, "What else do you want to know about me?"

"How did you get the name Seneca?"

"I was named for my paternal grandmother's people."

Booth's hooded lids lifted. "You're Native American?"

"Only one-eighth First Nation," she said, correcting him. My grandmother was half-Seneca."

"Do you want to be marketed as First Nation or African-American?"

"African-American."

"Are you versed in your grandmother's history?"

Seneca nodded, then remembered she was being taped. "Yes. Only because she was proud of her Indian heritage. The Seneca were the largest of the five tribes that comprised the Iroquois League, or Nations. They're the only Nation in the United States to own a U.S. city."

"What city is that?" Booth asked as he sat up straighter.

"Salamanca. It's situated on land owned by the Alleghany Indian reservation. I have relatives who still shave their heads in Mohawk fashion. They also tattooed their bodies with symbols that identified them as members of the Five Nations."

"Do you have any tattoos?"

"I have one," Seneca admitted.

Booth was aware that some designers wouldn't book a model with body art, but that was about to change. Temporary-tattoo-inspired bodies had been introduced on the Spring 2010 runways by fashion houses as different as Rodarte and Jean Paul Gaultier. Even Chanel had gotten in on the trend. Called Les Trompe L'Oeil de Chanel Temporary Skin Art, it was now available through their Internet Web site.

"Where is it?"

"It's at the small of my back."

"What is it?"

Seneca stared at the timepiece strapped to Booth's wrist, watching as the sweep hand made a full revolution. "It's a butterfly. To Native people, it's a symbol for joy."

Booth sighed inaudibly. He'd prayed she would say a

butterfly, because the beautiful insect would become her signature. "Do you want to be known as Seneca or Butterfly?"

"Butterfly."

He smiled. "I'd hoped you'd say that."

"Why?"

"Because *butterfly* can be translated into many languages, whereas *Seneca* can't. Once you sign the contract, I'll set you up with a runway coach. You're versatile enough to do commercial, print and runway." Booth paused, waiting for her to digest this information. "How much education have you had?"

Seneca recalled her mother's reaction to the news that she was dropping out of college. "I've just completed thirty college credits. I'm enrolled at NYU with a major in film and theater."

Booth found his potential client more interesting with every question he put to her. "Do you sing?"

"No."

"Dance?"

Seneca smiled tentatively. "Yes."

Lines fanned out around his eyes when he returned her smile. "How well, Butterfly?"

"Very well. I started dancing at four." The tape continued to roll when she told him about her grandmother, who'd appeared in more than two dozen independent black films and had passed her love of moviemaking on to her granddaughter. "Whereas my grandmother loved being in front of the camera, I prefer being behind the camera," Seneca explained.

"What's your ultimate goal?"

"I want to direct…" Her words trailed off when Booth shut off the recorder. "Why did you stop the tape?"

"I'm selling Butterfly, not Seneca Houston. Speaking of

your last name—you pronounce it like the street in downtown Manhattan."

"Yes," she confirmed.

"What if we change it to sound like the city in Texas?"

"No," Seneca said in protest. "It's always been House-stun, not Hugh-stun."

"Excuse me," Booth said when he felt his cell phone vibrating. He removed the tiny phone from the pocket of his shirt, staring at the display. "Yes, Raye. Hold on and I'll get it." He palmed the tiny instrument. "The contract is ready. I need your attorney's name and phone number."

Seneca retrieved her cell and scrolled through the directory for Electra's father's law firm, giving him the number, and he repeated it to the person on the other end of his line.

It's about to begin. The realization hit Seneca full force. Talking with Booth had just been that—talk—until he'd mentioned the contract. The legally binding document made it real. She would have an über-agent, publicist, makeup person and hairstylist. They were the team Booth had put together to turn her into a supermodel. He wanted twenty-five percent of her earnings, which to Seneca was tantamount to extortion. She was willing to give up twenty percent, and not one percent more.

Her cell phone rang before she could put it back in her handbag. The name that came up on the display sent her pulses racing. She pressed a button. "Please hold on. Excuse me, but I have to take this call, " she said to Booth. He half rose to his feet when she walked in the direction of the rest rooms.

Seneca put the tiny instrument to her ear as she pushed open the door to the ladies' lounge. "How did you get this number?"

"Booth gave it to me."

Sitting on a tufted chair, she crossed her legs at the knees.

"He told me you were coming back to New York for a photo shoot."

A deep chuckle caressed her ear. "A photo shoot I'm really looking forward to."

"So am I, Phillip," Seneca admitted.

"What do I have to do or say to convince you to hang out with me for a couple of days?"

She smiled. "All you have to do is ask me."

"Miss Houston, will you have breakfast, lunch and dinner with me?"

Seneca's smile was as dazzling as bright sunlight. "Yes, Mr. Kingston, I will have breakfast, lunch and dinner with you." She wanted to talk longer but didn't want Booth to send someone to look for her. "I'm going to have to ring off, because right now I'm meeting with *your* agent."

"Lucky you," Phillip teased, laughing.

"Goodbye, Phillip."

"Goodbye, baby."

She ended the call, left the rest room and returned to the table, ignoring the questioning look the agent gave her. "Where were we?" she asked.

"You seem quite pleased," Booth stated.

"I am."

"Who…" His words trailed off when he spotted someone he hadn't seen in months.

"Do you mind if I join you and the lovely lady?"

Pushing back his chair, Booth rose to his feet. "Rhys, when did you get back?"

"One day last week. But I must have caught something during the flight, because I was flat on my back for days. May I sit?"

A flush crept up Booth's neck to his hairline. He'd forgotten his manners. "Of course, please sit." He retook his seat when the fashion designer sat, in his opinion, a little too close to his client. "Rhys, this is Seneca Houston. Seneca, Rhys Calhoun."

Seneca offered her hand to the man who three years ago had exploded onto the fashion scene with an Asian-inspired collection of wedding dresses. Those in the industry referred to him as the male Vera Wang, which he'd accepted as the ultimate compliment.

Her eyes met a pair so dark she doubted whether light could penetrate their fathomless depths. Rhys had pulled his strawberry-blond hair back into a queue with a black silk ribbon. His skin was so pale it appeared translucent. Her eyes shifted from his eyes to his mouth, and she was hard-pressed not to laugh when she realized he was wearing lipstick. Putting her forefinger to her own lips, she made a sweeping motion.

Rhys reached for the handkerchief in the pocket of his jacket and blotted his mouth. He winked at Seneca. "Some ladies are a little frisky."

Booth didn't like that the designer was flirting with his client because Rhys had established a reputation for combining business and pleasure. "Where is your next show?"

"Miami. I've put together a swimwear collection that, as the kids say, is mad crazy. If she's available, I would like to have Seneca in the show."

Booth's eyebrows flickered. "I'll check her schedule and let you know."

Seneca stared at the flower petal that had fallen from the superb arrangement. *You lying, crafty fox.* Something told her Booth would hold out as long as possible to up the fee for her appearing in the show.

"Send me an e-mail," Rhys demanded. He touched the sleeve of Seneca's blouse, rubbing the fabric between his fingertips. "Where did you buy this?"

"I didn't. It's a Luis Navarro design."

Rhys angled his head. "Why haven't I heard of him?"

Opening her handbag, Seneca handed him one of Luis's business cards. She'd mentioned Luis's name to Booth at every opportunity, but he'd deigned to ignore the importance of the man who'd brought her to this point in her life. If not Booth, then she would make certain Rhys Calhoun was apprised of his fashion genius.

"Give Luis a call."

Rhys pocketed the card. "I will." He gestured to Booth. "Don't forget to e-mail about Seneca's availability. I have to be off," he said, rising to his feet and bowing gracefully to Seneca. "It's been a pleasure."

Booth's eyes turned frosty as he stared at Rhys' retreating broad back. "Why did you do that?"

"Do what?" Seneca asked.

"Don't play the innocent with me, Seneca."

She bristled at his acerbic tone; a tone that sounded too much like Dahlia's. "Don't talk to me like that."

"I'll talk to you any—"

"No, you won't," she countered, interrupting him. "Must I remind you that you're not my agent until I sign the contract. And even then, you will not talk to me as if I were chattel."

You just used up your second strike. Booth seethed, struggling and successfully curbing his explosive temper. If he hadn't had plans—grand plans—for Seneca Houston, he wouldn't have permitted the bitch to cross his threshold. He'd married and divorced two women because they'd continually forgotten their place. He'd grown up watching his overbearing mother browbeat and berate his father until the man couldn't get it up—not for her; however, there had been one exception. The woman who'd been his confidante.

The day he turned fifteen he left home, moving in with his

uncle and aunt. The childless couple gave him the affection so missing from his parents, and the first time his mother's brother took him to his office one weekend to show him what he did for a living Booth was hooked like an addict taking their first hit of crack. He started in the mailroom, then worked his way to gofer and finally got to sit in on the negotiations when his uncle signed an emerging actor to a daytime soap who a decade later would go on to become an A-list star. He'd learned the art of the deal from the best, but it was his natural instincts that had turned a mediocre entertainment and sports agency into one that rivaled William Morris and Creative Artists.

"I'm sorry, Seneca," he apologized insincerely, "if you take offense to my tone, but I deal with so much bullshit from men that I sometimes forget my manners."

Seneca leaned over the table. "I grew up having to bite my tongue, because my mother has a tongue that cuts like a cat-o'-nine-tails. And when I left home I swore an oath that I would never put up with that type of verbal abuse again. Please, Booth, don't make me regret signing with you."

There was an unidentifiable emotion in the eyes of the twenty-year-old woman-child that made Booth take note of her warning. Seneca Houston hadn't grown up in the slums, but there was something about her that said she could've easily been in a street gang. He recognized the latent dangerousness because his best friend had beaten another boy with a baseball bat when he wouldn't stop shaking him down for his lunch money. The bully lapsed into a coma and died before he could tell the police who'd attacked him, and Booth, who'd witnessed the assault, never told anyone what he'd seen. It was a secret he would take to his grave and Dennis Mayfield repaid him for his silence because whenever Booth wanted to apply a little pressure to close a deal, Dennis provided the needed incentive.

Booth flashed his practiced Cheshire-cat grin. "You won't." He winked at her. "My driver will take you back whenever you're ready."

Despite her annoyance, Seneca returned his smile. "Thank you for lunch. It was quite an experience."

His smile did not slip. "I should say it was." He signaled for the waiter, signed the check and then, looping an arm around Seneca's waist, he led her out of the restaurant. The car and driver appeared as if out of thin air. Cradling her face between his hands, Booth brushed a light kiss over her mouth. "Mitchell will call you to set up the shoot. Stay beautiful, baby."

Seneca didn't have time to react when she found her elbow cupped in the driver's hand as he escorted her to the car. She didn't know what to make of Booth's unexpected display of affection. He'd claimed he would never attempt to sleep with her, but on the other hand he was sending her mixed signals.

She managed to push all thoughts of the enigmatic agent to the farthest recesses of her mind when she recalled her conversation with Phillip Kingston. He was coming back to New York. They would do a photo shoot together, and if Booth was able to ink the deal, then they would appear in a television commercial together.

Butterfly was about to emerge from her cocoon to take flight.

Chapter Seven

Seneca harmonized with Alicia Keys singing "Like You'll Never See Me Again" as the warm spray of water beat down on her head. Booth had asked whether she sang, and her response had been no. But she did sing, only for herself. She'd lost count of the number of shower radios she'd gone through over the years. She stopped singing, listening intently, when she heard the distinctive squeak of the bathroom door opening.

"Seneca, my dad has been trying to reach you," Electra called out. "He called your cell, but it went straight to voice mail. I told him to call your other phone and leave a message."

It was apparent that William Jacobs wanted to talk to her about the contract. Whenever she charged her cell she always turned it off. "Thanks, Electra. I'll call him right back."

Ten minutes later, her body swaddled in a terry-cloth bathrobe and her hair under a matching towel, Seneca sat in a club chair in a corner of her bedroom with the cordless receiver cradled between her chin and shoulder, waiting for Electra's father to come on the line.

"Good morning, Seneca."

She smiled. If William Jacobs decided to give up practicing law, he could have a second career doing voice-overs. His sonorous voice was akin to thick velvet. "Good morning, Mr. Jacobs."

"First of all, congratulations on landing an agent, but before I give you the okay to sign your contract there are a few things I'd like to go over with you."

Her stomach made a flip-flop motion. It was apparent the attorney felt the contract was doable. "What are they?" she asked tentatively.

"What I want to ask is if you're willing to give up twenty-five percent of your earnings?"

It was as if the attorney had read her mind. "No. I'd prefer the prevailing fifteen percent, but if Booth Gordon balks at that figure then I'm willing to top out at twenty."

"Good girl," William crooned. "Let me play the numbers game with him. I'll throw out eighteen, but if he's not willing to accept that then we'll cap it at twenty. There's another thing you should know."

"What is that?" Seneca asked slowly.

"I had my investigator look up BG Management's corporate structure, and the public relations firm is under the umbrella of BGM. It's Booth Gordon's way of milking you for an additional five percent."

Seneca took in a deep breath. No wonder people referred to him as a barracuda. "What about the makeup person and hairstylist?"

"You don't need them, Seneca. Most designers have their own team that will include makeup personnel and stylists. Again, it's Gordon siphoning another five percent off the top.

You'd make out much better if you have your own stylist and makeup person."

A shadow of annoyance crossed her face, and she wondered how many unsuspecting people had contracted with Booth Gordon to represent them without the assistance of outside legal counsel. "Are you saying I shouldn't sign with BGM?"

"No, I'm not, Seneca. BGM is one of the leading talent and literary agencies headquartered in New York. It's just that I want you to be aware of hidden schemes some agencies use. Tell me what you want and I'll relay it to Gordon."

Seneca knew Booth was anxious to sign her, and that meant he would be willing to negotiate his fee. In fact, he was so certain she would sign that he'd planned to pair her with Phillip Kingston in a TV commercial. He'd disclosed that General Motors wanted Phillip as a pitchman for their luxury cars, and that meant Booth would reap hundreds of thousands in commissions. Yes, she mused, he wanted her, but was he willing to concede to her demands?

"Tell him I'll pay him twenty percent and no more. And if he asks about the makeup and stylist, tell him that I'll get my own." Securing a stylist and makeup artist would be an easy task; she could always ask her cousin Stefani, who worked in an upscale full-service salon in Harlem. Although a recent beauty-school graduate, Stefani's styling skills were awesome. Securing a publicist wouldn't be as easy, so she would let Booth handle the marketing and publicity.

"Good for you, Seneca. Gordon offered to pay for this deal, and I'm going to charge him through the nose. And if you want legal representation in the future, remember I'm always here for you."

"Thank you, Mr. Jacobs."

"After I hang up with you I'm going to call Gordon. If he agrees, then I'll have him download a revised contract. Once

I get it I'll messenger three copies to you. The courier will wait for your signature before he delivers them to BGM for Gordon to countersign. You should have a fully executed contract in your hands by tomorrow."

Seneca fought hard against the tears pricking the backs of her eyelids. She'd come to the Big Apple as an eighteen-year-old ingenue with dreams of making a name for herself in the theater. However, fate had intervened. Now she was a part-time model on the cusp of breaking into an industry where age and weight weren't only numbers but a death knell.

"Thank you," she repeated, the two words coming out in a trembling whisper. Depressing a button, she ended the call. The excitement that had been building for minutes bubbled up and exploded. "Yes!"

Tossing the phone on the bed, Seneca raced out of her bedroom and into the kitchen, where Electra sat at the table thumbing through the newspaper. Her roommate, who'd dyed her light-brown hair an inky black, smiled at her with large hazel eyes framed by a fringe of thick lashes.

"Good news?"

Seneca slid onto a chair at the table, unable to control her excitement. "I think so."

Electra closed the paper. "Well… don't keep me waiting," she wailed dramatically.

Seneca told her everything—from meeting Booth Gordon for the first time to her luncheon meeting at La Grenouille. However, she didn't tell Electra about Phillip Kingston. That would remain her secret—at least for the time being. Once the paparazzi spotted her and Phillip together there was certain to be a feeding frenzy as to who she was and their connection to each other.

Running a hand through her short, spiked hair, Electra shook her head. "I can't believe you're going to sign with

BGM. Do you realize they're referred to as CAA on the Hudson? CAA is Creative Artists Agency," she continued, as if Seneca didn't know who she was talking about. After all, they were both film and theater majors. "It's said they are the leading talent agency, whose clients include Oprah, LeBron James, Will Smith, Spielberg and Brad Pitt. Well, BGM is running a close second."

Seneca stared at the petite actress waiting for her big break who'd legally changed her name from Elaine Rachel Jacobs to Electra Reece-Jacobs because it had more of a theatrical flair. The first time she saw Electra in an audition for a role with a small theater group she'd been left speechless by her range of talent. Electra could do it all: sing, dance and act.

"Have you considered signing with them?" Seneca asked.

Electra emitted a low, throaty laugh. "Yeah, right," she drawled. "I couldn't get past the receptionist. That's why I signed with an agency with a small client list where I won't get lost in the huddled masses."

"You're going to make it big, roomie."

Electra rolled her expressive eyes upward. "From your lips to God's ears, roomie," she teased, smiling. "I told you the first time I saw you that you were too pretty to work behind the camera, and I'm proud to say I was right. And when you make it big, I'm going to tell everyone that Seneca Houston and I shared an apartment as college students."

Seneca sobered at the mention of college. She was going to have to withdraw from college, which meant the money her grandmother had put aside for her education would remain frozen in an account that had been set up expressly for that purpose. The executor for Ileana Houston's estate paid for her books and tuition and fees, and a small stipend for incidentals, leaving Seneca responsible for her room and board.

"You know I'm going to have to drop out."

"Pul-eeease," Electra drawled, again rolling her eyes. "You're about to blow up as an international supermodel and you're bitchin' about dropping out of college. There are plenty of very successful people on the Forbes list who've dropped out of college. Believe me—I'd drop out in a minute even if I landed a role in a B flick."

Seneca stared at the clock on the microwave. "I thought you were rehearsing with Jayson Brennan for his new play." Electra and the playwright had dated off and on for more than a year.

Electra exhaled an audible sigh of exasperation. "Jayson doesn't know his ass from his elbow. He hires a director to direct the play, and then decides at the last minute to rewrite a scene. It's the same with our relationship. He says he's in love with me, yet when we start getting close he says he needs his space."

"It sounds like a fear of commitment—to a woman and his work."

Electra combed her fingers through her hair in a nervous gesture. "I'm giving him until the end of the summer to get his shit together. After that, I'm done with him and his play. Now I know why you don't get involved with a man. It's much too emotionally draining."

"I can't afford to get involved with a man," Seneca countered. "If I'm going to give up my free time, then he's going to have to be worth it."

Electra put up her hand for a high-five handshake. "I should take your advice. I know you normally don't eat breakfast—"

"I eat breakfast," she insisted, interrupting Electra.

"Fruit with wheat germ and wheat toast."

"It's healthy and filling."

"It's boring, Seneca. I'm going to Zabar's. Do you want me to bring you back something?"

Moaning aloud, Seneca shook her head. "Oh, no, you didn't say *Zabar's*." The gourmet grocer was without a doubt the best in the city, if not the world. All of her self-control fled whenever she entered the perpetually crowded store at Broadway and West Eightieth.

"I'm only going there because I'm running out of coffee and cheese," Electra said.

Seneca stood up and walked over to the cookie jar that held her petty cash stash. She took out a twenty, handing it to Electra. "Smoked salmon on a bagel with scallion cream cheese."

"Do you want anything else?"

"I don't need anything else." The calorie-laden sandwich added up to one-fourth of her daily allowable caloric intake.

"I'll be back," Electra intoned in her best Arnold Schwarzenegger imitation.

Seneca returned to her bedroom to get dressed, snippets of the conversation she'd had with William Jacobs coming back to remind her that her future hung in the balance. If Booth Gordon didn't accept the terms Jacobs presented to him, then she would have to decide whether to give up modeling and resume her full-time student status or continue as she had for the past two years—modeling and attending classes part-time.

Regardless of the outcome, she would know for certain within a matter of hours.

Booth didn't bother to glance up when his executive assistant, the last employee holdover from his uncle's tenure, placed a cup of steaming black coffee on the corner of the rosewood desk at nine-ten. The cup sat for a full five minutes before he picked up the fragile china cup to take a sip. It was the perfect temperature, going down smoothly, the caffeine providing him with the energy he needed to stay alert throughout the morning.

He knew he had to stop sleeping with Krista. Either the woman was a nymphomaniac or she was trying to kill him. At forty he could get and sustain an erection, but he couldn't go as often as he had in his twenties and thirties. He'd literally thrown Krista out of his condo when she woke him up at three in the morning to complain that she was horny. Instead of banging the hell out of her he'd sent her packing.

His office ritual hadn't varied since he'd taken over as CEO of BGM. He came in at sunrise, worked out for an hour with his personal trainer at the in-office gym, showered and shaved, then selected what he would wear that day from a collection of tailored suits, custom-made shirts, ties and imported footwear. His office on the top floor of the four-story townhouse off Madison Avenue had become his home away from home.

"What's on today's calendar?" He knew he irked the woman because he never addressed her by name. Booth figured if he related to her like a piece of furniture she would get the hint and retire.

Joan Powers didn't bother to hide her disdain for her late boss's nephew when she glared at his lowered head. A few times she'd contemplated adding something to his coffee that would either make him sick or have to spend most of the day on the toilet, but then had to remind herself it wasn't good to harbor impure thoughts. Booth Gordon wasn't a tyrant—he was a monster.

"You have a meeting with the head of television at ten, and the head of music at eleven."

"What about lunch?"

"Lunch is open."

Booth raised his head, meeting the icy gaze of the woman whose loyalty was tied to a dead man. Joan didn't think he knew that she'd been his uncle's mistress for nearly forty years. She'd given up her youth and the chance to marry and have children because she'd been in love with a married man—a man who wasn't willing to leave his independently wealthy wife. He hated Joan and he knew she detested him. Why, he thought, didn't she just hand in her resignation? He was even willing to offer her a generous severance package just so he wouldn't have to put up with her cheerless expression.

"Order my usual. I also want you to call my barber."

"What time do you want him to come, Mr. Gordon?"

Booth lowered his eyes, staring at his manicured nails. His insisting Joan address him as Mr. Gordon was another source of contention for her. She'd called him Booth until he took the helm of the agency, then everything changed for her. She was still executive assistant to the CEO because she knew the functioning of the company in her sleep. In other words, she knew where all the bodies were buried.

His first order of business had been to get Joan Powers and every employee to sign a confidentiality agreement. Every piece of mail, telephone call and what was discussed in meetings had become sacrosanct. Booth knew he ran BGM like a despot, but it was necessary for continued success. Despot or not, he rewarded his employees with liberal salaries and year-end bonuses.

"See if he's available at two." He waved a hand, dismissing her. "That's all."

"What if he's not available for that time?"

"That's all," Booth repeated. He waited until the annoying woman walked out of his office, closing the door behind her, then shook his head. The only reason he hadn't given Joan her walking papers was because he'd promised his uncle that he would never fire her. And despite being the son of a bitch he was, he never would go back on an oath he'd made to the man who'd become his surrogate father.

Picking up the cup, he took a deep swallow of the premium brew. Good coffee, beautiful women and gourmet food topped Booth Gordon's favorite things list, but not necessarily in that order. His mind kept going back to his meeting with Seneca Houston. What he'd first interpreted as belligerence he now thought of as a banked fire that would serve her well once she waded into the treacherous and cutthroat world of international modeling. And, she would need the fire and everything she had to bring to stand out among women who were willing to sell an internal body part to make it big.

A soft chiming of the telephone claimed his attention. It was his private line. He depressed a button. "Yes?"

"There's a Mr. William Jacobs on the line for you. He says it's about Seneca Houston's contract."

"Put him through," he told Joan.

"Mr. Gordon?"

Booth sat up straighter in his executive leather chair. The voice coming through the speaker was deep, authoritative. "Yes."

"William Jacobs. I represent a potential client of yours, Seneca Houston. I'd like to talk to you about her contract. I need clarification as to the amount of your commission."

"What do you want to know?" Booth questioned.

"It's a little excessive."

"The contract stipulates a breakdown as to the percentage."

"It's still excessive. I've advised Ms. Houston to select her own makeup and hairstylists."

A muscle twitched nervously in Booth's jaw when he

clenched his teeth. "Has she gone along with your recommendations?"

"She has," the lawyer confirmed. "I've also recommended she sign the contract, but only if you're willing to cut your commission to twenty percent."

Booth's fingers curled into tight fists. It looked as if his golden goose was going to play hard to get. He'd promised to turn her into a supermodel if she gave him complete control of her career. Well, it appeared that wasn't going to happen.

What he couldn't afford to do was not sign her when he recalled her retort: *If not you, then there will be someone else.* There wasn't going to be someone else. BGM would represent Butterfly for ten percent. That was a fact no one other than Booth Wilkes Gordon needed to know.

"Twenty percent it is, Mr. Jacobs."

"Can you please revise the contract and download it to me, and I'll have Ms. Houston sign it. A courier will deliver it to you for your countersignature. I'll instruct him to wait for an executed copy."

A wry smile touched Booth's mouth. "I'll have my legal department make the revisions, and you have my word you will receive it today. Don't forget to e-mail your bill. Your payment will be in the same envelope as the executed contracts."

A deep chuckle came through the speaker. "It's been a pleasure doing business with you, Mr. Gordon. Perhaps one of these days we can get together over cocktails."

"I'd like that, Mr. Jacobs," Booth lied. He'd rather face a rabid dog than share a drink with a man who'd just robbed him of five percent of Butterfly's projected earnings.

He disconnected the call and then ordered Joan to connect him to the legal department, relaying his instructions before leaning back on his chair to study the financial statement on the agency's television division. Booth detested meetings but knew they were necessary. Whenever he sat at the head of the conference table in the boardroom it always solidified his position and power.

Power.

It was the only good thing he'd learned from his mother. Use it well and it would provide him with everything he'd ever want.

Misused or misguided power spelled certain disaster, and he would lose everything he'd sacrificed in order to make BGM into a full-service talent and literary agency. As head of a privately held company, Booth had established what he called his commandments: every employee had to be a team player, every client was deemed unique and irreplaceable, no one was to be placed on hold for more than a minute and whenever possible, telephone calls were returned promptly.

He'd achieved a pinnacle of success he hadn't thought possible while his personal life was in the toilet. What good was a continuous string of nameless, faceless women who managed to fill up the empty hours until he tired of their shenanigans?

Perhaps it was time, he mused, to settle down with one woman and father a child—or two. "Maybe next year," he whispered, smiling.

Chapter Eight

Seneca closed and locked the door behind the messenger, counting slowly to ten before opening the clasp on the envelope he'd given her. She removed a sheaf of papers with an envelope addressed to her bearing BMG Agency's return address. Flipping through the document, she fixed her gaze on the signatures on the last page, unable to decipher Booth Gordon's scrawl. It wouldn't matter if he'd signed *Barracuda* because the document was legally binding.

What she'd found surprising was that the length of the contract was only two years, containing a option clause for another two years if agreed upon by both parties. Seneca knew it would take her at least two years to become accustomed to the fast-paced, highly competitive world of high-fashion modeling, and no doubt she wouldn't be looked upon favorably by those who thought of any newcomer as direct competition. Not only did she have Booth Gordon as her agent but also a designer who'd called her his muse. Never would've she imagined that a tall, skinny girl from upstate New York would one day walk the runways wearing haute couture of world-famous designers. She wasn't lucky—she was blessed.

Removing the envelope, she opened it, her heart slamming against her ribs. There were two checks, payable to her in the amount of five thousand dollars each. The notation in the memo read *signing bonus.*

Walking on shaky knees, Seneca made it to her bedroom, closed the door and collapsed into the chair. There was no mention of a signing bonus in the contract, nor had Booth mentioned it during their lunch meeting. A ten-thousand-dollar windfall was more than a surprise—it was a shock. Now she would be able to repay Electra for the cost of the limo sooner than later.

Plucking the cordless phone off the cradle, she punched in a familiar number. The call was answered after the third ring. "This is Luis."

Heavy breathing came through the earpiece. "Did I catch you at a bad time?"

"No, no," he repeated. "I was just walking in the door when I heard the phone. What's up, Butterfly?"

"I'm in, Luis. Booth Gordon signed me."

"Congratulations, darling. Did you believe he wouldn't sign you?"

"There was no guarantee he would. I don't think he liked it when I told him I wasn't going to put up with him talking down to me."

"Gordon is a megalomaniac who is also a genius. His instincts to recognize talent are so finely honed that people believe he's clairvoyant. If he signed you, then he's knows he can sell you. Speaking of selling, I just got back from a meeting with Rhys Calhoun. He wants me to design a Butterfly collection of evening wear with a focus on gowns for Barcelona Fashion Week."

Seneca was glad she was sitting when she slumped back against the chair. Her meeting Booth Gordon, being signed to BGM, the unexpected signing bonus and Luis designing a collection for Rhys Calhoun with her as his inspiration was too much for her to process.

Her eyes filled with tears at the same time she pulled her lip between her teeth. "Congratulations, Luis."

"Butterfly?"

"What?" The word came out in a trembling whisper.

"Are you crying?"

"Yes-s-s."

"Dry it up, girl! You can't afford to end up with red, swollen eyes. What if you get a call for a shoot tomorrow?"

Wiping away her tears with her fingers, Seneca nodded before she remembered Luis couldn't see her. He was right. Not only did she make certain to get enough sleep, but she also made certain to drink enough water to keep her skin hydrated to offset dark circles under her eyes.

"You're right," she said. Her face and body were commodities—her moneymakers. Neglect one or both and her modeling career would come to a crashing end even before the ravages of age became a factor.

"Now, if you ate, I'd suggest taking you out for a congratulatory dinner," Luis teased.

"I eat as much as you do," she countered.

"Yeah, Butterfly. Just enough to stay alive. You know when I'm sketching or piecing garments I forget to eat."

"I never forget to eat, Luis."

"One of these days I'm going to take you to Puerto Rico, where my relatives will ply you delicious dishes ranging from carne guisada, empanadas to sancocho."

Seneca laughed softly. "If they cook like your mother and aunts, then I'll wait until I'm pregnant, when I have a good reason to eat." Every time she accompanied Luis to visit his relatives, she'd had to go on a weeklong fast.

"I hope that's a long way off."

"It is," she concurred. She chatted with Luis for another three minutes before ringing off.

Seneca didn't know why she'd mentioned becoming pregnant. At twenty she was much too young to become a mother when she was barely able to support herself. What she hadn't wanted was to end up like her mother. She'd wanted to believe that Dahlia's ongoing discontent had stemmed from the stigma she'd faced as a teenage mother and high school dropout.

Dahlia had been the only one among her peers who hadn't graduated from high school and gone on to college. Years later she'd earned a GED, but her dream to go to college to become a nurse had remained just that—a dream. The closest she got to a career in medicine was to become a medical secretary. Although Seneca had encouraged her mother to apply to nursing school, the older woman claimed there were times when she found it difficult to concentrate.

Moving off the chair, Seneca sat down at a computer workstation. She'd been forced to buy the unit because typing on her laptop while in bed had become a daunting task causing discomfort in her neck and back. The workstation with a hutch had taken three days to assemble, but in the end it was worth it. Textbooks that had been stacked on the floor were now filed on the hutch and papers and magazines were stored in a two-drawer file cabinet. There was enough space on the desk for her laptop and an all-in-one printer. After filing away the contract and checks, she thumbed through the directory at the back of her planner for the number of her cousin's salon.

She'd picked up the phone to dial the salon when her cell rang. Her heart kicked into a faster pace when she saw the display. "Hi."

"Hi yourself," crooned the deep voice she'd come to look for. "Can I interest you in an early dinner?"

Seneca sat up straighter. "Where are you, Phillip?"

"I'm in New York. My current contract is going to expire in a couple of months, so when I spoke to the owner of the team and told him I was coming back to the East Coast, he offered me a ride on his jet."

"That's what I call an accommodating boss," she teased.

"How about it, gorgeous?" Phillip asked.

"How about what?"

"Dinner."

"Okay. But…"

"But what, Seneca?"

"What if I cook dinner for you?"

"You cook?" he teased, laughing.

"Yeah, I cook. What makes you think I couldn't?"

"I don't know. Most young women I've met only know how to make reservations."

"You've hooked up with the wrong women, King Phillip."

"Don't ever call me that, Seneca!"

She recoiled as if he'd struck her. "I'm sorry, Phillip."

"Don't be sorry. Just don't do it again."

There was something in his tone that sent a shiver down her spine. It was more than a warning. It was a threat. A pregnant, uncomfortable silence followed his retort, giving Seneca the time she needed to compose herself.

"What's for dinner?" he asked. The hard edge in his voice was missing.

"What do you want?"

"Steak and potatoes."

Seneca smiled. She knew he would say that. "What about vegetables?"

"I really like asparagus."

"I'm certain I can pick up some from the greengrocer. Hang up, Phillip. I have to go shopping."

"I'll bring wine and dessert," he volunteered. "What time should I come over?"

Seneca noted the time on her cell. It was after three. "Six-thirty." She ended the call and then called the butcher where she bought her meat to order an aged, bone-in, cowboy rib eye steak for Phillip and a New York strip steak for herself.

She hadn't expected to see Phillip until the weekend. However, his return to New York was somewhat propitious, because he would celebrate her signing with BGM with her.

The planner, opened to the page with her cousin's number, reminded Seneca to call the Harlem-based salon. It took all of sixty seconds to inform Stefani that she wanted to hire her as her personal stylist. Stefani, who was either too choked up or stunned to respond, said she would call her back when she got home, because her boss was giving her a "screw face."

Kicking off her slippers, Seneca pushed her feet into a pair of mules, grabbed her wristlet, keys and a large canvas bag for her purchases and left for her shopping excursion. It would be the first time she would entertain a man since moving into the brownstone. She'd invited Phillip over because it was Thursday. Electra worked late on Thursdays, and instead of coming back to the Upper West Side she took a taxi to the East Village to spend the weekend with Jayson.

Seneca knew she could never have a relationship with a man like Electra had with Jayson. Even though Electra complained that it was emotionally draining, she seemed to wallow in the drama. The more drama the better.

Thanks, but no thanks, she mused. She'd grown up with drama every day of her life with Dahlia Houston, aka Drama Queen. If her father had had a different temperament he either would've left Dahlia a long time ago or not gotten involved with her.

Forty minutes later, Seneca returned home with the sail bag filled with prime cuts of meat, fresh white asparagus, small gold potatoes, salad fixings, a packet of quick-rising yeast for focaccia bread and a large bouquet of fresh flowers.

She unpacked her bag, washing and patting the steaks dry with a paper towel before sprinkling Oscar's special steak seasoning on them. Placing the steaks on a plate, she stored it on a lower shelf in the refrigerator. Working quickly, she mixed the yeast with warm water and added a leavening agent, then flour. Kneading the dough until it was smooth and elastic, she placed it in a small bowl coated with olive oil and covered it with a damp towel. The bowl went on the stove where the warmth from the pilot light would hasten the rising action.

It was six when Seneca had set the table, punched the dough down and kneaded it so it could rise a second time; she'd drained the water from the salad greens with a salad spinner. The asparagus were on a cookie sheet drizzled with virgin olive oil and a sprinkling of garlic powder and Parmesan cheese. The potatoes were washed, peeled and soaking in salted water. Two cruets, one with vinaigrette and the other with seasonings for what would become glazed rosemary and garlic potatoes, were on a shelf in the refrigerator.

She surveyed her handiwork. The bouquet of white baby roses, blue and green hydrangeas and yellow mini mums added a festive touch to the table with white china with a cobalt trim. Satisfied with the results, Seneca headed for the bathroom to shower.

Phillip mounted the steps to the brownstone, cradling a shopping bag with a bottle of champagne to his chest and another with a box filled with delicate Italian pastries. He rang the bell to Seneca's apartment and waited as the seconds ticked off.

"Who is it?" Seneca's slightly husky voice came through the small speaker on the intercom.

"Phillip."

A soft buzzing disengaged the locks. He opened the doors and walked into the foyer. He climbed the staircase to the top floor, and when he stepped off onto the fourth-floor landing he saw Seneca waiting for him outside her apartment. Phillip did not want to believe she could improve on perfection. Whether wearing haute couture or cropped pants and a white blouse, she was stunning.

He winked at her. "Like your shoes."

Seneca glanced down at her feet. The gray snakeskin Michael Kors "Famous" sandal was a favorite and the most comfortable in her shoe collection. A four-and-a-half-inch heel, half-inch platform and adjustable ankle strap with a buckle closure permitted her to stand for hours without discomfort.

Her head popped up and she stared up at Phillip through her lashes. "Thank you." She extended her arms. "Let me take one of those bags."

Phillip handed her the one with the pastries. "Do you always wear stilettos?"

"Every chance I get," she answered. "A lot of men feel intimidated when I tower over them, but I think of it as their problem, not mine."

Phillip followed Seneca into the apartment, pausing to close and lock the door behind them. "Do they complain about it?"

"Some do."

"How tall are you?" he asked, walking through the living room decorated with functional furniture seen in most moderately priced hotels: a beige-and-brown patterned sofa, love seat, mahogany coffee and end tables and ginger-jar lamps with white pleated shades. Shutters covered the tall, narrow windows instead of blinds or shades. The only item that made the space seem like home were plants—lots of potted plants.

"Five-ten in my bare feet."

"I don't have a problem with your height."

Seneca stopped at the entrance to the kitchen. "That's because you're what—six-seven?"

"Six-six."

She smiled up at the man who literally took her breath away. Today he was dressed in gray: a blue-gray silk shirt and a lightweight charcoal-gray suit. "Even with five-inch heels you still have three inches on me."

"Three inches and probably outweigh you by a buck fifty."

Seneca entered the kitchen and set the bag on the counter-top. "I will reveal my age, but not my weight."

Phillip removed the bottle of champagne from the box and placed it in the refrigerator. "What about dress size?"

"That, too." Crossing her arms under her breasts, she gave him a long, penetrating stare. "All a designer is concerned about is whether I can fit into the garment. It doesn't matter whether I'm a zero, two or a four. The bottom line is whether it fits."

Phillip's gaze roved lazily over her incredibly slender body. The stretch pants fit her body like a second skin, while the simple man-tailored white blouse with turned-back cuffs was in direct contrast to the sexy shoes. His gaze moved up to her face and hair. She wore little or no discernible makeup, and her hair was brushed back and secured in a knot on the nape of her long neck.

He'd spent days trying to remember every feature, every expression, but had failed miserably. Seneca Houston was a chameleon, changing and becoming whomever she wanted. Last week she'd been a siren, silently beckoning him when he hadn't wanted her to. And tonight she reminded him of a naughty schoolteacher or librarian with her conservative blouse, body-hugging slacks, sexy heels and bun.

And when the images of her long legs, sultry voice and sensual mouth had invaded his dreams, he'd awakened to find his thighs and the bed wet from his nocturnal emission. The last time he'd experienced a wet dream was as an adolescent. What he hadn't been able to understand was why, at twenty-six, he'd reverted to a time when women weren't readily available for his sexual pleasure and recreation?

All of that had changed once girls were cognizant of the scouts at many of the school's home games. They rang his phone and doorbell and some were even so brazen as to try and seduce him in the hope of becoming his baby mama. His father had lectured him about the pitfalls of having unprotected sex, and he'd heeded his father's warning. Not once, even when he'd been under the influence, had he not worn a condom when sleeping with a woman.

"Does it bother you that you make money because of your face and body?"

Seneca went still, only the rise and fall of her chest revealed that she was breathing. "No more than it bothers you to make millions tossing a ball through a hoop and net."

"It's different with me," Phillip countered.

"Why, Phillip?"

"I never would've become a professional athlete if I didn't have an exceptional physical skill."

Pinpoints of heat stung her cheeks. "And you believe modeling doesn't require any special skill?"

There came a beat of silence. "No," he finally said.

"If that's the case, then why can't every man or woman

model? Models are not only selling garments but also their persona. We are taught how to walk and what our best camera angles are. Even before modeling became so much a part of our society, folks were into people watching. Watching not only what they wore, but how they wore it."

Taking a step, Phillip dipped his head and kissed her cheek. "The only person I want to watch is you, Seneca."

"Can we change this subject?" He obviously disapproved of her profession, and she didn't want to continue to defend it.

Phillip increased the pressure, his mouth moving closer to the tempting curve of Seneca's lips. "What do you want to talk about?"

"Anything but us," she whispered.

"How am I going to get to know you better if you don't talk about yourself?"

Turning her head slightly, their mouths inches apart, Seneca stared at the strong mouth that made her feel things she didn't want to feel, emotions she'd forgotten existed when she'd walked away from the boy whom she'd believed she loved with all of her heart, body and soul; a boy to whom she'd offered her innocence in exchange for his passionate entreaty that he loved her.

There was something so strong in her attraction to Phillip Kingston that it was palpable, and she wondered whether it was because of his high-profile status as an athletic phenom, his eye candy appeal, if she'd been without a man for far too long or if she truly liked him.

She smiled, bringing his heated gaze to her parted lips. "You're going to have to date me, Phillip. And I don't mean you taking me out to dinner and then I become dessert when you expect me to crawl into bed with you."

His expressive eyebrows lifted a fraction. "Is that the way it's going to be?"

Seneca's expression changed as she sobered. "That's the only way it can be."

Phillip recognized the challenge. Seneca Houston wasn't going to be easy, and he liked that. It was why he'd told Booth he wanted Seneca in the Cadillac ad with him and then made the crafty agent swear an oath that he wouldn't tell her that it had been his suggestion.

There weren't too many things Phillip Park Kingston had been denied in his short lifetime. He wanted to become a doctor, and with a degree in premed he knew eventually he would earn a medical degree. He'd also wanted to become a professional basketball player, and that dream was manifested when he'd become a first-round draft pick for the NBA.

What he hadn't known before meeting Seneca Houston was his definitive ideal when it came to a woman. She had it all: beauty, confidence, intelligence and a smoldering fire that appealed to his very healthy sex drive.

"Okay, Seneca."

"Okay what?" she asked.

"I'll date you."

Leaning into his length, Seneca pressed her breasts to his hard chest. Tilting her head, she brushed her mouth over Phillip's. "Thank you."

Chapter Nine

Shrugging out of his jacket, Phillip draped it over the back of a chair at the table with place settings for two. "Can I help you with anything?" he asked Seneca as she emptied potatoes into a glass bowl. She'd opened the refrigerator, removing a cruet filled with what appeared to be salad dressing. She poured the mixture over the potatoes, tossing them with a large spoon.

Seneca shook her head. "Not right now. I have everything under control."

Crossing his arms over his chest, Phillip leaned against the countertop watching as she moved confidently around the kitchen. A platter with marinated steaks, a baking sheet with marinated asparagus and another pan with a mound of dough with a sprinkling of coarse salt, minced garlic, dried rosemary, grated Parmesan and drizzled with olive oil sat along the length of the countertop. Seneca moved over to the oven and turned it to a designated heating setting. Phillip was more than impressed with her culinary expertise. Not only could she cook, but she also made her own bread.

"How long have you lived here?" he asked.

Seneca crossed the kitchen, removed the bowl with salad greens from the fridge and placed it on the table. She also took out the vinaigrette to bring it to room temperature. "I moved in a little more than a year ago." She smiled at Phillip. "I'd shared an apartment with three other students on Avenue C, but when I was given the opportunity to not only have a roommate but also my own bedroom I jumped at it."

Phillip straightened. "You have a roommate?" He hoped her roommate wasn't male.

She nodded. "Most times I forget I have one because Electra and I rarely see each other. She's a full-time student, works part-time as a waitress, and she spends most weekends with her boyfriend when she doesn't go up to Connecticut to see her family."

Phillip, relieved that her roommate wasn't a man, told Seneca that being an only child hadn't prepared him for what he thought of as the pitfalls of dormitory life. "I grew up in a calm household, so having to put up with loud parties and people coming and going had become a problem, because I found I couldn't study. I spoke to my parents about moving off campus and into a nearby housing complex, and because I was on full scholarship they agreed to pay the rent."

"I'd read somewhere that you were premed, but where did you go to college?"

"UND. The University of North Dakota," he explained when she gave him a questioning look. "And before you ask," Phillip continued, smiling, "it was a bit of a shock going from Southern California to a state where temperatures sometimes dipped into double-digits below zero in the winter."

"How about snow?"

He shook his head. "I never ventured off campus after it'd snowed because all I thought about was ending up in a snowbank and not being discovered until the spring thaw. The landscape was incredible in the spring and summer."

"Did you stay year-round?"

Phillip shook his head again. "No. I usually went back to L.A. I'd delayed going back home the summer of my junior year when I drove from Grand Forks to Fargo, then over to the Badlands. From there I went up to Saskatchewan, Canada. What I hadn't realized until I was ready to check out of a motel was that I'd lost my wallet, passport and cell phone. The manager refused to let me use his phone to call my folks and contacted the police. The notion of being jailed in a foreign country scared the shit of me, so I convinced the police officer to call my coach at UND to verify who I was.

"It wasn't until I impressed upon them that my passport had been stolen that they were galvanized into action. The police contacted the Canadian and U.S. Border Patrol to look out for anyone attempting to cross into the States using my passport because after 9/11 border security had been on high alert. Thankfully, Coach came through for me. He paid for the motel room with his credit card and flew up to drive me back to Grand Rapids because I didn't have a driver's license. I'd promised the cop who helped me that when I made it to the pros I'd pay for him to come to the States to attend a game, but when he told me he preferred hockey I pledged he would get two season's tickets to every Minnesota Wild home game for as long as I remained in the pros."

"Isn't the Minnesota Wild an American hockey team?"

Phillip nodded. "It is, but St. Paul is closer to Winnipeg than Calgary, Edmonton or Vancouver."

Seneca glanced up from stir-frying the potatoes that she'd marinated with balsamic vinegar, stone-ground mustard, red chili flakes, minced garlic and chopped rosemary in a large frying pan. "How far it is it from Winnipeg to St. Paul?"

"It's a little more than seven hundred miles."

"Seven hundred miles!" she gasped. "You've got to be kidding me. Who would travel fourteen hundred miles to see a game?"

A smug smile softened Phillip's handsome features. "A real sports fan."

"No, Phillip. That's a fanatic," Seneca argued softly.

"Where do you think the word *fan* comes from? Thankfully, I've been able to keep my promise these past four years because he didn't have to make that call and I would've wound up with a criminal record. And there was no doubt I would've lost my scholarship."

Seneca added a half cup of broth to the pan, covered it tightly and lowered the flame. Wiping her hands on a towel, she walked over to Phillip, leaned in and kissed his smooth jaw. "Did anyone tell you that you're a very nice guy?"

Looping an arm around her waist, Phillip eased Seneca to stand between his legs, his eyes moving slowly over her face and committing it to memory. Now he didn't have to dream about her. She wasn't a specter, but real. Warm, breathing and his for the taking. Never had he wanted a woman as much as he craved Seneca Houston. Would he, he wondered, still crave her once they'd slept together, or was it because she was so unattainable that he hungered after her?

"Not lately," he crooned.

"Well, you are, Phillip Kingston. You're also a gentleman."

His hands came up to frame her face. "What I'm thinking right now isn't very gentlemanly, baby."

With wide eyes, Seneca met his penetrating stare. "What are you thinking about?"

"Do you really want to know?" he asked, answering her question with his own.

"Yes, Phillip. I really want to know."

"I want to…"

"You want to what?"

Phillip had stopped himself before he could say he wanted to fuck her. That was what most of the women he'd slept with wanted him to do. When they'd asked him to fuck them, he did. And when they'd asked him to make love to them, he did that, too. With Seneca he wasn't sure what she'd want: fucking or lovemaking.

"I want to make love to you." He'd decided on the latter.

Seneca felt Phillip's heart, keeping tempo with her own. She knew he was as physically attracted to her as she was to him; however, she wasn't going to jump into bed with him because he was basketball phenom King Phillip. It didn't matter if Booth planned to market them as a couple. The decision as to whether she would or wouldn't sleep with Phillip was hers and hers alone. Who and what she wanted to know was Phillip, and not the baller who ignited the arenas with adoring, rabid fans when he executed his dazzling three-point plays.

"You just may get what you want one of these days," she said cryptically, "but you'll have to—"

"I'll have to date you," Philip said, interrupting and completing her statement.

She affected a sexy moue. "Yes. Did I tell you that I'm now a BGM client?"

Phillip pulled her closer. "It looks as if the Barracuda didn't waste any time signing you."

"Does he know people call him that?"

"I don't know, and I doubt if Booth cares as long as he makes money." Phillip kissed the end of her nose. "I brought a bottle of champagne, not knowing whether you'd want to share it with me, but I think your good news calls for at least one sip of bubbly."

Putting her arms around his neck, Seneca pressed a kiss to Phillip's brown throat. She couldn't believe he could look, smell and feel so good. Maybe it was her prolonged celibacy that made her respond to him like a cat in heat, rubbing against him, while using every opportunity to touch his magnificent body.

"Tonight I'll have more than a sip."

"Are you sure you can handle it?" he teased.

"We'll have to wait and see, won't we?"

Phillip chewed slowly, savoring the ingredients that made up the dry rub on the perfectly grilled rib eye steak. The flavor of mesquite lingered on his palate. "Damn, girl, I'm surprised some man hadn't married you before now."

Touching the corners of her mouth with a linen napkin, Seneca smiled across the table at her dining partner. "Why would someone want to marry me?"

"You've got skills—mad cooking skills, baby."

She inclined her head. "I thank you and my father thanks you."

Phillip cut another piece from the steak that had exceeded his expectation. He'd told Seneca he wanted his meat cooked medium-well and it was just that—medium-well. "I take it your father is a chef."

Seneca picked up a goblet filled with icy-cold water. She'd alternated drinking water and sipping champagne, which had affected her within seconds of taking a mouthful. "Not professionally. He learned to cook after he'd become a merchant seaman."

"Does your mama cook?"

"Yes. But she didn't do much cooking before she married Daddy. Everything she knows she learned from him."

Phillip raised his flute. "My compliments to the cook *and* her daddy. Dinner was superb."

Following suit, Seneca raised her half-filled flute. "Thank you."

"No, Seneca, thank *you*."

"Do you cook, Phillip?"

He peered at her over the rim of the delicate wineglass. "The question should be *can* I cook. And the answer is hell no, even though my grandparents own a restaurant in Koreatown."

"No, you didn't say Koreatown."

Phillip drained his flute and refilled it before topping off Seneca's. "Yes, I did. If you come to L.A. you'll see a City of Los Angeles Koreatown marker. The locals call it K-town."

"Did you grow up there?" Seneca asked, eager to know more about the man sitting at her kitchen table.

"I did the first ten years of my life. It took that long for my parents to pay off their student loans and save enough money to buy a house of their own. Both my parents are doctors. My father is a microbiologist working on infectious diseases, while my mother is a medical examiner."

"What will be your specialty?"

"Pediatric orthopedics."

Seneca smiled. "So when someone calls Dr. Kingston they'll have to identify which one."

Phillip also smiled. "My parents had a problem with that until my mother decided to use her maiden name. She's Dr. Park and my father is Dr. Kingston."

"What will you be?"

"Dr. Park-Kingston."

Picking up her wineglass, Seneca took a sip. The champagne made her feel sleepy, languid, as if she didn't have a bone in her body. Her eyelids drooped. "When are you going to medical school?"

"I've decided to give the NBA another four years, and then I'm out."

This disclosure made her suddenly alert. "Is Booth aware of your future plan?"

Phillip slowly shook his head. "No. And there's no reason for him to know. Don't get me wrong, Seneca. Basketball has been very good to and for me. It paid for my undergraduate education and it will pay for medical school. I've made a lot of money—much more money than I'd ever earn practicing medicine—but there has to be a time I have to sacrifice something in order to fulfill my dreams.

"My grandparents came to this country literally with the clothes on their backs and the address of a relative willing to take them in until they got on their feet. They worked sixteen-hour days in a family-owned restaurant while sleeping on a pallet in a hallway between the kitchen and bathroom. It took years, but they managed to save enough money to rent an apartment."

"Did they still work at the restaurant?"

"Yes. My grandmother never missed a day of work. She took time off when my mother was born, but her goal was to buy the restaurant from her uncle. And she had one dream, and that was for her daughter to graduate from college. My mother was a very good student, graduating at the top of her class, and that was a first for a Korean-American at her high school. She got into Stanford as a premed student. That's where she met my father. They managed to keep their liaison secret until Mom found out a month before they were to graduate that she was pregnant.

"To say all hell broke loose is an understatement," Phillip drawled, smiling. "Both families declared war on one another, and while they were threatening to take the other out, my parents drove down to Mexico and got married."

"Did they ever declare a truce?"

"Yes, but it took my birth to make them somewhat rational. While my parents were working on their internships and residencies, I spent the week in the restaurant with my grandparents and was shuttled to my father's people on the weekends. Korean had become my first language, and then English. I'd become a black and Korean prince to both sets of grandparents."

"Now you're a prince to hordes of screaming women," Seneca drawled.

Phillip's expression changed, becoming a mask of stone. "I don't accept everything that's offered."

She sat up straighter, meeting his angry gaze. "I didn't say you were a dog, Phillip. I said what I said because you're known as a sex symbol. Oh, come on now, don't act as if you've never heard anyone call you that."

"I don't believe everything I hear."

Seneca took a deep swallow of champagne, holding it in her mouth for several seconds before letting the dry wine slide down the back of her throat. "You and I are about to become the living Ken and Barbie of color, so don't pretend that you don't know what you look like. The difference between you and me is that I'm comfortable using my face and body to earn a living, while you believe it's your basketball skill that has allowed you to become a pitchman for certain products. Don't kid yourself, Phillip. It's the fact that you are intelligent, articulate *and* certifiably eye candy that are the reasons Booth wants us together."

"And you're not," he retorted.

"I know who and what I am," she countered. "If I can make a lot of money using this face and body, then I'll do it as long as I can." She made a sweeping motion with her hand over her face and chest. "Some people sell drugs, others sex. I sell face and clothes, Phillip." Pushing back her chair, she reached for his plate, but he caught her wrist.

Phillip stood up. "What are you doing?"

"What does it look like? I'm clearing the table."

"I'll do it. You cooked, so I'll do the dishes."

Seneca peered up at him through her lashes. She was slightly inebriated but didn't want him to know that. For her, drinking champagne was akin to taking a sleeping pill.

"Don't look at me like that," Phillip continued. "I used to clean up my grandparents' restaurant."

"Okay. Just don't put the flutes in the dishwasher."

Resting his hands on her shoulders, Phillip angled his head and kissed her cheek. "Go relax. That's not a request, but an order."

"Okay. I'm going to lie down, because my legs aren't working so good right about now." Before the last word was off her lips, Seneca found herself swept up in Phillip's arms. "What are you doing?"

"I'm putting you to bed. After you get your legs back I'd like you to pack enough clothes to spend the weekend with me. You did agree that we'd have breakfast, lunch and dinner together," Phillip quickly reminded Seneca. "Where's your bedroom?"

"It's down the hall on the right. Remember, we're scheduled for a photo shoot this weekend," she reminded Phillip when he carried her across the kitchen.

"Why don't you call the photographer and ask him what he wants. You can ask him what he wants me to bring, too."

"O-k-ay," she slurred, closing her eyes while resting her head on his shoulder.

Phillip shifted the slight weight in his arms. "Damn, baby, you'd be a very cheap date," he teased.

Seneca opened her eyes. "Don't play yourself, Phillip Kingston. There's nothing cheap about Butterfly."

"Who's butterfly?"

"I'm Butterfly."

He walked into her bedroom and stopped. Whoever had chosen the Asian-inspired head and footboard design of the queen-size bed, bedside tables, double dresser and lingerie chest was obviously very discriminating. A workstation and club chair with a matching footstool were positioned under a trio of tall, narrow windows. A flat-screen television, resting on a stand, was positioned so Seneca could view it whenever she lay in bed.

"Put me down on the chair. If I get into bed, then I'm not getting out."

"Who decorated your bedroom?"

Seneca smothered a yawn behind her hand. "I did."

"What happened to the living room?"

She smiled up at Phillip when he loomed over her. "I had nothing to do with that. At least once a month Electra threatens to put everything out on the curb, but the furniture was a gift from her favorite aunt."

Phillip grimaced. "It looks more like a charitable donation."

Seneca giggled. "You're bad, Phillip Kingston."

He leaned closer, brushing a kiss over her mouth. "Relax."

Waiting until she was alone, Seneca picked up her cell and dialed Mitchell Leon's number. She informed him that Phillip Kingston was back in town and wanted to know what they should bring to the shoot. Reaching for a pen and pad, she jotted down the outfits and accessories Mitchell had requested.

"What about makeup and hair?" she asked. It was almost

nine, and Seneca still hadn't heard from her cousin. She knew Stefani wanted to leave the salon where she'd become a glorified shampoo girl.

"I'll have people on hand who will do your hair and face."

"What day and what time should we get to your place?"

"Sunday at eight. I'm projecting it should take about four hours to get what I want, so figure finishing up around noon."

"We'll see you Sunday," she said in parting, and rang off.

Slumping back against the chair, Seneca closed her eyes, chiding herself for drinking the second glass of wine. It wasn't the calories that worried her, but the dizzying effects. It was apparent she had very little tolerance for alcohol.

"Seneca, baby, wake up."

Eyelids fluttering wildly, Seneca came awake. She moaned when she realized she'd fallen asleep. Phillip sat on the footstool, her bare feet in his lap. She hadn't remembered taking off her shoes.

"How long have I been asleep?"

"Not long."

"How long is not long, Phillip?" From where she was sitting she couldn't see the clock or the readout on the cable box.

"About forty minutes."

"I have to pack." She attempted to get up, but his hands tightened on her ankles.

"Don't get up," Phillip urged softly. "You don't have to go home with me tonight."

"Really?"

Phillip smiled. Seneca reminded him of a trusting child. And that's what he wanted. He wanted her to trust him. "Yes, really. But I wouldn't mind if you let me stay here with you."

Her eyes grew wider. "You want to sleep with me?"

Again, Seneca had shown him another side of her personality—vulnerability. He liked this better than her getting in his face. "We can *share* the bed."

Something should've alerted Seneca that she and Phillip were moving too quickly, that they hadn't known each other a week, but her limited experience with men had her committing to sharing his hotel suite. She'd successfully parried the advances of every man who'd professed to be attracted to her, yet she found herself unable to escape the sensual masculine magnetism Phillip emitted like a force field. Whenever they shared the same space he seemed to suck her in while making her his willing captive.

"Okay. But if you start anything, I'll dial nine-eleven."

"What will I be charged with?" he teased, grinning.

"It won't be for you, but me when they arrest me for manslaughter."

"Damn, baby. Why are you so hard?"

"Would you like me better if I were a doormat?" she asked.

"Nah," Phillip drawled.

Raising her arms above her head, Seneca arched her back. "Please let me up so I can change into my jammies. If you want, you can select a movie." She pointed to the lateral file cabinet under the workstation.

Phillip stood, offering his hand and pulling her gently off the chair. "It can't be movie night without popcorn and soda."

Seneca rolled her eyes. "Sorry, my brother, but the concession stand is closed, because the workers wanted to unionize and management wasn't having it."

Throwing back his head, Phillip laughed loudly. "Go change and I'll pick out one that doesn't require tissues."

"I don't know what you're talking about, but I don't cry when viewing a movie."

Phillip slapped his forehead with the heel of his hand. "Oops, I forgot. Seneca Houston is hard."

"You better get used to calling me Butterfly."

"Why Butterfly?"

Turning and presenting him with her back, Seneca pulled the hem of her blouse from the waistband of her slacks, showing Phillip the delicate tattoo of a monarch butterfly. The artist had drawn the insect with orange-brown wings with black veins and borders to appear as if floating in flight.

Phillip closed the distance between them, tracing the outline of the permanent ink at the small of her back with his forefinger. Wrapping one arm around her waist, he eased her forward and kissed the tattoo. "Whoever inked you is incredible. The little bugger looks real."

Seneca smiled. "I got it the day I turned eighteen." She straightened, turning around to face Phillip when dropped his arm. "Do you have any?"

Unbuttoning his shirt, he bared his chest. Black Asian characters were tattooed over his heart. He pointed to the first one. "This is Korean for 'now is the time.' The next one is a Chinese symbol for 'health,' and the last one is Japanese for 'long life.'"

"They're nice."

Seneca had said they were nice when she meant they were tasteful. She liked tattoos but couldn't understand how some people resorted to covering large parts of their body with the colorful ink designs. She'd gotten hers before she'd begun modeling, but if she'd known she was going to become a model she would've held off getting one until she'd left the business.

"I'll leave a toothbrush and towel for you on the table in the bathroom."

Phillip nodded. "Thank you." He waited for Seneca to leave the bedroom before he stripped down to his boxer briefs, leaving his clothes folded neatly on the chair. When he'd gotten up that morning he never would've expected to be invited to Seneca's apartment for dinner or to sleep with her. And she didn't have to concern herself with him attempting to seduce her, because he hadn't brought condoms with him.

Phillip Park Kingston wasn't about to join the ranks of other high-profile athletes who'd become fodder for the tabloids when they were thrust into the spotlight with paternity suits and/or baby-mama drama. If or when he fathered a child, it would be with his wife and not some chicken head crooning that he would "make some pretty babies."

Seneca returned, wearing a white tank top with a pair of peppermint-striped cotton drawstring pants. Her curly hair floated around her face like a cloud. "You can use the bathroom now." She ran over the bed, falling on it like a mischievous child. "I always run and jump on the bed," she explained when Phillip stared at her as if she'd taken leave of her senses.

Crossing his arms over his chest, he shook his head. "One of these days you're going to break down the bed and land on the floor."

Kicking her legs as if she were riding a bicycle, Seneca gave him a sexy smile. "That means I'll just have to buy another one."

In that instant Phillip realized that underneath her so-called tough-girl exterior, Seneca Houston was still a kid—a kid who was about to be thrust into a world where everyone would want a piece of her. And if she wasn't strong enough, she would come to believe the hype. Then, if and when the fickle public moved on to the next "It" girl, would she be prepared for the fallout? He'd planned to give the NBA four more years before walking away to follow his ultimate dream to become a doctor. What were Seneca's long-term plans? She'd gone from full-time to part-time and now a college dropout to embark on a full-time modeling career. Who, he pondered, would be there for her when it ended?

I will, said the voice in his head.

"Hurry up and come to bed, Phillip. The movie is going to begin in ten minutes."

Seneca's sultry voice broke into his thoughts. He'd selected *Blood Diamond* because he hadn't seen the movie. "I'll be right back." Sleeping with Seneca and not making love to her was going to be a first for him, because whenever he crawled into bed with a woman it was because they'd mutually agreed to have sex.

Smiling, he entered the bathroom. Hanging out with Butterfly was not only going to be profitable but also a great deal of fun. Not only was she sexy but she had a wicked sense of humor that complemented what sports writers called his impenetrable mask of perfection.

He was King Phillip, the automaton on the hardwood, master of the three-point shot, while shooting ninety-seven percent from the free-throw line. He rarely gave interviews, and when he did sports writers were always frustrated, because in an age where a minor infraction was headline news he hadn't obliged them. One writer had hinted he had the tendency to be a bad boy, and Phillip reminded him that there was only one Dennis Rodman.

Now he wondered what they would say once the news got out that Phillip Kingston was dating supermodel Butterfly. Their association would prove a win-win for BGM, Phillip Kingston *and* Seneca Houston.

He would get to date a woman he sincerely liked while providing her with male protection. What he didn't want to do was think about the money Booth would earn from booking the beautiful model. Phillip brushed his teeth and splashed water on his face, patting it dry with a thick, thirsty towel before returning to the bedroom and slipping into bed beside Seneca.

She lowered the lamp setting, picked up the remote and activated the play button. Halfway into the movie Phillip realized Seneca had fallen asleep. Gently easing her down from the mound of pillows supporting her back, he covered her with the sheet. He viewed the rest of the movie, and when the credits started to roll across the screen, he stopped the disk, ejected it and turned off the television. Walking on bare feet, he returned to the bed, extinguished the lamp and lay beside the woman who'd managed to slip under the barrier he'd erected to keep them at a distance.

He cradled her to his chest and fell into a deep, dreamless sleep.

Chapter Ten

"I can't believe I had two of them," Seneca moaned. She'd eaten two hot dogs, smothered with mustard and grilled onions. On impulse, she and Phillip had stopped and ordered the franks and hot sausage from the man who'd parked his food cart several blocks from Macy's. Reaching up, she blotted away a smudge of mustard at the corner of Phillip's mouth with a napkin.

"Don't worry about it, baby," he crooned, smiling. "You'll work off the extra calories on the walk back to Battery Park."

Seneca glared up at Phillip from behind the lenses of her oversized sunglasses. They'd left her apartment at nine that morning when the driver arrived to take them to the Ritz-Carlton. A bellhop carried the garment bags filled with the outfits Mitchell had requested she bring to the shoot and her overnight bag to Phillip's suite. She'd hung everything in the closet in the adjoining suite while Phillip called room service, requesting a continental breakfast for her and an all-American

breakfast for himself. Seneca managed to conceal her aston-
ishment at the amount of calories he'd consumed, marveling
that there wasn't an ounce of fat on his hard muscular body.

They'd shared her bed, she waking before him to shower.
She'd altered her routine to dress in the bathroom rather than
in her bedroom. When she'd returned to the bedroom she was
met with the sight of Phillip executing push-ups, not anchor-
ing his hands but his fists on the floor. Watching the flexing
muscles in his back, arms, and buttocks had left her gasping
for breath. Seneca wasn't certain how she'd done it, but she'd
backed out of the bedroom without making a sound. However,
the image of Phillip's nearly nude body lingered for hours.

"I am not walking back, Phillip." Unfortunately, she'd worn
high-heeled sandals.

She'd whispered his name because Phillip had managed a
modicum of anonymity with a baseball cap pulled low over
his forehead and sunglasses. He'd blended in with crowds of
New Yorkers going about their business and wide-eyed tourists
taking in the sights of the city. They'd walked from Battery
Park to Herald Square, stopping en route at an outdoor café
in the West Village to share a Caesar salad and a bottle of
mineral water.

Wrapping an arm around her waist, Phillip pulled Seneca
close to his side. "We don't have to walk. I'll hail a taxi."

Going on tiptoe, Seneca pressed a kiss to his firm mouth.
"Thank you, my love."

He increased the pressure. "You're most welcome, my
love."

"Do you know what else I'm going to need, Phillip?"

"What?" he whispered against the column of her neck.

"A massage." Tightness in her calves was a sure sign that she
would wake up with pain in her legs the next day; she needed
complete flexibility for the shoot.

"Do you have a preference?" Phillip asked.

"What do you mean?"

"Male or female?"

Seneca gave him a Cheshire-cat grin. "Male, of course."

Reaching for her hand, Phillip laced their fingers together. "I'll call the concierge and see if they can reserve one for you."

"Thank you."

His eyebrows lifted a fraction. "You're quite welcome." Walking to the corner, Phillip raised his hand, and within seconds a taxi maneuvered along to the curb. He opened the rear door, waiting for Seneca to get in before he slid in beside her. "Ritz-Carlton at Battery Park," he directed the driver through the Plexiglas partition. The words were barely off his tongue when the taxi took off like a rocket.

"I'm going to soak in the tub," Seneca said over her shoulder as she walked in the direction of her suite.

"Do you want company?" Phillip asked, staring at her slender hips in the fitted jeans.

Seneca did not break stride. "No, thank you."

Phillip smiled. "Just trying to help a sister out."

She halted, turning slowly. Phillip's voice had changed. It was lower, almost coaxing. Seneca knew what he wanted, and no matter how much she'd denied the strong passions within her, she wanted the same: sex. Her first and only sexual liaison had ended badly, leaving her to blame the entire human male species for the debacle.

Something innate communicated that it would be different with Phillip. As a high-profile sports figure with a brand sponsorship tied to his not behaving badly, he couldn't afford a scandal. While she, on the other hand, with her star on the crest of rising, could not afford to take up with a purported bad boy. And Phillip Kingston was anything but a bad boy.

"Are you good with your hands?"

Raising his right hand, Phillip stared at the broad palm and long fingers. "I can palm a basketball with one hand."

A mysterious smile played at the corners of Seneca's mouth. "Have you ever given a massage?"

He approached her, his gaze never leaving her mouth. "Yes, I have."

"Are you any good?"

Phillip recognized an open invitation in the eyes meeting his. "I've never had any complaints."

"If that's the case, then you're hired," Seneca whispered.

His hands went to her shoulders, pulling her to his chest. "Can you afford me, baby?"

Seneca exhaled an audible breath. Sexually sparring with Phillip was new for her, something she hadn't experienced with her first lover. But then, she had to remind herself that Phillip Kingston wasn't a boy but a man.

"What if I can't?" she asked, purring like a cat.

"Then we'll have to come up with something that's amenable to both of us."

"Do you have any suggestions?"

Phillip's impassive expression successfully concealed the satisfaction coursing throughout his body. He finally had Seneca Houston where he'd wanted her since coming face-to-face with her for the first time. When he'd glanced across the living room in Booth Gordon's condo and saw the woman who seemingly had floated in with a garment draped over her slender body that revealed as much as it concealed, he knew he had to have her; he wanted Seneca like he'd wanted to join the NBA, like he wanted to become a doctor.

He'd approached her, the slogan of his favorite tattoo, "Now

Is The Time," echoing in his head. Phillip had hoped to catch her unawares, but she'd turned the tables because she knew who he was. She hadn't gushed, gone mushy or thrown herself at him like so many other women did once they were cognizant of his carefully scripted superstar status. However, Seneca Houston had flipped the script, leaving him to do the chasing.

"I'm mulling over a few, but there is one we can do right now," he said after a pregnant pause.

Seneca's eyes narrowed suspiciously. "What's that?"

"I shared your bed last night, so I'm inviting you to share my bathtub."

"Okay," she agreed, flippantly.

The look of shock freezing Phillip's features was priceless. "Really?"

"How many models have you dated?"

He blinked once. "You're the first one."

She gave him a look that parents, whenever exasperated, usually reserved for their children. "One thing models aren't and that's modest. Taking off my clothes for you isn't any different from my posing nude for an artist."

Phillip gritted his teeth in frustration. It was as if Seneca was testing his very manhood. He swallowed the expletive poised on the tip of his tongue. "Go get what you need from *your* suite, and I'll fill the bathtub." He'd wanted to tell her that athletes also weren't reticent about taking off their clothes. All she had to do was visit a locker room before or after a game to know that.

"Are you angry with me, Phillip?"

His eyebrows flickered. "Why would you ask me that?"

Reaching up, Seneca ran a fingertip over his right eyebrow. "This eyebrow lifts just a fraction whenever you're upset about something."

He caught her wrist. "Do you really think you know me that well?" Seneca tried pulling away, but he increased his grip.

"No, I don't know you *that* well," she countered. "But what I do know is that you have a nasty habit of grabbing me."

Phillip dropped her hand. "I'm sorry, baby. I'd never hurt you."

Going on tiptoe, Seneca pressed a kiss to his throat. "I know you wouldn't. But you probably aren't aware of your own strength."

Cupping the back of her head in his hand, Philip buried his face in her hair. "You're right. Anytime I go Neanderthal on you, please stop me."

He always meditated before every game in order to turn on the switch in his head when he'd become a fierce and aggressive competitor. At six-six, he was shorter than many of the other players, but he made up for the difference with tenacity and excellent hand-eye control. His stats included leading the league in the highest number of three-point totals two years running.

Seneca nodded, smiling. "I will." She kissed his chin. "I'll see you in a little bit."

Phillip watched her walk, her hips swaying sensually, as if she were on a runway. A knowing smile softened his features. *Yes,* he mused. Seneca Houston fit perfectly into his plans for his future. However, he had to tread carefully or he would lose her. Although he liked her spirited personality, her mouthing off at him was bothersome.

When he'd first joined the NBA he'd overheard some black players say they didn't date black women because they always had attitude. In other words, they didn't know their place, that when given the opportunity they tended to emasculate a man. Phillip had thought it was an excuse for them to date or marry women outside of their race.

It hadn't happened with him, therefore, he considered himself luckier than the others. It wasn't that Seneca had an attitude but that she was as derisive as she was beautiful. What she didn't know was that he had the perfect remedy to counter her acerbic tongue, and it was between his legs.

Seneca stripped off her clothes, leaving them in a large wicker basket that doubled as a hamper in her en suite bathroom. She hadn't spent a night in the hotel but knew she could very easily get used to living there. The thought that Phillip could get anything he wanted with a single telephone call astounded her. During the ride back to the hotel he'd disclosed that he'd ordered dinner in his suite for later that evening, and she would have the option of dressing up. When she'd tried to get him to divulge what they were celebrating he'd remained tight-lipped, which led her to believe the dinner was going to be more than room service bringing a cart with covered dishes.

She lingered in the bathroom long enough to remove the elastic band from her hair and comb it with a wide-tooth comb before she brushed her teeth. Returning to her bedroom, she picked up a blood-red kimono off the foot of the bed and slipped it on. Walking on bare feet, she went through the door connecting the suites and into Phillip's bathroom.

Leaning against the door frame, Seneca smiled at the man lounging in the tub; the swirling water from the Jacuzzi lapped against his chest. "Waiting long?" she asked, her sultry voice lowering an octave.

Phillip, stretching his arms along the ledge of the tub, nodded. The motion accentuated the corded muscles in his long arms. "Yes," he confirmed verbally. "I've been waiting all of my life for someone like you."

Seneca opened her mouth to tell him that he was being overdramatic, that he'd probably seen too many romantic-themed movies, but she wasn't able to get the words out. It was as if her tongue was glued to the roof of her mouth.

"Same here," she whispered, not knowing where the admission had come from.

Had she lost her mind? What spell, she mused, had Phillip Kingston cast over her, that she'd agreed to stay with him in his hotel suite like a kept woman? She was Seneca Ileana Houston, soon-to-be Butterfly, and she'd permitted herself to succumb to the good looks and superstar status of a man adored by the sports world and women from coast to coast.

She'd been one of those who'd opened a copy of *Essence* magazine to find Phillip Kingston staring out from the glossy page and had experienced a rush of moisture flowing between her legs. It was the first and only time she'd found herself enthralled with the face and body of a man who'd become eye candy for millions of women. She never would've imagined meeting the man, or agreeing to share a bathtub with him.

With wide eyes, she stared as Phillip pushed to his feet, water streaming off his magnificent body. Her gaze went to the thick length of flesh hanging between muscled thighs. "Come on in, baby. The water's perfect."

Seneca shook her head. If Phillip hadn't stood up she would've gotten into the tub with him. But just seeing how well he was endowed frightened her. He didn't have an erection, but he was *huge!* There was no way he could fit inside her.

"No, Phillip," she whispered.

He beckoned to her. "It's all right. I'm not going to do anything you don't want me to do."

She took several steps. "It's not you."

"Who is it?"

Seneca forced a smile she didn't feel. "It's me, Phillip. It's been almost two years since I've slept with a man, and to say I'm horny is an understatement. I've told myself that I don't want or need a man, but I know that's a lie. The truth is I need one in the worst way. I never thought I would ever resort to masturbating, but I do it just to get some relief."

Phillip whispered a silent prayer of thanks. Seneca was so pumped and primed he could almost smell sex coming off her in waves. He beckoned again. "Come get in."

Moving as if she were being pulled by an invisible wire, she approached the tub and untied the sash to the kimono, letting it fall to the floor. A modicum of bravado returned when she heard the soft whoosh of breath from Phillip. He extended his hand and she took it like a trusting child. His free arm went around her waist and he hoisted her into the tub.

Never had Seneca been more aware of the differences in their bodies as she was now. Pressed to his length, she felt the raw power in Phillip's arms and hands as they moved up to her neck. His fingers circled her neck. A smile flitted across her face when his lips parted seconds before his head lowered and he slanted his mouth over hers.

Breathing the raw essence of his masculinity, she opened her mouth to his rapacious tongue. She went still when the tip of his tongue touched her palate before she collapsed against his chest.

Phillip felt Seneca go pliant in his arms. She was his, his for the taking. At that point he knew he could do anything to her that he wanted to do. But he didn't, only because of her sexual inexperience. Although she'd admitted to sleeping with one man, he still thought of her as a virgin. What, he mused, could she have learned from an insensitive and no doubt bumbling adolescent boy?

His first sexual encounter was at sixteen, when an older and very experienced woman offered to "make him feel good." She did, and then the tables were turned when he was the one who'd made her feel good. She was an incredible teacher and he a willing and apt student. Phillip continued to sleep with her until he left for college, and whenever he returned for school breaks he sought her out. It ended when she left L.A. to marry a man who lived in Florida. Her send-off gift was to keep him in bed for three days. When he was finally able to escape, his penis, despite his wearing a condom, felt as if it had been put through a meat grinder.

The one thing his sexual mentor had taught him, and he never forgot, was to make certain a woman was satisfied before he was. Phillip found meditating helped him to focus—spiritually and physically. However, upon awakening to discover that he'd had a wet dream had left him baffled *and* uneasy, because he feared losing control with Seneca.

"Come on, baby, let's sit down," he urged, as much for his benefit as hers.

Seneca held on to Phillip as if he were her lifeline when he eased her into the warm, swirling water to sit between his legs. "Aaagh! That feels wonderful."

Phillip emitted a low moan. The water felt good, his hands splayed over Seneca's flat belly felt good, and his semierect penis bobbing up and down against her hips felt very, very good.

"Are you okay?" Seneca asked.

He moaned again. "I've never been better."

Turning her head, she stared out the window above the marble ledge with a vase of fresh flowers and candles in varying heights and shapes. Phillip had slid back the privacy screen. The sky was awash with streaks of blue and orange as the sun sunk lower in the horizon.

"If I lived here I'd turn off the light, light candles and sit in the tub to watch the sun set." Her voice was pregnant with longing.

Phillip traced the outline of her ear with his tongue. "That can be arranged."

She closed her eyes. "What are you saying?"

"Move in with me."

Seneca's eyes opened, shifting slightly to stare over her shoulder at Phillip. "You're kidding, aren't you?"

His expression was unreadable. "No, I'm not. You can have your own suite."

"What about your parents?" she asked.

"I'll put them up in another suite. Besides, they don't come to New York that often."

She shook her head. "Thanks, but no thanks. I'm comfortable living where I am."

"You wouldn't have to worry about paying rent."

Shifting until she was facing Phillip, Seneca straddled him, her arms going around his neck. "Do you invite every woman you sleep with to live with you?"

Staring at her under lowered lids, Phillip smiled at the woman who'd become in his estimation the epitome of perfection. "No."

"Then why me, Phillip?"

He dropped a kiss on the end of her nose. "I haven't slept with you. Sharing a bed doesn't count," he said when she opened her mouth to refute him.

"All right," Seneca conceded, "let me rephrase my question. You've just met me, in fact know nothing more about me than what I've told you, yet you want me to live with you."

Phillip mentally shifted gears. He *had* to hook up with Seneca Houston before she became the supermodel Booth had promised to make her into. And knowing Booth Gordon as well as he did, there was little doubt the reincarnated Svengali/Rasputin clone would make Butterfly one of the most sought-out high-fashion models in the world.

"It would work well if we're going to be a couple."

"What about Electra?"

"What about her, Seneca?" he asked, answering her question with another one.

"I'm committed to half the rent."

"I'll pay her for you."

Again, Seneca felt a flicker of apprehension course through her. She couldn't wrap her head around someone like Phillip Kingston pursuing her like a large cat stalking prey. She had barely walked into Booth's condo when he'd approached her. Men who looked like Phillip and earned millions a year usually didn't do the chasing but were chased by women plotting and scheming to get them into bed with them, regardless whether their ulterior motive was sex, marriage or a baby—of which she wanted none. No, she corrected—she didn't want sex as much as she needed it. "Can you slow it down a little, Phillip?" she asked. "Let's give ourselves the summer to see if we're able to get along with each other. It's one thing to play to the camera and another once we go home and close the door."

The tense lines in Phillip's face relaxed. He knew he was coming on strong, but he'd hoped Seneca would jump at his offer. She would have her own suite, and he would leave it to her discretion whether she wanted to sleep with him. What he'd wanted to do was to make her unavailable for other men.

"Do you want to set a date?"

"How about Labor Day?"

He smiled. "That sounds reasonable. By that time I'll have to report for preseason practice."

Seneca pressed her breasts to his muscled chest. "I think we'll get along well if you don't put too much pressure on me."

Phillip's smile grew wider. He splayed his hands over her back, pulling her closer. "I know you'll stop me if I do."

Burying her face between his neck and shoulder, Seneca closed her eyes. "You can count on that."

"Do you mind if I ask you a very personal question?"

"No. What is it?"

"How did you get that Charlie Chaplin mustache on your beaver patch?"

She eased back, her gaze meeting and fusing with an amused one that sent a rush of heat across her face. Her mouth opened and closed several times. "I can't believe you'd ask me that!"

His eyebrows lifted. "I did ask your permission." There was a hint of laughter in his voice.

Seneca swallowed back her embarrassment. "I had it threaded."

Lines deepened around Phillip's eyes when he laughed. "You have your pussy threaded?"

She rolled her eyes. "Yes, I have my pubic area threaded. Whenever I model lingerie or swimwear I can't have any superfluous body hair. The first time I tried waxing I ended up with a reaction. And shaving leaves little bumps, so I went the threading route."

Phillip's fingers grazed her mound. "I think it's cute. Scoot down so I can massage your legs."

He'd told her he wanted to massage her legs when it was another part of her body he wanted to touch. Seneca had asked that he slow down his pursuit of her, and he would. She wasn't going anywhere and neither was he. His one consolation was her revelation that her sexual urges were strong enough for her to resort to masturbating.

Now all he had to do was wait, wait for her to come to him to take care of her sexual needs. One of his favorite Seal songs was "Waiting for You." He hadn't realized the significance of the lyrics until he met Seneca Houston.

Chapter Eleven

Seneca woke Saturday morning disoriented. She wasn't in her bed, she wore a T-shirt instead of pajamas or a nightgown, and it wasn't until she sat up to see the drawn drapes that was she aware of her surroundings. She wasn't in her own bedroom in the Upper West Side brownstone but in Phillip's hotel suite. Closing her eyes, she remembered drinking the second glass of wine but didn't remember going to bed.

Dinner the night before had been nothing short of perfection. Phillip had ordered room service, and the chef had prepared the dishes while they'd looked on; a waiter stood at the ready to take care of all their dining needs. He had refilled their water goblets and wineglasses and picked up and set down each course with expert precision. Once the chef and waiter left, she and Phillip lay on the chaise, staring out the window talking and listening to music. After a while, the effects of the wine won out and she fell asleep.

Throwing off the sheet, she walked on unsteady legs to the

bathroom. Despite spending time in the Jacuzzi and Phillip's massage, the muscles in her calves were still somewhat tight.

Seneca brushed her teeth, followed by rinsing her mouth with a peppermint mouthwash, then stepped into the shower stall. The shower had become the magic cure. She felt almost normal. Damp curls hung around her face as she pulled on a set of underwear and a pair of lounging pants with an oversize T-shirt.

Opening the drapes, she discovered she couldn't see through the thick fog obscuring the harbor. It was one of those days she always referred to as "pea soup weather." The time on her cell phone read 8:17 a.m. She checked her home phone for messages. Stefani still hadn't called her. It had become apparent that her cousin had changed her mind about leaving the salon.

"I need water," she murmured under her breath. Not only did she need water but lots of it to offset the effects of the wine she'd drunk and also the slight puffiness under her eyes. If she was going to be photographed the following day, she didn't want the makeup artist to apply layers of foundation and concealer to correct the imperfections. Adequate sleep and remaining hydrated were the cure to a model's overall physical well-being. Opening the mini bar, she took out a bottle of water. She finished the bottle, temporarily assuaging her thirst. Not bothering to put on shoes, Seneca went in search of Phillip.

She found him in the living room, lounging on a chaise in a T-shirt and shorts, bare feet crossed at the ankles, reading the newspaper. "Good morning."

Phillip's head popped up when he heard the dulcet voice. Sitting up straight, he swung his legs over the chaise with Seneca's approach, coming to his feet. "Good morning, beautiful. How do you feel?" He extended his arms, and he wasn't disappointed when Seneca came into his embrace. He sat down again, bringing her down with him.

"Okay."

"Why just okay? Didn't you sleep well? Talk to me, baby."

Straddling his lap, Seneca pressed her cheek to the column of his thick neck. He smelled of soap and clean laundry as she melted into his protective strength. "I have no tolerance for alcohol."

"Do you have a hangover?"

"No."

Phillip buried his face in her damp hair. "Perhaps you should limit yourself to one glass."

Easing back, she stared up at him through her lashes. "Perhaps I should swear off wine completely."

He smiled. "You'll be all right as long as you hang out with me. I'll always be the designated driver, and if or when you fall asleep on me, I'll put you to bed."

She returned his smile. "I'm surprised I didn't wake up in your bed."

"You sleeping in my bed would've really been too much of a temptation, and I probably would've broken my promise not to make love to you until you say yes. After all, you did say you wanted me to date you. But now that I think about it, having dinner here was a date," he said, as if it were an afterthought.

Seneca smiled. Their walking from Battery Park to Herald Square while stopping en route to have lunch was a date. Sharing dinner in his suite last night was again a date. "Is that what you're waiting for?" Her voice had lowered seductively. "Are you waiting for me to say yes?"

Phillip slid his hands under her shirt and covered her breasts, discovering that Seneca's slimness was deceiving. She had curves where a real woman should have curves. "The answer to both questions is a resounding yes."

Seneca inhaled sharply, then bit down on her lip when she felt the growing hardness under her hips. The seconds ticked as they stared at each other. She wanted him to make love to her.

"What do you want?" he asked, reading her mind.

"I want you to make love to me."

The instant the revelation rolled off her tongue Seneca felt as a weight had been lifted. She'd spent two years denying her femininity, but a single glance from Phillip Kingston had left her breathless and the area between her legs moist and pulsing.

"Are you certain that's what you want, Seneca?" Phillip chided himself when he'd asked the question. He'd spent a week fantasizing about making love to her. She nodded. "You know what this means?"

Her mouth formed a sexy moue. "What *does* it mean?"

Cradling her face in his hands, he kissed her soft mouth. "This is about us, not a publicity stunt. It doesn't matter why you want me to make love to you, but let me warn you that I'm not into playing head games."

Seneca felt the strong, steady beating of his heart against her breasts and she wondered if he could feel the runaway rhythm of hers. "Why do *you* want to make love to me?"

"Isn't it obvious, baby? I like you."

What he didn't say was that Seneca Houston fit perfectly into his future plans. She was attractive, intelligent, articulate and, more important, she wasn't needy. He'd found her to be as self-centered as he was. Their careers were first and a relationship secondary.

The truth was, long before he'd met Seneca he'd tired of dating different women, whether it was by mutual consent or if it was a prearranged publicity stunt. Some of them he'd slept with and some he hadn't.

He was only twenty-six yet felt years older. Playing professional ball was physical enough, but Booth Gordon's carefully orchestrated plan to turn him into a sex symbol had become emotionally challenging. Each and every time he slept with a woman he'd run the risk of scandal, which could jeopardize his lucrative contracts—on and off the court. It was a risk he wanted to do away with. His having a relationship with Seneca "Butterfly" Houston would serve as a feeding frenzy for the paparazzi and fodder for the tabloids while turning them into international celebrities.

Seneca's smile was as tender as a kiss. "I like you, too," she whispered, curving her arms under his shoulders.

She liked him because she knew she could trust him. He'd admitted he wasn't one to kiss and tell, and that he couldn't afford to do anything that would put his basketball career, his endorsements and his future plans to become a physician at risk. Whether Phillip realized it or not, *she* was the one who could make him sorry he'd ever come on to her if he ever did or said anything to jeopardize *her* career.

"I'm not using protection," she said when he swung her up in his arms and headed in the direction of his bedroom. Seneca couldn't afford an unplanned pregnancy, and being faced with the decision of terminating a pregnancy was not an option. Her rationale was if she was woman enough to lie with a man, then she was woman enough to deal with the consequences.

"Don't worry about it, baby. I have condoms." She didn't want a baby *and* he couldn't afford to father a child—not at this time in his life.

Phillip placed her on his unmade bed; she closed her eyes for several seconds, but when she'd opened them she saw that he'd drawn the drapes. Everything seemed to move in slow motion. He sat down on the side of the bed, opening the drawer in the bedside table. With wide eyes, Seneca stared at the small square packet on the pillow next to her head. Her gaze shifted to the muscles rippling in Phillip's back as he leaned over to remove his shirt and shorts. He turned and loomed over her. A small gasp escaped her when his penis, swaying heavily between his legs, brushed across her belly.

Phillip followed the direction of her gaze. "It's okay, baby. I'll try not to hurt you." He knew he had to make certain Seneca was fully aroused before he penetrated her. "If I do something you don't like, please let me know."

Seneca nodded. If she hadn't been attracted to Phillip, or sexually deprived, she never would've asked him to make love to her. Masturbating while viewing a porn flick had become her guilty pleasure. Heat, then chills, swept over her body, bringing with them a rush of wetness in her vagina as she struggled not to move her hips. She was literally gawking at Phillip's dick as he opened the packet and rolled the latex down his erection.

Inhaling through her nose and breathing out through her mouth, she slowed her breathing until she was back in control. His fingers grazed the hem of her shirt, and he eased it up and over her chest. Her lounging pants and panties quickly followed, as if he'd performed the task countless times.

Supporting his weight on his elbows, Phillip rained feathery kisses down the column of Seneca's neck, lingering at the rapidly beating pulse in her throat. He caught her hands, threading their fingers together when she reached out to touch him. Her touch was like pouring gasoline on a fire. It would excite him to the point where he wouldn't be able to control himself, and he would take her without a pretense of foreplay.

His mouth covered her breasts, tongue and teeth, making

the nipples hard as tiny pebbles. Sliding down the length of her smooth, silken body, Phillip inhaled the musky scent wafting from the apex of her thighs. Tentatively, he flicked his tongue over her mound, the tip tracing the small patch of soft hair, ignoring the gasp from Seneca. He didn't know whether a man had gone down on her; if not, then he wanted to be her first.

"Are you okay with this?" Phillip asked.

His query penetrated the sensual fog pulling Seneca into an abyss she hadn't known existed. Phillip's lovemaking was so different from what she'd had with her first lover. Vincent had always kissed her hard, then squeezed her breasts a few times before pushing inside like a battering ram. He pumped like a jackrabbit, came and then collapsed on her, all the while whispering how good she was. It took a while, but she finally told him that he had to slow down so she, too, could climax. He'd stomped off angry, telling her no girl had ever complained about his "fuckin'," to which she replied that he should go back to those girls.

He'd returned a few days later, apologizing profusely and asking Seneca to give him another chance. She did give him another chance, and Vincent must have heeded her advice, because she'd had her first orgasm. It had also been the last time they'd slept together. The next day Vincent spread the rumor that her best friend gave him better oral sex than she did, and that she'd gone down on a group of guys.

"Yes-s-s," she stuttered.

It was the last intelligible word she'd uttered when moist heat seared the area between her legs and turned her into a trembling mass of helplessness. The tip of Phillip's tongue swept over her clitoris in a slow back-and-forth motion, causing her hips to rise off the mattress. The tiny flutters increased in intensity as moisture bathed her labia. Then it happened—the first orgasm seized Seneca, holding her captive as she arched her back, gasping.

Holding his penis while moving up Seneca's bucking body, Phillip eased his erection into her vagina at the same time as another orgasm gripped her. She was tight, but because she was so wet it aided his attempt to push inside her.

Fastening his mouth to the side of her neck, he opened his mouth to brand her, then remembered she had a photo shoot the next day. It wouldn't do for her to show up with love bites on her body. He nuzzled her instead as he counted the number of seconds to penetrate her—inch by each deliciously slow inch. It took nine seconds, and when he was fully sheathed inside her hot, wet body, it was his turn to moan. They were a perfect fit.

Damn, she felt good, better than he'd fantasized. She'd breathed out the last of her climax when he began moving. Her eyes opened, and she smiled the smile of a completely satiated woman.

Bracing himself on his hands as if he were doing push-ups, Phillip stared at his dick moving in and out of her pussy, the sight making him harder, longer. He leaned forward, the motion causing friction against her swollen clit. His head came up, his gaze meeting the stunned stare of the woman beneath him. Her hips had begun to move again, rising to meet his strong thrusts. A knowing smile softened his mouth. He was going to make her come again. And she did. This time the contractions were stronger, Seneca bucking like a wild mare, the walls of her vagina squeezing him like a too-tight rubber band.

Phillip saw her eyes glaze over. He lowered his arms, supporting his greater weight on his elbows as he ejaculated into the condom. "Oh fuck! Oh fuck!" he chanted like a litany.

"Oh shit!" he finally groaned out, then collapsed heavily on her slight body.

They lay motionless, only the sound of heavy breathing indicating they were still alive.

Seneca recovered first. Phillip was crushing her. "Baby, please get up."

It took Herculean strength for him to roll off her body. He lay on his back, staring up at the ceiling and waiting for his respiration to return to normal. Reaching for her hand, he laced their fingers together. When he'd asked his father why he'd married his mother and not some other woman, Richard Kingston's response had been, "When you meet the right woman something deep inside of you will let you know she's the one."

Phillip let out an audible sigh. His father was right. He'd met the right woman—the one lying beside him. He felt the blood pooling in his groin again, but instead of discarding the condom and putting on a new one, he left the bed to wash off the semen.

When he returned to the bed, he found Seneca lying on her side, asleep. Smiling, he got into bed. It took a while before he was able to relax enough to sleep, but when he did his mind was filled with images of Seneca as his wife and the mother of their children.

Seneca slipped out of bed, moving slowly not only because she didn't want to wake Phillip but also because muscles she'd forgotten she had slowed motion. She hadn't gotten into a routine of working out, because first, she couldn't afford the membership fees at Manhattan sports clubs and second, she didn't like to exercise. The closest she got to exercising was walking. Everyone who lived or worked in Manhattan walked.

However, her walking regime was relegated to running shoes, not high-heeled sandals.

The ache between her legs wasn't as uncomfortable as it was a reminder of how long it'd been since she'd shared her body with a man. A sensual smile softened her eyes when she remembered making love with Phillip. He was more than she'd expected, making certain she climaxed before he came. Her smile faded when she recalled the explosion of profanity he'd spewed when ejaculating. For a brief moment she'd been so frightened by the intensity and ferocity that she'd feared for her well-being. Her limited experience with the opposite sex hadn't prepared her for Phillip's reaction, but it was something to bear watching.

When she'd shared the apartment with three other girls, Seneca had been drawn into their conversations about the men they'd slept with. Although she'd had only one prior romantic affair, she'd found herself engrossed in the discussions. And only one of the four hadn't had a kiss-and-tell experience, while one had admitted to breaking up with a guy who'd cursed and called her *bitch* during sex. His outbursts had escalated, reaching a point where she'd feared for her life after he was diagnosed with schizophrenia.

Walking into her en suite bathroom, Seneca brushed her teeth, stepped into the shower stall, turned on the water, adjusting the temperature, and then moved under the showerhead. She let the water beat down on her head and face for a full minute before picking up the bath sponge and gel and lathering her body from neck to toes. A gasp escaped her when the door opened and Phillip stepped in and closed the door behind him. Not only did she find breathing difficult, but there didn't seem to be enough room for her to move without her body brushing against his.

"What are you doing?" she asked, breathlessly.

Resting his hands on her hips, Phillip moved Seneca close, her breasts flattening against his chest. He dipped his head, brushing a kiss over her parted lips. "I came to say good morning."

Smiling, Seneca inhaled his mint-flavored breath. "I like the way you say good morning." Going up on tiptoe, she curved her arms under his broad shoulders. "Thank you, and good morning to you, too." She gasped again—this time when his hand moved over the curve of her hip to between her thighs.

"Are you sore?" he whispered in her ear.

"A little," Seneca said truthfully. "I want us to wait until—"

"Don't worry, baby," Phillip crooned, kissing Seneca and stopping her words. "I won't touch you until you're feeling better. But that doesn't mean you can't touch me."

Tilting her head, Seneca stared up at him through spiked lashes. "What are you talking about?"

He went completely still, his eyes searching hers and seeing indecision. She didn't know. Seneca didn't know what he wanted her to do. Then realization dawned when he realized her age and limited experience with men.

Reaching for her hand, he guided her fingers to his semierect penis. "Jerk me off, baby."

A shudder swept over Seneca from the top of her head to the soles of her feet when the flesh in her hand stirred to life, growing harder and longer. Phillip wanted her to jerk him off, and what he didn't know was that she used to masturbate Vincent whenever she was on her menses.

"How do you want it, Phillip? Fast, slow, hard, easy?"

Resting his back against the tiled wall, Phillip closed his eyes. "You're in the driver's seat, beautiful. Do whatever you want."

It was the first time, other than with the woman who'd taught him everything he knew about pleasuring a woman, that he'd relinquished control. There was something about Seneca Houston that was different, unique, and he intended to find out exactly what it was.

"Aren't you afraid I'll do something you don't want me to do?" Seneca asked.

He opened his eyes, glaring at her. What was she trying to do? Make his hard-on go down? "No, Seneca," he said between clenched teeth. "Just do it."

"Sit down, Phillip."

"What?"

"I said sit down."

Phillip complied, sliding down to the floor of the stall, Seneca following and straddling his thighs. Grasping his penis with both hands, she pressed it against his belly while moving it up and down, around and around, as if she were churning cream into butter.

The guttural sounds coming from deep within Phillip's heaving chest competed with the rhythmic tapping of water splashing over their bodies. Excitement—raw, untamed— quickened Seneca's breathing, her heart pumping wildly against her rib cage. Never had she felt so powerful, so in control as she manipulated the rigid length of blood-engorged flesh.

"Don't stop! Please don't stop, baby. It's so-oo good."

She didn't want to believe that Phillip Kingston—touted as the most focused player in the NBA—was sitting on the floor of a shower stall, quivering and blathering like someone possessed while she masturbated him.

Seneca felt her tender flesh respond to her own rising desire as Phillip jerked wildly, bellowing, then groaning as he ejaculated, semen spurting into her hand and onto his belly; she opened and closed her fist until the strong pulsing ebbed, then stopped.

It was her turn to moan softly as orgasms seized her in a maelstrom of dizzying ecstasy that left her calling his name while she collapsed to his chest. They lay together, breathing heavily.

Bracing himself on one hand, Phillip came to a stand, bringing Seneca up with him. Fastening his mouth to hers, he pressed her back to the wall, slamming his pelvis against hers and simulating making love to her. Lust clouded his mind when he realized he was getting hard again. Holding his erection in one hand, he guided it between Seneca's legs, but she managed to slip away from him.

"What the hell do you think you're doing?" Seneca wasn't aware that she was screaming until she saw Phillip's shocked expression. She backed away from him. "You promised to use protection."

He blinked, as if coming out of a trance, and his erection went down like someone letting the air out of a balloon. It wasn't her yelling at him as much as the look on Seneca's face that had jerked him back to reality. She looked frightened. *No,* he thought, *the girl was terrified.* But what, he mused, was she so frightened of?

He reached out to touch her, but she pulled away. "What's the matter, Seneca?"

"What's the matter?" she spat out. "You were going to go inside of me without a condom."

"I know I promised to protect you, but if I were to get you pregnant then I'd marry you."

Seneca reached over to turn off the water. She didn't want to believe what she'd just heard. A man she'd known exactly one week was talking about babies and marriage. "You're delusional, Phillip. I don't know you, and you certainly know nothing about me."

Crossing muscular arms over an equally muscular chest, Phillip rested his back against the wall, his hungry gaze moving slowly over her face and body. "What don't I know about you?"

"I don't want a baby. No, let me correct myself. I don't *need* a baby. Not when I have to concentrate on my career." Phillip's right eyebrow flickered, and Seneca sensed he was upset with her response.

"I understand." The two words were flat, cold.

She shook her head. "No, you don't understand, Phillip. At twenty you knew exactly what you wanted and where you were going. You even have your life planned out for yourself. You say you want to give the NBA ten years, and then it's on to medical school. Well, my life isn't wrapped up in a neat little package with a bow like yours. I'm twenty years old, or should I say I'll be twenty-one, *if* or *when* I'm regarded as a full-time professional model. And that's old, Phillip. I'll be lucky if I can stay in the game ten years, not when fifteen- and sixteen-year-olds are looking to push me off the runway. I plan to work as often as I can and for as long as I can before I give it all up for marriage and a family. I'd also like to go back to school and get my degree. Those are *my* long-term plans."

Phillip realized he'd underestimated Seneca Houston. She could care less about his superstar status. She was Butterfly— purported by Booth Gordon to be the world's next super-model. And something said she would reach her goal, because she wanted it as much as he'd wanted to play in the NBA.

"I'm sorry, Seneca. It won't happen again." He held out his arms. "Come here, baby." She took a step, then another, and he cradled her to his body. "Why the hell do you have to be so damn sexy?"

Tilting her chin, Seneca smiled. "I should ask you the same thing. I came in here to take a shower, but someone interrupted me," she continued, deftly changing the subject. "Remember, Mitchell expects us to be at his place around eight."

Phillip patted her behind. "I'll let you shower while I go and shave. I've already reserved a car, and the bellhop will take the garments down to the car whenever we're ready to leave."

"What time are we leaving?"

"I told the driver between seven-thirty and seven forty-five. It shouldn't take more than ten to fifteen minutes to get to Tribeca, even with traffic."

Seneca patted and then pinched his tight butt. "Go, baby. I'll meet you in the living room."

It was only when the door opened, then closed behind Phillip's departing figure that she was able to draw a normal breath. Seneca knew she'd dodged a bullet when she'd stopped him from penetrating her. She didn't know if he'd been so caught up in the moment that he wanted to make love to her without using protection. What she wasn't willing to do was risk it again.

Come Monday she would call her gynecologist for an appointment to be fitted for an IUD. Women probably fantasized about having Phillip Kingston's baby, but she couldn't be counted among them.

He was King Phillip on the hardwood, and she was to become Butterfly on the runway. And that wasn't going to happen if she found herself carrying his child. Dahlia's dreams were dashed when she'd found herself pregnant. When she'd overheard her mother talking to her sister about the pitfalls of becoming a single mother, Seneca had vowed it would never happen to her.

And as long as she remained in control of her mind *and* her body—it wouldn't.

Chapter Twelve

Booth Gordon glanced at the clock on a far wall; standing, he reached for his suit jacket folded over the back of the chair next to his desk. The excitement rushing throughout his body made him feel as if he were having sex instead of preparing to meet the account executives for the Super Bowl ad. He'd instructed Joan to set up the luncheon meeting in his on-premise apartment instead of scheduling the meeting at La Grenouille. He'd taken the liberty of asking the men their dining preferences and had a chef prepare the dishes in the kitchen off the living/dining room in the fourth-floor office, which was larger and more luxurious than many Manhattan apartments.

The buzzing of the intercom caught his attention. He'd instructed Joan to call him when the men arrived. He picked up the receiver rather than activate the speaker feature. "Yes?"

"Mr. Gordon, there's a Mr. Browning here to see you—"

"I don't know a Mr. Browning. And you know I never see

anyone without an appointment," Gordon practically growled into the mouthpiece.

"I know that, Mr. Gordon. But Mr. Browning was referred to you by Dennis Mayfield."

The intermittent euphoria Booth had experienced when viewing the photographs Mitchell Leon had taken of Seneca Houston and Phillip Kingston vanished as if he'd been doused with a bucket of ice-cold water. Dennis knew better than to send anyone to his office. He always met with the professional enforcer at his condo, because not only did his boyhood friend have to be announced but because his image was also captured on closed-circuit cameras. If Dennis had decided to turn on him, the police would have a name, face and a time of departure as a lead.

"Tell Mr. Browning that I'm coming out to see him."

Gordon hung up, slipped into his suit jacket and walked out of his office. His gaze swept over the slender blond man sitting on the chair in the anteroom where Joan Powers presided like a sentinel, guarding and providing her boss with the utmost security. He estimated the man was somewhere in his late twenties or early thirties, and he looked as if he'd stepped off the glossy pages of a Ralph Lauren ad.

"Mr. Browning?"

The younger man popped up as if released from a tightly coiled spring. "It's Carter. Carter Browning." He extended his hand, but when Booth glared at it he slowly let it drop.

"Mr. Browning, I never see anyone without a prior appointment, but because you claim Dennis Mayfield referred you—"

"Claim?" The contrast of added color under a light summer tan made Carter's natural ash-blond hair even more startling. Patrician features twisted into a scowl. "Dennis *did* send me," he said in dangerously soft voice.

Nothing in Booth's expression indicated the rage making it almost impossible for him to move or speak. "Joan, this won't take long. Mr. Browning, please come with me." He led the way back to his office, closing the door quietly before he rounded on the unsuspecting man. "Listen to me, you little arrogant fuck! No one comes to see me without a prior appointment. Even Dennis knows that, so don't try and shit me by dropping his name."

Carter recoiled as if he'd been punched in the gut, but then recovered quickly. He hadn't expected the elegant-looking, well-dressed man to come at him like a pit bull. "Dennis didn't tell me I needed an appointment."

"Well, you do!" Booth spat out. "Now, I want you to go out that door and have my assistant give you my private number. Call me anytime after six and I'll let you know when and where we'll meet. And tell Dennis that he fucked up and not to do it again."

Carter nodded, his blue eyes hard and cold as chipped ice. "Okay, Mr. Gordon."

In a gesture that surprised even him, Booth gave Carter a comforting pat on the back. "Call me Booth."

Carter Browning smiled for the first time. "No problem, Booth."

Booth waited two minutes and then buzzed Joan. She picked up immediately. "How did he get past reception?"

"I don't know, Mr. Gordon. They never bothered to announce him."

"Find out who let him through and take care of it."

"I'll do that," Joan said, her voice pregnant with pride.

Booth slammed the received in the cradle. He knew Joan hated him, but he could also trust her to act as his office enforcer whenever she redirected her rage onto another hapless employee.

Reaching up and adjusting his tie, he walked through the door leading to the private dining area with the table set with silver, crystal and china. Delicious aromas wafted from the nearby kitchen. He'd planned for them to eat, drink and then discuss business. That was something he'd learned from his uncle. Seth Rockwell's mantra was "Feed them, drink them, and then kill the bastards with kindness." Booth was willing to exercise the first two, but kindness was not a part of his business repertoire. His approach was straight, no chaser.

Ten minutes later Joan ushered the advertising executives into the space that on occasion doubled as her boss's second home. Her late lover's nephew had renovated the entire floor to suit his personality. The furnishings were expensive yet not ostentatious. There was nothing wrong with what she'd selected for Seth Rockwell, but after Seth died, it was as if Booth sought to erase every trace of the man whom she'd promised to love—even in death. However, the upside of Booth taking over the helm was that he'd expanded the agency beyond anything Seth could've imagined. Seth had done business the old way, with a smile and a handshake, while Booth relied on Machiavellian machinations.

Booth was smiling, but his eyes weren't. They quickly assessed the well-dressed men, instinctually identifying the weaker of the two when he offered his hand. His fingernails were bitten to the quick.

Both were named John, and with the exception of the gnawed fingernails, they were Tweedledum and Tweedledee, indistinguishable: gray-flecked brown hair, gray eyes and clean-shaven. Both favored brown suits, shoes, white shirts and brown-and-white ties with differing patterns. Even their haircuts were the same, close-cropped and parted on the right side. They were updated versions of TV's *Mad Men*.

He gestured to the sideboard, where a white-jacketed waiter

stood in front of a well-stocked bar. "Gentlemen, may I offer you something to drink?"

Tweedledum, the senior account manager, ordered a caipirinha and Tweedledee a suffering bastard. Booth nodded to the bartender, grinning and exhibiting porcelain veneers. Cocktails, rich food and casual conversation before talking business were the prerequisites for closing a deal. Normally he would've had wine, but today he would take his lead from the ad execs.

"Ricky, I'll have a smoky martini."

The mixologist nodded. "I'm on it, Mr. Gordon."

Booth was hard-pressed not to laugh when the two men strolled across the room to stare at the images flickering across the large wall-mounted flat-screen television. Their stunned expressions were priceless, and he wished he had a camera to capture them for posterity. He'd instructed an intern to set up a PowerPoint presentation with the frames of film Mitchell Leon had taken of Seneca and Phillip with the intention of whetting the creative appetites of the advertising executives before they sat down to negotiate the terms of signing Phillip Kingston as pitchman for the luxury crossover vehicle.

The ice in John Waller's suffering bastard rattled like dice as he clasped his hands around the icy-cold concoction to keep his hands still. Whenever he was excited or exasperated, the fingers found their way to his mouth. "Who is she?" he whispered.

This time Booth did laugh, the warm rich sound bubbling up from his chest. His ploy had worked. The image of Seneca Houston's face as she peered over her shoulder was mesmerizing. Her startled expression, wide-set eyes filled with indecision, slightly parted full lips, the profusion of raven curls around her face and sweeping over her bared shoulders, the sensual curve of her back, the distinctive, colorful butterfly tattoo at the base of her spine and the outstretched legs and arched feet in a pair of stilettos as she straddled Philip Kingston's lap were cause to give most men—if they were normal—an instantaneous erection. He had been no exception.

Booth took his drink from the bartender, picked up the remote, freezing the frame, and walked over to stand beside Waller. "She's Phillip Kingston's girlfriend."

John Alexander joined them, staring numbly at the frozen images on the screen. "Holy shit!"

"Are you talking about Kingston or the girl?" Booth asked Tweedledum.

"Both. They're perfect together. Maybe we can use her for something. Do you know how we can get in touch with her?" The words rushed off his tongue.

Gotcha! Booth mused. He'd gotten their rapt attention even before sitting down to discuss business. "That's easy, because she's a BGM client."

The Johns extended their glasses as if they'd choreographed the motion countless times. "I think we're onto something," Waller announced proudly. "We plan to run the ad with Kingston during the Super Bowl, and what better time than to feature him with a beautiful woman who just happens to be his girlfriend?"

John Alexander took a long swallow of his caipirinha. "What happens if they break up before the ad airs?"

Booth's eyes darkened until all traces of blue had disappeared, leaving them a frosty green. "That shouldn't concern you. Remember, Kingston and Butterfly—"

"Butterfly?" the two men chorused, interrupting him.

"Sixties supermodel Lesley Hornby went by the name of Twiggy, and Seneca Houston is Butterfly. As I was saying, their relationship should not concern you. You're selling a product, and BGM is responsible for its clients' image. And, if they do break up, then our publicity department will handle it so that it doesn't impact negatively on either of them."

He depressed the pause button and the frozen image switched to one of Seneca and Phillip in wedding attire. Booth sipped his drink, watching the reaction of the men who were transfixed by the photographs of the attractive couple.

He did the calculations in his head. If the auto company was willing to offer Kingston twenty mil over four years to endorse their product, then he would ask for ten percent for Butterfly. Earning a cool two hundred thousand, less commission, for appearing in a ten-second spot with Phillip Kingston was a very nice start for a twenty-year-old girl from upstate New York.

Ricky, doubling as a waiter, approached with a tray of hors d'oeuvres. "I have barbecued tandoori shrimp, mini deviled crab cakes with tomato remoulade and potato rosti with crème fraiche, caviar and dill."

Waller set his drink on a nearby glass-topped table, accepted a cocktail napkin from Ricky and selected a rosti with caviar. "I think I'm going to like doing business with you, Gordon. Nice office, good drinks and wonderful food."

Booth gave him a facetious grin. "I've always said that if you can't do it well, then don't bother to do it at all."

John Alexander nodded, smiling. "It's the same with Norman, Kilburn and Spencer. We've staked our reputation as being one of the best advertising agencies in the country. That's why we're very excited to come up with a campaign to promote one of the most electrifying vehicles to come along in years. And having Phillip Kingston as the spokesperson is as phenomenal as his stats."

John Waller took a crab cake and popped it into his mouth. "Don't forget to warn Kingston that if he's a bad boy not only will he lose the endorsement but he'll have to repay all monies for that particular year. You know how some of *these people* act when they get two nickels to rub together. It goes to their head."

Booth counted slowly to ten, hoping to defuse his quick temper before he said something he would later come to regret. He'd worked hard to get the endorsement for Phillip, and he would be damned if he'd let a tight-ass bigot take money out of his pocket.

"You take care of the advertising campaign and I'll take care of my clients. And, in case you're not aware of it, 'these people' is hardly politically correct." Sarcasm marred his forced polite tone.

John Alexander shot his assistant a disapproving look. "There are times when my associate forgets himself."

Booth waved his hand as if brushing away an annoying insect. "Please don't apologize for him. I'm relieved that neither of my clients heard it, because it wouldn't bode too well for your company. Would it, Mr. Waller?"

A bright flush crept up his neck to his hairline. "Sorry about that," he said, apologizing.

"Apology accepted," Booth said grudgingly. "Ricky, please freshen up everyone's drink. After we eat, I'll have the head of legal join us. The sooner we ink this deal, the sooner you can begin to put your campaign together. I also want you to keep in mind that Ms. Houston will probably be out of the country in the fall, because she'll be involved in several fashion shows for next year's spring line."

"We'll work around her schedule," Alexander said. "We just picked up another client who might be interested in your Butterfly."

"Who are they?" He'd piqued Booth's curiosity.

"I can't divulge the name, because we haven't finalized the deal. But they are a cosmetics company and they're looking for a new fresh face. As soon as we bring them on board, I'll contact you for headshots."

Booth nodded, watching in smug delight that the ad execs couldn't keep their eyes from straying to the television screen. Seneca Houston had become his secret weapon. Once her face appeared on the pages and covers of glossy magazines, she could name her price. He knew he could sell her, because everyone had a price, and he would make certain she wouldn't get out of bed for less than ten thousand a day.

Chapter Thirteen

"No! No! Stop, Butterfly, before I hurl my lunch."

Seneca halted midstride. "Is something wrong?" she asked the runway coach, who when meeting her had seemingly sniffed her like a dog familiarizing itself with his new surroundings.

Keane Thomas waved his arms. "Wrong, Butterfly? What's wrong is that you have a beautiful face, the perfect body, yet you walk like hundreds of other models."

Staring at the tall, slender man with a shaved pate who favored large red horn-rims, she rested her hands at her hips. His black-and-white striped T-shirt and black slacks reminded her of a mime. "What's wrong with walking like a model?"

Keane moved closer to the raised stage doubling as a runway. He squinted, mounting the stairs and bringing him face-to-face with the most naturally beautiful woman he'd encountered in years, and in the past decade since he'd become involved in fashion he'd seen more women than he could remember.

He'd grown up believing modeling was about a pretty face

and a tall, thin body. But once he got into the business, Keane realized it was more than that. And for a runway model she had to have the *goods:* face, body and a signature walk. Seneca "Butterfly" Houston had everything but a signature walk.

"You don't look like any other model, Butterfly. So why do you want to walk like everyone else?"

Seneca blinked. She'd practiced ad nauseam, perfecting her walk until she could execute it in her sleep. "What can I do to change it and still feel natural?"

"Have you seen Tyra or Naomi on the catwalk?" Keane asked. She nodded. "They have signature walks, Butterfly," he continued. "Even if you didn't or couldn't see their faces, you would still know it was them. That's what I want for you. From the moment your stiletto hits that runway for the first time I want every eye on you. It's not going to be enough for photographers to snap pictures of you, but for them to wait for you to come down that runway again. You've got a dancer's body, Butterfly. I want you to use it."

Seneca thought of Miss J, runway coach on *America's Next Top Model*. He didn't walk down a runway, he literally glided. And that's what Keane wanted. He wanted her to glide instead of walk.

She pointed to a stereo unit on a table. "Can you put on some music?"

Keane's inky-black eyes lifted in his sun-browned face, a tan further enhanced by spending time in a tanning bed. "What kind of music?"

"I need something with a heavy baseline beat."

"Hip-hop or heavy rock?"

Seneca smiled. "Hip-hop."

Keane nimbly hopped off the stage and turned on the unit. The distinctive voice of 50 Cent flowed through speakers. Turning around, he stared at Seneca. She'd closed her eyes, one hand tapping against her thigh. Crossing his arms over his chest, he watched in awe as she morphed into Butterfly, floating down the runway, her arms swinging gently, her hips swaying sensuously and her feet in a pair of strappy stilettos crossing in front of one another, taking her to the edge of the platform. She paused for three seconds, hands at her waist, then pivoted gracefully, retracing her steps.

Smiling and applauding softly, Keane congratulated himself. She got it! All he'd had to do was talk to Seneca Houston and she got it, unlike some models, with whom he worked hours and still they couldn't master the technique.

"That's it, Butterfly," he crooned. "Now I need you to do it again. This time without the music." He punched a button and the room went silent.

Seneca closed her eyes and exhaled a breath. She felt the music, but wondered if she could do it again without it. Recounting the tune in her head, she opened her eyes and walked, her hips and shoulders keeping time with the silent rhythm. She didn't see Keane as he walked along the length of the platform, his gaze following her every motion from head to toe.

"How was that?" she asked.

"That was better than the first time. I want you to take a five-minute break, then we'll do it again and again until it becomes second nature. When you get up in the morning and before your feet hit the floor I want you to think about your walk. It doesn't matter where you are or what you're doing, you must remember you're always Butterfly."

Extending his hand, he assisted Seneca as she walked off the stage and went over to retrieve a bottle of water. Keane watched Seneca uncap the bottle and put it to her mouth. She was a rare find, and he knew she would become an instant sensation with her first show.

Sitting on a folding chair, Seneca sipped the water, enjoying the cooling liquid sliding down the back of her throat. She was looking forward to driving up to Ithaca for the weekend if only for a change of scenery. After her photo shoot with Phillip, she'd called Yancy to meet with him about her hair. It took four days of playing phone tag for them to connect.

The talented stylist, who rented a chair at an Upper East Side salon, had so many private clients that he was rarely seen in the salon. She finally set up an appointment with him, and after spending three hours in his chair she'd emerged from the upscale establishment with a chocolate shade shimmering with red and gold highlights.

Seneca knew she'd shocked Luis Navarro when she walked into his apartment, because it had taken a full minute for the designer to utter a word. And when he did it was to go on and on about her new hair color. He liked it because it brought out the gold undertones in her complexion.

Luis had wanted her to see the sketches of the new Butterfly collection he was working on for Rhys Calhoun. It was her turn to become mute when she'd stared at his sketches of skirts, dresses, slacks, blouses and jackets in every conceivable color and fabric. She still hadn't figured out what it was about her that inspired Luis to design clothes for her. The first time she'd asked, his response was that she'd become his muse. However, there were times when she felt that she'd become more to him than his creative inspiration.

As promised, Phillip called her several times a week, asking when he was going to see her again. Seneca knew it had been impossible to give him a definitive answer because she was dividing her time between fittings with Luis and meeting with Rhys to discuss her involvement with his swimwear show in Miami.

She'd also visited her gynecologist, who'd fitted her with

an intrauterine device. Seneca knew she couldn't afford to get pregnant—not when she was on the threshold of breaking into the world of high-fashion modeling. She liked Phillip, liked sleeping with him, but not enough to marry him or become the mother of his children.

"Are you ready to try it again?"

Keane's query pulled Seneca out of her reverie. She glanced at the watch on her wrist. Booth had asked her to have dinner with him at his condo later that evening, and while she'd tried to come up with a plausible excuse why she didn't want to meet him at his home, she'd found herself agreeing.

"I'm ready," she said, pushing to her feet.

This time she didn't need music to inspire her as she strutted down the runway as if she were wearing Givenchy or de la Renta instead of a pair of cropped jeans, tank top and four-inch sandals. She knew she'd shocked Keane when she executed a flawless pirouette that would have made her former ballet teacher proud when he gasped audibly, then applauded.

"You're more than ready," he said, smiling.

Seneca took his hand as he helped her down the three steps. Putting her arms around his neck, she kissed his smooth cheek. "Thank you."

Easing back he stared at her. "No, thank *you*, Butterfly. Not only do you make my job easy, but you also reaffirm my self-confidence that I'm very good at what I do."

She kissed his other cheek. "I promise to make you proud of me."

He cradled her face. "Make yourself proud first." Keane dropped his hands, watching Seneca as she sat and exchanged her heels for a pair of running shoes. His gaze lingered on her until she walked out, closing the door behind her.

Booth didn't bother to stand when his housekeeper escorted Carter Browning into his home office. Although Joan had given the young man his private number, he hadn't called until earlier that morning. And it was curiosity more than anything else that had him agreeing to a meeting.

"Mr. Gordon—"

"Sit down and start talking," Booth ordered, waving his hand in a dismissive gesture. Despite the hot, humid weather, Carter Browning looked cool, fresh in a lightweight suit, white shirt and silk tie. "I'm expecting a dinner guest and I want you out of here before she arrives. Now tell me what your connection to Dennis Mayfield is."

"I was introduced to your boyhood friend by a third party." Tenting his fingers, Carter brought them to his mouth as he gave Booth Gordon a long, penetrating stare. "After you hear what I have to say you will probably invite me to stay for dinner."

Booth's eyes narrowed. "Get the hell out of my home!"

Carter lowered his hands. "Not so fast, *cousin*."

A hint of a smile touched the agent's thin lips. "I don't have any cousins. So, whatever your con is, Mr. Ivy League, let me warn you that you can't out-hustle a hustler."

Carter's impassive expression did not change. "I'm not trying to hustle you, Booth. I'm your uncle Seth's boy."

"My uncle and his wife didn't have any children."

"Your aunt didn't have any children because she couldn't have any. She'd had a botched abortion as a college freshman that resulted in a hysterectomy. Why do you think she was so taken with you? You'd become the son she never had. It was your uncle who'd fathered a child. Me," he said after a long pause.

Booth didn't know whether to reach into a drawer of his desk where he kept a registered handgun and blow the lying bastard's head off or continue to entertain the preppie punk who'd claimed they were related.

"Who was my uncle screwing?"

"I'll give you one guess. How do you think I was able to gain access to your office so easily?"

Booth flinched as if he'd been jabbed with a sharp instrument. Realization suddenly dawned. No one, and that included BGM employees, ever walked into his office without prior approval.

"Joan Powers."

Carter nodded. "Good ole mommy dearest. But I really don't think of her as my mother because she didn't raise me."

"Who did?"

"Arthur and Pamela Browning. Pamela is Joan's sister. The Brownings and Seth had arranged for the adoption before I was born." He pulled an envelope from his jacket and placed it on the desk. "That envelope contains my birth certificate and adoption papers. Both have official seals. Those copies are for you."

"How old are you?" Booth asked.

"Thirty. Joan managed to conceal her pregnancy until the last three months. It was then that she took a medical leave of absence."

Booth shook his head, not wanting to believe Carter, yet not ready to discount his claim. "That must have been when she claimed she'd undergone gall bladder surgery."

"It was. You probably didn't pay her much attention, because you were too involved in learning the business so you could take over after Seth died."

Slumping back in the leather executive chair, Booth swiveled, his back to Carter, and stared out the window. "Why did you get in touch with Dennis?"

"I needed a name in case you wouldn't talk to me. It worked, didn't it?"

Booth spun around. He stared at Carter, trying to see some resemblance between the younger man and his late uncle. The forehead was the same, as was his nose. Everything else, including his mouth, blond hair and blue eyes, were Joan's.

"Only because I was curious about you. When I called Dennis, the only thing he said was that he'd met you. Now tell me why you're here, other than to claim we're blood relatives."

Carter looped one leg over the opposite knee. "I need you to hold on to some money for me."

Booth's temper exploded. "Get the fuck outta here! I'm not going to use my business to launder money for you."

"You won't be laundering money, cousin. What I need is for you to open an account and hold the money for me until I need it. You'll get ten percent of every cent you deposit."

"It's called money laundering, *cousin*," Booth spat out. "The last I heard that's illegal."

Carter's lips twisted into a cynical smile. "And so is paying your *good* friend to put the muscle on clients who are reluctant to sign with *your* agency."

Fisting his hands under the desk, Booth flashed a defiant grin. "You don't know what you're talking about."

"You think not?" Carter countered. "Dennis didn't tell me about your little business arrangement, only because he's like a loyal puppy. For some reason I fail to understand, he'd give up his life for you. It was Joan who told me everything. She hates you even more than she loved your uncle, but you already know that. After Seth died, she waited for you to go on vacation and had your office bugged. Every meeting, conference and telephone call is recorded."

"Where are the tapes?" Booth's calm voice belied the rage making it difficult for him to draw a normal breath.

"They're in a safe-deposit box in an upstate bank." Reaching inside the breast pocket of his suit jacket, Carter pulled out a palm-size recorder. "Here's a little of what's on one of the tapes."

Booth listened to the recording of himself when he directed Dennis to convince an ambivalent actor it would be in his best interest to renew his contract. "I've heard enough," he spat out. Crossing his arms over his chest, he angled his head. "What is it you want? A piece of the agency?"

"I want nothing to do with the agency. I just need some-place to safeguard a client's money."

"Why don't you open your own account?"

Tilting his head, Carter stared up at the ceiling. "I run a small law firm with no more than half a dozen clients. I just picked up one who has a great of money but prefers to keep a low profile."

Booth knew when he'd been bested. Even if he hadn't believed Carter Browning was related to him, his voice on the tape telling Dennis to strong-arm an actor he'd identified by name was damning. "How much money are you talking about?"

"A couple of mil."

"A couple of million," Booth repeated. "There's no way I can hide that much money."

"You can begin with small amounts under ten thousand. That way the bank won't report it to the Internal Revenue. Or you could use your client's accounts. Just earmark the monies, so you don't comingle the funds."

"You could do the same. Open several accounts and make deposits."

Carter lowered his head. "No, I can't. I neglected to tell you that I'm renting an office in a larger law firm off Madison Avenue. Some months I don't bill enough hours to cover the rent, so that's why—"

"You consort with criminals," Booth said, finishing his statement. He leaned forward. "Why didn't you come to me sooner? Let me know that you're Seth's kid? Instead you turn to blackmail. You're no better than the scum you represent." He waved his hand. "Get the hell outta here and let me sleep on this shit. Meanwhile, I want you to call that bitch who birthed you and tell her if she comes into the office tomorrow I'll have her arrested for illegal wiretapping."

Pale eyebrows lifted a fraction. "She's gone, Booth."

His eyebrows nearly met in a frown. "What do you mean?"

"When I told Joan I was meeting you tonight she knew it would be her last day at BGM. And don't bother looking for her because she's on her way to a country in South America. When she signed over the deed to her condo to me she wouldn't tell me where she was going."

A light knock on the door garnered Booth's attention. His housekeeper's gaze shifted to Carter. "Yes, Alice?"

"Miss Houston is on her way up."

"Thank you, Alice. Please see Mr. Browning to the door."

Realizing he'd been unceremoniously dismissed, Carter took the tape recorder, stood up and walked out of the home office of a man with whom he hadn't known he'd shared a bloodline until six months ago. It'd taken him that long to work up enough nerve to approach Booth Gordon. He wasn't certain whether his cousin would go along with his scheme, but he had to take the risk. The other alternative was if Booth went to the police, then he would lose his license to practice law. For Carter, that was not an option.

With wide eyes, he watched an incredibly beautiful woman coming closer and closer, walking into his cousin's condo as he walked out. He saw Booth grasp her hand and press a kiss to her fingers before the door closed. Carter wasn't certain how long he stood just staring into space; when the elevator door opened again and a middle-aged couple emerged he was galvanized into action. Moving quickly, he caught the door before the car moved again. He rode to the lobby and walked out of the luxury high-rise; standing on the sidewalk breathing in the hot, humid city air, he felt a sudden surge of bravado.

Joan Powers had told him that if he left the condo alive, then he could consider himself blessed and her scheme a success. She claimed Booth Wilkes Gordon operated on the principle of power, money and ego. Carter smiled. It appeared as if the old girl was right.

Chapter Fourteen

Booth knew that meeting with Seneca Houston was the magic cure to dispel the rage he'd experienced when he'd sat entertaining the preposterous scheme outlined by Carter Browning. There was no way he was going to take the word of a stranger that they were related until he'd had Carter investigated.

Although it was his voice on the tape, Booth knew enough lawyers to get the tapes thrown out as inadmissible. And there was still the question of taping private conversations. If Joan Powers hadn't left the States, he would have made certain to find her and make her pay for her betrayal.

His eyes swept over Seneca, finding her changed, more beautiful. Her hair was lighter, and the pale gray silk chiffon ruffle sundress was virginal and seductive. Tonight she wore a pair of black leather flats instead of the stilettos she favored. He could look her in the eye instead of having to tilt his head.

"You look beautiful," he crooned, curbing the urge to brush his mouth over hers. She smelled as delicious as she looked.

Red and gold wisps had escaped the loose knot at the top of her head.

Seneca smiled, her rose-colored lips parting. "Thank you, Booth. I like your hair." He hadn't just shortened the back but had shorn his salt-and-pepper hair to where it lay against his scalp like feathers on a raven. Dressed entirely in black linen, he radiated masculinity *and* power.

Booth smiled, the warmth in the expression reaching his brilliant eyes. "Thank you. It took some getting used to, but I must say I like it. And I thank you for being so candid." Tucking her hand in the curve of his elbow, he led her into the living room. He seated her on a chair, taking one facing her. His gaze went to her long bare legs when she crossed them at the knee.

Leaning over, he picked up a water goblet filled with sparkling water and a sliver of lime, handing it to Seneca, then picked up a glass of his favorite rosé. He raised his glass in a toast. "To Butterfly."

Seneca flashed a demure smile. "Butterfly," she said softly, inclining her head.

Booth took a long swallow of his wine, holding it in his mouth before letting the premium vintage slide down the back of his throat. "I saw the photos of you and Kingston, and to say I was blown away is an understatement."

"Mitchell is an incredible photographer," Seneca said.

"No, baby. He has to have something to work with."

Seneca felt a shiver of annoyance when Booth called her baby; she wasn't his baby or anything close to it. What she'd found strange was that she didn't resent Phillip using the endearment. Perhaps it was because they were closer in age than she and Booth, who was twice her age and old enough to be her father.

"You're right," she agreed. Posing with Phillip was akin to their making love again.

Booth pointed to the small, gaily wrapped box on the table. "That's a little something from me to you. Take it," he urged, when Seneca stared at it without moving.

She picked up the package, carefully peeling away the black velvet bow and glossy black-and-yellow foil. She couldn't stop the rush of air coming from her mouth when she saw what Booth had given her. Suspended on a gold chain, with stations of diamonds, was a large pear-shaped blue topaz with delicate butterflies and flower petals encrusted with emeralds, diamonds and rubies. There were even diamonds on the bail.

"What…why are you giving me this?"

"You earned it, Seneca."

Her eyes narrowed. "What do you mean, I earned it?"

"You're going to be in a commercial with Phillip Kingston that will air for the first time during the Super Bowl. A production company has arranged for you to come to L.A. this weekend for rehearsals. You'll fly first-class into LAX, where a driver will be at your disposal for as long as you remain there. I've also arranged for you to stay at L'Ermitage in Beverly Hills. It's a five-star hotel designed to combine elegance with privacy. I'm certain you'll enjoy your stay there."

Seneca's eyelids fluttered wildly. Booth had shocked her with the gift of the pendant, and now he'd planned for her to fly to California. "I can't go."

"Why not?" Booth didn't bother to hide his exasperation.

"I promised my family I would get together with them for the holiday weekend."

Looping one leg over the opposite knee, the agent peered at his client through narrowed eyes. "It's time you grew up, Seneca. I'm not going to lose forty-thousand dollars because you want to go home to see mummy and daddy," he sneered.

Her smooth brow furrowed. "What are you talking about?"

"You'll be paid two-hundred thousand dollars for a ten-second ad. Do you know how many twenty-year-old girls would jump at an opportunity like the one presented to you? Millions," he said, answering his own question. He placed both feet on the carpeted floor. "You're going to L.A., Seneca, and you're going to perform like you've never performed, or I'll sue you for everything you have or ever hope to have."

The enormity of what Booth was offering was mind-boggling. A company was willing to pay her almost a quarter of a million dollars to be in a commercial with Phillip Kingston for a mere ten seconds. That computed into her earning twenty-thousand dollars per second. She knew her parents would be disappointed not to have her join them, but she had to think of her career *and* her future.

"Okay, Booth, I'll go."

"Don't make it sound as if you're doing me a favor, Seneca. This is your career, and do not forget there are thousands of young women who would love to be where you are now. You're going to be in Rhys Calhoun's Miami show, and I'm currently talking to a designer who may find a spot for you in his show this coming fall."

"Where is it?"

A beat passed. "Paris."

Pinpoints of heat pricked Seneca's face and armpits. She couldn't believe Booth had said Paris. It was the world's fashion capital, even though Milan was actively vying for the title.

Every girl who'd dreamed of a modeling career set her sights on walking down a Parisian runway, and she was no exception. Booth was right. She had to grow—and quickly.

A mysterious smile touched her lips. "I took your advice and renewed my passport."

Leaning over, Booth rested a hand on her knee. "Good girl." He winked at her. "I had my housekeeper prepare salmon. If you'd prefer something—"

"The salmon is fine," Seneca said softly. Her dark eyes met and fused with a green-blue pair that reminded her of the Caribbean Sea. "Thank you again, Booth, for the gift and for helping me get the ad with Phillip."

Booth removed his hand when what he'd wanted to do was slide it up her thigh to her crotch. "You like Kingston, don't you?" A becoming blush gave him his answer before Seneca spoke.

"Yes, I do. I like him a lot."

"And he likes you, Seneca. That was obvious from your expressions in the photographs. I'm not usually into match-making, but I've invited Kingston to spend the weekend with me when I go out to my rental property in Southampton. I'd like for you to join us."

"What weekend are you talking about?"

"The third weekend in July. A good friend is celebrating his birthday on the fifteenth, and he would have my head if I didn't show up."

"My birthday is also on the fifteenth."

"Okay. That means you'll be celebrating a milestone birthday. If that's the case, then I'm going to invite Mitchell, Luis Navarro and Rhys to join us to celebrate you becoming legal. Is there anyone else you'd like to invite?"

Seneca groaned inwardly for the second time within minutes. First she was going to miss seeing her family for the Fourth of July weekend, and now Booth had arranged for her celebrate her twenty-first birthday with him instead of her family. She knew she had to call her mother to let her know she wouldn't be able to come to Ithaca as planned.

"I'll ask my roommate if she'd like to come with her boyfriend."

Booth counted on his fingers. "Do you mind rooming with Kingston? The house has six bedrooms and I'm not certain whether Mitchell and Luis will bring someone with them. I know for certain Rhys doesn't go anywhere without a woman."

"No, I don't mind." One thing Seneca had decided to be adult about was her relationship with Phillip. She didn't plan to take out an ad to tell the world they were sleeping together, but she didn't intend to hide it either.

Clasping his hands together in a prayerful gesture, Booth nodded. "Good." He rose to his feet, extended his hand and helped Seneca to her feet. "I think it's time we ate."

Seneca felt the comforting warmth of Booth's hand, feeling completely at ease with her agent. He'd promised to make her a supermodel, and with him negotiating a deal to have her appear in a commercial with Phillip Kingston, she'd taken her first step in the journey.

Seneca held the receiver away from her ear when Dahlia's voice rose to ear-shattering decibels. "How can hanging out with a bunch of fake-ass plastic people be more important than your family, Seneca?"

"Why do you make it sound as if I'm hanging out?" she asked her mother. "I'll be working."

"Sure!" Dahlia spat out. "Taking off your clothes and spreading your legs for every pervert to gawk at."

Red-hot rage swept over Seneca. "For your information, I won't be taking off my clothes."

"But isn't that what slutty models do? Take off their clothes?"

"No, Mother, they don't."

"Don't call me Mother!"

"And don't try to *fuck* with my head." The expletive slipped out. "Just because your life didn't turn out the way you wanted, don't try to rain on my parade. I thought mothers wanted more for their daughters than they had for themselves, but it looks as if my *mother* wants me to be as miserable as she is. All of my life I've put up with your toxic negativity, but it stops today—now. If you can't give me your blessing, then so be it. But I'm not going to let you stop me from realizing my dreams. Goodbye."

Seneca's hand was shaking uncontrollably when she hung up the phone. She'd known her mother would be disappointed that she wouldn't join the family for what was always viewed as an unofficial family reunion, but she'd hoped at least she would be happy that her daughter would appear in a commercial with a high-profile athlete. It would give her something to brag about—but no, not Dahlia Houston. If the attention wasn't on Dahlia, then she pouted and acted out like a child who couldn't get her way.

Booth had told Seneca to grow up, but it was Dahlia who needed to grow up. At forty-two she was much too old to engage in temper tantrums. The phone rang, startling her and she picked it up before it rang a second time.

"Hello."

"Seneca, this is your father."

Closing her eyes, she exhaled an audible sigh. "Yes, Daddy."

"What's with you cursing your mother?"

"I didn't mean to curse at her, but she's impossible, Daddy. I called to tell her that I can't come up this weekend because

I have to shoot a commercial in L.A. and she called me a slut. What my mother and your wife forgets is that I'm a grown-ass woman. I can't get any more grown, just older. I'll respect her as a grown woman, but only if she's willing to reciprocate."

"I don't want to get into this middle of this, but—"

"Then don't, Daddy. Mom spews her venom, but when someone gives it back to her she runs to you to fight her battles. You're her husband, not her father. You shouldn't be defending her."

There came a long pause before Oscar said, "Where is all of this hostility coming from, Seneca?"

"Someone told me to grow up when I thought about turning down a six-figure deal because I didn't want to miss seeing my family for our annual Fourth of July gathering, and I took his advice. I told him that I was going to L.A. because there would be many more Fourths of July for me and my family to get together. If Mom can't understand that, then I don't know what to say. And by the way, I won't see you for my birthday, because I have other plans for that weekend, too."

"Are you doing this to punish your mother?"

"No, I'm not, Daddy. I love my mother and I wouldn't deliberately hurt her, but she has to stop trying to control everyone's life. She's upset because I dropped out of school, upset because I've chosen to model, and she's angry because I won't let her control my life."

"That's who she is, Seneca," Oscar argued softly.

"She wouldn't have to be who she is if you didn't put up with her theatrics. She's probably gloating right now because you're talking to me and hoping you'll get me to change my mind. But it's not going to happen, Daddy. Being an adult is all about being responsible. I've committed to going to L.A. and to Southampton for my birthday. I'm not certain when

I'll be able to come up, but I promise I'll see you before the end of the summer."

"What about the Labor Day weekend?"

"My agent has booked me for a show in Paris in early September. As soon as I get all the details, I'll let you know."

"You're really serious about this modeling, aren't you?"

Seneca smiled for the first time since she'd dialed her parents' number. "Very serious, Daddy. I can't explain it, but I'm someone else when the camera and lights are on me. It's like having an out-of-body experience. People don't see Seneca Houston, but Butterfly."

Oscar chuckled softly. "So, my baby has become a butterfly."

Tears filled her eyes. "Yes, she has."

"I just wish your grandmother could see you now. She would be so proud."

The tears filling Seneca's eyes spilled over. "I know that."

"I'm going to let you go, because I know you have to get ready for your flight. Don't let your mother stress you, baby. Once she sees the commercial she'll change her mind."

Seneca wanted to tell her father she didn't care if Dahlia did or didn't approve of her modeling career, because even if any one of her children was fortunate enough to become President of the United States, she would still find fault and complain. Some people were placed on the earth to be chronic complainers, and Dahlia Houston was counted among them.

"I hope she will. I'm going to ring off now because I have to meet with a designer to select what I'm going to take with me. Love you, Daddy."

"Love you back, baby."

Wiping her tears with her fingers, Seneca walked out of the bedroom to the bathroom to wash her face. During the taxi ride from Booth's condo to her apartment, she'd called Luis to tell him that she was flying to L.A. to shoot a commercial and had nothing to wear. Luis had laughed, then told her to come over and see what she could find.

She returned to her bedroom and scribbled a note to Electra, inviting her and Jayson to come to Long Island for her twenty-first-birthday celebration. Booth had made all the arrangements for a car to take her to the airport, the hotel reservation and having a driver available 24/7 once she arrived in L.A.

Instead of Phillip coming to New York, she was going across the country to see him. Booth had asked if she liked him, and she was forthcoming when she confirmed she did. However, there were times when she was unable to distinguish between what was real and what was fantasy.

She had to be very careful or she would blur the lines between acting and reality. Phillip Kingston was too potent, too masculine to play with and then run away from. Maybe she wouldn't find herself in an emotional dilemma if she hadn't slept with him. But it was too late to turn back the clock. Even if she didn't consciously crave him, her body did.

Each and every time she replayed their lovemaking, her body betrayed her. She'd awake moist, with the area between her legs pulsing with the aftermath of orgasms so strong she had to clench her teeth to keep from crying from the pleasure shaking her from head to toe.

She was looking forward to going to Los Angeles with the excitement of a child waking up on Christmas morning, not only for the experience of shooting a commercial but also to sleep with Phillip Kingston again.

Chapter Fifteen

Seneca strutted toward the baggage claim area at LAX to meet her driver, ignoring the admiring glances directed at her. She could've been wearing haute couture instead of a pair of fitted jeans, a man-tailored shirt, a pullover thrown over her shoulders and tied at the neck and four-inch pumps. There was just enough sway and dip in her slender hips to capture the attention of most men and a few women. Oversize sunglasses shielded her eyes from the curious onlookers as she stared straight ahead.

Within minutes of touching down, she'd called Phillip to let him know that she was in Los Angeles and give him the name of her hotel. Something in his voice indicated she'd disturbed him, and she hung up quickly rather than imagine that she'd interrupted his making love to a woman.

She entered baggage claim and spied Phillip wearing a base-ball cap and sunglasses standing behind a black-suited man holding up a sign with her name. A smile spread over her face like the rays of the rising sun. When she'd called him he hadn't been at home but at the airport waiting for her.

"I'm Seneca Houston," she told the driver, handing him a garment bag and oversize tote.

The driver lowered his gaze in order not to be caught openly gawking. "Do you have any other bags?"

Seneca shook her head. "No." She stepped around the man and found herself molded to Phillip's hard body. Tilting her head, she brushed her mouth over his. "Thank you for meeting me."

Phillip deepened the kiss, caressing her mouth. "Welcome to the City of Angels. I love what you've done with your hair."

Curving her arms under his broad shoulders, she attempted to get closer. "Thank you."

"Let's get out of here," Phillip whispered against her lips. Someone had recognized him, calling him by name, but he hadn't turned to acknowledge him. They hadn't taken more than half a dozen steps when a flashbulb went off.

"King Phillip, who's the girl?"

Heads snapped, necks craned, as people turned to stare at Phillip and Seneca when they quickened their pace to follow the driver. People were reaching for cameras and camera phones, flashes lighting up the area like a light show. They were practically running to the area where the chauffeur had parked his car, and Seneca prayed she wouldn't turn an ankle in the heels.

"Is it always like this?" she asked Phillip once they were seated in the rear of the limousine. "Having to run from the paparazzi?"

Taking off his cap, Phillip ran a hand over his cropped hair. His face was flushed with high color. "No."

"No?" she repeated. "I didn't know that being with you I would have to run track," she teased.

"What can I say, baby. This is L.A.—land of the paparazzi."

"They usually don't bother people in New York the way they do here. I've lost count of the number of actors, models and sports figures I've seen strolling the streets of the Big Apple."

"That's because people who live in New York believe everyone's a celebrity—including themselves. No one is more important than a native New Yorker."

"Which do you prefer, Phillip? New York or L.A.?"

He took off his glasses and stared out the side window at the passing landscape. "I like them both. L.A. is my home, while I do enjoy the modicum of anonymity New York offers."

Seneca slumped against Phillip while attempting to smother a yawn. Her body was still in East Coast time. "I hope you don't mind if I use you for a pillow."

Reaching over, he cradled her head against his chest. "Go to sleep, baby. I'll wake you when we get to the hotel."

"Are...are you staying with your parents?" she slurred.

Phillip ruffled her hair. "No. We have adjoining suites at the hotel."

"Oh." That was the last word she said before slipping into the comforting embrace of Morpheus.

Seneca woke, not knowing where she was or the time of day. She rolled over, encountering an unmovable, solid object. She sniffed the air, inhaling what was now a familiar aftershave.

"Phillip?"

"She awakens."

"What time is it?"

Going on an elbow, Phillip peered at the clock on the bedside table. "Four-fifteen."

She moaned softly. "That's seven-fifteen in New York." Pushing into a sitting position, Seneca saw a sliver of light coming through drawn drapes. Phillip had undressed her but hadn't removed her underwear.

"Is that your belly talking?" he asked.

Seneca buried her face against his bare shoulder. "I guess it is."

"Didn't you eat during the flight?"

She shook her head, then realized he couldn't see her in the darkened room. "Not really."

Swinging his legs over the side the bed, Phillip flicked on the table lamp. "Do you want room service, or would you prefer to eat at the hotel's restaurant?"

Seneca stared at the corded muscles in his broad back. Phillip Kingston's body was so beautifully proportioned for a very tall man. He was all muscle and sinew. He probably had less than two percent body fat.

"I don't mind eating in the restaurant." She had to get out of the suite or she would end up back in bed. She met Phillip's gaze when he peered at her over his shoulder and winked at her. "What are you thinking about?"

"My shower or yours?"

Leaning forward, she pressed a kiss to his shoulder blade. "You shower in your suite and I'll shower in mine."

"Are you scared something's going to happen, baby?"

Seneca wrapped her arms around his waist. "No, I'm not, baby. You know if we share a shower we're going to end up making love *and* ordering room service." She trailed tiny kisses down his spine. "Go, so I can get up."

A change in his breathing told her that Phillip was becoming aroused. He eased her hands from his waist, stood up and walked across the room to the door connecting her suite to his. He opened and closed the door with a soft click, and Seneca slipped out of bed, retrieved a change of clothes and walked into the en suite bathroom.

Seneca dabbed her mouth with a cloth napkin, folded it, and then placed it beside her plate. She hadn't realized how hungry and thirsty she'd been until she'd sat down to eat. Having to get up at an ungodly hour to be ready for the car service to drive her to airport had put her out of sorts.

Then there was the interminable waiting to go through airport security and another ninety minutes of waiting to board the jet. Despite flying first-class, she'd been too exhausted to eat, preferring instead to drink water during the six-hour flight. The three-hour time difference also played havoc with her body's circadian rhythm.

Phillip had made reservations for them at the hotel restaurant. Jaan featured modern French cuisine with Indochinese and California influences. They'd waited in the Writer's Bar enjoying predinner cocktails until their table was ready. Seneca had enjoyed sitting in the private area that boasted a working fireplace.

"What are you smiling about?" she asked Phillip. They'd hardly exchanged a word over dinner.

His smile grew wider. "You."

"What about me?" Seneca questioned defensively.

Placing his left hand on the tablecloth, Phillip stared at his outstretched fingers, fingers that could easily palm a basketball, and fingers that he prayed he would someday use to help heal sick and broken bodies.

"Do you realize that you're very anal? That everything has to be in its own place?" He pointed to her napkin. "Take that napkin. It looks the same as when we first sat down. You even folded it where smudges of lipstick can't be seen."

Although Seneca's mouth was smiling, her eyes weren't. "Perhaps it's because I'm a neat freak."

"It's more than that, baby."

Her eyebrows lifted. "If it is, then you tell me what it is," she challenged.

"You feel this need to be in control." Phillip ignored her soft exhalation of breath. "Even during the photo shoot you were controlling the action."

"Perhaps it was because I have more experience in front of the camera than you do."

Phillip shook his head. "It's more than that."

Propping her elbow on the table, Seneca rested her chin on the heel of her hand. "I thought you wanted to go into rehab medicine, not psychiatry."

"Don't try and change the subject, Seneca. Why does it always have to be your way?"

She didn't like the timbre of Phillip's voice, and where the topic of conversation was going even less. "Where is all of this coming from, Phillip? Are you upset because I'm not falling all over you, because as basketball phenom King Phillip I should be grateful that you even look at me?"

His right eyebrow shot up. "You need to watch your mouth, Seneca. Some of the things that come out of it aren't very becoming."

Lowering her arm, Seneca glared across the small expanse of the table separating her from Phillip. "Don't ever tell me what I can or cannot say."

"I'm not telling you what not to say. I'm just commenting—"

"Don't," she said, cutting him off. "Don't comment, Phillip." Pushing back her chair, she stood up and walked out of the restaurant.

Phillip popped up like a jack-in-the-box, staring at her retreating figure. He glanced around the restaurant to find every
man looking in the direction where Seneca had been. Seneca
Houston was the most exciting and exasperating woman he'd
ever met. Signaling the waiter, he signed the check and left
the restaurant.

He returned to his suite, literally tearing off his jacket and
tie, throwing them on a chair. His frustration level was off the
chart. Seneca wasn't making it easy for him to, as his father
would put it, court her. As per her directive, he called her several times a week. Then he had a standing order from a local
florist to send her flowers every week. That was something
he'd never done with any other woman.

Phillip had wanted to tell Seneca that he was falling in
love with her, but he shuddered to think of her response to
his passionate revelation. It wasn't ego that told him that he
could have his pick of any woman he wanted but a fact. He'd
slept with women old enough to be his mother and some who
were unadulterated freaks. Those were the ones who let him
do whatever he wanted with them.

Although he wasn't the first man to sleep with Seneca Houston, he felt as if he had been. Her response to him was natural
and unrehearsed, and that was something he hadn't found with
the other women who'd shared his bed.

There were times when he'd believed it was her effortless,
timeless beauty that had him lusting after her, but a separation
of three thousand miles and sleeping with another woman had
proved him wrong. Even before getting into bed with the aspiring actress, Phillip realized she'd become a mere substitute
for a woman who'd touched him as no other. He'd had sex
with her, got out of bed to shower and then walked out of
her North Hollywood apartment, knowing he would never
return. A few days later, he dropped by the restaurant where

she waited tables and gave her enough money to pay her rent for the next six months. When she asked him if it was over, he hadn't lied and told her he had fallen in love. She kissed him, wishing him the best. What Phillip hadn't realized at the time was that the best would walk away, leaving him staring at her back in a hotel restaurant. Walking across the room, he tapped on the door connecting his suite to Seneca's.

"What is it?" came her muffled reply.

"May I come in?"

"The door's unlocked."

Phillip smiled. She hadn't locked the door, which meant she hadn't shut him out completely. Turning the knob, he walked into Seneca's suite to find her standing at the window staring at the lights of nighttime L.A. She'd taken off her shoes but still hadn't removed the body-hugging black dress that revealed every curve of her slender body.

"I'm sorry, Seneca."

"I'm sorry, Phillip."

They'd apologized in unison. Turning from the window, Seneca stared at the broad shoulders filling out the breadth of the doorway. "I don't know what it is about you that sets me off," she whispered.

Leaning against the door frame, Phillip crossed his arms over his chest. "It's called passion, baby."

A smile tilted the corners of her mouth upward. "Is that what it is?" He nodded. She took one step, then another, until they were less than an arm's-length apart. "What are we going to do about it, Phillip?"

Staring down at Seneca's upturned face, he committed her features to memory. "We're going to get married." He knew he'd shocked her, because her mouth opened but nothing came out.

"Married?" she finally gasped.

His arms came down and he cradled her face as gently as he would've a newborn. "Yes. I'm in love with you, Seneca Houston."

Seneca blinked as if coming out of a trance. "But...but I don't—"

Phillip stopped her words with a kiss that communicated everything he felt for the woman who'd turned his world upside down. "Shush, baby. The only thing I want you to say is 'I do' when asked if you take me to be your lawfully wedded husband."

Seneca did speak when she asked, "When?"

"Tonight. Pack an overnight bag. We're going to Vegas."

The princess-set diamonds in the bangle on Seneca's right wrist competed with those in a matching band on the third finger of her left hand. She hadn't believed she'd consented to become Mrs. Phillip Kingston until the official at one of Vegas's many wedding chapels had announced that they were husband and wife.

The world appeared to have stopped spinning on its axis when she changed into a conservative pantsuit while Phillip made arrangements for a car to drive them to the airport where they'd boarded a private jet for Las Vegas. Her heart had beaten a rapid tattoo against her ribs when the sleek jet circled over millions of lights as nightfall descended on the desert.

They hadn't bothered to check into a hotel, because Phillip wanted to acquire a marriage license before midnight. She'd followed Phillip as if in a trance to a jewelry store where he'd purchased the bracelet as an engagement gift and the wedding band. She slid her plastic across the counter when she paid for an unadorned gold band for her groom. Two hours after stepping foot on Nevada soil for the first time, she'd become a married woman.

Wrapping her arms around her waist over the thick velour robe the hotel had made available for guests in their bridal suite, she closed her eyes and let out a long sigh. Seneca had never fantasized about getting married like most girls. However, even in her wildest dreams she would never have believed that she would marry a man she'd known for only a month. She really didn't know him, because at that moment she didn't know who Seneca Houston was.

What nagged at her was that she wasn't impulsive. Never had she done anything without giving it a great deal of thought. The decision not to attend Cornell had not been an easy one for Seneca. She'd wrestled with the notion for weeks until she'd found it hard to go to sleep and sleep throughout the night. Not only had she stopped sleeping but eating as well, losing weight she could ill afford to lose.

When she'd given the clerk her New York State driver's license as a government-issued photo ID to secure the license, a voice had told her to run and not stop running until she was back in New York in her bedroom in the Upper West Side brownstone. However, Seneca ignored the silent voice and was now a married woman.

She hadn't mentioned a prenuptial agreement and neither had Phillip, because she realized she hadn't been thinking clearly. For that matter, she hadn't been thinking—not until now. They would spend the night in the Vegas hotel before flying back to L.A. to meet with the production company that was to shoot the commercial.

"I thought you would've been in bed."

She turned around slowly. Phillip had come out of the bathroom wearing nothing more than a towel around his hips. "I was waiting for you."

His hands went to the towel, it falling to the carpeted floor. "I'm ready."

Seneca swallowed when she saw the heavy sex jutting from between muscular thighs. How had she forgotten the size, length and width of his prodigious sex? She closed her eyes, moaning softly when she felt a rush of moisture bathe her vagina.

Taking long strides, Phillip closed the distance between them. The rush of color to his wife's face was all he needed to know what she was feeling and needed. Scooping her up as if she were a child, he carried her to the large bed and placed her on it, his body following hers down.

Reaching over, he turned off the lamp. He hadn't bothered to close the drapes at the wall-to-wall, floor-to-ceiling windows. There weren't as many lights dotting the desert, but there were enough to let him know the city was still filled with an energy that waned slightly but only to return with the rising sun. Phillip hadn't thought he would spend his wedding night in a Vegas hotel penthouse. But then, he hadn't given marriage much thought, either. His focus was playing basketball, then a career in medicine. Now it would shift to include his wife.

"How are you doing, Mrs. Kingston?" he whispered in his wife's ear.

"I'm good, Mr. Kingston."

And she was good. She wasn't in love with Phillip, but Seneca knew she could grow to love him. Perhaps that was better than being so madly in love with someone that she'd lose all sense of perspective. "Remember, you have to use a condom," she reminded him.

Seneca knew being able to trust Phillip surpassed her wanting to love him. She hadn't disclosed that she was fitted with a birth control device because she wanted to see if he would keep his promise to protect her from an unplanned pregnancy. Phillip could afford to father as many children as he could financially afford, but for her it was different. Her body was her moneymaker, and becoming pregnant was certain to short-circuit her career.

"Don't worry, sweetheart," Phillip crooned.

Deftly, he took off Seneca's robe, tossing it on the floor beside the bed. They hadn't talked about children—in fact they hadn't talked about anything other than to exchange vows. He'd promised to protect her, and he would until the time came for them to start a family.

Rolling over on his back, he searched under a mound of pillows for the condom he'd placed there when Seneca had gone into the bathroom. He opened the packet and rolled the latex sheath down the length of his erection. Just once, he wanted to experience the sensation of going inside Seneca without the barrier of latex between them. But he knew that wasn't possible, recalling when she'd said: "I don't need a baby. Not when I have to concentrate on my career." She was right. *They* didn't need a baby. It would take time for them to get to know each other; their careers would take them away from each other whenever he played an away game or she had a show out of the country. They would make New York their home base only because his team was in New York.

Trailing kisses down the column of her long neck, Phillip spread her legs with his knee. He'd wanted a prolonged session of foreplay but realized it was not to be. His dick was so hard it hurt, and only Seneca could assuage the pain. He rubbed the head over her clit, achieving the reaction he sought when she raised her hips and spread her legs.

He pushed inside her, acutely aware of the change in her breathing. How had he forgotten in a few short weeks? Her feminine scent, the tight fit. Everything outside the room ceased to exist for Phillip Kingston as he found himself falling into a sexual abyss from which he didn't want to escape.

The contractions began for Seneca within seconds of Phillip penetrating her. She tried to hold back, but to no avail. The orgasms came, one after the other, then overlapping to where she didn't know where one began and the other ended.

However, it did come to a crashing end, with her soaring beyond herself, seemingly speaking in tongues while Phillip pumped faster, harder before collapsing heavily atop her. They lay joined together, their chests rising and falling in unison. Seneca managed a small moan of protest when Phillip pulled out. He left the bed to discard the condom.

She never knew when her husband returned to the bed. She'd fallen asleep.

Chapter Sixteen

Seneca slipped quietly out of bed in an attempt not to wake Phillip. She showered, dressed and was lounging in the living room, watching the sun rise over the desert, when he walked in. Her body was still on East Coast time. She averted her gaze rather than stare at his male body in its entire naked splendor. The sun pouring into the room turned him into a statue of gold.

Yawning and scratching his chest, Phillip stared at his wife. "What are you doing up so early?"

"I'm still on New York time. Besides, I want to call my parents to let them know I'm now a married woman."

He yawned again. "What do you think they're going to say?"

Seneca turned to look at him. "I don't know. My dad will probably be shocked. I can't anticipate what my mother will say."

"It'll be easier breaking it to my folks because I've already told them about you."

She sat up straight. "When?"

"When I returned to see you. My father wanted to know what had me flying back to New York after I'd only been home a few days."

"Am I going to meet your parents before I go back?"

"No."

"No!" Shock was evident in the single word and her stunned expression.

"You'll get to meet them at some other time. They're in Malaysia for an international medical conference." Phillip studied Seneca, still unable to believe his good fortune. With her flawless complexion and the ends of her hair curling around her incredible face, she continued to take his breath away. "Are you coming back to bed?"

Seneca shook her head. "In a little while. I want to make the phone calls before my folks read about it in a supermarket tabloid."

"I suggest you call Booth, so he'll know how to spin it."

"How do you want him to spin it, Phillip?"

"I'm going to leave that up to the Barracuda. Knowing him, he'll milk it for all it's worth. Who is she? Are they a couple, or just friends? Weren't King Phillip and Butterfly spotted together wearing wedding bands? Is she pregnant? Yada, yada, yada."

Throwing back her head and baring her throat, Seneca laughed uncontrollably. "It sounds as if you know the drill."

Phillip chuckled. He liked hearing Seneca laugh. For someone so young she was much too serious. "It's a well-rehearsed script, baby. Prepare yourself for an onslaught from tabloid, magazine and television entertainment reporters. BGM's publicity department will schedule the interviews based on how much they're willing to pay for a story. They'll try to get as much as they can, only because Booth Gordon is a greedy bastard."

Seneca sobered. Her private life was about to be played out in public. She knew she would've been able to maintain a modicum of privacy, away from the runway, as Seneca Houston. However, her confidence wavered when she realized she would be hurled into the spotlight as Mrs. Phillip Kingston.

Was she prepared for the close scrutiny that was certain to occur? Unknowingly, it would be a question she would ask herself over and over in the next few weeks. She picked up her cell phone and punched in the speed dial for her parents' house. It rang six times before going to voice mail. Not bothering to leave a message, Seneca called her mother's cell. It, too, went directly to voice mail.

Lines of consternation appeared between her eyes. It was odd that Dahlia hadn't picked up, because she was fanatical about keeping her cell charged and on. Seneca tried one more number—Robyn's cell. She smiled when hearing her sister's voice.

"Hey, Robbie, it's Seneca. Is Mom around?"

"Yeah. I just left her downstairs in the kitchen. What's up?"

"Did you hear the house phone ring?"

"Yeah," Robyn repeated. "But I thought Mom got it."

"Can you do me a favor, Robbie?"

"Sure. What is it?"

"Go downstairs and see if Mom is okay."

"No problem. I'm on my way down. Daddy told me you're not coming up for the Fourth."

"I'm in California."

"Doing what?"

"I'm shooting a commercial with Phillip Kingston." Seneca

held the tiny phone away from her ear when Robyn screamed into the mouthpiece.

"Omigod, Seneca! He is so fuc—freakin' hot!"

She smiled, wanting to tell Robyn that Phillip was now her brother-in-law. "He is kind of nice on the eyes," she said instead. Seneca couldn't hear what Robyn had told Dahlia, but the older woman's reply knifed through her like an ice pick. Dahlia had heard the phone, but after seeing the caller ID hadn't wanted to speak to her.

"She doesn't want—"

"I heard her, Robbie. It's okay."

"What's going on between you and Mom?"

"Nothing," Seneca lied smoothly. She didn't want to bring her sister into her quarrel with their mother. "I'm not going to see you for my birthday, because I have another event that weekend."

"When am I going to see you?" Robyn whined.

"As soon as I finalize my summer calendar, I'll ask Daddy if you can come down and spend some time with me."

"I'll come if you promise to introduce me to Phillip Kingston…"

Seneca smiled. "I promise."

She talked to her sister for another minute and then rang off. Her smile faded, replaced by unshed tears. She knew Dahlia was notorious for holding grudges, but that did little to relieve the feeling of sadness holding her captive. Seneca had tired of fighting with her mother years before, and once she'd moved out she'd thought things would change. Apparently they hadn't—at least not for Dahlia.

"I can't let her do this to me," she whispered, pushing to her feet. If she continued to dwell on the friction between her and her mother, Seneca knew she would become an emotional wreck.

Sniffling and squaring her shoulders, she raced into the bed-room and flopped on the bed, Phillip catching her in midair. They rolled around and around on the large bed, stopping long enough for Phillip to slip on a condom. This coming together was different from their wedding night. There was no frantic coupling and when it ended they'd ceased to exist as separate entities.

Seneca closed her eyes when she felt the flutter of nerves seize her as she stood on the mark from which she would move once filming began. The set was in a large warehouse that had been converted into studios where a popular daytime soap opera was in production. The commercial was prom-ised to be as stunningly visual as the crossover vehicle being showcased. Well-dressed actors spanning six decades filled the room, talking quietly, most holding flutes with sparkling cider. Classical music played softly in the background as the actors examined and gestured toward sculpture and framed prints on the stark-white walls.

There were no lines for them to memorize. She and Phillip had been directed to stroll around what would become an art gallery exchanging sultry glances, in keeping with the vehicle's tagline: "Words are unnecessary."

Clad in a black sheath dress with an asymmetrical neckline and black Studio Pollini suede-and-patent-leather pumps, a strand of thirteen-millimeter pearls, matching studs, dramatic makeup and with her hair fashioned into an elaborate chignon, Seneca found herself transformed into a young sophisticate. She opened her eyes. The butterflies were gone, replaced by adrenaline.

Seneca hadn't seen Phillip since he'd disappeared behind a door marked *Wardrobe/Makeup,* and when he walked onto the set the reaction the director wanted from her was evident when she stared, an expression of awe filling her eyes. She couldn't pull her gaze away from the tall figure dressed in a navy tailored suit, stark-white shirt, charcoal-gray silk tie and black imported slip-ons.

Spotlights bathed Seneca and Phillip in warm, flattering light as the director yelled "action" and they began walking in opposite directions, their eyes following the other as they glanced over their shoulders. The camera angle changed, pulling back to capture a full shot of her from head to toe. Phillip stopped, lifted his eyebrows questioningly, and was rewarded with a coy smile and lowered lids from Seneca. She hadn't accepted his unspoken advance, but her expression communicated that she hadn't rejected him either.

"Cut!" The director's voice echoed throughout the set. "Let's set up for scene two." He'd captured the scene in one take.

The second scene, an outdoor shot, showed Phillip leaning against the bumper of the crossover, waiting for Seneca to emerge from the gallery. He nods to her, but she shakes her head and gets into a waiting limo. Phillip watches her car take off, then slips into the SRX, maneuvering smoothly away from the curb.

The edited ten-second spot concludes with Phillip slowing down when he sees Seneca standing on the side of the road with her thumb up. He gets out and opens the passenger-side door, but she rounds the SRX and slips in behind the wheel. She motions for him to get in and the scene ends with them sharing a smile as she drives off.

The director was effusive with his praise when Seneca climbed out of the luxury car, kissing her cheeks. "You were incredible. I occasionally direct a daytime drama and the writers have come up with a new storyline where one of the principal characters discovers he's the father of a biracial daughter after he'd had a brief affair with a former business associate. You would be perfect for the part."

Seneca patted his shoulder. "Talk to my agent."

She'd never thought saying those four words would leave her feeling euphoric. *"Tell your agent to call my agent."* If she had a dollar every time she'd heard that line of dialogue in the movies, she could've saved enough to spend the night in the Waldorf-Astoria's ultra-exclusive Towers.

"I'll do that," he promised.

Seneca's head popped up when she felt the punishing grip of Phillip's fingers around her upper arm. "What are you doing?" she asked whispering, when he led her back to the building.

"We have to talk," he said between clenched teeth.

"We're not going to talk about anything until you let go of my arm. Not only are you hurting me but you'll probably leave a bruise."

She'd learned early in her adolescence not to pick her zits, because the result was bruises that took weeks to fade. Phillip loosened his hold, but not enough for her to escape him. Waiting until he closed the door to the dressing room to which he'd been assigned, Seneca rounded on Phillip. "What's up with the caveman act?"

"I'm sorry, baby. You know I'd never hurt you."

"No, I don't know that," Seneca countered. "This is the second time I've asked you to take your hand off me."

Phillip flashed a sheepish grin. "I guess I don't know my own strength." He hadn't lied to Seneca. He would never deliberately cause her physical harm.

Walking over and flopping down on a sofa, Seneca stared at the toes of the designer pumps. "What do you want to talk about?"

Taking two long strides, Phillip leaned against a lighted

vanity. "How can you tell that man to talk to your agent before you talk to me?"

"What?"

Shifting and resting his hands on his thighs, he leaned toward her. "I am your husband, Seneca. Instead of telling him to call Booth, you should've told him that you'll get back to him."

She blinked. "Get back to him after I talk to you?"

"Dah!" he drawled.

Seneca paused as she tried analyzing Phillip's reaction to her interaction with the film director. "What's obvious to you isn't *that* obvious to me, Phillip."

"How can you commit to a job without consulting with me first?"

Emotions ranging from shock, incredulity and anger gripped her. "Are you saying I have to get your approval where it concerns *my career?* I'm only asking because I don't believe you would permit me to control yours."

"It's not about control, Seneca."

"If it's not, then what is it, Phillip?"

"If you get the part for the soap, then you'd have to work in L.A."

Seneca swallowed hard, trying not to reveal the inner turmoil turning her stomach muscles into knots. "You're projecting. I haven't even auditioned for the part, so your saying I'd have to work in L.A. is pointless. You're jumping the gun because you don't know the details."

"It's not business as usual, Seneca. You can't make a decision without first checking with me."

"Check with you!" she shouted. "I am not a little girl where I had to check in with my father, or get his approval before I could do something or go somewhere. You knew before you asked me to marry you what our marriage would be like."

Phillip nodded. "That's true. But I'd expected you to do fashion shows, magazine layouts or even an occasional commercial. But not a daytime soap opera."

"Now you want to pick and choose the course of my career?"

"No."

"Yes, Phillip," Seneca countered angrily. "Yes, you do. Are you telling me it's okay to do runway shows or pose for a magazine, but I can't act because it would take me away from New York? What about you?" she spat out. "You're a professional athlete. One night you may play in New York, then the next night in Miami, and a couple of days later you're in Chicago. You start preseason play in early October and the regular basketball season doesn't end until mid-April. Then there are the play-offs, and if you're lucky to make it to the championship that's another month. So in all there are six to seven months of the year when I'm lucky if I get my husband all to myself for six or seven consecutive days.

"You may have caught me off guard when you asked me to marry you, but I had to weigh all my options. Even if I wasn't a model I had to be willing to accept that you wouldn't be coming home every night to sit down to dinner with me. If I can sacrifice not seeing you whenever I want, or sharing you with millions of adorning fans, then you should at least do the same for me. I'm just starting out, and what I need from you more than love is respect and support. Respect for what I do, and to support me as I begin my journey into the only profession where having a good face and body counts for something."

Phillip's face had become a mask of stone during Seneca's lengthy monologue. He knew if he'd interrupted they would've engaged in an all-out verbal assault on each other. So he'd remained silent and let her have her say. She believed he didn't want her to have a successful career, but she was wrong. He wanted Butterfly to soar, to become the supermodel Booth Gordon had predicted. What she'd failed to understand was that now they were a team, and if a team didn't confer and play together, then they were doomed and certain to fail.

"Are you finished?"

Seneca recoiled as if he'd struck her across the face. Not only was his voice cold, but it was cutting. "Yes, I am."

Phillip stood up. "Good. As soon as you're ready, we'll go back to the hotel, call the carrier and hopefully book a flight out today." Booth hadn't booked a return flight because he didn't know how long it would take to shoot the commercial. Fortunately, it had taken only one day.

Seneca stood up and walked out of the dressing room, slamming the door behind her. Red-hot rage made it almost impossible for her to think clearly. She didn't need a clairvoyant to tell her that her marriage was in trouble, although she hadn't been married a week.

When she'd called to tell Booth that she had married Phillip, his advice was to keep their marriage a secret until he met with the agency's publicity department. The news of her marrying one of the country's most eligible bachelors was cause to sell millions of supermarket tabloids and entertainment magazines. He would also arrange for them to be interviewed by all of the television entertainment journalists individually and as a couple. He'd predicted the hype would thrust her into the spotlight where she and Phillip would become another beautiful, high-profile celebrity couple.

She entered her dressing room, closed the door and sat down at the vanity to begin removing the makeup that always had a tendency to make her face feel heavy. However, wearing makeup had its advantages. It forced her into a daily regimen of caring for her skin. For Seneca, cleansing facial lotions, eye-makeup remover and moisturizers were as essential as food, water, deodorant and toothpaste.

Using a tissue, she removed the last of the makeup, dabbed her face with a deep-cleaning astringent for sensitive skin, making certain to avoid the eye area, then applied an oil-free moisturizer. It had been a while, but she never knew when a pimple would remind her that she still hadn't reached the stage where adolescent acne was a thing of the past.

Seneca changed out of the dress and into a pair of jeans, an oversize T-shirt and running shoes. Removing the pins from her hair, she swept it up in a ponytail, securing it with a red elastic band, then pulled a worn denim baseball cap over her head. When she walked out of the dressing room no one would recognize her as the actress who'd silently seduced basketball phenom Phillip Kingston into letting her drive his prized vehicle.

Phillip, who'd also changed, was waiting for her in the parking lot. He opened the rear door to the limo and waited for her to get in before he slid onto the leather seat next to her. Reaching for her hand, he laced their fingers together as the driver maneuvered out of the lot and onto the road that led to their hotel. It was as if they were reliving the commercial. No words were exchanged, but that was a good thing, because the last thing Phillip wanted to do was argue with his wife.

Chapter Seventeen

"Why aren't you dressed?" Seneca asked Phillip when she walked into the bedroom at the Ritz-Carlton. He lay on the bed, eyes closed. Although he'd covered his lower body with the sheet, it couldn't conceal his erection.

When they'd returned to New York they'd stopped at her apartment, where she'd packed enough clothes to last a week. She'd also left a note for Electra with the arrangements for their weekend in Southampton. Booth had reserved a car for her and Phillip. The driver was scheduled to arrive at the hotel at eleven, then pick up Electra and Jayson in the Village before taking the Queens Midtown Tunnel to the Long Island Expressway.

Although Electra had asked her a thousand and one questions about PK, Seneca still hadn't revealed his name, or that she'd married him. In fact, no one knew she was married except Booth. She hadn't called her parents again, deciding when she did tell them it would be in person.

"I'm not going to Southampton this weekend with you."

"What! Why?"

Phillip opened his eyes and glared at his *wife*. He'd had a problem thinking of her as his wife because she wasn't performing her wifely duties. They hadn't had sex since returning from California. Reaching for his erection, he waved it back and forth like a baton.

"I'll go with you if you give me *some*."

Seneca blinked, stunned, unable to believe what she was hearing. Her eyes narrowed. "Do you know what you're saying?"

Rising and supporting himself on an elbow, Phillip continued to massage the hardened flesh. "I know exactly what I'm saying, Mrs. Kingston. I need you to come and fuck me." He pulled back the sheet to show her his swollen member. "I need some relief, Seneca. Don't make me take care of myself."

"I'm not your whore, Phillip, and I'm not going to *fuck* you." He slipped off the bed, and she took a step backward.

"If you're not my wife, then you have to be my whore."

Seneca knew Phillip was still harboring some hostility because Booth had negotiated for her to return to L.A. to audition for a role in the daytime soap opera. The character would appear in ten episodes, and based on ratings and Internet feedback, the role could possibly become a recurring one.

Resting her hands on her hips, she went on tiptoe and thrust her face close to his. "Do you want out of this marriage, Phillip? Because if you do, then I'm gone."

The skin tightened over his high cheekbones when he pulled his lips back over straight teeth. "Is that what you want?"

"No, it's not, Phillip. What I don't want is for you to ever refer to me as a whore again. Because if you do, then whatever we have will be over. Don't touch me," she shouted when he reached out for her. "Please, don't touch me." Her voice had softened.

"Why don't you want me to touch you, Seneca?"

"Because having sex isn't going to solve our problem. We don't talk."

"What do we do?"

"We make love, and that's not enough to hold a marriage together. Maybe I made a mistake when I fell into bed with you so quickly. And I know I made a mistake when I agreed to marry you knowing I wasn't in love with you."

His stoic expression did not change. "I need you to answer one question for me."

Seneca nodded. "What do you want to know?"

"Do you love me?"

She didn't know why, but Seneca felt like crying. "No, Phillip, I don't love you. I was beginning to fall in love with you until…" Her words trailed off.

His right eyebrow lifted. "Until you thought I wanted to sabotage your career," he said, completing her statement. "It's not that I don't want you to be successful."

"If it's not that, then what is it, Phillip?"

"I don't want to lose you." He held up a hand when she opened her mouth. "Please, don't interrupt me," he warned softly. "I asked you to marry me not because I'm in love with you. It was lust and obsession. I didn't want another man to have you. Don't look at me like that, Seneca."

With wide eyes, she asked, "How else can I look at you? You just made me feel like some…some object you just had to have."

"I'm sorry, baby."

"So am I, Phillip. I'm so sorry it didn't work out between us."

Phillip took a step, cradling her face between his palms. "Will you forgive me for deceiving you?"

Her eyes filling with tears, Seneca gave him a reassuring

smile. "Yes. And thank you for being honest." She sniffled. "It looks as if keeping our marriage a secret turned out to be a good thing."

Phillip gave her a sad smile. "I guess you can say it's a blessing in disguise."

"We'll annul it," she suggested. "I'll have my attorney handle everything."

Phillip angled his head, brushing his mouth over Seneca's. His attempt at subterfuge had backfired. He'd accused her of not knowing him when it was she whom he hadn't even tried to get to know. In fact, he hadn't even scratched the surface. She was much more complex than she seemed.

"Do you think it's possible for us to remain friends?" he asked.

The tears Seneca had struggled to hold back fell; they streamed down her face, wetting Phillip's fingers. "Of course."

His hands moved to her waist, pulling her closer as he pressed a kiss to her forehead. "Don't run away. As soon as I shower and throw a few things in a bag I'll be ready to go to Southampton with you."

Seneca waited until Phillip had walked into the bathroom before slumping down on the unmade bed. Nothing had changed, yet at the same time everything had changed. She and Phillip would annul their marriage and no longer sleep together. But they would share a connection, because for a brief moment in time they'd come together as one.

"Do you mind if we continue this tomorrow?" Seneca asked Hans Lindquist. She'd talked throughout breakfast, while she'd cleared the table and loaded the dishwasher, and had continued to talk after she and the photojournalist retired to the family room.

"Not at all. How's your voice holding up?" he asked when she rested her hand over her throat.

"All I need is a cup of hot water with lemon and honey." She stood up. "I'll be right back."

Seneca returned to the kitchen, filled the electric kettle with water and plugged it in. Opening an overhead cabinet, she removed a mug. By the time the water had boiled, she'd added a tablespoon of honey and lemon juice to the mug. She lingered in the kitchen, recalling all she'd divulged to Hans. Her secret marriage to Phillip Kingston had remained that over the years—a secret, until her world as she'd known it at that time was turned upside down. She wasn't certain that what she'd told Hans would end up in the book, but whatever it was that hadn't been made public would thrust the former Butterfly back into the public eye.

Before agreeing to grant the interview, Seneca had discussed it with her husband. His response was to tell the truth, because lies would only come back to haunt her and disrupt the lives of their children.

There was a time when her mother, father, sister and brother were her family—but everything had changed when she'd decided it was time for Butterfly to put away her colorful wings and join the ranks of former supermodels who'd gone on to establish new careers.

Try as she would, Seneca wasn't able to make the transition, to leave the glare of the spotlights and flashbulbs, so she was forced to do what she hadn't wanted to do—make others happy. It wasn't about what had made Butterfly happy, and so she had continued to agree to photo shoots and fashion shows and accept cameo roles in movies and popular television shows.

It had taken Herculean strength, but Butterfly underwent another metamorphosis in an attempt to survive, not for others but to secure her own future. By this time she'd wanted what most women wanted—a husband, children and a normal life. It was one thing to ask for these and another to fight for them. For her it had been the latter.

Cradling the mug between her hands, she retraced her steps. Walking into the family room, she stopped abruptly. Hans was flipping through a photo album she'd left on the table next to the love seat.

"I meant to put that away."

Hans spun away, embarrassed that she'd caught him snooping. "I'm sorry. I should've asked your permission."

Seneca shook her head. "It's okay. You already know more about me than most people."

"Where were you when those photos were taken?"

Closing the distance between them, she sat at the opposite end of the love seat. "I was at Booth Gordon's house in the Caribbean. I'd gone there to recuperate."

"Were you sick?"

She took a sip of the warm honey-and-lemon-infused water. "Not physically sick. I was close to burnout, or what is commonly known as a nervous breakdown. It took at least a month before I began to feel like myself." She took another swallow of the liquid, then cleared her throat. "No more questions, Hans, or I'll be completely hoarse tomorrow. Let me show you to the guesthouse. As soon as you're settled in I'll take you on a tour of the property and the surrounding area. If you're up to it later on, we can visit some of the vineyards, where you can do a little wine tasting."

Hans flashed a wide smile. "I like the sound of that. Let me get my bags from the car and I'll meet you around the back."

Seneca retrieved the key to the guesthouse from the small box on the fireplace mantelpiece and left the room through a side door. Once she'd received confirmation that Hans was coming, she'd made arrangements for the smaller version of the main house to be cleaned and aired out. Unlocking the door, she left the key in the lock, leaving the door ajar. Hans arrived, carrying a garment bag and matching Pullman.

"Come in and rest yourself." Seneca closed her eyes, remembering that it was a phrase her grandmother always used when she welcomed someone into her home.

Hans walked in, peering around at the French country furnishings. It was the perfect place to kick back and relax. "Very nice."

"Thank you. I restocked the pantry, refrigerator and the bar. If there is anything you need and it's not there, please let me know."

He set down the Pullman that contained his photography equipment. "Right about now I'm craving a shower and a firm bed. If you don't see me in a couple of hours, that means I'm down for the count."

Hans didn't tell Seneca that he'd left Los Angeles and was on the road minutes after midnight to arrive at her house before eight. She'd explained to him that she'd wanted to begin the interview early in the morning and conclude by noon.

"If I don't see you later, then it'll be tomorrow morning." Turning on her heels, she walked out, feeling the heat from Hans's gaze on her back.

Seneca had returned to the main house after her early-morning walk and had just finished slicing fruit when she heard the thud of the door knocker. She walked out of the kitchen, through the living room to the front door. Peering through the security eye, she recognized the face and opened the door.

"Good morning."

Hans winked at the former model, whose smoky voice, sensual smile and perfectly symmetrical features had invaded his dream. "That it is, Seneca. It's a beautiful morning." He brought his right hand up. "May I take a few candid shots of you before we begin the interview?"

Seneca ran her hand over the hair she'd secured in a ponytail. "You know I don't model anymore."

"This is not for the book. I'd like to add it to my personal collection. And if I decide to include it in a book of models unplugged, I'll be certain to get your release."

A beat passed as she pondered his request. "Okay." What did she have to lose? After all, she'd literally spilled her guts to Hans. Having him take a few candid photographs paled in comparison.

Hans raised the camera, peered through the lens finder and got off a shot, then showed Seneca the digital image. "Is that candid enough?"

A smile softened Seneca's mouth when she recognized the wide-eyed expression that had appeared on so many covers of glossy fashion magazines. Butterfly had walked away from the fashion world at thirty, and seven years later she still had a good face.

"It's nice, Hans."

He got two more frames. "It's more than nice, Seneca. You're that rare find, because you're stunning with or without makeup."

"Come on in," she ordered. "Yesterday I told you about Seneca Houston. Today's Butterfly's turn."

Hans walked into the entryway and closed the door behind them. "Is Butterfly as interesting as Seneca?" he asked, staring at Seneca's hips in a pair of cropped black pants in a stretchy fabric. She'd replaced her man-tailored shirt with a black tank top. Today she'd pushed her feet into a pair of sandals with wedge heels that put her close to the six-foot mark.

"Butterfly is synonymous with drama."

Hans sat at the cooking island and took out the tape recorder. "I don't remember reading about you having to deal with catwalk drama."

"Most of my drama was off the catwalk." She handed Hans a glass of freshly squeezed orange juice. "Butterfly emerged from her cocoon the weekend I celebrated my twenty-first birthday. What I didn't know at the time was that it would change my life, and not necessarily for the better."

Part Two

Butterfly

Chapter Eighteen

"I've got a bone to pick with you," Electra whispered sotto voce when she slipped into the rear of the town car next to Seneca.

"What are you talking about?" Seneca whispered back.

"Why didn't you tell me you were dating Phillip Kingston?"

Seneca glanced at the man who was about to become her ex-husband. When they'd stopped to pick up Electra and her boyfriend, within a minute of introducing Phillip to the couple Jayson had launched into an in-depth discussion of basketball.

"I wanted to surprise you."

Electra pushed out her lower lip. "Well, you did. How is he?"

"How is he how?"

Shaking her head and rolling her eyes, Electra didn't want to believe her roommate was so gauche. She was dating one of the most beautiful men on the planet; meanwhile she acted as if he was nothing more than the young college student who bagged groceries at their local supermarket. As much as she wanted to break into the movies as a serious actress, she would give it all up for the man known as King Phillip of the hardwood.

"Fuhgeddaboudit," she drawled in her best Brooklyn dialect.

Seneca laughed. "We'll talk later." She closed her eyes, feigning sleep while listening to the conversations going on around her. Mixed emotions assailed her when she realized this weekend would signal the end of her relationship with Phillip, although they'd promised to remain friends. A friend she'd married; a friend with whom she'd shared the most incredible sex.

And she'd been forthcoming when she'd told Phillip that sex wasn't enough to save their marriage. There had never been a time when she hadn't enjoyed making love with him, but she wanted and needed more than multiple orgasms. She needed him to love her, trust her and above all else support her enough to help her realize her dreams.

The smooth motion of the car lulled her into a state of total relaxation, and she temporarily shut out everything going on around her, including the expression of pain in Phillip's eyes whenever their gazes met.

Booth Gordon's summer rental was magnificent. The six-bedroom, six-bathroom farmhouse was built on a rise overlooking the ocean. A household staff of four was on hand to see to the needs of Booth's guests.

Rhys had arrived, and he and the woman who looked young enough to be his daughter were assigned the bedroom next to the one where Seneca would stay with Phillip. Electra and Jayson were across the hall, and Luis and Mitchell, who'd come unaccompanied, were in bedrooms at the rear of the house. Seneca looked around for the young woman who'd looked so forlorn at Booth's dinner party. When she got the opportunity to ask Mitchell, the photographer said he'd heard that Booth had given the needy woman her walking papers.

Mitchell, resplendent in white linen, leaned in close to her. "Be careful, Seneca. Even though I know you're involved with Phillip, that doesn't preclude Booth from trying to hit on you."

Seneca met his resolute gaze before he slipped on a pair of sunglasses. "Phillip and I are just friends."

"Either you're a better actress than I'd imagined you to be or you're an incredible liar." Mitchell ran a finger along the curve of her delicate jaw. "The camera doesn't lie, beautiful. You and your baller were on fire during that shoot."

"It's called acting, Mitchell."

"Don't try and shit me, Butterfly," he drawled. "You don't have to worry. Your secret is safe with me."

Seneca spied their host as he walked out onto the patio where a small crowd had gathered. Booth was hosting an afternoon soirée for his guests and several neighbors, and later that evening everyone would drive a short distance to attend the birthday celebration for the movie director whose films were viewed in the industry as innovative, revolutionary and avant-garde in the same breath. It was the reason why she'd wanted to invite Electra and Jayson. Meeting the director would offer them an opportunity to talk to the quixotic filmmaker about their projects.

She signaled to Booth, smiling as he closed the distance between them. Like his guests, he wore lightweight loose-fitting attire and sandals. A light breeze off the ocean ruffled his shirt and slacks.

Slipping her hand in his, Seneca squeezed his fingers. "I need to talk to you where no one can overhear what I want to tell you."

Booth blanched under his deep summer tan. "Please don't tell me you're pregnant."

Seneca gave him an incredulous look. "Of course I'm not."

"Come with me." Booth steered her away from the rear of the house to a side door that led directly into a room off the kitchen that doubled as a pantry and laundry room. He flicked on a light and locked the door behind them. "What's going on?"

Leaning her hip against a table, Seneca told Booth everything, from leaving his condo, going with Phillip to his hotel suite, their going to Vegas to marry before the shoot, and the reason why she wanted to annul their short-lived marriage.

Booth rolled his eyes. "If you'd told me this I wouldn't have put you in the same room with him."

"It doesn't matter now."

A savage curse escaped the agent's compressed lips. "I thought Kingston was smarter than that."

"Don't blame him," Seneca in defense of her husband. "We never should've married. If I was thinking beyond the next orgasm I would've rejected his proposal—at least until I'd gotten to know him better."

Flashing a sardonic smile, Booth shook his head. "That's no guarantee, baby. I've been married twice, and each time I thought I knew my ex-wives, but something would jump off where we were unable to work through it, so it was the lawyers who made out like bandits when they charged me through the nose to get rid of them." He sobered. "Did you have a prenup?"

"No. It doesn't matter, because I don't want Phillip's money."

Booth's eyebrows lifted a fraction. "The man's a fool. He could've had it all—a beautiful wife, half a billion in endorsements and a multimillion dollar basketball contract—yet his fuckin' insecurities had to blow it."

It was Seneca's turn to lift her eyebrows. "We've decided to remain friends."

"No, Seneca. That's not going to happen. The man has confessed to being obsessed with you, so you continuing to see him will just feed into his sick shit. He's one of those guys who believe if they can't have you, then no one will. You will cut the ties after this weekend. And I'll talk to Kingston and let him know the deal."

"What makes you think he'll listen to you?"

The blue-green eyes hardened like stones. "He'll listen to me. I've saved his ass more than a few times when he got a little too rough with several of his girlfriends."

"What do you mean about *too rough?*"

"Either that or Kingston doesn't know his own strength, because some of them wound up with some pretty nasty bruises."

Seneca's mouth opened, and she wasn't able to utter a word, recalling the two times she'd had to warn Phillip about grabbing and holding her too tightly. She would be hard-pressed to explain the bruises if she were to do a shoot.

"Okay, Booth. I'll stop seeing him."

"Did he hurt you?"

She shook her head. "No."

"You're not lying to me, are you, Seneca?"

The seconds ticked as they stared at each other. "No."

Booth gave her a thin-lipped smile. "After the Super Bowl

ad airs I'm certain you'll get tons of offers to appear with him again, but that decision will have to be yours."

"Do you think it would be wise to work with him again?"

"You're going to have to learn to separate business from personal. If you're going to feel uncomfortable working with him, then I'd say don't do it. But, if not, then go for it."

"I need you to answer one question for me, Booth."

"What is it?"

"Why didn't you tell me about Phillip's proclivity for roughing up women?"

"I don't involve myself in my clients' private lives until they involve me. I've been in this business long enough to see how young men become victims to their own hype. Either they come from a single-parent family or from one where their parents are struggling to make ends meet, then suddenly they're being bombarded with offers from people for more money than they could ever hope to earn in ten lifetimes.

"There are the cars, jewelry, drugs, mansions, and let's not forget the women. Women who would never give them a second look if not for their multimillion-dollar contracts. It doesn't matter if they come from the projects or the trailer park, it's just too much for them to digest. I picked up Phillip because he was different. He comes from a good family, he's intelligent and without peer when it comes to making three-pointers. But unfortunately, he feels the need to hurt women every once in a while, and mark my words, there *is* going to come a time when I'm not going to be able to cover for him. You're a young, beautiful woman, Seneca, and I'd hate for you to have to give up your career because some man decided to rearrange your face."

Seneca couldn't stop the audible gasp when she processed what her agent had just revealed. "He hit them in the face?"

Booth nodded. "Not only did he have to pay their medical bills but he agreed to pay them for pain and suffering to the tune of millions. He had to give one ten million. His only consolation is that the money is paid out over twenty years— half a mil for each year. If she decides to get diarrhea of the tongue, then she's cut off and legally must repay what he's given her."

"Why don't you turn him in?"

"You have to remember that he's not beating my ass. It's up to the women to press charges."

Seneca recalled the first time when Phillip grabbed her and she'd threatened to sue him if he'd bruised her. Little had she known that other women *had* sued him. She said a silent prayer of thanks that she'd gotten out unscathed.

Looping her arms around Booth's neck, she pressed a kiss to his smooth jaw. "Thank you for telling me."

Booth's hands went to her waist, and he resisted pulling her closer. "You and Phillip are my clients, but morally, it's my responsibility to protect you from him. When you told me you'd married him I freaked. That's why I cautioned you about telling anyone. You say he didn't hit you, and that leads me to believe that hopefully he's learned his lesson." He kissed her forehead. "Let's get back to the others before tongues start wagging about us sleeping together."

Seneca sucked her teeth loudly. "That's never going to happen," she said confidently. She walked out into the bright sunlight, leaving Booth to follow a minute later.

Talking with the agent was enlightening *and* frightening, only because she'd been unaware that the man she'd been sleeping with and had married was an abuser. She forced a brittle smile when she returned to the large tent that had been set up to protect everyone from the harmful rays of the hot summer sun.

Seneca sidled up to Phillip when he stood in line waiting for the bartender to take his beverage request. "I know everything," she said in a quiet voice.

Phillip angled his head, staring at his soon-to-be ex-wife as if she were a stranger. "What?"

"Booth told me about the other women," she continued sotto voce. "After this weekend I think it best if we do not see each other again. Get some help, Phillip, or you can kiss your dreams of becoming a doctor bye-bye."

Phillip, who'd decided it was better not to pretend he didn't know what she was talking about, nodded. "I'm seeing a therapist."

Seneca placed a hand on his back in a comforting gesture. "Good for you."

"I was going to tell you—"

"Don't, Phillip. It's okay."

"The first time I saw you," Phillip continued as if she hadn't spoken, "I knew I wanted to marry you. All I thought about was you having our children and our growing old together."

Turning on her heel, Seneca walked away from him. She'd heard enough. His obsession was frightening, and she feared what he could possibly do to her. There was no way she was going to share a bedroom with him ever again.

Thankfully, she'd packed the clothes she'd left at his hotel suite and her luggage was stored in the trunk of the limo that would take her back to Manhattan. She bumped into Luis, who caught her before she lost her balance.

"*¿Cómo estás, Mariposa?*"

"Do you mind sharing your bedroom with me?"

"What's up?"

"Answer the question, Luis."

"Of course you can."

She grabbed his hand. "Come and help me move my things."

Luis's eyes narrowed. "What's going on, Seneca?"

"I just don't want to share a room with Phillip Kingston."

Luis recognized fear in the eyes of the woman who'd become the inspiration for most of his creations. "Okay. I'll help you move your things."

Seneca chewed her lower lip, praying not to break down. "Thank you, Luis." The skirt of the ankle-length tank dress swirled around her long legs as she and Luis returned to the house.

Phillip watched his wife and the designer through narrow eyes until they disappeared from his line of vision.

"Now is the time to let her go," said a familiar voice next to him. He turned to see his agent standing only a few feet away.

"What if I don't want to let her go?"

A feral smile twisted the agent's face. "You will let her go, Kingston, or you're done with a capital D."

"Don't worry, Gordon. I'm not going to hurt her."

"I know you're not, because if anyone's going to get hurt it's you. I'm tired of cleaning up your messes, Kingston. And I blame myself for letting you go after Butterfly."

"Butterfly?" he spat out. "You're nothing but a greedy bastard, Gordon. This is not about Seneca."

"You tell me what it's about, Kingston."

"It's the money. Everyone who signs with BGM is nothing more than a dollar sign to you."

Crossing his arms over his chest, Booth rocked back on his heels. "Listen and listen well, my *boy*. I didn't sign a document stating I wouldn't divulge the details of your physical altercations with several women who will remain nameless. Fuck with me and I'll not only drop you, but I'll also make an anonymous phone call to a friend who works for a newspaper that thrives on salacious gossip. I told you before. Even if you were my one and only client, I'm not going to stand by and let you hit another woman. What is it going to be, Kingston? Are you going to stay away from her?"

The sweep hand on Phillip's watch made a full revolution. "I'll think about it."

"You do more than think about it!" Booth countered. Physically, he knew he was no match for the ballplayer, knowing he would have to even the odds. That's where Dennis Mayfield's special skills came in. He never asked his boyhood friend how he managed to coerce people into seeing things his way. All he was concerned about were the results.

But one thing Booth Wilkes Gordon was not, and that was easily frightened. He hadn't issued an idle threat when he'd mentioned leaking information that Phillip Kingston had battered women. "After this weekend, you will never contact Seneca Houston again." He gestured to the bartender. "Take his drink order. He's holding up the line."

A ripple of silence descended over the two hundred guests who'd gathered on the property of Francisco Abrams when Booth Gordon walked onto the property with Seneca Houston clinging to his arm. Those close enough to glimpse her tall, thin figure draped in a short, backless, silk chiffon dress in flattering colors of tangerine and cream whispered among themselves while wondering who she was. The flared skirt, ending at midthigh, showed off her long legs to their best advantage. Five inches of Christian Louboutin black patent-leather pumps had her towering over many of the men in attendance.

Booth introduced Seneca to the Argentinean-born director who lived half of the year in the States and the other half in Buenos Aires. Francisco cradled her hands, kissing her knuckles. His sharp brown eyes took in everything about her in a single glance.

"When Gordon told me he was bringing me a gift, I never thought it would be so incredibly beautiful."

Seneca laughed, the sultry sound catching and floating on the rising wind off the water. She'd found the tall, slender man charming. His slightly accented English was musical, and he was attractive without being handsome.

"Since today is also my birthday, are you going to be my gift?"

Throwing back his head, Francisco roared in delight. "It would be my pleasure to be your gift." He released her hands and peered around her back. He smiled. "Lovely dress. Ah—you have a tattoo. What is it?"

"It's a monarch butterfly and my signature."

"Your signature?"

Seneca pointed to Luis, who was attempting to extricate himself from a woman who'd latched onto him like a ravenous predator. "That's Luis Navarro, and he designed this dress. He claims I'm his muse and his *mariposa*."

"It's a fitting signature. Booth told me you're a model. Do you have any acting experience?"

Seneca affected a sexy moue. "I have a little."

"How much is a little?"

"Do you mind if we don't talk shop tonight?" she asked.

"When do you wish to talk, *Mariposa?*"

Booth moved closer. "I'll call you, Frankie, and set up a day and time when the three of us can get together. Now, if you'll excuse me, I'd like to introduce Butterfly to a few other people."

"Thanks," Seneca whispered when he wrapped an arm around her waist and led her away from Francisco. "I was running out of witty repartee."

"You do all right for a twenty-one-year-old. How about a drink—now that you're legal?"

"No, thank you." She didn't want to tell Booth that turning twenty-one wasn't an excuse for her to drink.

"Don't you feel like celebrating?"

"Being here is a celebration. When I used to read *Vanity Fair* and *Town and Country* and see photos of celebrities vacationing and partying in the Hamptons, I never would've imagined being here."

Booth gave Seneca a sidelong glance. "So, you like hanging out with counterfeit people?"

"Why are you so cynical, Booth?"

His fingers tightened on her tiny waist. "I'm getting old, Butterfly. Old, tired and crotchety."

"You need a wife."

"I don't know if getting married again would mellow me out."

Booth was still faced with the Carter Browning dilemma. He had hired a private investigator to have the man checked out. He'd also had a security technician come and sweep the entire building for electronic listening devices. Carter hadn't lied. The technician discovered a total of eighteen bugs, and if Joan Powers hadn't disappeared he would've personally strangled her.

"Let's go down to the beach," Seneca urged Booth when she spied Phillip with a buxom redhead clinging to his arm as if he were her lifeline. It was apparent he was ready to move on.

Seneca returned nods and exchanged smiles with invited guests as she followed Booth down to the beach. Leaning against him for support, she slipped out of her shoes and dug her bare toes in the sand. "It's going to be a long time before I'll be thinking about getting married again."

"Now who's being cynical?" Booth teased.

"I'm being realistic," she countered.

"May I give you a little advice?" Seneca nodded. "Don't get married again until you retire from modeling."

She nodded again. "That sounds like good advice."

"I'm going to set you up with my lawyer, who will handle your annulment."

"Is he going to charge me through the nose?" Seneca teased, repeating what Booth said about his divorces.

"No. There's no division of property or children, so it should be short and sweet." Booth gave her a peck on the cheek. "I'm going to get something to drink. Try and stay out of trouble."

Seneca noticed the beach was becoming crowded as party-goers carrying cups and plates of food sat on the sand to watch the awe-inspiring sunset. Electra joined her, balancing a plate piled high with food.

"I got enough for both of us," she explained, handing Seneca several cocktail napkins.

Seneca took a large prawn and a skewer with grilled chicken. "Where's Jayson?"

"He's hanging around the pool waiting for you to introduce him to Francisco Abrams."

"Why is he waiting for me?"

"We're your guests, Seneca."

"And I'm Booth's guest. Tell Jayson to go over and introduce himself."

Electra pushed out her lower lip. "Why are you being a bitch, Seneca?"

She glared at her roommate as if she'd suddenly taken leave

of her senses. "I'm a bitch because I won't take your bitch-ass, poor excuse for a man by the hand and introduce him to someone he wants to meet?"

"Who the fuck are you to call my boyfriend a bitch?"

Seneca struggled not to lose her temper. "I'll call him any-thing I want. When Booth told me we were going to Francisco Abrams's soirée, I thought of you and Jayson and that he could possibly connect with the man."

"What if he introduces himself and Mr. Abrams gives him the brush-off?"

"That's his problem. He's just going to have to learn to deal with rejection, Electra. You're his girlfriend, not his mother. You can't pick him up when he falls and scrapes his knees."

Electra went completely still, her eyes filling with tears. "I thought you were my friend."

"I am your friend, Electra, but I'm not a bitch."

"What I don't need is a shady friend. Ever since you signed on with BGM you've changed. It's like you're breathing rari-fied air and you don't have time for us common people. You're dating Phillip Kingston, yet when I asked who PK was you acted as if I'd asked you something that would jeopardize national security. Now you get a one-on-one with Francisco Abrams and you refuse to introduce your friends to him. Has he asked you to appear in one of his films?"

Seneca didn't know where Electra was coming from or what had set her off. "I don't have to deal with this." She walked off down the beach without giving her roommate a backward glance. Hot tears pricked the back of her eyelids, but she refused to cry—not on her birthday.

Turning twenty-one had become a sobering experience. She planned to dissolve her two-week marriage, and the woman she'd called *friend* had just turned on her.

Chapter Nineteen

Seneca found Booth's driver and had him drive her back to the house, where she locked herself in the bedroom she would share with Luis. She went through the ritual of removing the makeup from her face before she showered and pulled on a pair of lounging pants and tee. Sitting yoga-style on the twin bed, she called Ithaca. Her father answered the phone. The instant she heard his deep voice her eyes filled with tears.

"Hi, Daddy."

"How's my birthday girl?"

"She's good," she lied, blinking back tears.

"You don't sound so good."

"That's because I miss you guys."

"What's the matter, Seneca?"

"I can't talk about it now."

There came a pregnant pause before Oscar Houston said, "What's going on, Seneca? You call to say you miss us, yet you're too busy to come and visit with your family. You act as if we live on the other side of the world. Not only are we in the same time zone but we also live in the same state. I try not to take sides, but this time I'm going to agree with your mother when she says you're only thinking of yourself. I've always tried to support you when you say you want to do something, but I'm not so certain about this modeling business."

"What's wrong with it, Daddy?"

"The question should be what's right with it."

"I like it."

"Do you love it, Seneca?"

Seneca chewed her lower lip as she thought about her father's question. "I can't answer that."

"You can't because the answer is no. You can't give something a hundred percent of yourself if you don't love it. Your grandmother loved being an actress more than she loved being a wife and mother, and she wasn't ashamed to admit it. What you're going to have ask yourself is if modeling will be worth the sacrifices that you're going to face in the future."

"What sacrifices?"

"Your first sacrifice is giving up your education and—"

"I'm going to go back to school," she said, interrupting him.

"Please let me finish, Seneca. The second sacrifice will be friends and family, because everybody is going to want a piece of you. And you're going to want to please them. Designers will line up like vehicles at a car wash to beg you to wear their clothes. Then it's the folks who want you to promote their products. People are going to expect you to smile when you don't feel like smiling, and if a photographer happens to take a picture of you when you're having a bad hair day, then tongues start wagging about what's going on in your life. It's going to happen, baby girl. I just want you to be prepared when it comes."

Seneca cried silent tears. Her father's words cut her to the quick. Had he always harbored reservations about her becoming a model, or had Dahlia brainwashed him? Her mother equated models to whores and sluts. But she wasn't a whore or a slut. What she'd done was marry the wrong man.

"Thanks for the advice."

"You don't have to take it, Seneca. Just think about what I've said. No matter what happens, always remember that I'll be here for you."

"I know that, Daddy. I'm going to Miami next week for my first show in the States. Instead of coming back to the city I'll fly up and see you, Mama and Robbie."

"That sounds good."

"Don't say anything to Mama and Robbie. I want it to be a surprise."

"I won't say a mumbling word."

Seneca laughed for the first time since hearing her father's voice. "By the way, how is Mama?"

"Other than complaining about hot flashes, she's all right."

"She's too young to have hot flashes."

"That's what I told her, but she insists she's going through the change."

"When I see her I'm going to try and convince her to have her estrogen levels checked."

"Good luck with that, baby girl. Did you have a drink to celebrate becoming legal?"

"No."

"Good for you. The stuff can be poison to some people."

Seneca knew Oscar was talking about his younger brother, who'd been in and out of alcohol rehab for most of his life before he died of liver disease.

"If I start drinking, then I'll eat all the wrong foods."

Oscar's deep laugh caressed her ear. "I suppose modeling has a few good perks."

"It does. It forces me to eat healthy."

"Look, baby, I'm going to ring off because I promised the ladies of the house that I would take them to the movies, and if we don't head out now we're going to miss that last show."

"Have fun."

"Thanks. Bye, and happy birthday."

Seneca held the tiny phone to her ear, then punched the end button. Her father had hung up. Slipping off the bed, she went into the bathroom to splash cold water on her face. Staring at her reflection in the mirror over the pedestal sink, she hardly recognized the face staring back at her. Puffy red eyes were a telltale sign that she'd been crying.

She was crying and hiding behind a locked door on what should've been one of the momentous days of her life. Seneca wasn't as unsettled about her father's change of heart about her modeling as she'd been about the altercation with Electra. That was totally unexpected. Now she knew what people meant when they said something came at them out of left field.

She'd gotten Booth to agree to let her invite Electra and her playwright boyfriend to Francisco Abrams's birthday celebration, and yet Electra wanted her to take Jayson by the hand and personally introduce him to the director. She didn't expect her roommate to bow and kiss her hand, but Electra verbally attacked her—calling her a bitch—because Jayson was too timid to take care of his own business. She'd seen girls punched out because they'd called another girl the B-word.

Seneca Houston was nobody's bitch, and she knew that sharing an apartment with Electra was no longer an option. Finding another apartment in Manhattan and paying what she did for rent was nearly impossible, but she was confident she could find something. She would give Electra two month's notice, and even if she didn't find another place to live she knew she couldn't continue to share the apartment.

Seneca felt the comforting press of Mitchell's hand on hers as the jet picked up speed in preparation for liftoff. She was flying to Miami to walk in Rhys Calhoun's swimsuit show, and Mitchell Leon was going along as the photographer for *Elle* magazine.

When she'd returned to Manhattan after her weekend on Long Island's South Shore, it wasn't to the Upper West Side brownstone. She'd checked into a moderately priced hotel near the Hudson River, spending hours on her cell calling Realtors and scouring classified ads for apartment rentals. What she didn't want to do was share an apartment again, but with the price of New York City real estate she'd concluded her best option was renting in one of the other boroughs. Brooklyn had become her first choice, because it was easily accessible by public transportation.

Mitchell had attempted to resolve her problem when he'd called to invite her out to a vegetarian restaurant they both liked, offering to pick her up. However, when she told him she was staying at the hotel, he calmly told her to check out and stay with him. He'd deflected her rejection, reminding her that she'd put him up on her sofa when he hadn't had anyplace to stay. Her last comment to him on the matter was that she would think about it. After dinner, they returned to the hotel, and Mitchell took her luggage back to his loft.

"Have you thought about it, Butterfly?"

Seneca pulled her gaze away from the window where the tarmac whizzed dizzily by. "Thought about what?" She closed her eyes briefly as the jet gained altitude.

"Moving in with me?"

She opened her eyes, her gaze moving slowly over the

sculpted mahogany face with mesmerizing gold eyes. "I'll *stay* with you, but only until I find my own place."

Mitchell smiled, flashing his beautiful white teeth. When they'd walked through the terminal to their gate, stares and whispers had followed. Mitchell Leon hadn't been away from the world of modeling long enough for people to have forgotten his tall, slender body and dynamic face. Both were flying first-class and had elected to carry on their luggage.

Mitchell gave Seneca's fingers a gentle squeeze. "Good. Now, are you going to tell me why you're moving out, or do you want me to take a wild guess?"

"There's no need to play twenty questions." Seneca recounted the conversation she'd had with Electra at Francisco Abrams's beachfront home. "I'd never seen her so upset. I think it's because she wants more for her boyfriend than he wants for himself. I would've excused her if she hadn't called me a bitch."

"No, she didn't."

"Yes, she did. I prayed to the ancestors to keep me from stomping a mud hole in her ass. Five-inch stilettos can double as lethal weapons."

Mitchell laughed despite the seriousness of the situation. "I see why you checked into that hotel. I don't want to say anything but…"

"But what, Mitchell?" Seneca asked when he stopped talking.

"You've got to toughen up," he said cryptically. "You have what Electra wants—fame."

"You're wrong. I'm *not* famous."

"Not yet. And she knows that. Remember, you invited her to come along to the Hamptons, not the other way around. You're a BGM client, you know Phillip Kingston and she saw Francisco Abrams's reaction when he met you. Your roommate wants to be you. She wants to be Butterfly. And because she isn't, she turned on you."

"She can't be jealous."

"No. She's not jealous. She's envious. Don't forget envy is one of the seven deadly sins. And you're not going to only get it from friends but also from family."

"You went through something like I did with Electra?"

"If I'd had an Electra moment, then I would've thought of myself as blessed. Once I returned to the States after my first European show, every friend and relative I'd ever known had their hand out. If they weren't asking for a little 'spare change' they were hounding me about how to break into modeling." Mitchell leaned closer to Seneca. "Guys I'd gone to school with called me *faggot* and *dick sucker,* because they believed I'd prostituted myself to get modeling jobs," he said in her ear. "Women I wouldn't sleep with perpetuated the rumors and gossip because they weren't used to men turning them down. As my grandmother used to say, God bless the dead, 'Gird your loins, boy, 'cause theys gonna come afta ya.'"

Seneca laughed when she didn't feel like laughing and prayed Mitchell was wrong. Her family wasn't destitute, so she doubted whether they'd ask her for money. Even her few distant cousins, Stefani included among them, rarely interacted with her. She hadn't reconnected with Stefani until she'd graduated from cosmetology school. Her cousin had called to let her know she was working in a salon in Harlem.

The flipside was that her cousin didn't want her to come to the salon but to her apartment in Brooklyn to do her hair. The experience was one Seneca would never forget. Between screaming at her three children, all under the age of six, and attempting to appease her grumpy husband when he wanted her to stop what she was doing and cook dinner for him, it had taken more than four hours for Stefani to wash, deep-condition, set, dry and blow-dry her hair.

She didn't say anything to Mitchell, but she prayed he was wrong. The jet had reached cruising altitude and the flight attendants began serving breakfast. It was an added perk when airlines had downsized to the point where they charged for checked bags, snacks, pillows and blankets. She and Phillip had flown first class to L.A. and had taken a private jet to Vegas. It was a practice she could easily get used to.

Chapter Twenty

"Come on, ladies, it's time for you to get into hair and makeup!"

Seneca felt the pulsing excitement heating her blood. When they'd walked out of Miami International she'd been taken aback by the blast of heat and humidity. The hair she'd pulled into a ponytail frizzed and curled within minutes. As she sat in front of the mirror, wearing a dressing gown over a pair of bikini panties, she watched the stylist as he ran his fingers through her hair.

"I'll take this one," said a familiar voice behind her. Seneca smiled when she saw Yancy's reflection in the mirror.

Reaching up, she caught his hand. "Hey, you."

Leaning down, Yancy pressed a kiss to her temple. "Hey, yourself." He massaged her scalp, pulling her hair back off her face. "You ladies are going to be birds—beautiful, colorful, exotic birds."

"Does that mean I'm going to be wearing feathers?"

Yancy nodded. "Lots and lots of colorful feathers." He

released her hair, resting his hands at his hips. "Only because you have the longest legs I've ever seen on a woman, I'm going to turn you into a flamingo."

Seneca clapped her hands as she'd done when she was a child, her eyes shimmering with excitement, praying she wouldn't lose focus. When she and Mitchell had checked into their respective hotel rooms, she'd drunk a bottle of chilled water, then practiced her walk until she could do it perfectly in her sleep. The show was scheduled to be held later that evening in the ballroom of a newly constructed cultural arts center in Miami's South Beach.

She watched, transfixed, as Yancy, wielding a large brush and blow-dryer, straightened the front of her hair before securing it with an elastic band. He pinned up the rest of her hair into a tight knot on the crown of her head. The headpiece came next. Pure white feathers tipped with pink and orange were pinned tightly into the knot, truly making her look like an exotic bird. With her heels and the feathers she would appear even taller.

Seneca was hustled over to makeup, where the artist applied bright splashes of red, orange, white and pink to her face. Her eyes seemed to disappear under the garish paint until they were outlined with kohl. The show's coordinator was shouting orders like a marine drill sergeant.

"Butterfly! Who the hell is Butterfly?"

Seneca raced over the frantic man who wore entirely too much makeup. "I'm Butterfly."

"Rhys wants you to open and close. So please get to wardrobe and into your first outfit."

Seneca felt her heart kick into a higher gear as she was handed a two-piece red-and-yellow swimsuit that wasn't much more than a scrap of fabric and ribbon. Taking off the dressing gown and her panties, she stepped into the bottom as a young woman tied the ribbons below her hipbones. Seconds later she had on the top and was pushing her feet into a pair of silk stilettos with ties that wrapped around her ankles. Rhys, who'd walked backstage, came over to her.

He looked her over, his eyes narrowing. "Exquisite, but you need something." He snapped his fingers. "She needs chicken fillets." Within seconds she'd achieved a larger cup size when the rubbery breast enhancers were inserted into her top.

The sounds of voices speaking English and Spanish and music with an infectious Latin-infused beat drifted backstage. Seneca closed her eyes, her hips swaying in time to the music. She shook her arms at her sides to relax them. If this was to be her first runway show, then she wanted it to be a memorable one—for the spectators and for herself.

She'd come to the center earlier than scheduled and had walked the length of the runway, counting the number of steps it took for her to get to the end before falling off. Keane had cautioned her about knowing exactly when the end of the runway was, because too often he'd witnessed models falling after they were stunned by flashbulbs. Not only did she know how many steps it took to the end of the runway, but she was also cognizant of its width. There wasn't much room if she had to pass another model coming from the opposite direction.

The show's coordinator peered through the curtain. "It's a full house. Two minutes, Butterfly, and you're on."

Seneca schooled her face until there was no expression. It wasn't about selling her smile but the garment she was wearing. She waited for the signal, then the curtain parted and, wearing a designer garment, she stepped out on the runway for the first time.

She registered the gasps as her red heel hit the floor, her arms swinging loosely at her sides. Halfway down she folded her hands at her hips, and when she reached the end of the runway she stopped, counted three seconds, then raised her hands with the fluid grace of a flamenco dancer wielding a set of castanets, rested her hands on her hips and strutted back the way she'd come. A roar went up as flashbulbs caught the action. The curtain opened and she raced in to change into another outfit.

Seneca changed her shoes for a pair of high-heeled mules and a one-piece suit that showed a liberal amount of her toned buttocks and barely covered her breasts. The crowd roared when she reappeared, and in that instant Butterfly took flight. She was high on adrenaline, drunk on the excitement that all eyes were watching her every move.

She gave them high fashion and then some. When she returned for her final walk wearing a minuscule sheer black two-piece with a matching flowing sheer black sarong, the crowd went wild when she pirouetted and snapped the sarong as if she were a matador.

All the models lined up for their final walk, applauding, Seneca in the lead. Rhys appeared onstage and bowed gracefully, his strawberry-blond hair sweeping over his shoulder. Turning, he applauded his models, then cradling Seneca's face, he kissed her flush on the mouth. Taking her hand, he bowed again, and she following suit.

The curtain opened and the beautiful birds fluttered backstage, where they promptly slipped out of the uncomfortable shoes. One model had had to wear a pair that were a size too small and stomp through the pain. Fortunately for Seneca, she wore a size seven and was able to find a pair in her size.

Rhys walked backstage, grinning from ear to ear. "Ladies, you were the most beautiful birds on the planet. Thank you for making the show a rousing success. Of course, you are all invited to the reception."

He approached Seneca and kissed her cheek. "You know you were magnificent."

Her eyelids fluttered wildly. "It was my first show and..."

Rhys put his finger over her lips, stopping her words. "Every show will be your first show when people see you for the first time. You're going to take the fashion world by storm, because every designer from Givenchy to de la Renta will want you," he predicted. "You have something very special, so if you keep your wits about you, you will never have to worry about where your next dollar or meal is coming from."

Seneca swallowed the lump that had risen in her throat. "Thank you for giving me the opportunity to work for you."

"Stop being so modest, Butterfly." He gave her a gentle pat on her behind. "Go change and I'll meet you at the reception."

When Seneca returned to the makeup room, she noticed several models standing in a group talking quietly to one another. All conversation stopped when they saw her, and she suspected they were talking about her. *Bitches!* Mitchell had warned her about envy and she was witnessing it live and in living color. Lifting her chin, she sniffed as if she'd smelled something malodorous; totally ignoring them, she sat down and began removing the black makeup ringing her eyes.

Seneca felt the power of fame when she walked into the reception with Mitchell Leon. Conversations stopped, then started up again as eyes followed their progress. She'd sent Mitchell a text, asking that he escort her to the reception. He'd returned her text saying that he would. After removing the makeup, she made up her face, using the subtle technique that enhanced her best features. The jeans and T-shirt she'd worn to the center were replaced by a one-shoulder dress in a flaming hot-pink and orange that hugged every line and curve of her body. It ended at midcalf with a provocative slit up the back. The bright-orange silk stilettos pulled her sexy look together. She'd sprayed her hair with a lotion that gave her curly hair a wet look without feeling sticky. The only allowance for jewelry was Booth's gift: the blue topaz butterfly pendant.

A woman dressed to the nines in couture and dripping with priceless jewels approached Seneca and Mitchell. "You were magnificent on the runway. I told my friend that I'd never seen anyone glide the way do you."

Seneca smiled through lowered lashes. "Thank you so much. I hope you're going to order at least a few swimsuits from the collection."

"My *friend* has promised to take me to the Greek Isles for Christmas, so you know I must have a few new suits."

"Good for you," she drawled.

"You're getting good at this," Mitchell whispered when the woman walked away. He gave her fingers a gentle squeeze. "She's right, Butterfly. You were magnificent, and I have the photographs to prove it."

"All I wanted to do was make it down the runway and back without falling on my face."

Mitchell, dressed in a black linen suit with a white silk shirt opened at the throat, did not want to believe Seneca could be that naive. She had to know she had something special that made her a standout. And if she didn't know now, she was certain to believe the hype when she walked a European runway for the first time.

Seneca paid the driver, then alighted from the taxi. As promised, she'd come to Ithaca. Dahlia, who was sitting on the porch, sat up straight, and before Seneca placed her foot on the first step her mother had disappeared inside the house.

Dropping her luggage and tote and moving quickly, she mounted the porch and threw open the screen door. "Mother!"

Dahlia stopped and turned, drilling her to the spot with her wild stare. "Get the hell out of my house!"

"I'm not going anywhere. This is also happens to be my *home*."

"It stopped being your home when you ran away because everyone was talking about you being a slut."

Seneca bit her tongue to keep from reminding her mother that she wasn't the one who'd become a teenage mother at sixteen. "Mother, please don't."

Dahlia pointed to the door. "Get out! Get out now!"

"What the hell…. What's all the shouting about?" Oscar Houston had come into the house through the back door.

"I want her out of this house," Dahlia snarled through clenched teeth. Spittle had formed at the corners of her mouth.

Oscar closed the distance between him and his wife, pulling her stiff body close to his chest. "Calm down, sweetheart. Seneca told me she was coming."

Dahlia rounded on her husband. "You knew she was coming and you didn't tell me?"

Oscar dropped a kiss on the top of her head. "We wanted it to be a surprise."

"You know I don't like surprises. I still don't want her here."

Seneca saw the indecision on her father's face, wondering how many times he would have to run interference between his wife and his daughters. "It's all right, Daddy. I'll stay at a motel. I'll call you and we can get together before I go back."

"No, Seneca. I'm not going to let you check into some motel

when you have a bedroom upstairs." What was it about his girls, he mused, that made their mother come down so hard on them? It hadn't been that way with Dahlia and Jerome. It was as if he was exempt from Dahlia's rage and hostility.

"I'm going, Daddy." She'd just turned to walk to the door when she heard the heavy thud. Seneca turned back to find her father on the floor, clutching his chest. "Oh my God, oh my God," she chanted over and over. Her father was having a heart attack. Reaching for the cell phone in the back pocket of her jeans, she dialed 9-1-1. "My father is having a heart attack!" she screamed into the tiny instrument. The dispatcher on the other end of the line spoke in a monotone, asking the address like one of those recorded messages.

"Hold on, miss. An ambulance is on the way."

She ended the call, then sank to the floor beside her father. Dahlia sat beside him, his head on her lap. "Mom?"

Dahlia's head popped up, and she gave her a blank stare. "Who are you and what are you doing in my house?"

Chapter Twenty-One

Seneca knew from the doctor's expression what he was going to say before he'd opened his mouth. "He's gone, isn't he?"

The doctor placed a comforting hand on her shoulder as she slumped against the wall to support her shaking knees. "I'm sorry, Miss Houston, but we couldn't save him. If it's any comfort, he went quickly."

Her eyes filling with tears, her legs shaking like Jell-O, Seneca buried her face in her hands and sobbed. Her father was dead. She would never again hear his deep voice, his booming laugh, his comforting touch and his undying pledge to protect *his girls*. Well, his girls had killed him with their squabbling and inability to get along with one another. Her kind, gentle father who'd run interference and played referee between her mother...

"My mother!" Seneca wiped her tears with her fingertips. When she and Dahlia had arrived at the hospital, the admitting doctor had recommended keeping Dahlia for observation.

"Your mother has been sedated. Would you like to see her?"

"May—may I see my father first?"

"Of course, Miss Houston. Right this way."

She followed him past several cubicles in the emergency room, stopping at one with a drawn curtain. Seneca pulled back the curtain and walked into the small space. Her hand trembled uncontrollably when she trailed her fingers over his forehead. The EMTs had performed a tracheotomy to assist Oscar in breathing, and the instrument hadn't been removed.

"Can't you take that out?"

"We'll remove it later. Let me check with the desk and I'll let you know in which room you'll find your mother."

Seneca wanted to cry again, but she knew she had to pull it together before seeing Dahlia. She didn't know what had frightened her more—seeing her father lying motionlessly on the floor, or her mother not knowing who she was when minutes before she'd ordered her out of the house where she'd lived when her parents brought her home from the hospital. Dahlia said it was her house; it wasn't her house, but Oscar's. He'd used his G.I. bill benefit to buy the house after he'd gone to work for the postal service. Dahlia had redeemed herself when she managed to snag a single man with no children and a house of his own.

Leaning over, she kissed Oscar's cold cheek. "I'm sorry, Daddy, about fighting with Mom. I promise it will never happen again." She teared up again as she ran a hand over her hair. She had to be going crazy—talking to a dead man. "Goodbye, Daddy. Tell Grandma I said hello."

Seneca walked out of the cubicle and over to the nurses' station. The doctor handed her a slip of paper. "Mrs. Houston is in room 247. When you take the elevator to the second floor, follow the yellow stripe. It will lead you directly to the psychiatric wing."

She froze, staring at the doctor's I.D. "Psychiatric wing? Dr. Pino, my mother is not crazy."

"Your mother's in shock. We want to keep her overnight to make certain she's not a danger to herself or anyone else. If she's okay tomorrow, you can take her home."

Seneca followed the signs leading to the elevator, a gamut of puzzling emotions tying her into knots. She'd lost her father; she couldn't lose her mother, no matter how much they'd argued. Dahlia wasn't a bad mother; she was a controlling mother.

There was no question her mother loved her children, but she didn't have the same expectations for Jerome as she had for her daughters. Standardized tests revealed that he was gifted. Her brother had graduated from high school at fifteen, college at nineteen and by the age of twenty-three had earned two post-graduate degrees. Since Jerome was a mathematics and science prodigy, NASA had come knocking, but he politely turned them down to teach high school math.

Stepping into the elevator, Seneca punched the button for the second floor. The car rose swiftly, the doors opening in a soft whooshing sound. Remembering the doctor's directions, she followed the wide yellow stripe along the wall until she saw the signs pointing the way to the psychiatric wing. She stopped at room 247. *D. Houston* occupied the top slot on a name plaque outside the door.

The door to the semiprivate room was ajar. Seneca walked in, her eyes going to the empty bed nearest the door, then to the other behind the curtain. Her mother was in the bed closest to the window. She moved over to the bed, staring down at the woman who was so still that Seneca's eyes went to her chest to make certain she was breathing.

Pulling over a chair, she reached for Dahlia's hand. It was warm, pulsing with life, when Oscar's was cold. "Hi, Mom. I know you can't hear me, but it's Seneca. Daddy's gone. The doctor said he didn't suffer. I suppose he said it to make me feel better. It's as if that's something they teach them in medical school.

"Why didn't you tell me Daddy had a weak heart? You had to know. He told you everything." She exhaled an audible sigh. "It all makes sense why he wanted to retire. Why didn't you tell us, Mama?"

Seneca went completely still. It'd been years since she'd called Dahlia *Mama*. Once she'd entered her teens she'd started calling her Mom. "Mama, how am I going to tell Robbie Daddy's gone?" Her eyes welled up yet again. "I'm going to call Jerome and let him know, too. I don't want you to worry about anything. We'll take care of the funeral arrangements. I want you to rest. I'll be back tomorrow to bring you home."

Pushing to her feet, she reached for a tissue from a box on the metal table next to the bed. As she'd done with her father, Seneca leaned over and kissed Dahlia's forehead, the familiar scent of her mother's favorite perfume wafting in her nose.

"I'll see you tomorrow."

Now it begins.

The realization slammed into Seneca as she left the hospital and made her way to the parking area. She didn't know how she'd accomplished it, but she'd managed to drive to the hospital in her mother's car, following closely behind the wailing ambulance without mishap, while Dahlia had ridden in the ambulance with her stricken husband.

Thankfully, her mother's car was equipped with Bluetooth, making it easier for Seneca to talk and drive at the same time. She dialed Robyn's cell phone, drumming her fingers on the steering wheel while she waited for a break in the connection. Robyn answered after the third ring.

"What is it, Mom?"

"This is not Mom."

"Seneca? Why are you using Mom's cell?"

"I'm here—in Ithaca. Where are you?"

"I'm at Keisha's house."

"Go home and stay. I'll meet you there."

"What's up, Seneca?"

"I'll tell you when I get home. Now do as I say, Robbie."

"Okay. There's no need to go mad hard and try to sound like Mom."

Seneca hadn't realized she sounded like their mother. "I'm sorry, Robbie."

"Okay."

One down and one to go. Now she had to call her brother. It wouldn't be as easy to talk to Jerome as it had been with Robyn. Seneca wouldn't tell her sister that their father had died until they were face-to-face. But there was no way she could tell Jerome to leave D.C. and come to New York without divulging the reason.

She dialed her brother's home first. It rang half a dozen times before going to voice mail. She scrolled through her directory for his cell. Jerome's voice came through the speaker after his cell phone rang twice.

"This is Jerome."

Why, Seneca mused, hadn't she realized how deep her brother's voice was? "Jerome, this is Seneca."

"Hey, sis. What's up?"

Slowing, she stopped for a red light. "Where are you?"

"What does that matter?"

"Is Maya with you?"

"As a matter of fact she is. What's going on, Seneca?"

"Dad died about…" She couldn't finish. The dreaded words had fallen from her lips, landing on her heart like large stones.

"What do you mean, he died?"

"He had a heart attack. It was a massive coronary. The doctor said he went quickly."

The seconds ticked. "Where's Mom?"

"She's in the hospital."

"She's in or at the hospital, Seneca?"

"She's in the hospital. The doctor had to sedate her, and they recommended keeping her overnight."

"Is she all right?"

Jerome was asking questions to which Seneca didn't have an answer. But she knew there were going to be *the* questions. Why had she come to Ithaca? What was Oscar Houston doing when he'd suffered his fatal heart attack? Other than the shock of her husband's death, what had sent Dahlia over the edge where she had to be hospitalized *and* sedated? Seneca knew the questions would come, and she would be called on to answer.

"I won't know that until she's evaluated."

"Why would they want to evaluate her? Was she hysterical?"

Someone in the car behind Seneca honked, and she realized the light had changed. "Yes." She'd lied. Dahlia wasn't hysterical. It was as if she'd gone into a trance. She believed the term was *catatonic*.

There came another pause. "I'm at Maya's parents' place in Orlando. It's going to take us a couple of days to drive up. If it was just me and Maya we would drive straight through. But with the baby we'll have to stop and stay in a motel overnight."

"Why don't you fly up, Jerome? I need you to help me with the funeral arrangements as soon as possible."

"The cost of three airlines tickets from Orlando to New York would put a real strain on my budget."

"I'll pay for the tickets."

"Are you aware how much it would cost—"

"I said I will pay you whatever it costs to fly here. Pay for the tickets, let me know, and I'll reimburse you when you get here."

"Okay. Hang up so I can go online and buy the tickets. I'll call you back when I finalize everything."

"Thank you, Jerome."

"I'm sorry about Dad, but I'm glad you were there when it happened. By the way, where's Robyn?"

"She's at Keisha's house. She doesn't know yet. I told her to meet me at the house."

"That's good. I'll talk to you later."

Seneca disconnected the call. She'd offered to underwrite the cost of Jerome, Maya and their baby to fly up to New York because she didn't want to wait two days for them to drive from Florida. Jerome and Maya were like so many other young couples trying to live a middle-class life. There were no luxury items and very few extras.

Seneca didn't have much more than Jerome, but the difference was she didn't have a mortgage, car payments or a family to support. She had only herself. What she also had was the ten-thousand-dollar signing bonus. She was also expecting payment from Booth for shooting the Cadillac ad and for appearing in Rhys's swimsuit show. There was still the matter of funeral costs, but Seneca was certain her parents had put aside monies for emergencies *and* the inevitable.

She was only twenty-one, but Seneca felt three times that age. It was as if she'd been in a rosy bubble that had exploded into millions of little irretrievable pieces. When she'd told Robyn their father had died from a heart attack, Robyn had become so distraught that she'd locked herself in her room, refusing to come out. In the end, Jerome was forced to take the door off the hinges.

Seneca managed to get her sister out of bed and into a shower where she shampooed her hair and washed her body. They got into bed together, talking quietly as they'd done when they were younger.

Dahlia was home, but monosyllabic. She didn't know where Oscar kept his financial records or official documents like his military discharge papers. Jerome had assumed the task of notifying Oscar's employer of his passing, while Seneca and Maya visited the local funeral home to make arrangements for the funeral and burial.

When Seneca called Booth to inform him that her father had died and she wasn't able to locate any of his bank documents, the agent volunteered to overnight a check, less his commission, for the Cadillac ad. True to his word, after she'd signed confirming she'd received the envelope, she opened it to find four checks payable to Seneca Houston in the amount of forty thousand dollars each. She'd earned one hundred sixty thousand dollars for a ten-second commercial. She drove to the bank, signed the checks and deposited them in her accounts.

Seneca sat in the kitchen with Jerome and Maya. Robyn had taken James Scott and sat on the porch with her nephew while keeping an eye on Dahlia.

She met her brother's eyes across the table. "Funeral expenses total twelve thousand dollars."

Jerome closed his eyes and ran a hand over his face. "Where are we going to come up with that kind of money?"

"Don't worry about it, Jerome."

His hand came down, he glaring at his sister. "What the hell do you mean, 'don't worry about it?'"

Maya placed a hand on his shoulder. "Please, Jerry."

He glared at the pale hand for a long moment before she dropped it. "Don't get into this, Maya. It concerns family."

Her face paled before becoming flushed with color. "What the hell am I, if not family? That little boy on the porch with your mother and sister is proof that I am a part of this family."

Despite the gravity of the situation, Seneca smiled. *Oh, the girl does have a backbone.* When she'd first met Maya, Seneca had felt she was too submissive. If Jerome said jump, she jumped, and that was why he'd married her.

"Answer me, Jerome Houston."

Jerome dropped his gaze. "You're right, Maya. You are a part of this family."

He knew the importance of family more than anyone sitting at the table. After Oscar married his mother he'd come to Jerome telling him that he wanted to adopt him, making him legally his son. His rationale was that they were now a family, and family members shared the same last name. It was the same thing he'd said to Maya on their wedding day. She was now a Houston and therefore family.

Maya assumed a brittle smile. "Thank you, darling." She directed her attention to her sister-in-law. "Why are you saying 'don't worry about it?'"

"I said that because I'm willing to pay for the funeral."

A frown furrowed Jerome's forehead. "You know you can't use the money from the fund set up for your education."

"I know that," Seneca said. "I have some money from one of my modeling assignments."

An expression of surprise replaced Jerome's frown. "Modeling must be good. You just gave me a check for three thousand for the airline tickets, and now you're willing to put out twelve thousand on Dad's funeral."

"We do what we have to do, Jerome. The only thing we've found is Dad's ATM card, and without his PIN it's useless. Mom's not talking, so we don't know where his financial documents are, or how much he has. She has a few credit cards in her purse, but I'm not going to try and access them to find the credit limits. I have the money, so let's not beat our gums over what doesn't need to be discussed."

She crossed that item off the list. "Have you called all of our relatives?" Seneca asked her brother.

"Yes. I gave them the day, time and address for the funeral home."

"What about his coworkers at the post office?"

"I called the postmaster and gave her the information," Jerome confirmed.

Seneca put a line through that item. "I'm thinking we should have a repast here at the house after the burial. What do you think?" Jerome exchanged a look with his wife and Seneca knew again, Jerome was thinking about money. "I'll pay to have it catered."

Jerome nodded. "That's better than asking people to bring something."

"That does it. I'm going to need you to pick out a suit for Daddy, Jerome, so I can bring it to the funeral home. I've already ordered flowers from his children and grandchild. I also ordered a separate one from Mom. Can you think of anything else we're going to need?"

"How about cars?" Maya asked.

"I ordered one limo for the immediate family. Do you think that's enough?"

Jerome counted on his fingers. "There's five of us, plus the baby, who'll be on Maya's lap. Yes, one is enough."

"We're through. I'm going over to the funeral home to give them a check, then I'll stop at Webber's to order the food."

"How many people do you anticipate coming?" Maya asked.

"Probably eighty. But, I think I'll have them cater for one hundred. There's the family, the people Mom works with, Dad's coworkers, and don't forget the people in the neighborhood. Dad had this route when he first became a letter carrier."

"Look, Seneca, when Maya and I get back on our feet financially we're going to give you something. I feel bad that you're underwriting the cost of everything."

Seneca kept all expression from her voice and face. She'd wanted to tell Jerome that Oscar Houston was *her* father *and* as his oldest child that she should assume the responsibility of paying for his funeral. She wasn't looking Jerome to repay her only because she had the money.

"I'd feel bad if I didn't have it," she said instead. "You have a house, two cars and a family, while I rent and there's only me. Now, please go and pick out a suit for Daddy so I can do what I have to do, then come back here and relax."

She was exhausted, averaging as little as four hours of sleep, which was beginning to tell on her face. Her eyes appeared shrunken, her cheeks gaunt, and the dark circles under her eyes would require layers of concealer if she were to have a photo shoot. All she wanted was to put her father in the ground—then she would have to concern herself with what to do with her mother.

Chapter Twenty-Two

When Seneca had flown from Miami to Ithaca she never would've imagined her stay would stretch beyond a month. It was nearing the end of August and she hadn't returned to New York City. She'd mailed Electra a check for rent for August and the remaining four months of the year with a note that when her lease expired December thirty-first she would be vacating the apartment.

Not only did she have enough money to rent an apartment in a "good" neighborhood, but she also had enough money to purchase a co-op. She favored the Upper West Side, so that's where she planned to concentrate her search.

Dahlia was slowly returning to the woman with whom she was familiar. She stored the flag that had draped Oscar's casket in a box on the fireplace mantel, cleaned out his closet and donated his clothes to a homeless shelter, and had retrieved her late husband's financial documents, which had been stored in a safe-deposit box at a local bank. He had an insurance policy with Robyn listed as his beneficiary. Dahlia explained that the money was earmarked for Robyn's college education.

Other financial documents revealed that Oscar had taken out a second mortgage on the house without Dahlia's knowledge, ballooning their current mortgage payments to nearly four thousand a month; it took hours to read every piece of paper in the box, but Seneca was able to locate what Oscar had done with the money: he'd invested in a new Florida retirement community. Unfortunately, the builder had filed for bankruptcy when the housing bubble burst. His investors suffered a double loss: money and unfinished structures.

"Mom, you're going to have to put together a budget," Seneca told Dahlia.

"I don't need no damned budget."

Ignoring her mother's acerbic tone, Seneca smiled. "Yes, you do. Do you know how much your mortgage payments are?"

"Why would I know that? Oscar paid all the bills."

"Mom, the mortgage is more than four thousand a month. And don't forget, you have your car and Daddy's truck. In another couple of months you'll have to heat the house and—"

"I don't need you lecturing me about what is none of your business," Dahlia snapped angrily. "You only paid for Oscar's funeral out of guilt."

Seneca narrowed her eyes at Dahlia. "What did I have to feel guilty about?"

"You killed him."

The venom dripping from Dahlia was so potent it was palpable. Seneca stared at her mother, complete surprise freezing her features. Dahlia blamed her for Oscar's heart attack, when a medical examination revealed he'd had a history of heart disease—disease he'd kept hidden from his family.

"Guilt tribute," Dahlia continued, sneering. "You felt bad about killing your daddy, so you tried to cover up everything by throwing the money around you made posing naked." She shook her head. "Where did I go wrong? I tried to raise you and Robyn to be ladies, but you wind up with everyone talking about you sucking some boy's dick, while Robyn brings some no-account, wannabe pimp into our home and spreads her legs for him. The only reason I didn't tell Oscar was because I knew it would kill him."

But my coming home to visit my family killed my father, Seneca thought. She knew arguing with Dahlia wasn't going to change anything, so she decided on another approach. "Mom, I know you don't want me and Robyn to repeat your life, because you were a teenage mother. I'm twenty-one, too old to be one, and Robyn told me that you found condoms in the house. I got on her about it. But you should be grateful that she did use protection."

Dahlia fell silent, and Seneca prayed she'd gotten through to her mother. She could not have imagined what the older woman had gone through when she had to tell her parents she'd been sleeping with a married man who'd gotten her pregnant, that she'd slept with him because he'd given her money and gifts, making her nothing more than a prostitute.

"You want gratitude, Seneca?"

"What are you talking about, Mother?"

Dahlia's delicate features were frozen into a sinister grin. "The only thing I'd be grateful for is if you leave *my* house and never come back."

Seneca jumped, the chair she'd just vacated clattering noisily to the kitchen floor. "Do you know something, Mother? I'm going to grant your wish. I'm leaving."

Turning on her heels, she stalked out of the kitchen, stomped up the staircase and into her bedroom to pack her clothes. She'd had enough. She'd tried over and over to make peace with her mother. Over and over holding her tongue so she wouldn't be looked upon as disrespectful.

"Grandma, why did you have to die?" she sobbed, opening and slamming dresser draws as she threw clothes haphazardly into her bag. Whenever Dahlia got into a funk, Ileana would come to pick up her grandbabies. Her excuse was she'd wanted to give her daughter-in-law a break. When Seneca told her grandmother that Dahlia was crazy, Ileana hushed her, saying she suffered from stress and depression.

"Where are you going?"

Seneca turned to find Robyn standing in the doorway. "I'm going back home."

Robyn walked into the bedroom. "Why?"

"I have a modeling assignment," she lied smoothly. Seneca didn't want to bring her sister into her altercation with their mother.

"When are you coming back?"

"I don't know, Robbie. I have a show in Paris in a couple of weeks and I also have to look for an apartment."

"You're moving?"

She nodded. "I'm going to buy a co-op."

Robyn sat on the foot of Seneca's bed, watching her throw things into her luggage. "Why aren't you folding anything?"

"I'm in a hurry," she lied again. "I have to get to the airport. If I don't get the seven o'clock flight, then I'll have to wait until tomorrow, and that's going to be too late."

What she planned was to take a taxi to the regional airport, then rent a car and drive down to New York City. Although Mitchell had given her a key to his loft, she would call to let him know she was coming back. She'd reached a decision to take the photographer up on his offer to live with him until she found her own place. Meanwhile, she planned to move all of her possessions from the brownstone and into storage.

"You're going to have to look after Mom, Robbie."

Robyn nodded. "I know. I don't know why, but I'm getting used to her craziness. Sometimes she can be so sweet, then *bam!* she turns into this freaky-ass monster that is so scary. One of my friends says Mom is bipolar."

"Is your friend a doctor?"

"No."

"Then tell her to keep her comments to herself and stop trying to diagnose what's wrong with people who don't concern her."

"I can't tell her that, Seneca."

"Why not, Robyn?"

"Because she's my friend. She's the only good friend I have."

Seneca wanted to tell her sister that Electra was the only good friend she'd had in the whole of the eight million who made up New York City, and she'd turned on her. "Just watch your friends, Robbie."

She finished packing, then called for a taxi to take her to the Ithaca Tompkins Regional airport. Once in the taxi she would reserve a rental car. She would also call Jerome to let him know she was returning to New York City and that he should call Dahlia several times a week to check up on her. Even if Dahlia resented her interference, she'd welcome Jerome's. Seneca knew Dahlia loved Oscar but had always suspected she'd loved Jerome's father more.

"Let's go, ladies! We have a show to put on. Butterfly, you're up first."

Hopping on one foot while pulling the jeweled strap of a stiletto over her heel, Seneca shouldered her way through waiflike models, makeup, wardrobe and hairstylists to take her position at the head of the line. She still had to pinch herself to make certain she wasn't dreaming. She was in Paris, the City of Lights. There were eight models, each wearing a collection from an up-and-coming designer. Seneca was on hand to introduce the world to Luis Navarro's Butterfly line.

She recognized the music coming from the powerful sound system. It was Enigma. Seneca had found herself intrigued with their electronic old-world, New Age sound. The music was conducive to the setting. The show was held in a restored château several kilometers from the capital city.

Peering through the curtain, she spotted her cheering section sitting in the front row. Booth Gordon and Mitchell Leon had come over together on a private jet. Rhys Calhoun, who was already in Paris, had joined the other two men.

Luis had designed a collection that included lingerie, evening gowns, sportswear, a dress that was draped across her body and an outfit with a vivid jungle, or as Luis referred to it, tribal print. She would begin with a gold sporty jacket, slacks and a sheer white man-tailored shirt and end with an elegant wedding gown.

She checked the front of the blouse. Luis hadn't buttoned the top three buttons. He wanted enough of a display of flesh to titillate. Seneca knew she was going to do more than titillate once she began walking. Her unbound breasts would definitely put on a show of their own. Her hair was styled for simplicity: blown-out and pulled tightly into a chignon with a large jeweled butterfly pin resting on the coil of hair at the nape of her long neck. The makeup artist had emphasized her eyes with dramatic shadows, liner and individually applied lashes. Her mouth was a soft rose pink, an almost muted contrast to her eyes.

"I want you to stomp your ass off, *Mariposa*."

Seneca smiled at Luis. He'd finally gotten his big break, and she intended to make him proud. Leaning forward, she pressed her cheek to his while affecting an air kiss. "I will," she promised.

"One minute."

It was her cue to ready herself to introduce the Parisian fashion world to Butterfly. Nothing had changed, only the venue. Instead of being in Miami, Florida, she was in Paris, France. Her feet glided down the runway to gasps and a flash of bulbs. She heard comments from "the Amazon is magnificent" to "she's the hottest thing since sliced toast." The other comments went past her because she didn't understand French. Halfway down the runway her stoic expression changed when she winked at Booth and Mitchell. Luis wanted her to stomp and she did not more stomp.

Butterfly was soaring higher than she had in Miami, and by the time she'd returned wearing a black lace demi-bra and matching bikini panties, black silk bows on her hips moving sensuously with every step, she felt the heat from every gaze on her tall, slender body. When she paused the requisite three seconds, she gave them an unobstructed view of the butterfly tattoo at the base of her spine.

Seneca felt light-headed and struggled to breathe when she stepped into the evening gown. "Someone, please give me some water," she gasped. Miraculously, she grasped a bottle of water and almost poured it down her throat. The spinning stopped and she nodded to the dresser. "Finish."

She picked up the skirt of the platinum silk, chiffon and tulle garment embroidered with thousands of tiny pearls and slipped her feet into a pair of matching silk pumps. Bending slightly, she permitted the woman who'd dressed her to slip a silver necklace with a brilliant crystal-encrusted butterfly around her neck. Matching earrings were inserted in her pierced lobes.

Pressing her lips together, she nodded at the backstage co-ordinator. She was ready for her final walk. Yards of fabric trailed behind her as she floated like a graceful swan down the runway. Each time she stopped, took her hands off her waist and rolled her wrists a roar shook the large room. Smiling from under lowered lashes, she twirled, fabric billowing out from her feet, and retraced her steps. The crowd went wild when she winked at the photographers racing along the catwalk to capture her image for posterity.

Luis was there to meet her when she collapsed into his arms. "Don't fall apart now, Butterfly. We have to take our final walk."

Her head moved up and down like a bobble-head doll's. "Okay."

Seneca doubted whether she would've been able to support herself if Luis hadn't put his arm around her waist when it came time for them to walk the catwalk together. She felt a resurgence of energy with the thunderous applause. Suddenly it hit her—Butterfly was high, high on fame and the newfound power she wielded over the fashion industry. She knew some of the people crowded into the great hall at the château were fashion professionals while others were photographers and journalists. But those who'd come because of sheer curiosity had witnessed something in the making. Seneca Houston, also known as Butterfly, had become fashion's new darling and supermodel.

Seneca, her hand resting on Luis's jacket, walked into the private cocktail party and was met with applause. Four-inch heels and the black silk slip dress floating around her feet made her look thinner than she actually was.

"They love you, Luis," she said close to his ear.

"No, *Mariposa,* they love *you.*"

"I'm just the vessel through which they see your designs."

Luis covered her hand with his. "You are the vessel that inspires me."

Seneca jumped slightly when a flute of champagne was thrust at her. A wide smile parted her lips when she realized it was Booth. "Thanks," she said, accepting the pale bubbling wine.

His blue-green eyes were sparkling. "You were absolutely magnificent. I didn't want to believe Rhys when he told me about the Miami show. I'm willing to bet that every man watching you had a hard-on, yours truly included among them."

Seneca blushed, then put the flute to her mouth and took a sip of the cool liquid. It was excellent. "I try, Booth."

Leaning closer, he brushed a kiss over her soft lips. "You don't have to try, baby."

She didn't know why, but Seneca felt uncomfortable. Perhaps it was what Booth said about having a hard-on, or it was because he'd kissed her. She hoped he didn't have thoughts about crossing the line between agent and client. "Could someone please get me something to eat?"

"What do you want?" Luis asked.

She smiled. "Anything salty."

He lifted his eyebrows questioningly. "Caviar?"

"That'll do."

Waiting until the designer walked away to get Seneca's request, Booth cupped her elbow and led her to where they couldn't be overheard. "I just want to tell you to clear your calendar for the next five years to eight years."

"Why?"

"I've booked you for Fashion Week in Bangkok, Buenos

Aires, of course Paris, Mumbai, London, New York City, Hong Kong, Kingston for Caribbean Fashion Week. Dubai, Cape Town, Barcelona…" He stopped, trying to recall the list. "Oh, there's Auckland, New Zealand, Montréal and Milan. I'm certain there are many others, but I can't remember them right now."

"But I'll never be home," she said in protest.

"The schedule begins with New York, followed by London, Milan and Paris. These four cities are the traditional big four fashion weeks. They are followed by new emerging fashion weeks globally. I promised to make you a supermodel, and you are, Butterfly. Isn't that what you wanted?" Booth asked when he saw her crestfallen expression.

"Yes. It is what I want."

Seneca did want to become a supermodel, but at what cost? She wanted to buy property—some place she came home to where she could be Seneca and not Butterfly. Even before her final walk she'd felt faint, as if the crowd had sucked up all of her strength.

"I got a call from the producer of a daytime soap who wanted you to come to L.A. to audition for a limited run, but I told him you'd just lost your father and wouldn't be available. I thought it best you stay away from television at this time. I'd prefer you stick to fashion: runway shows, magazine covers and photo shoots. There's more money in it and higher visibility. I'm going to try and get you on the cover of *Vogue, Vanity Fair, W, British Vogue, Elle* and the *Sports Illustrated* swimsuit issue. I want you to become most men's fantasy."

"That sounds scary, Booth."

"Don't worry, baby. I'll make certain you move into a very secure building and whenever you travel you'll have a personal bodyguard with you. No more commercial carriers and taxis.

It's going to be private jets and car service. After all, I have to protect my client."

She gave him a strained smile—a smile she didn't feel. Seneca had told Booth she wanted to be a supermodel yet hadn't thought about what went with it. There was no doubt she would make a lot of money, but what good was money when she didn't have time to enjoy it?

Her agent had asked for the next eight years of her life, and she would give it to him and an additional two. By the time she celebrated her thirtieth birthday, she planned to get out and go back to school. She'd promised her grandmother and parents that she would finish college, and if she survived the world of high-fashion modeling, she would.

Luis returned with a small plate with caviar on wafer-thin crackers. He fed her one, and she closed her eyes when the salty fish eggs exploded in her mouth like Pop Rocks. She took another sip of champagne and opened her mouth for another.

At that very instant a flash bulb caught the scene of Luis feeding her caviar while she held a flute of champagne between her fingers. The expression on her face was blissful and serene. It was only one of her that appeared in the fashion section of newspapers around the world. Most captions read: *Stunning!*

Chapter Twenty-Three

Seneca opened her eyes when she felt the car stop. She'd slept during the transatlantic flight, but her body still felt as if she'd been punched repeatedly. Peering out the side window, she noticed a man standing about thirty feet from the entrance to the building where she'd purchased a duplex.

"Dwight."

The muscular man sitting beside the driver nodded. "I see him."

After so many years, she knew the drill. Do not get out of the car until her bodyguard was beside her. She'd gotten a restraining order prohibiting the tabloid reporter to come within two hundred feet of where she lived, but it was apparent the man was either persistent or he liked being locked up.

Dwight Hudson opened the passenger-side door and stepped onto the sidewalk. His broad shoulders and six-foot-four frame of unadulterated muscle were imposing *and* threatening. He glared at the reporter who had had the nerve to move to the end of the block. It was only then that Dwight returned to the town car, opening the rear door and extending his hand to assist Seneca Houston alight.

"Thank you, Dwight," she whispered. She'd come down with a case of laryngitis within days of arriving in Rome. Her throat didn't hurt, but it was frustrating not being able to talk.

"Don't move," he ordered again. "I need to get your luggage." The driver lifted a lever, opening the trunk.

Seneca closed her eyes again while inhaling a lungful of humid New York City air. No city smelled like the one that been her home for the past four years. She'd come to the Big Apple at eighteen, with stars in her eyes when she'd enrolled in New York University. She'd planned to become a movie director, but a meeting with an aspiring fashion designer had become a temporary detour. Seneca thought of it as temporary because she hadn't given up her dream to direct movies.

"Miss Houston, is it true you were once married to Phillip Kingston?"

With wide eyes, she turned to find the reporter standing only a few feet away. Then, without warning, the flash of light distorted her vision. "Dwight!" His name came out in a croak instead of a scream.

The bodyguard moved quickly, reaching under his jacket for the firearm concealed in a shoulder holster. However, he wasn't quick enough when two men took off running in opposite directions. He rushed back to his client. "Are you okay?"

Seneca nodded. "They just startled me," she rasped.

"Go into the lobby and wait for me while I get your luggage." Dwight watched as the liveried doorman waited with Seneca in the building vestibule before he returned to the car to retrieve her luggage. Five minutes later he left her bags on the floor near a closet in a spacious entryway.

"Call me if you need me."

Seneca rolled her head on her neck. "I don't plan to go anywhere for the next three days." She extended her hand, staring up at the man with the dark-brown shaved pate. "Thank you, Dwight."

He took her hand, which disappeared in his large one. "You're welcome, Miss Houston." Dropping her hand, he walked to the door, opened it and then closed it softly behind him.

Kicking off her running shoes, Seneca slowly made her way into the living room and the staircase leading to the second floor. After showering, she planned to get into bed and sleep until hunger or nature forced her from it.

She was exhausted from the never-ending shows, posing for magazine layouts and a relationship with a financial planner that was going nowhere. Malcolm had begun whining that they never got to see each other, and the last time she listened to his voice on her voice mail, she deleted the message, then called to tell him she thought it best if they stopped dating.

Seneca stopped halfway up the staircase, sighed, then continued to the top. Booth had said she had eight good years in the business. Her projection was ten. Now she wasn't certain she could make five. At twenty-two, she was contemplating retirement.

Reaching into the pocket of her hoodie, she took out her cell phone. She'd neglected to pack her charger, and after two days she had a dead phone. Plugging in the cell, she walked over to the bedside table and checked the house phone. A blinking red light indicated someone had called.

"Damn," she whispered while staring at the display. She had eleven missed calls. Scrolling through the CID, Seneca felt her heart lurch in her chest. All of the calls were from her brother. Without bothering to activate voice mail, she punched in Jerome's number.

"Hello."

Her sister-in-law had answered. "Maya, this is Seneca. What's going on?"

"Hold on, Seneca. Let me get Jerry for you."

"What's up, Jerome?" she asked when hearing her brother's voice.

"Where the hell have you been? And why weren't you answering your cell?"

"I just got back from Rome. My cell is dead because I forgot to bring my charger. What is going on?"

"Why didn't you tell me Mom wasn't paying her mortgage?"

"Me!" Oh, how Seneca wished she could scream. "I told you to check with her to make certain she was paying her bills. How far behind is she?"

"They've foreclosed on the house."

"What!"

"The bank took the house and they've sold it to someone else. Our mother and sister have a thirty-day vacate order."

Biting on her lip, Seneca willed the tears welling in her eyes not to fall. "Jerome, you know Mom won't speak to me, that's why I told you to check in with her at least once a week."

"I do, but she says everything is okay."

"How can it be okay when she's about to be homeless?"

"That's why I called you, Seneca. We have to figure out something."

"We! What's this *we* shit, Jerome? I ask you to do one thing for me and you drop the ball."

"Cut the bullshit, Seneca! You don't have chick or child, while I have to take care of my family. Maya is pregnant again. This time with twins."

Seneca didn't want to believe it. Her brother was living on one salary while his wife managed to get herself pregnant again. She'd promised Jerome that she would return to teaching when James Scott turned two.

She cradled her forehead. "I can't think right now. I'll call you tomorrow."

"Remember, they have to be out by the end of September."

"There's no way I'm going to allow my mother or my sister to be homeless. Goodbye, Jerome." She slammed the receiver so hard in the cradle that Seneca feared she'd broken the phone.

"Mother, mother, mother. Why have you become the bane of my existence?"

Seneca picked up the phone when she heard the buzzer from the building lobby. "Miss Houston."

"There's a Jerome Houston asking for you."

"Please send him up." She'd arranged for her brother to fly into LaGuardia airport, where a driver awaited his arrival. Whatever she had to say to her brother needed to be done in person.

Seneca stood at the door when Jerome stepped out of the elevator, watching as he came closer. He'd lost weight, and she wondered if it was deliberate or if he wasn't eating. Tilting her chin, she offered her cheek for his kiss. "Thank you for coming."

"It's your dime, Seneca."

She rolled her eyes at him, but he didn't see her because he was staring over her shoulder. "Come in."

Jerome Houston walked into his sister's apartment, his jaw dropping in awe. It was like a layout in *Architectural Digest*.

His gaze went to the high ceilings and the curving staircase leading to another floor.

"Very nice," he drawled facetiously. "It looks as if you're doing well for yourself."

Seneca led him into a room where she spent most of her time whenever she had the luxury of leisure time in her home. "I'm working hard, not smart, Jerome." Bright sunlight poured in through the floor-to-ceiling windows. She gestured to a table set for two in a corner. "I know you want to get back to D.C. before the last shuttle, so I arranged for you to share dinner with me."

Instead of being buoyed by his sister's success, Jerome suddenly felt a rush of resentment so bitter that he believed he'd just downed a potion of bile. It was as if she was showing off. All she had to do was pick up the phone and order airline tickets, arrange for a chauffer to carry his bags and drive him wherever he wanted. She lived in a duplex in a luxury high-rise overlooking Central Park. She jetted all over the world, and since she'd stared out from the cover of *Vogue* she'd become fashion's "It" girl.

"I know you like steak, so my chef will prepare it any way you like."

Inky-black eyebrows lifted in an equally dark face with features much too delicate for a man. "You have a chef?"

"He only cooks for me when I spend more than a week in town. If he didn't cook for me I wouldn't eat. Most times I'm too tired," Seneca explained when Jerome gave her an incredulous stare.

"But you're a fabulous cook, Seneca."

"Thanks, but I can't remember the last time I cooked for myself. Why don't you wash up before you sit down. There's a bathroom through that door." She pointed to the door at the far end of the room. "How do you like your steak?"

"Medium well," Jerome threw over his shoulder as he walked to the bathroom.

Seneca halted putting a forkful of spinach in her mouth when she watched Jerome cut into a piece of aged rib eye steak. He was shoveling food into his mouth as if he hadn't eaten in days. She made a mental note to send him an order of frozen steaks from a gourmet steakhouse.

"I want to pay you to take care of Mom and Robbie."

Jerome stopped chewing, his eyes wide. "You want to pay me?"

"Yes," she said confidently. What she was going to propose to Jerome she'd given a great deal of thought to. "I know you haven't completed renovating your house. I'll pay for the renovations. And I'll also pay for an architect to draw up plans to add an extension, so Mom and Robbie can have their own place with two bedrooms, two baths, full kitchen, living room and dining area. There is space where they can park their cars."

Jerome set down his knife and fork. "You want our mother and sister to live with me and Maya."

"Are you listening to what I've been saying, Jerome? They won't be living in your house. The addition will be like a guesthouse. When you told me that Maya is pregnant again, I knew there wouldn't be enough room for two more people. Mom's social security for Robyn will stop once she turns eighteen, and Daddy's stipulation that Mom can't collect his pension until she's fifty-five isn't going to kick in for another ten years. And because of this, I'll pay you and Maya to look after them. I had someone look into how much Maya would earn if she'd returned to teaching. I'll pay you what she would earn—before taxes."

"Will we have to pay taxes on the money?"

"No, Jerome. It will be a gift."

"You're going pay to complete the renovations, build a guesthouse *and* pay me and Maya to look in on Mom and Robyn?"

"You're going to do more than "look" in, Jerome. You're going to take care of them like you do your son. Robbie tells me Mom has been acting strangely. She's forgetting things, names, and she's having a problem getting words out. I want you to take her to a neurologist."

"Mom's too young to have Alzheimer's."

"She can be the exception. Either you do it, Jerome, or I'll bring Robbie here to live with me. I'll hire a live-in house-keeper who will look after her when I'm out of town or out of the country. She only has another year before she's off to college. Somehow I will get Mom evaluated, and if she is ill, then I'll obtain power of attorney to have her committed to a skilled nursing facility. That way the pressure's off you and Maya, especially since you're growing your family."

"You have money like that to throw around?"

"How much money I make or have is none of your concern," Seneca retorted. "Talk it over with Maya, and let me know tomorrow if you will or won't do it."

"Why the rush, Seneca?"

"I have to be in Madrid the second week in October, and I'd like to get them settled before that time. If you agree, then I want you to register Robbie in your high school. I'll arrange for someone to pack up the house and put everything in stor-age. I know there are furnished apartments in D.C. that offer short-term lease agreements. Mom and Robbie can live in an apartment until their place is ready.

"I will not leave the States worrying whether my sister and mother are being taken care of. It doesn't matter whether

Mom hates me, or she doesn't want me in her house. I will not abandon her, Jerome."

"I won't either. I don't have to talk it over with Maya. Dahlia Houston is my mother, and I *can't* abandon her. She and Robyn will move in with us."

Two hours after Jerome Houston walked into her condo, Seneca closed the door behind him. The driver in front of the building waited to take him back to the airport for his return flight to D.C. She wasn't certain her brother was willing to become a caretaker for their mother, but knowing someone was looking after Dahlia had alleviated some of her anxiety.

She still blamed Jerome for not being as vigilant as he should've been. However, she was certain that would change with Dahlia living within earshot.

Chapter Twenty-Four

Seneca had been awake for hours, yet she couldn't force her legs to move so she could get out of bed. It was as if she was temporarily paralyzed. It didn't take the IQ of a rocket scientist to tell her that she was exhausted—totally burned out.

Butterfly had strutted up and down runways on every continent, with the exception of Antarctica, for thirteen years. She'd appeared in fashion-week shows from Amsterdam to Zagreb.

Butterfly had become a multimillion-dollar supermodel who'd didn't know how much she earned until Booth mailed her the requisite 1099s. What had remained constant were the checks that were transferred from her account to her brother's for their mother's care. Dahlia, now fifty-five, was a shadow of her former self.

She had begun the practice of going to D.C. during her downtime, only because her mother didn't recognize her and therefore couldn't order her out of her house.

Robyn had finally graduated from college the year before.

She'd dropped out in her sophomore year in an attempt to break into modeling. Although she'd signed with a leading modeling agency, designers were reluctant to use her because they didn't want another Butterfly. Robyn blamed Seneca for not using her influence to help her, and had stopped speaking to her for several years.

The sisters reconciled after Robyn, who'd become engaged to a legislative aide, asked Seneca to be her maid of honor. The wedding had become a media spectacle because supermodel Butterfly was a part of the wedding party. Seneca's gift had been a check for the down payment on the property Robyn and her husband had planned to purchase.

Seneca had discovered recently that everything annoyed her: loud noises, ribald laughter and people who invaded her personal space. And those people were the media. There had been a time when she'd pose and preen as if on cue from a director, stopped to scrawl her signature on napkins, scraps of paper, even skin, but that too had changed. The reporter who'd harangued her constantly about being married to Phillip Kingston was currently serving a year in jail. He'd violated his order of protection and had continued to stalk her.

A sad smile parted her lips. Phillip Kingston. Other than Britney Spears, they probably were in the running for shortest celebrity marriage. Phillip had shocked the sports world when he decided not to renew his basketball contract, citing that his passion for practicing medicine had surpassed playing ball. Gordon didn't appear fazed that he'd lost his most valuable client, because he hadn't had to go looking for big-name clients—they'd come looking for him to represent them. Seneca moved, rolling over to pick up the cordless phone on the bedside table. She dialed seven digits and felt a surge of courage when she heard his voice.

"Hello, beautiful."

"You ought to stop, Booth."

"Why should I, when it's true?"

"Dial down the bull, Booth."

"What's going on, Seneca?" His voice had changed, becoming sober.

"I'm retiring from modeling."

"You can't!"

"I can, Booth! I'm tired, burned out. I've been awake for hours, yet I can't force myself to get out of bed."

"Look, baby—"

"Don't fuckin' baby me, Booth! You hear me, but you're not listening to me. I'm not eating, losing weight I can't afford to lose. I'm five-ten and my weight has dropped from one twenty-five to one-ten. I'm willing to bet my next check that most doctors would tell me that I'm dangerously close to being anorexic."

"I hear you, baby. What if you take some time off?"

Seneca stared at the bedroom ceiling, her eyes tracing the design of the crown molding. "How much time are you talking about?"

"Three months. Six months. You tell me."

"Six months," she said.

"You've got it, Butterfly. And to let you know I support you, I'm offering my vacation home in the Dominican Republic. You can stay there for as long as you want. I'll let the staff know you're coming, and everything you want or need will be at your disposal. Let me know when you're ready to leave and I'll have my assistant make travel arrangements."

Seneca thought about Booth's offer, her sluggish mind clearing as if jolted by an lightning bolt. "What if you put out a press release announcing my retirement? I go into hiding for six months, and when I resurface you can capitalize on the media hype."

What she hadn't told her agent was that her future plans did not include returning to the runway. She'd earned enough money to support her current lifestyle. There was no mortgage on her condo, she hadn't made risky investments and she was debt-free. Even if she didn't work another day in her life she would be able to live a comfortable, uneventful life.

"You've missed your calling, baby. You should consider a second career in television. You'd do great as a correspondent with one of those entertainment shows like *The Insider, Entertainment Today* or *Extra*."

"No, thanks, Booth. I've been the topic of their salacious innuendos much too often to join their ranks."

"How would you like your own talk show?"

Seneca paused. She'd always wanted to be behind the camera, not in front of it. However, having her own talk show was something she'd possibly consider. Since the Cadillac spot she'd shot with Phillip, which took the honor of being the sexiest Super Bowl commercial, she'd become a much-sought-after model/actress.

Booth had secured contracts for her for cosmetics, jeans, perfume and luggage companies. She'd appeared in ads for Chanel Boutiques, Patek Philippe, and all of the major designers, including Yves Saint Laurent, Michael Kors, Gucci, Marc Jacobs and Giorgio Armani. Her face on the cover of *Vogue* had introduced her to the world; however, it was when her swimsuit-clad body appeared on the *Sports Illustrated* swimsuit issue, not once but twice that she was acknowledged as a sex symbol.

"That's something I would consider," she told the agent.

"Let me work on it, Seneca. It just might take six months before I hear anything. Now, when do you think you'll be ready to leave?"

"Not until next week. I have to go to D.C. to see my mother."

What was there to think about? It was winter in the northeast. Snow had lingered on grassy surfaces after a storm had dumped more than eighteen inches of the white stuff on the tristate area the week before. She had to stop her mail and alert the cleaning service that she would be away for an extended period of time.

"I could arrange for you to fly out of Dulles International instead of you coming back to New York."

"That sounds like a plan. I'll call you a couple of days before I finish my business in D.C."

Booth Gordon gently replaced the receiver in the cradle when he wanted to slam it down. When he recognized the number that had appeared on his private line, he'd thought Seneca Houston was calling to chat. It was something they did every couple of months. However, her pronouncement that was she was retiring was totally unexpected. Even at thirty-three, after thirteen years in the business, she hadn't lost her edge; she was still was the world's top supermodel. When girls were asked about role models, Butterfly's name was always at the top of the list.

She'd become a celebrity without the negative baggage that followed many young women who'd become victims of their own success and carefully scripted hype. Seneca had walked the red carpet at various media events with A-list actors, athletes and the occasional bad-boy hip-hop performer. All of her high-profile liaisons were put together by the agency's publicity department, and Seneca had become the consummate actress in whatever role they wanted her to play.

Booth suspected she was seeing someone in New York but had managed not to involve himself in her private life.

His attorney had taken care of her annulment from Phillip Kingston, quickly and quietly. However, there had been one persistent reporter from a leading tabloid who was like a dog with a bone when he'd uncovered information about Butterfly and King Phillip's secret marriage. His subsequent investigation was stymied when documentation attesting to the Vegas marriage was mysteriously deleted from the records when a computer virus attached itself to the files, causing the system to crash.

Disclosure of their short-lived marriage would've proved damaging if word of Kingston physically abusing women were made public. In the end it had become a moot point when Kingston quit basketball to attend medical school. Booth hadn't been bothered about losing Kingston because of his disdain of domestic abuse—whether verbal or physical. Seeing his mother verbally abuse his father on a daily basis would stay with him for the rest of his life.

Booth didn't want to lose Seneca, not because he would lose twenty percent of everything she earned but because he was using her account to launder money for his cousin. She was his only client who didn't call and hound him for her checks.

He'd hired a PI to do an extensive investigation, including DNA testing, on Carter Browning. The tests revealed that Carter *was* his uncle's son *and* his cousin. It had taken a while, but one night when his younger cousin had had too much to drink he'd let it slip that his client was a member of the Russian mob who was involved in everything from drugs to human trafficking.

When he'd asked Carter for the damaging tapes, the younger man refused to return them, claiming they were his insurance just in case any "shit jumped off." In the end, Booth had to admit that he'd been out-hustled by an Ivy League–educated preppy thug. Joan Powers had gotten her revenge. Wherever the duplicitous bitch was, he hoped she would burn in hell.

Seneca maneuvered the rental car into the driveway leading to the rear of the property, where Jerome had built a charming two-bedroom apartment for their mother. She didn't see Maya's minivan and assumed she'd gone out. All her children were now in school. The money she gave Jerome to take care of their mother allowed Maya the luxury of being a stay-at-home mom.

The clothes she needed for a tropical climate were in the luggage in the trunk of the car. She planned to drive the rental to the airport and leave it before boarding the jet Booth had arranged to take her to Punta Cana. Reaching into her tote, she removed a set of keys. She'd asked Jerome to make her a set of keys to the apartment. Seneca unlocked the door, wrinkling her nose when a foul odor hit her. Dropping her tote, she closed the door and walked through the foyer and into the living room, the odor growing stronger.

Seneca felt her knees go weak when she stood at the entrance to the bathroom. Her mother sat on a hospital potty chair, her wrists secured to the arms of the chair by restraints. Dahlia's salt-and-pepper hair was uncombed and she was thin, much thinner than she'd been during her last visit.

Curses, raw and savage, spewed from her mouth when she saw the condition in which her mother had been left. Moving quickly, she undid the restraints. "It's okay, Mama," she crooned when Dahlia looked up at her with the familiar expression frozen on her face.

She managed to get her mother into the tub to bathe her, beginning with shampooing her hair. Dahlia's hair was short, so she toweled it dry instead of using a blow-dryer. She guided her to a chair in the bedroom, raising her feet to the footstool, then stripped the bed and changed the linen. Seneca put her mother into bed, covering her with a lightweight comforter.

Some of her white-hot rage had subsided when she'd cleaned the bathroom and lit a scented candle to offset the cloying odor of feces. Seneca knew if Maya had been there she would've kicked the bitch's ass. Her trifling sister-in-law hadn't returned when she'd managed to get Dahlia to eat a small portion of oatmeal to which she'd added an overripe banana.

"It's okay," she repeated, gently wiping Dahlia's mouth with a warm facecloth. "I'm going to get you out of this hell."

She remembered researching skilled nursing facilities when her mother's condition had taken a drastic decline, but Jerome had reassured her that he and Maya could care for her. She'd trusted her brother to keep his word, but apparently he'd lied. There were dishes in the kitchen sink that had to have been there for days. And how could Maya go out and leave her mother-in-law tied to a chair?

Opening and closing utility drawers in the kitchen, Seneca found the sheet of paper listing the facilities. Thankfully, she'd visited each one to assess the level of care. She dialed the number of the one she'd starred. The admissions director confirmed that they had a bed and that if she brought in the patient they could begin the intake process. A staff neurologist would evaluate Dahlia to ascertain the level of care she required.

Seneca liked the facility because it was clean and modern and the doctors and nurses who were on staff were experts in geriatric care. After packing a bag with clothes and personal items Dahlia would need, she dressed her for the weather and assisted her out to the car. Maya was arriving when they were leaving. She got out of the minivan cradling shopping bags bearing the names of upscale shops.

"Where are you going?" she called out cheerfully as Seneca backed out of the wide driveway. Maya wore a three-quarter bottle-green shearling that had to have cost more than a thousand dollars. One thing Seneca had learned to recognize was quality when it came to clothes.

She forced a smile when she wanted to get and put her hands around the woman's neck, squeezing until she stopped breathing. "I'm taking Mom for a drive." Her tone was so sweet and syrupy that Seneca almost laughed aloud. "We'll probably stop and get something to eat before we come back."

"You know she doesn't eat much."

Seneca nodded. "I know. That's why I'm going to try and order something she likes." She waved. "I'll see you later."

Seneca sat, shocked, when the doctor detailed the results of Dahlia Houston's medical examination. "You should be thankful you brought your mother in when you did, Ms. Houston. She doesn't have Alzheimer's disease but something much worse. Your mother has frontotemporal dementia, or what we call FTD. It's typically a fast-progressing neurodegenerative disease that can lead patients to experience speech and memory difficulties."

A shudder raced throughout Seneca as she digested this information. "When you mention frontotemporal, I take that to mean the brain." The doctor nodded. "Can the condition be slowed or corrected with surgery?"

"I'm sorry, but the disease is incurable and will only get worse with time. Your mother requires twenty-four-hour care."

"What about medication?" she asked.

"Some patients react favorably to selective SSRIs, or serotonin reuptake inhibitors. They are the same drugs used to treat depression and anxiety."

"How many years do you expect people who're diagnosed with FTD to survive?"

"A rough estimate is five to ten years. What I don't know is how long your mother has had the disease."

"It started, or we became aware of it, about ten years ago."

"Maybe your mother is one of the luckier one who will beat the odds. I'm hopeful, because there are new drugs coming out for these types of disorders, and an increase in research into curing the disease. I give you my word that your mother will be well cared for here. We have a complete open-door policy where we encourage family members to stop in any time of the day or night to look in on their loved ones."

Smiling, Seneca offered her hand. "Thank you, Dr. Marks."

"You're welcome." He pushed a pad across the desk stamped with the logo of a pharmaceutical. "Would you mind giving me an autograph? My teenage daughter will think I'm the coolest dad in the world when I tell her that I talked to Butterfly."

Taking his pen, she scrawled her signature on the square of paper, then drew the facsimile of a butterfly underneath. Pushing to her feet, she walked out of the doctor's office and to the room where her mother had been assigned. The facility, situated on two hundred acres in northern Virginia, looked like a small private college with apartment-like dorm rooms. She'd requested a private room for Dahlia. Medicare and Oscar's pension would cover most of the cost, while Seneca would subsidize the balance.

She found her mother sitting in a chair watching a flat-screen television. Seneca smiled. "Mom?"

Dahlia looked at her, her brow furrowing as she tried remembering who she was. "What a pretty girl." That said, she returned her attention to the images on the screen.

"Stay well, Mama," she whispered.

Seneca felt a gentle peace, knowing her mother was going to get the best medical care available. She returned to the parking area to retrieve her car. Her hands grasped the steering wheel in a death grip as she followed road signs leading back to D.C. Her first impulse was to check into a hotel near the airport, then call Booth to let him know she'd taken care of her business and she was ready to leave the country. But that couldn't happen until she confronted her brother and sister-in-law.

Maya answered the door, peering around Seneca. "Where's Mom?"

"She's in bed." Seneca didn't tell her *which* bed.

"Come on in. I just put the kids to bed."

"That's okay. I'm not going to stay long. Where's Jerome?"

"He's in his study marking papers. I'll get him."

Seneca sat down on a butter-soft leather sofa. The renovations and furnishings had turned a formerly dilapidated house into a showplace. She didn't stand when Jerome walked in and leaned over to kiss her cheek.

He sat on a matching chair, Maya hovering over his back. "Maya told me you took Mom out today."

Her face was a mask of stone. "I did. In fact, I took her out of here."

Jerome leaned forward. "What are you saying?"

"Our mother is now in a skilled nursing facility not far from here." She took a business card from the back pocket of her jeans. "You can visit her whenever you want, but you're not allowed to remove her from the premises, or you'll be arrested for kidnapping. Maya is on their 'no entry' list."

"What the…"

"Shut up, Jerome, and let me finish," Seneca snapped.

Maya blanched. "Remember, you're in my home."

Seneca pointed at her. "Look, bitch, you need not speak to me, because I'm less than a minute off your ass. You left my mother tied to a chair sitting in her own waste while you went shopping. If you'd been here when I arrived I know I'd be in jail for manslaughter right now." She popped up as if pulled by a taut spring. "The money stops today. I've already notified my bank not to send any more checks. Dad's pension and Mom's disability checks will go directly to the facility to cover her care. Jerome, you're my brother and I love you, but I'll never forgive *your* wife for what she did today. No need to get up. I'll find my way out."

Chapter Twenty-Five

It took Seneca two days of waking up to bright sunlight, warm breezes, the sight of palm trees and the blue-green waters of the Caribbean to make her feel as if she'd been reborn. The first night on the island she'd dreamed of her mother. It wasn't the image of the frail woman staring blankly into space but the pretty, vibrant woman who'd become a mother when she should've been dating, going to football games and hanging out with her friends.

Seneca had experienced a modicum of guilt that she'd left Dahlia behind when she boarded the jet. However, when she rethought her conversation with the neurologist, she knew her mother was in a better place—a place where medical experts would see to her every need. She still was unable to fathom how Maya could tie a harmless and defenseless woman to a chair and then go and leave her. If she hadn't been so desperate to free her mother and clean her up, Seneca would've called the police. Not only would Maya have faced arrest and charges of abuse, but it would also impact on her children. There was no way Jerome could work and be Mr. Mom to three young children. Her brother couldn't boil water without burning the pot.

When she'd arrived at the palatial house overlooking the ocean, it was too dark for her to survey the landscape. A middle-aged dark-skinned woman with a dimpled smile and accented English had shown her to an apartment on the second floor's west wing. Ynes told Seneca if she needed anything all she had to do was ask her.

There wasn't much she needed. She slept in late, went to bed after midnight and had developed a fondness for their strong black coffee and freshly baked crusty bread. She also ate three meals a day—something she hadn't done in years. It no longer mattered if she did gain weight, because she wanted to regain the fifteen pounds she'd lost. The solution for stained teeth from the black coffee was bleaching. When she wasn't eating or watching television novellas she spent most of her time lounging on the terrace outside her bedroom.

She'd just taken off the top to her swimsuit when she heard a knock on the door. Slipping her arms into the cotton wrap, Seneca walked across the room and opened the door. "Yes, Ynes."

The housekeeper handed her an envelope. "Señor Rollins ask that you get this."

"Who is Señor Rollins?"

Ynes grasped her hand and led her out to the terrace. Leaning forward, she pointed to a house partially concealed by a copse of palm trees. "He lives in that house."

Shading her eyes with her hand against the bright sunlight, Seneca spied a stucco structure with a red tiled roof. "Who is he?"

Ynes debated whether to answer the question. Mr. Gordon didn't like his employees to gossip. "He is a very famous doctor in your country. He said I should wait for you to read it and give him an answer." She gestured to the envelope.

Sliding her finger under the flap, Seneca took out a square of vellum: "Please have dinner with me. I have something you should see—ER." She reread the invitation twice, then a third time. Ynes said Rollins was a famous doctor in the States, yet his name wasn't familiar. "Tell him I will have dinner with him, but not at his house. If he wants to see me, then he must come here."

Ynes turned her head in an attempt to conceal a smile. "I will tell him."

Seneca rose gracefully to her feet when Ynes escorted a tall, slender bespectacled man with ebony skin onto the loggia where she'd set a table for two. He wore a white shirt with bright green leaves, black linen slacks and matching woven slip-ons with the aplomb of a male model. Stubble covered his well-shaped head.

Smiling, she offered him her hand. "Dr. Rollins, I presume."

Eliot Rollins took the hand of the woman with the perfect face, a face he'd seen on the covers of fashion and entertainment magazines. He nodded. "Yes, Miss—"

"Houston. Seneca Houston."

Large, penetrating dark eyes narrowed behind the lenses of the wire glasses. "Why is your name so familiar?" he asked innocently.

Seneca shrugged her shoulders. "Maybe we've met before."

"I don't think so. You're not one of my patients."

Seneca pointed to the chair opposite hers. "Please sit down, Dr. Rollins."

"Eliot," he said, taking the chair after Seneca sat. "I know you're not one of my patients because I'd recognize my work. I'm a plastic surgeon," he explained.

Seneca touched her face. "I've never had any work done—at least not yet."

"I doubt if you'll ever have to be nipped and tucked."

"What makes you so certain of that?"

"You have good skin and an even better bone structure. Your hair will turn gray years before you'll discover your first wrinkle."

Delicately arched eyebrows lifted. "What about my body?"

"You probably can have at least four children before considering a tummy tuck." Eliot found her body was as exquisite as her face, even if she was a little too thin.

"I'll keep that in mind, Dr. Rollins, after I push out my fourth baby."

"It's Eliot. I'm only Dr. Rollins to my patients."

She inclined her head. "Okay, Eliot. Your note said you have something I should see." She held out her hand, palm up. "May I see it?"

Reaching into the pocket of his shirt, Eliot placed a memory card on her outstretched hand. "I took this from a trespassing paparazzo who was hiding on my second-floor veranda taking photos of you."

Seneca went completely still. She'd come to the island to get away from the glare of spotlights and flashbulbs distorting her vision; however, it appeared she wasn't as cloistered as she'd thought.

"What did you do to him?"

Eliot met the eyes of the most exquisite woman he'd ever seen. He had female patients who'd bankrupted their wealthy husbands to get the face and body of the woman sitting opposite him. She'd pulled her curly back and tied it with a yellow ribbon that matched the midriff top and hip-hugging long skirt.

"I took his camera. That's a lot more punitive than reporting him to the police."

"Have you looked at what's on this?"

Eliot shook his head. "No. The only thing I'll say is the pervert was photographing you sunbathing."

"You looked?"

"No, I didn't look."

"But you said you saw me sunbathing," she countered.

"I said when I caught the creep I wanted to see what he was looking at, so I peered over the veranda and saw you sunbathing."

Throwing back her head, Seneca laughed uncontrollably, the sultry sound caressing Eliot like the brush of a feather. "What's so funny, Butterfly?"

Seneca sobered immediately. "So you do know who I am?"

"Only someone who'd been living on another planet wouldn't know who you are. Do photographers always stalk you?"

"Not usually. Living in New York allows me to have some anonymity. I'm certain it would very different if I lived in L.A."

"You don't like L.A.?"

"It's nice, but I prefer living in New York. Have you ever been to New York?" she asked Eliot. She liked the way he angled his head as if he were deep in thought, or contemplating the answers to the questions she put to him. It was difficult to pinpoint his age, but she estimated he was somewhere between thirty and forty.

"I visit New York several times a year."

Propping her arm on the table, Seneca rested her chin on the heel of her hand. "Business or personal?"

"It's always business." Eliot assumed a similar position, his gaze burning into Seneca's. "If I decide to come to New York and it's not business-related, would you show me around?"

"What would you like to see?"

"A Broadway play, museums, go to a Yankees game, and maybe a jazz club."

"No famous restaurants, Dr. Rollins?"

Eliot lowered his arm. "Do you have an Eliot in your past you don't like, because you seem to have a problem saying my name."

"No. I've never met an Eliot."

"Then why do you insist on calling me Dr. Rollins?"

"I don't know. Maybe it's because when the housekeeper gave me your note she identified you as Dr. Rollins.

"I…" Whatever Seneca was going to say was preempted when Ynes and another older woman entered the loggia pushing a serving cart from which wafted the most delicious aromas.

Her eyes met Eliot's as the women set out platters of thinly sliced grilled steak with onions, white rice, red beans and sweet plantains. Ynes was smiling when she filled two goblets with sangria.

Waiting for the two women to return to the house, Seneca raised her wineglass. "It's very nice meeting you, Eliot Rollins."

Smiling and following suit, Eliot raised his glass. "And I'm honored to meet you, Seneca Houston." He took a deep swallow of the chilled red wine. "How long are you going to be in Punta Cana?"

Seneca traced the rim of her glass with a forefinger. "I'm not certain. I've decided to play it by ear."

"Which means?"

"The length of my stay is open-ended." She paused. "I suppose you're curious as to why I'm hanging out here."

"A little. But you don't have to tell me if you don't want to."

How could Seneca tell Eliot that it wasn't that she didn't want to tell him but she needed to tell him, because she had come to the realization that she didn't have a close girlfriend in whom she could confide, and just when her off-again, on-again relationship with her sister had stabilized, the focus of Robyn's life had shifted to her husband and his widening political social circle. Robyn had attended so many D.C. parties that she'd hired a part-time social secretary.

"I've decided to retire from modeling." A feeling of inner peace that had evaded her for years swept over Seneca with the pronouncement, and she felt almost giddy with relief.

"Aren't you too young to retire?" Eliot asked.

"Not from modeling. I started modeling part-time at eighteen, and three years later I had my first runway show in Miami. Since then, all the years have become a blur."

Eliot extended his hand. "Give me your plate and I'll serve you. There's no way we're going let this delicious-looking food go to waste." He took her plate, spooning a small portion of each dish on her plate, then handed it back to her. "You take more if you want."

Seneca looked at the food on her plate. The portions were for a small child. Her head came up. "I do eat."

Eliot smiled. "You don't have to try and convince me that you don't have an eating disorder."

"I don't," she said defensively. "I've lost fifteen pounds in the past three months."

"Why?"

"I was working too hard and traveling much too much,

so I had to decide to whether to continue to model and drop dead from exhaustion or give it up and live a normal life."

"Eat, Seneca. You can talk later."

She did eat, taking two servings of everything, while Eliot talked. He told her he'd always wanted to be a doctor but hadn't decided on a specialty until his last year of medical school. He'd become a dermatologist, practicing for several years before choosing cosmetic and reconstructive surgery.

"What is your most popular procedure?" Seneca asked after swallowing the red wine.

"I'd have to say rhinoplasty closely followed by breast enhancement."

Seneca wrinkled her nose. "Do people really hate how they look that much?"

Eliot lifted broad shoulders under the colorful shirt. "Hate is a strong word. I'd like to believe they're uncomfortable with themselves whenever they look in the mirror. They see something that doesn't fit their perception of perfect. But then you have to ask yourself, what is perfection? Do you like what you see in the mirror?"

"We're not talking about me, Eliot."

"But I am talking about you, Seneca. I've had a few women come to me and ask if I can give them a nose or eyes like some model or actress they admire. Your name has come up a few times. We're a society that has become obsessed with looks and youth. And it isn't just women. I have almost as many male patients who want larger calves and penises. Why a man would want a ten-inch penis boggles my mind."

"Do you give it to them?"

"I give my patients whatever they want as long as it doesn't compromise medical ethics."

"How do you decide how to change just, say, a too-wide nose or heavy eyelids?"

"With today's technology, before-and-after photos are placed side by side, giving the patient an opportunity to approve of the result. To determine the width of your nose you should draw a vertical line from the inner corner of your eye. It should fall somewhere near the outer edge of the nostril. Patients are told to smile in their photos because nostrils tend to spread out.

"I perform what is called an ABR, or alar base reduction, to narrow the width and opening size of the nostrils. It's performed under local anesthesia and downtime is usually two to three days, with the sutures removed on the fifth day."

Seneca affected a noticeable shudder. "It sounds painful."

"It is, but patients are given pain medication."

"How much is a rhinoplasty?"

"It can range between twenty-five hundred and five thousand."

"How many breast enhancements do you perform a year?"

Eliot's eyelids lowered behind the lenses of his glasses. "Too many," he admitted. "Are you considering implants?"

Seneca glanced down at the front of her top. Whenever she lost weight she usually lost a cup size. "No. I have enough for my size, thank you."

"I wouldn't take you on as a patient even if you asked me."

"Why would you say something like that, Eliot?"

"You have a perfectly symmetrical face. Only a doctor out to make money would change your features. I read somewhere that ten billion was spent on cosmetic procedures in 2008, and that's about ten percent less than was spent in 2007 because of surgery alternatives."

"Are you talking about Botox?"

Attractive lines deepened around Eliot's eyes when he

smiled. "Fillers like Botox and Restylane, laser skin resurfacing and laser treatments for leg veins have surged in popularity, while there has been a decrease in liposuction, tummy tucks and face-lifts. A weakened economy will also impact the price of beauty."

Seneca found herself intrigued by the doctor, who kept her entertained with stories about some of his patients who traded up husbands when he refused to pay for another procedure. "I assume you have an office in Beverly Hills?"

"You assume correctly. If you ever find yourself in L.A., I'd like for you to call me. I'd love to show you places where most tourists don't visit." Eliot noticed her frown. "Did I say something wrong, Seneca?"

Her eyelids fluttered wildly. "No."

"You said *no* much too quickly," he said perceptively.

Again, Seneca felt the need to bare her soul. "I want you to pretend that I'm your patient and you're bound by doctor-patient confidentiality."

Leaning back in his chair, Eliot crossed his arms over his chest. "It doesn't have to go that far. Whatever you tell me will never be repeated."

Seneca told Eliot everything, from meeting Phillip Kingston, their over-the-top sex, impulsive, short-lived marriage and eventual annulment. She stopped talking when Ynes came over to clear the table. Once the floodgates had opened, she talked about her relationship with her mother and having to put her in a skilled nursing facility.

Tears were streaming unchecked down her face, and she was helpless to stop them. "I wanted to bring her home with me..."

Pushing back his chair, Eliot stood and came around the table, pulling Seneca gently to her feet. He wrapped his arms around her body, appalled at the fragility. "How can you take care of a sick woman when you don't have the strength to take care of yourself?" he crooned in her ear. Reaching into the pocket of his slacks, he took out a handkerchief and gently blotted her face. "Come on, let's go for a walk along the beach."

They walked hand in hand along the stretch of sand. The soft sound of the incoming surf was hypnotic, and there was no need to talk. Just being together had become a soothing balm for Seneca. She didn't know if Dr. Eliot Rollins was married, single, divorced, living with a woman or had fathered a bunch of kids, but that didn't matter. For the first time in her adult life she discovered what it felt to be *at peace.*

She was at peace with herself and with the world. There were those who'd helped her achieve her dream of becoming a supermodel, and then there were those she'd helped, and they'd either turned on her or wanted much more than she could give.

Dating a financial planner had come with a bonus: he'd put together two ten-year income-projection statements. One included real assets and liabilities. The other included the monies she would pay Jerome as Dahlia's caretaker and the costs to complete the renovations and expansion to house Dahlia and Robyn.

He'd cautioned that even with her conservative investments, she wouldn't have enough money to maintain her current lifestyle or take her into old age if she'd continued to subsidize her family. She heeded his advice when her wedding gift to Robyn wasn't to purchase a house for her but to give her the down payment. Seneca realized she'd made a faux pas when she'd promised to Robyn that she would buy the house, but her new brother-in-law was effusive when he received the check covering the down payment. Robyn pouted and sulked openly until her husband told her she should be grateful for the generous gift.

She'd told Booth she wanted to retire, but her agent wanted her to take six months to think about it. Well, she'd thought about it. She was leaving modeling and not going back.

"Thank you, Eliot."

"For what?"

"For being a good listener."

"How good a listener are you?" he asked.

Seneca gave him a sidelong glance in the encroaching darkness. The sun had slipped behind the horizon and stars were now visible in the darkening sky. "Maybe not as good as you, but I'll do my best."

"If that's the case, then I'd like you to have dinner at my place tomorrow. It will be my turn to tell you about Eliot Othello Rollins."

"Othello?" she asked laughing softly.

"What can I say. When my mother discovered Shakespeare had written a play with a black man as a lead character she wanted to name me for the Moor. But my dad overruled her, so they compromised, and Othello became my middle name. You didn't answer my question, Seneca."

"Yes."

"Yes, what?"

"I'll have dinner with you tomorrow."

Chapter Twenty-Six

Seneca slept soundly and woke at sunrise. She showered, slipped into a pair of panties, then pulled a sundress over her head and left the house to walk along the beach. Talking with Eliot was better than spending countless sessions with a therapist. He hadn't interrupted her monologue, and for that she was grateful, because she feared she wouldn't have been able to continue; he hadn't commented, and again she was grateful. She'd needed to unload and he'd become the receptacle for her fears, doubts and frustration.

She walked past his house, which was a smaller version of the one where she was staying, and farther down the beach another quarter of a mile, then turned to retrace her steps. Ynes greeted her with a cup of hot coffee liberally laced with milk and sugar. She sat on the loggia, enjoying the panoramic landscape spreading out before her. Picking up her cell phone, she hit speed dial for Booth's private number. He answered on the first ring.

"How are you, baby?"

She smiled, wondering if Booth called her *baby* because he couldn't remember her name. "I'm wonderful, Booth. Can you believe that a paparazzo tried taking pictures of me sunbathing?"

Booth laughed. "Sure I can. Especially if they know where to find you."

Her heart stopped, then started up again with a pounding that hurt her chest. "You told him that I was staying here?"

"Don't get your cute nose bent out of shape, baby. Our publicity department put out the word that Butterfly was MIA, so we arranged for the man to take the photos. He planned to wait a couple of weeks, then sell them to the tabloids."

"I don't know if he's told you, but he's not going to be selling them. Dr. Rollins caught him and took his camera and memory card. So he *gots nuthin'*," she drawled. A raw curse came through the earpiece. "Your little stunt just helped me to make up my mind. I'm out, Booth." Seneca didn't tell the agent that she'd already made up her mind. "Put out the press release that Butterfly has hung up her wings. You have three days to do it, and not one day more, or I'll return to the States and call my own news conference."

"You don't have to do that. I'll put out the release. I'm glad you called, because I have some good news about a proposed talk-show format for you. One network is very interested since Tyra Banks released a statement that she wants to end her show to focus on her film company. You would be perfect to fill that void."

"When do you think it might happen?"

"They're projecting a year to eighteen months."

Her smile was dazzling. "That's doable. Where would it be filmed?"

"L.A. Speaking of Los Angeles..."

"What about Los Angeles, Booth?"

"Someone in our publicity department heard a rumor, which still has to be substantiated, about your marriage to Kingston."

"Do they know who started the rumor?"

"It looks as if Kingston's estranged wife is looking for her fifteen minutes of fame. He had to tell her, Seneca, otherwise how would she know?"

"I don't know, Booth, and I don't care. I'm going into retirement, so it's moot."

"Remember, baby, news like this sells copy."

"What I want to do is forget. I don't care what you do except put the word out that Butterfly has left the catwalk."

"Consider it done. I'll send you a copy of the tapes from the networks."

"Thank, Booth."

Seneca rang off. She'd started to dial the number of Manor Oaks to check on Dahlia when the phone rang; the ring tone was the one she'd assigned to Robyn's number. "Hey, Robbie."

"Where the fuck is Mom?"

"What!"

"You heard what I said, Seneca. I'm at Jerome's and Mom isn't here."

"Is Jerome there?"

"Yeah. But you didn't answer my question."

"Jerome knows where Mom is. I gave him the information after I checked her into Manor Oaks."

"He says he doesn't know where she is. And, Maya's hysterical because she says her children are crying themselves to sleep because they can't see their grandmother."

Seneca's free hand curled into a tight fist. "I don't know what kind of game Jerome and Maya are playing, but—"

"Why did you move her, Seneca?" Robyn interrupted.

"I moved her because when I found her she was sitting in feces."

"She occasionally soils herself. You would know that if you weren't gallivanting all over the world. You think throwing a few dollars around absolves you of the responsibility of taking care of our mother? I wonder what your adorning fans would think if we were to tell them that you locked your mother away because you're ashamed of her."

Seneca gripped the tiny phone so tightly it left a distinct imprint on her palm. "I'm going to hang up before I forget you're my sister. And in case Jerome still hasn't regained his memory, I'll tell you that Mom is a resident of Manor Oaks, which is about a half mile outside Reston. Don't think of signing her out, because you'll need my approval for that. And there's another thing you should know. Maya is not allowed to see her."

"When did you become such a cunt!?"

Seneca felt her temper rise in response to the slur, then forced herself not to react in kind because that's what Robyn wanted. "You've been hanging out with so many men that you're beginning to sound like one," she crooned. "FYI, the reason Maya's not permitted to see Mom is because she left her home alone—tied to a chair. Now who's the *cunt?*"

There came a beat. "You're a liar!"

"Why don't you ask your wonderful sister-in-law? Goodbye, Robyn."

Seneca disconnected her sister and dialed the number of Manor Oaks. She refused to let Robyn upset her.

Not today.

Not tomorrow.

Not ever.

Today was the beginning of the rest of her life.

After talking to the floor nurse, she was told her mother

hadn't had any visitors, but the staff had coaxed Dahlia to leave her room to sit with the other residents in the solarium. The resident psychiatrist had prescribed a low dose of SSRIs to monitor her reaction to the drugs and recommended physical therapy in an attempt to improve her circulation and muscle tone. Dahlia Houston's legs had atrophied from sitting in the same position day after day.

Seneca wasn't certain how long she would remain on the Caribbean island; her plans included returning to the D.C. area before going back to New York. Her decision to retire now freed her up where she could rent an apartment in the capital city and commute between New York and D.C. every week.

Eliot came around the table and eased Seneca to her feet. She was stunning in a fitted white tank dress. He'd given his housekeeper and her husband the night off while assuming the cooking duties. What he hadn't anticipated was Seneca volunteering to cook with him.

She'd prepared a tropical salad with sour oranges, mango, papaya, Bermuda onion, sliced beets and avocado, while he'd broiled marinated butterflied lamb on the gas grill. She'd passed on the wine in lieu of sparkling water.

"I ate and drank too much. Let's go for a walk before I fall asleep on you," Eliot whispered in her ear.

Tilting her chin, Seneca smiled up at the man whom she thought of as a tranquilizer. Just being with him was calming and soothing, and she didn't have to pretend to be Butterfly. Seneca slipped her hand in his as they headed down to the beach.

"Where did you learn to cook, Eliot?"

"I was ten when my mother died in childbirth, and my grandmother came to live with us. She had rheumatoid arthritis that impeded her mobility. It took her most of the day to clean the house. Her rule was everyone had a chore. My two sisters learned to do laundry and iron, my younger brother had to keep the grass mowed and the yard clean. I was assigned cooking duties. She would sit on a stool and tell me exactly what needed to be done. By the time I was sixteen I could prepare a four-course dinner in under an hour."

As they strolled barefoot along the beach, Seneca listened as Eliot Rollins talked about himself. He was forty. He'd married twice—the first time to an older wealthy widow who'd paid for him to attend medical school. She'd died within days of his graduation, leaving him a small fortune and the vacation home in Punta Cana.

He'd remarried five years later to an aspiring actress when he discovered she was pregnant with his child. His wife lost the baby at the beginning of the second trimester when the car in which she was driving was hit head-on by an unlicensed teenage driver. Eliot reconstructed her face, but their marriage couldn't survive the psychological damage. They divorced quietly and she went on to land a recurring role with a daytime soap.

"I have a condo in the Hollywood Hills and share a practice with another plastic surgeon in Beverly Hills." Eliot pulled Seneca's hand into the bend of his elbow. "You're life is so much more interesting and exciting than mine."

Seneca dug her bare toes into the soft sand with each step. "My life is crazy. No, let me rephrase that. My life *was* crazy. I called my agent earlier this morning and officially retired. No more watching everything I eat or drink, jet lag, frenetic runway shows and no more skinnin' and grinnin' while strolling the red carpet."

Eliot patted her hand. "What's next for Seneca Houston?"

"It's not what I want but what I need."

"And that is?"

"Normalcy."

"What about a husband and children?" he asked.

She smiled. "That, too."

"Does Booth know this?"

"Why should he?" Seneca asked. Suddenly she didn't like the direction which the conversation was going. "Why are you mentioning Booth Gordon?"

"Aren't you Booth's woman?"

Seneca didn't know whether to laugh or scream at Eliot for being presumptuous. She decided on the former, if only to remain on friendly terms with her temporary neighbor. "No, I'm not his *woman*. Booth Gordon is my agent. Why did you assume I was involved with him?"

Eliot realized he'd just come down with a serious case of foot-in-mouth. "All of the women I've seen Gordon with here in Punta Cana…just say it's obvious they were more than friends."

"How long have you known Booth?" she asked.

"Probably six, maybe seven years. The property had been on the market awhile, because the former owner didn't want to drop the price. Once he did, Gordon bought it. The first couple of years he hosted some very lavish parties; they stopped abruptly when a young Russian woman drowned in his pool. There were rumors she hadn't drowned but was murdered. Gordon closed up the house for a while, and then when he came back it was maybe one or two times a year, and always with a woman."

"And you assumed I was one of his women?"

"I'm sorry about that," Eliot apologized.

"Apology accepted."

Eliot smiled. "Now that I'm forgiven, I'd like to ask you something."

Seneca stared at a flock of seagulls swooping down on the sand, fighting one another for food left by the incoming tide. "What is it, Eliot?" Her voice was a monotone.

"Why do you make it sound as if you're dreading my question?"

"I'm trying to imagine what you want to ask me."

"Did anyone ever tell you projecting can sometimes be bad for you?"

She smiled. "As a matter of fact he did, and I married him."

Eliot chuckled. "That's probably not going to happen with us."

"You're right about that," Seneca concurred. She wasn't going to make the same mistake twice in one lifetime, because of the similarities between the two men: Phillip, who was now Dr. Kingston, and Dr. Rollins both practiced medicine in L.A.

"Damn, Seneca," Eliot drawled. "You really know how to wreck a dude's ego."

"You were the one who said we'd never marry, and I just agreed with you."

"I said probably."

"What do you want to ask me, Eliot?" Her voice had taken on a bored tone again.

"When was the last time you went out dancing?"

She gave him a quizzical look. "I can't remember."

Dropping her hand, Eliot wrapped an arm around her waist and steered her back in the direction from where they'd come. "If you can't remember, then that means it's been too long. I know a little club in a resort not far from here that offers the best live music on this part of the island."

Seneca felt a warm glow flow through her. The last time she'd gone out dancing was in high school. She'd spent the past thirteen years working so hard that she'd forgotten how to enjoy life. Unlike other high-profile celebrities, she hadn't been one to make the rounds of clubs or after-parties. She showed up, posed for photographs, nibbled on finger food, drank sparkling water and mouthed the appropriate inane responses before her date dropped her off at her hotel. She didn't ask them in, because she hadn't wanted a repeat of what she'd had with Phillip.

She'd been on an emotional merry-go-round for thirteen years, and now it was time for her to catch the brass ring so she could get off. Becoming friends with Eliot Rollins would offer a modicum of the normalcy she wanted *and* needed.

Seneca's idyllic world came crashing down when she answered her cell phone. Dr. Marks had called to tell her that Dahlia Houston had slipped into a coma, and because she hadn't signed a DNR she was being kept alive with machines.

"I'll be there as soon as I can get a flight."

Everything seemed to fast-forward like a movie. She'd called Eliot to tell him she had to leave because of the turn in her mother's condition. He told her quietly to pack her travel documents and that he would arrange for her to return to the States. She'd been too shocked to realize he'd chartered a private jet to fly from Punta Cana directly into a private airstrip in Washington, D.C.

After spending two glorious weeks in the tropical sun, eating regularly and swimming or walking the beach with Eliot, Seneca felt stronger than she had in a long time. She'd called Manor Oaks every three days to check up on Dahlia, and the feedback was always positive: her condition hadn't deteriorated. She'd wanted to ask Dr. Marks what happened, then remembered his prognosis that victims of the fast-progressing neurodegenerative disease could expect to live five to ten years after diagnosis. Dahlia Houston had beaten the odds because she'd been living with the disease for more than a decade.

Seneca stared out the small oval window when the skyline of D.C. came into view. "You know you didn't have to come with me."

Leaning to his left, Eliot squeezed the hand gripping the armrest. "I wanted to come, Seneca. This is a time when you don't need to be alone."

"I called my brother and sister." She had called and left messages for Jerome and Robyn, hoping they could get past their resentment and meet her at the facility. Whenever she called Manor Oaks, she'd stopped asking whether her mother had had any visitors. If her siblings didn't want to visit Dahlia, then there was nothing Seneca could do about it.

Shifting her gaze from the window, Seneca met Eliot's gentle eyes behind the lenses of his glasses. Whenever he wore glasses he looked like Dr. Rollins. The first time she saw him without them he'd explained that he usually wore contacts.

Her gaze lingered on the slight cleft in his strong chin before moving up to his head, where coarse salt-and-pepper hair had replaced the stubble. "I really appreciate you coming with me, but I feel guilty that you—"

Eliot brushed his mouth over hers. "Stop it, Seneca. We're friends, and friends are supposed to help each other. And don't worry about me cutting my vacation short. Remember, I can always go back whenever I want." Pressing his thumb between her eyes, he smoothed away the frown lines. "Keep frowning and you're going to need a shot of Botox."

She gave him a sad smile. Eliot was a friend. Mitchell Leon was a friend. Luis Navarro was a friend. Seneca found it odd that her only friends were male. What was it about her that she didn't have or couldn't keep a female friend?

The jet touched down smoothly, and ten minutes later they

left Customs and made their way to where a car awaited them. Once they were seated in the back of the warm automobile, Seneca realized she wouldn't have been able to make it back to the States so quickly without Eliot's assistance. She could've called Booth, but he wasn't the first person she'd thought of. She didn't know when it had happened, but Eliot Rollins had become more to her than she could have imagined. He was someone she had come to depend on for emotional support.

The driver stopped at the checkpoint, and the guard in the booth gave him a ticket and instructions on where to park. Everyone coming or going was monitored by cameras. The driver maneuvered into the curving driveway at the entrance to the beautifully maintained medical facility, then continued to the parking area.

Seneca walked into the reception area, welcoming the heat wrapping around her like a comforting blanket. The temperature in Virginia registered forty-two degrees, forty degrees lower than what she'd left in the Dominican Republic.

"I'm Seneca Houston. I'm here to see Dahlia Houston. This is Dr. Rollins," she added, when the dour-faced woman glared at Eliot after she'd pulled up the computerized information on Dahlia.

"I need to see some ID, Dr. Rollins."

Reaching into the breast pocket of a waist-length black leather jacket, Eliot took out a case and handed the woman a card identifying him as a Fellow of the American College of Surgeons.

The receptionist gave him a warm smile. "Thank you, Dr. Rollins. Miss Houston, your mother is in ICU."

Eliot felt Seneca trembling when he placed his arm around her waist. There were so many things he wanted to say to her. That if she needed him—for anything—he would be there for her.

"It's okay, baby," he whispered in her ear. "I won't leave you."

Biting on her lip, Seneca nodded when she saw her brother and sister together. Both stood up when they spied her. Their expressions spoke volumes. She was too late. Jerome's face looked as if it was carved out of wood, while Robyn's puffy red eyes indicated she'd been crying.

Seneca held out her arms to Robyn, but her sister didn't move. It was Jerome who came over and folded her against his chest. Robyn was galvanized into action when she put her arms around her brother and sister.

Eliot watched the Houstons comfort one another, remembering when he'd huddled with his younger siblings after their father told them their mother had left to sleep with the angels. It was Eliot, Sr.'s way of telling his children that their mother wasn't coming home.

Chapter Twenty-Seven

BGM's spin that Butterfly hadn't shown up at a show in Southeast Asia, then the announcement that she was walking away from high-fashion modeling, had worked too well. The result was that Dahlia Houston's funeral had become a media spectacle. Reporters and photographers had respected the family's wish not to crowd into the small church in the Ithaca suburb where longtime friends and family had gathered, waiting instead in and around the cemetery where Dahlia was to be buried beside her late husband.

They hadn't come to pay their respects but to catch a glimpse of Butterfly, the supermodel who'd reigned as queen of the catwalk for more than a decade. When she hadn't shown up for Bangkok Fashion Week, rumors circulated that she was either pregnant or she'd come down with food poisoning because some unnamed source remembered seeing her retching. Another rumor was that she'd gone to the Caribbean to recover from a bout of influenza. Those who were close enough to get a glimpse of Seneca Houston were awed by her poise and natural beauty. Her deeply tanned face bore little traces of makeup when she emerged from the rear of the limo to take her place near the open grave.

Long-range lenses caught and captured the images of what had become a who's who of fashion. There were familiar and not-so-familiar faces. One photographer snapped a photo of Seneca's gloved hand reaching for the hand of Dr. Eliot Rollins, the renowned Beverly Hills plastic surgeon to the rich and famous. He moved closer, taking frame after frame of the tall couple at the exact moment Seneca rested her head on his shoulder.

Seneca closed her eyes as she leaned into Eliot's length. He'd promised not to leave her, and he hadn't. His presence had served as the buffer between her and her siblings when they'd sat down to make funeral arrangements. When it had come to the delicate topic of money, she'd preempted the discussion, informing her brother and sister that she'd prepaid Dahlia's funeral when they'd buried Oscar. The only expense was transporting the body from D.C. to Ithaca, which she'd offered to pay when Jerome looked as if he was going to panic.

Jerome and Robyn had made arrangements to spend several days with their Ithaca relatives, who'd opened their home to them and their families, but Seneca had decided not to join them. Who she would miss were her twin nieces who were carbon copies of their mother. She'd informed Eliot that she wanted to leave following the burial observance, and he'd arranged for a driver to take them back to Manhattan. She would return to her condo; he'd reserved a suite in a hotel near Kennedy Airport. Instead of returning to the Caribbean, he planned to go back to California.

Seneca hadn't wanted to be a hypocrite and pretend all was well between her and her siblings when it wasn't. She still hadn't forgiven Jerome for not telling Robyn where she'd taken their mother. And she wasn't certain whether she would ever forgive Maya for leaving Dahlia tied to the chair.

The graveside prayers concluded, Seneca turned to meet a pair of blue-green eyes. Booth Gordon had come to pay his respects. She dropped Eliot's hand and hugged her agent. "Thank you for coming."

"How are you holding up, Butterfly?"

"As well as can be expected."

Booth stared at the woman who was the epitome of beauty and grace even in mourning. His gaze shifted to his Punta Cana neighbor. They exchanged handshakes, Booth pulling the doctor out of earshot from Seneca. "Take her out of here as soon as this over," he whispered harshly. "She's going to need your protection."

Eliot didn't have time to react to the cryptic demand when two men wearing dark suits and topcoats walked up behind Booth. "Mr. Gordon, will you please come with us," said the taller of the two.

Booth frowned. "Who's asking?"

The man opened his hand, flashing a small gold badge. "FBI. Special Agent Richman."

Booth's face seemed to crumple like an accordion. "Am I under arrest?"

The federal agent's expression never changed. "Sir, we can do this quietly, or you can embarrass yourself *and* Miss Houston."

"Do I have time to speak to Miss Houston?"

"No, Mr. Gordon."

A cynical smile twisted Booth's thin mouth. "Time," he drawled, "is an uncompromising *bitch*." He spat out the last word.

Eliot watched, stunned, as Booth was led away. *"Take her*

out of here. She's going to need your protection." He hadn't wanted to believe Seneca was involved with something that required FBI scrutiny.

The agent's parting words lingered with him as he returned to Seneca, who was hugging and thanking those who'd come to support her in her time of grief as photographers, standing a respectable distance away, snapped frame after frame. Several reporters were talking to Jerome and Maya, a few handing them business cards.

They reminded him of vultures feeding on carrion. He'd seen enough. Eliot waited five minutes and then closed the distance between himself and Seneca. Cupping her elbow, he led her away from the crowd to where automobiles were parked.

"I want you to come to L.A. with me."

Seneca stopped in midstride, losing her balance but for the firm grip of Eliot's hand on her arm that prevented her from falling. "Why?"

Eliot knew he couldn't reveal what he'd just witnessed, or Booth's warning, so he decided to do something he rarely did: lie. "I'm not ready to let you go."

Unconsciously her smooth brow furrowed. She'd spent two weeks with Eliot Rollins and at no time had he openly demonstrated he wanted anything more than friendship. When they'd arrived in Ithaca they'd checked into adjoining hotel suites, and when she'd offered him the extra bedroom in her condo in lieu of his spending the night at an airport hotel he'd quickly turned her down. Now he wanted her to go to L.A. with him.

Seneca shook her head. "I don't understand something."

"What is it?" Eliot said, leading her to their car as the driver got out and opened the rear door.

Waiting until they were seated on the leather seat, Seneca

turned to face him. "You rejected my invitation to spend the night at my condo, because you said it was best we said goodbye tonight. Now you talk about not letting me go. It's just not adding up, Eliot."

"Don't women change their minds?"

She smiled. "Yes, but—"

"Well, men change their minds, too. I have a confession to make."

"What's that?"

"The real reason I want you to come with me is that I don't think you should be alone."

Stretching out and crossing her legs at the ankles, Seneca stared straight ahead. "If you're worried about me harming myself, then you're wrong. I don't take pills and—"

"It's not about you harming yourself," he said, cutting her off. "Instead of sharing your grief with your relatives, you're running away—"

"I'm not running away, Eliot!" she snapped angrily.

"Then please tell me exactly what are you doing?"

"I'm going home."

"To do what? To do what?" he repeated, taunting her. "You're going to wind up staying in bed and not eating. Then you're going to start crying and won't be able to stop. No, Seneca. That's not going to happen, because I care about you. In fact, I find myself caring a little too much, and I'd promised myself that I never wanted to feel that way again about *any* woman."

Eliot realized as soon as he'd finished his rant that his wanting Seneca to come with him had little to do with Booth Gordon asking him to take care of her and everything to do with what he'd felt and was beginning to feel for Seneca Houston.

He didn't see her as the beautiful woman everyone sought

to have a piece of but a young woman who'd been forced to grow up too early. The first time they'd gone dancing she was like a child in a candy shop. She hadn't sat out a dance for as long as they'd remained at the club. She presented herself as elegant and stylish, but whenever he scratched her surface she emerged as naive and childlike.

Seneca shook her head. "I can't do this again."

Moving closer, Eliot reached for her hands and removed her gloves. "Do what, baby?"

"Get involved again."

He smiled. "Did I ask you to become involved with me?"

Turning her head, she gave him a shy smile. "No, you didn't."

Eliot winked at her. "Come hang out with me, Seneca. My place is large enough for you to have your space when you feel you want to be alone. And there will be no pressure to do anything you don't want to do."

Seneca sobered as she pressed her lips together. "Does that include not sleeping with you?"

Eliot's lids came down, hiding his innermost feelings from her. He'd thought about sleeping with Seneca, yet he knew that would ruin their easygoing friendship. It had been six years since his divorce, and he hadn't lived a monastic lifestyle. However, there was something about Seneca Houston that kept him from crossing the line, physically and emotionally. He was more than content to remain friends—unless she communicated she wanted more.

"Especially *not* sleeping with me."

Looking at him through lowered lashes, Seneca said, "Eliot Rollins, it looks as if you have yourself a houseguest."

Seneca lay sprawled over Eliot like a sinewy cat, watching the large wall-mounted television. Footage of her walking the runway filled the screen as the voice of the cable channel's fashion editor added the commentary.

"Butterfly has taken her final walk. At the age of thirty-three, supermodel Seneca Houston has retired from modeling after a career that spanned fifteen years. Beginning tomorrow we'll cover the metamorphosis of Butterfly from a young girl from upstate New York to print model and queen of the runway."

"Where did they find that picture?" Seneca whispered. It was a photograph of her at her tenth-birthday party.

Eliot chuckled. "I think you look rather cute."

"Yeah, right." She rolled her eyes.

"I'm going to set it to TiVo so we won't miss it tomorrow."

Seneca combed her fingers through her hair, holding it off her face. "I'm never comfortable watching myself."

"You don't have to. I'll watch for both of us."

Glancing up at Eliot over her shoulder, she gave him the smile photographers had captured for an eternity. The past three days had been nothing short of perfection. Eliot, who always took a month off during the winter and another month over the summer, was scheduled to return to his practice next week.

Eliot had admitted to caring a little too much for her, while she was too much of a coward to let him know how she felt about him. Her emotions went deeper than liking or caring. It was different, exciting, and of all of the men who'd passed in and out of her life it was Eliot Rollins who'd gotten her to fall in love with him.

Seneca shuttered her gaze against the stare that seemed to penetrate the wall she'd put up to keep all men since her decision to end her marriage to Phillip Kingston, at a distance. She hadn't come to California with Eliot because he'd coerced her, but because she *had* wanted what had begun the night he'd given her the memory card bearing photographs of her sunbathing partially nude to continue. Booth had paid the man to take pictures of her as a publicity ploy, but his Caribbean island neighbor had foiled the scheme. It was apparent the Barracuda hadn't lost any of his edge. He was still wheeling and dealing.

"What are you smiling about?" Eliot asked Seneca.

"I was thinking about Booth."

"What about him?"

"The man is still a barracuda."

Eliot had wrestled with his conscience since Seneca had moved in under his roof as to whether he should tell her about Booth Gordon. After all, he was her agent and she deserved to know what the government had accused him of.

Reaching for the remote device, he switched to an all-news channel, muting the sound. "I *need* to tell you something."

Seneca heard dread in Eliot's voice. "If it's something that's going to make me sad, Eliot, then I don't want to hear it." She closed her eyes for several seconds. "I've finally found what I hadn't realized I'd been looking for, and that's an inner peace that can't be bartered for or negotiated. And for that I thank you."

"Don't thank me, Seneca. I had nothing to do with it."

She shifted, straddling his lap. "If you don't want to take credit for it, then consider you're a conduit in my journey to discover who I am and what I need to do to make Seneca Houston happy. You were right when you said I was unable to care for my mother when I couldn't take care of myself."

Cradling her face, Eliot kissed the end of her nose. "Are you happy, Seneca?"

"Delirious."

He angled his head and pressed a gentle kiss to her parted lips. "Good."

Seneca knew she was wading into dangerous territory sitting on Eliot's lap; she could feel his erection pressing against her hips and making it virtually impossible for her not to move. Her celibate body screamed in frustration; she'd spent over ten years denying her femininity because she hadn't wanted a repeat of what she'd had with Phillip Kingston.

However, her body betrayed her shamelessly when the pulsing between her legs grew stronger and stronger, her moaning when the orgasm that held her captive finally released her, leaving her shaking like a fragile leaf in the wind.

Eliot felt Seneca breathe the last of her passion into his mouth. He'd convinced himself that he didn't want or need a woman except for sex. But Seneca Houston had proven him wrong. He moved off the chaise, bringing her up with him.

"Seneca?"

She opened her eyes. "Yes, you can."

Eliot had his answer. He carried her out of the den and into his bedroom. He'd drawn the drapes, shutting out the millions of lights coming from the valley, but had left the lamp on the bedside table on its lowest setting.

He placed Seneca on the turned-down bed as if she were a piece of fragile crystal. Eliot took his time undressing her, because all they had was time. Time to discover each other and time to uncover whether she would become the last woman in his life.

Tank top, shorts and panties lay at the foot of the large bed. His gaze never left hers when he divested himself of his T-shirt, briefs and shorts. With wide eyes she watched as he removed a condom from the drawer of the table and slipped it on to protect her from an unplanned pregnancy.

The mattress dipped slightly when he got into bed beside her. "Tell me what you want, baby."

Seneca felt hot tears prick the backs of her eyes. It was the first time a man had asked her what she wanted. It was always what he'd wanted. "I want you to make love to me, Eliot." She'd asked him to make love to her when she'd wanted him to fall in love with her. She wanted and needed him to love her as much as she was beginning to love him.

Eliot took his time arousing her again, his mouth charting a sensual path from her lips to her feet. His hands and mouth left no part of her body untouched, and when he'd reached the point when he was afraid he wasn't able to hold off ejaculating, he eased his sex into her body, both of them groaning in exquisite pleasure.

I've come home! That was all Seneca could think when Eliot moved inside her, taking her to sensual heights that left her gasping for her next breath. She came again, the orgasms overlapping one another as she surrendered to an ecstasy that took her beyond herself, screaming and crying when she and Eliot climaxed together.

Eliot waited for his heart to slow to a normal rate. He buried his face in the curly hair fanning out on his pillow. "I can't let you go," he whispered.

Seneca smiled. "And I don't want you to."

Chapter Twenty-Eight

A mere twenty-four hours later, Seneca felt as if her world had come crashing down on her. The news that her bank account was frozen by the federal government because Booth Gordon had used it to funnel drug money was compounded with details of her personal life that had become the grist for the entertainment rumor mill.

"Calm down, Seneca, before I'm forced to sedate you."

Eyes, wide with fear and pain, implored him to understand her. "They are lying, Eliot! Why would my family turn on me like that?"

Forcibly pulling her against his body, Eliot wouldn't permit Seneca to escape him. "Viewers don't know they're lying, because they haven't heard from you."

Seneca stopped struggling. Her eyes met Eliot's. "What do you mean?"

"You have to counter their lies with the truth."

"You want me to go on the air and spill my guts?"

"Either that, or do or say nothing. And if you do that, then the public will draw its own conclusions and you'll be hounded by the media for the rest of your life."

Seneca wasn't certain who in her family had talked to the investigative reporter, but the segment on the rise of Butterfly was rife with innuendos and lies. What if she married again? Had children? Would they be forced to defend their mother?

"Okay, Eliot. Who do I talk to? Larry King? Oprah?"

"Let me make a phone call. I know a correspondent who is just breaking into the business. She owes me a favor, so let's see if she can come through for you."

Seneca stared at the man with the smooth black skin and penetrating deep eyes that seemed to know her better than she knew herself. "Why does she owe you?"

"That's something I can't tell you, baby. Doctor-patient privilege. But if she can get her network to approve the interview, then we can have more control than if someone like Barbara Walters or Larry King conducted the interview. I'll ask Debrah to let us know which questions she'll ask beforehand."

Seneca smiled despite the seriousness of the situation. Eliot had said *we* and *us*. It was apparent they were in this together. "Call her, Eliot."

"Two minutes and we're ready."

Seneca felt as if she'd stepped back in time when she'd prepared for the shoot with Phillip Kingston. She'd asked Kathie to come to L.A. to do her makeup and Yancy to style her hair. Eliot had paid their expenses because the FBI still hadn't removed the lien from her bank accounts. If it hadn't been for Eliot Rollins, Seneca Houston would've become a part of the *system.*

She'd returned to New York, taking a red-eye and wearing

a wig and several layers of clothes in an attempt to conceal her identity. She knew the paparazzi were camped out in and around her apartment building; in an attempt to evade them she slipped into the building using the service entrance. Although she didn't have access to her bank accounts, she wasn't cash-poor. Seneca had secreted five thousand dollars in cash, along with jewelry—mostly gifts from admirers—in a safe built into the floor of a bedroom closet. The cash, two pairs of diamond studs, totaling six carats, and the diamond band and bracelet Phillip had given her were in the tote she carried on when she took a return flight to the West Coast.

Eliot, who hadn't known of her escapade because he was working a three-day shift at the medical facility where he and his partner had set up their practice, was waiting for her when she walked into the condo. They had their first serious disagreement, with her seeing another side of the soft-spoken man who'd made the most exquisite and tender love to her. He accused her of stealing away like a thief to retrieve a stash he'd hidden away from his cohorts. When Seneca told him she didn't want to have to rely on him for her existence, his rejoinder had shocked her into silence. *When I love someone, I tend to take care of them. That's what I do, Seneca.*

She'd walked into the bathroom, showered and then crawled into bed with Eliot. They'd slept with their backs to each other until she crawled over Eliot, begging him to make love to her. He did, and without a condom. When she woke hours later to find dried semen on her thighs she hadn't panicked. She was thirty-three and ready to give motherhood a try. Her period was late, but she hadn't told Eliot. And Seneca knew if she was pregnant she wouldn't be able to hide it from him. After all, he was a doctor.

The cameraman checked the lighting for the last time, while Debrah White checked and rechecked her notes. Her career was certain to take off because she'd landed the exclusive live interview with the former supermodel Butterfly. Seneca Houston had agreed to the interview in a private room at a popular Beverly Hills restaurant. Dr. Eliot Rollins had suggested the venue because it would provide complete anonymity for the woman with whom it was obvious he'd fallen in love.

She met the eyes of the woman with raven-black hair styled in a loose twist on the nape of her long slender neck. Her makeup was so subtle it appeared as if she wasn't wearing any. A sleeveless black sheath dress with an asymmetrical neckline showed off her toned arms to their best advantage. Pearl studs and a matching strand around her neck complemented her sleek, sophisticated style. She crossed one long, bare leg over the opposite knee, the gesture attracting the attention of every man in the room.

Debrah affected her professional expression when the producer gave the signal to begin taping. "Good evening. I'm Debrah White, and I'm here with Seneca Houston, the former supermodel known as Butterfly, to get answers firsthand from the woman about whom there's been a great deal of talk and interest. First, Seneca, I would like to thank you for agreeing to this interview."

Seneca smiled. "Thank you for agreeing to meet with me."

"I find it strange that throughout your thirteen-year career as a model you were never the topic of any scandal, but with your retirement there seems to be a maelstrom of innuendos and attacks upon your character. How do you explain this?"

"What I find so strange is that I can't explain it. I've worked with some of the most temperamental, egotistical women on the planet, yet I never had a problem with any of them. I retire and all of a sudden I've become a pariah—which is shocking and hurtful, because it comes from my family."

"Speaking of family, I'd like to extend my condolences on the recent loss of your mother."

Seneca closed her eyes, sucking in her cheeks, visibly moved. "Thank you," she said after a pregnant pause.

Debrah leaned forward. "Do you want me to give you a minute?"

Seneca smiled again at the attractive reporter with the round face, flawless sable complexion and large dark eyes. With her pixie-styled haircut she looked like a chocolate doll. "I'm okay, thank you."

"There have been quite a few men in your life. Can you tell me about them?"

"Which one?" Seneca asked, her expression impassive.

"Let's start with Luis Navarro."

"I credit Luis with starting my career and giving me my signature name. I was Luis's muse and his inspiration for his Butterfly collection."

"Mitchell Leon."

"Mitchell took photos of me when I didn't have the money to pay him. But I was able to repay him when he photographed me for the cover of *Cosmopolitan,* the *Sports Illustrated* swimsuit issue and *Vogue.* In my opinion, Mitchell Leon is in the same class as Annie Leibovitz, Richard Avedon and Francesco Scavullo."

"Tell me about Phillip Kingston."

"What about him?" Seneca asked.

"I spoke to your former college roommate, and she said you and Phillip Kingston dated for a while."

Seneca stared at the toe of her black patent-leather stiletto. Phillip's estranged wife had tried and failed to secure a televised interview where she could talk about her soon-to-be ex-husband, so she posted it on an online blog.

She and Eliot had talked about how she would answer the

battery of questions Debrah had forwarded to her. Debrah had listed more than fifty but had to narrow the list to fit the show's time format.

"Phillip and I were married briefly, but decided we'd acted impulsively so we agreed to have it annulled."

"How long were you married?"

"Not long," Seneca replied.

"Were you in love with him?"

"Phillip and I were in *lust* with each other," she said smiling.

Debrah smiled for the first time. "Okay, let move on. Booth Gordon."

"Booth is my agent."

"Is or was?"

"Booth Gordon is still my agent."

"I know Mr. Gordon is currently out on bail, but are you at liberty to talk about the allegation that he had been laundering money for a Russian drug lord?"

"I haven't seen or spoken to Booth Gordon since my mother's funeral." Seneca stared directly at the camera, placed her fingertips to her lips and threw him a kiss. "That one is for you, Booth." Instead of giving him an air kiss, Seneca wanted to give her agent the kiss of death. His using her account to launder drug money was something she still couldn't fathom.

"I've spoken to your brother and sister-in-law, and both claim you came to their home, took your mother and moved her to a medical facility, without letting them know where you'd taken her."

I should've kicked that bitch's ass when I had the chance, Seneca seethed inwardly. She clenched her teeth, then forced herself to relax. "My mother needed medical care my brother and sister-in-law could not provide. She wasn't eating and had lost control of her bodily functions. I did what I thought best for my mother's well-being, and I stand behind my decision."

"Your sister-in-law said your mother told her you'd killed your father. Why would she say that?"

"Dahlia Houston said a lot of things, but that didn't necessarily make them true. She was diagnosed with FTD—frontotemporal dementia. It is a disease that robbed her of her memory in her early forties." Seneca paused. "Let me set the record straight. My father died of coronary heart disease."

Debrah rearranged her cards. "A month before you announced your retirement footage shows you thinner than usual. You were observed vomiting. There is speculation that you are bulimic, had come down with the flu or food poisoning, or you were pregnant. Which one is it?"

Throwing back her head and baring her throat, Seneca laughed. "I'm sorry, but none of the above." She sobered quickly. "I'd become dehydrated during the overseas flight, and when I checked in at my hotel I'd drunk too much water. The water had to go somewhere."

Debrah shifted another card. "Nicely put. You've been photographed with heads of state and celebrities all over the world. Perhaps you can identify a few of them for us." The camera shifted to a large flat-screen television.

"I can't remember or pronounce all of the names, but I can tell you who they are." Seneca was able to identify eight photos before Debrah resumed her questioning. She took a sip of water from the glass on the table beside her chair.

"I have to keep coming back to your family." Seneca lowered her lids and nodded. "Your sister-in-law—"

"Maya," Seneca said, supplying the name.

"Maya told me you resented her because your brother married out of his race."

"How resentful could I have been if I was one of her

bridesmaids? I'm also godmother to her son. Does that sound like resentment to you?"

"No, it doesn't. I spoke to your sister and she told me that she once harbored a lot of resentment because she felt you wouldn't help with her modeling career. What do say about this?"

"I know how Robyn felt because there's one thing my sister isn't and that's shy."

Debrah smiled. "I got the same impression when I spoke to her. But on a more serious note, she told me if she had the opportunity to choose any sister she wanted, she would pick you again."

Seneca winked at the camera. "Love you, Robbie."

"She says you're generous to a fault, and that people tend to take advantage of your generosity. Is she talking about your brother and his wife?"

"No comment."

"Is it true you renovated your brother's house and paid him a small fortune to take care of your mother after she was unable to live alone?"

"No comment," Seneca repeated.

There was a charged silence as the two women stared at each other. "What's next for Butterfly?"

"Butterfly has taken off her wings."

"Will you ever return to the runway?"

"Maybe if someone decides to put together an old-school fashion show I'll consider it. But only if I don't have to wear five-inch heels."

"Are they really that uncomfortable?"

"They are if they're a size too small." Seneca made a fist. "This is how a foot looks when you finally release the dogs."

Debrah laughed softly. "What's next for Seneca Houston?"

Seneca pressed her hand to her throat. "I don't know. I'm still trying to get used to keeping my feet on the ground. There have been days when I wake thinking I've overslept and will miss my flight to Europe or Asia."

"Are you enjoying retirement?"

"I love it."

"What about marriage and children?" Debrah asked.

A dreamy expression softened Seneca's face. "Maybe one of these days."

Leaning forward, Debrah extended both hands as Seneca grasped her fingers. "Thank you for being so candid. Good luck." The camera focused on the journalist as she issued her closing statement.

Seneca stood up and a technician removed the microphone attached to her neckline. "Debrah, thank you so much for allowing me to tell my side of the story."

The petite woman steered Seneca away from the technicians. "I'm sorry if I blindsided you when I mentioned you paying your brother to take care of your mother."

"It's all right. As annoyed as I am with my brother and sister-in-law, I don't plan to out them publicly. After all, I'm godmother and aunt to their three children.

"You sister's right, Seneca. You're generous to a fault. I don't think I could be as forgiving," Debrah admitted.

"I understand where my brother is coming from. His wife has to leave her children and go back to the classroom because they're not able to maintain their current lifestyle on one paycheck. It's not going to be easy for them, but they'll make it. Maya's lucky she has a degree to fall back on, so my heart isn't bleeding for her." Seneca saw Eliot walk into the room. "My ride's here, so this is goodbye."

"I'm sure I'll see you around," Debrah said confidently.

She watched Seneca walk across the room and put her arm around Eliot's waist. His hand slid down her back to her hips. It had been a while since the man who'd put her face back together after a jealous boyfriend beat her until she was unrecognizable had shown an interest in a woman. He'd hit the jackpot, because Seneca Houston was the antithesis of the bad-tempered diva who made everyone's life around her a living hell.

Seneca pressed her mouth to Eliot's ear. "Let's go home. I have something to tell you."

Hans let the tape run until he realized Seneca had finished. "What did you tell Eliot?"

"Turn off the recorder." Seneca waited until he pushed the button, stopped the tape. "I told Eliot that I suspected I was carrying his baby."

"Were you?"

Seneca nodded. "Yes. We had a City Hall wedding, with his partner and a nurse as our witnesses. It took more than seven months for the FBI to audit BGM's books. There was such a backlash from the agency's clients when they couldn't get their money that the government was forced to lift the liens."

"Did they indict Gordon?"

"No. He worked out a deal where he rolled over on his cousin, who in turn gave up the drug lord. Booth sold the agency and left the country for parts unknown; his cousin testified against the Russian, and a year later his body was found on the beach off Long Island Sound, minus the tongue. I still own the condo in Manhattan. My children love staying there whenever we visit New York."

"How is your sister?" Hans asked.

"She's great. Robbie went back to school to get a master's and doctorate. She's teaching political science at Georgetown. She and her husband decided not to have children, but they treat their two dogs as if they were kids. I saw my brother's children for the first time in years. His oldest, my godson, graduated from high school last year, and I wanted to be on hand to see him walk across the stage to get his diploma. Maya started with the apology and the tears, but I told her to dry it up. By the time we left D.C. everyone was one big happy family unit."

Hans sat up straighter. "I hear a car."

"That must be my husband and children."

Minutes later Dr. Eliot Rollins, his son and daughter walked into the kitchen, stopping when they saw the strange man sitting at the cooking island. Seneca walked over to Eliot, raising her face for his kiss. She then bent down to kiss her four-year-old son and toddler daughter.

"Russell, please take your sister into the bathroom and make certain she washes her hands."

"She always wants to stand on the stool," Russell mumbled.

Seneca ran her fingers through his curly hair. She'd told Eliot to get the boy's hair cut. He was beginning to look like the wolf man. "She has to stand on the stool because she can't reach the sink."

"That's because she's a baby."

"I'm not a baby," Abigail shouted while stomping her little foot.

Eliot bent down and swung his daughter up in his arms when Hans came over to meet him. "I'm Eliot. You must be Hans."

"I'm honored to meet you, Dr. Rollins. Your wife just finished telling me about her very exciting life."

Eliot lifted his eyebrows. "Please, call me Eliot. And, yes my wife has had quite a life for someone who has yet to celebrate her fortieth birthday. Are you going to hang around until tomorrow?" he asked.

"I hadn't planned to."

"You don't have to run off. The weather's nice, so we'll cook and eat outdoors. We don't get many visitors up here, so when we do we like to drag it out a bit."

Hans found the plastic surgeon as open and friendly as his wife. They were living a fairy-tale life with two homes in California, one in New York and the fourth on a Caribbean island. They had two beautiful, bright children, and the former supermodel seemed to be enjoying her life as wife and mother.

He'd spent more time with her than with the other models who would grace the pages of his coffee-table book. Perhaps, he thought, if he was persuasive enough, he could get Seneca Houston to agree to his devoting the entire volume to her. It wasn't often that a model started out electrifying the runway and thirteen years later still hadn't lost her spark or edge.

It is said that beauty has a price. Butterfly had sold it to the highest bidder, and in the end had reaped more than she'd sown: love.

★ ★ ★ ★ ★

National bestselling author

ROCHELLE ALERS

Naughty

Parties, paparazzi, red-carpet catfights…

Wild child Breanna Parker's antics have always been a ploy to gain attention from her diva mother and record-producer father. As her marriage implodes, Bree moves to Rome. There she meets charismatic Reuben, who becomes both her romantic and business partner. But just as she's enjoying her successful new life, Bree is confronted with a devastating scandal that threatens everything she's worked so hard for….

Coming the first week of March 2009 wherever books are sold.

KIMANI PRESS™

www.kimanipress.com
www.myspace.com/kimanipress

KPRA1280309TR

NATIONAL BESTSELLING AUTHOR

ROCHELLE ALERS

INVITES YOU TO MEET THE BEST MEN...

Close friends Kyle, Duncan and Ivan have become rich,
successful co-owners of a beautiful Harlem brownstone. But
they lack the perfect women to share their lives with—until
true love transforms them into grooms-to-be....

Man of Fate
June 2009

Man of Fortune
July 2009

Man of Fantasy
August 2009

ARABESQUE®

www.kimanipress.com
www.myspace.com/kimanipress